ST. MARTIN'S

MINOTAUR
MYSTERIES

Be the first to hear the latest mystery book news…

With the St. Martin's Minotaur monthly newsletter, you'll learn about the hottest new Minotaur books, receive advance excerpts from newly published works, read exclusive original material from feature mystery writers, and be able to enter to win free books!

Sign up on the Minotaur Web site at:
www.minotaurbooks.com

THE CRITICS LOVE BEN REHDER'S NEWEST BLANCO COUNTY NOVEL

BONE DRY

"You don't need an invite to the Bush ranch to have fun in Texas. Ben Rehder, whose *Buck Fever* earned him an Edgar nomination for best first mystery last year, is back."

—Chicago Tribune

"Fans of Rehder's rollicking debut, *Buck Fever* (2002), which was nominated for both Edgar and Lefty awards, will welcome the sequel, an over-the-top tale of sex, mayhem and murder in Texas's hill country."

—Publishers Weekly

"More funny adventures of John Marlin, amiable, estimable game warden of Blanco County, Texas . . . [a] winning sequel to *Buck Fever* . . . characters to chuckle at, yes, but Rehder never forgets he's got clues to furnish and a story to tell."

—Kirkus Reviews

"A humdinger. Funny, sardonic, and filled with clever metaphors and similes, *Bone Dry* is as cool and satisfying as a Lone Star beer on a hot Texas afternoon."

—Sports Afield

MORE . . .

"A deserving, character-rich atmospheric crime novel that is deserving of the Edgar nomination."

—*Deadly Pleasures*

"Imagine Carl Hiaasen with a Texas accent. *Buck Fever* is a laugh-filled riot."

—*Denver Post*

"This debut novel is a complete success. The writing here is confident and vigorous; the tone is quintessentially Texan and relentlessly wry. There's sure to be a long career for this wacky, happy series."

—*Publishers Weekly* (starred review)

"Briskly paced, amusing, spiced with deftly drawn good-old-boy portraits; an altogether promising debut."

—*Kirkus Reviews*

"This fast-paced comic thriller comes within shooting distance of Hiaasen and Leonard territory. . . . a promising debut."

—*Booklist*

"A wild and crazy first novel."

—*Library Journal* (starred review)

ALSO BY BEN REHDER

Guilt Trip

Flat Crazy

Buck Fever

AVAILABLE FROM
ST. MARTIN'S/MINOTAUR
PAPERBACKS

BONE DRY

A BLANCO COUNTY MYSTERY

BEN REHDER

St. Martin's Paperbacks

BONE DRY

Library of Congress Catalog Card Number: 2003050625

ISBN: 0-312-99460-5
EAN: 80312-99460-0

Printed in the United States of America

St. Martin's Press hardcover edition / September 2003
St. Martin's Paperbacks edition / August 2004

St. Martin's Paperbacks are published by St. Martin's Press, 175 Fifth Avenue, New York, NY 10010.

10 9 8 7 6 5 4 3

For Becky,

with all my love

ACKNOWLEDGMENTS

Once again, a slew of people helped make this book better than it would have been.

Thanks go to my "pre-editors": Becky Rehder, Helen Fanick, Mary Summerall, Kate Donaho, and Stacia Hernstrom, as well as my copyeditor, Christine Aebi.

Much appreciation to my expert sources of information: Trey Carpenter (wildlife biology), Jim Lindeman (game warden procedures and hunting laws), Tommy Blackwell (law enforcement), Martin Grantham (firearms), Kevin Critendon and B. R. Critendon (water issues), Joe Summy (Blanco County anecdotes), Ted Levay (scuba diving), Cisco Hobbs (construction), Don Gray (hunting anecdotes), and Michael Perna (dialect assistance). Any errors or distortions of reality are mine, not theirs.

Thanks to the people of Blanco County for providing such enthusiastic support, and to the booksellers across the nation for welcoming me so warmly at every turn.

And, of course, a huge debt of gratitude to my agent, Nancy Love, and my editor, Ben Sevier, for guiding me with skilled hands and good humor.

ACKNOWLEDGMENTS

CHAPTER ONE

On the morning of Saturday, November 5—opening day of deer season—a statuesque blonde beauty strolled out of the trees, pulled down her khaki shorts, and peed beneath Cecil Pritchard's deer feeder.

"Well, suck a nut," Cecil said to himself, sitting in his deer blind a hundred yards away. He looked down at his coffee mug, blinking dumbly. Maybe he'd added a little too much Wild Turkey. And this *was* his fourth cup. But when he looked up again, the Nordic goddess was still there, hiking up her shorts. His brother-in-law would never believe it.

The day had started normally enough. Cecil climbed out of bed at four A.M. sharp, pulled on his camo coveralls, and brewed a pot of Folgers. *Nothing gets you going like the smell of fresh coffee,* Cecil thought, whistling happily. He would have loved a big plate of scrambled eggs, bacon on the side, and a basketful of biscuits, but Cecil wasn't much of a cook, and his wife, Beth, was still drowsing in bed. Goddamn woman was as useless as a negligee on a nun. On weekdays, when he'd come home from the machine shop at lunchtime, he'd usually find

Beth staring at the soap operas or Jerry Springer on TV, and Cecil would be left to make his own lunch. The way Cecil saw it, that was a serious infraction of the marriage vows. So, as he had prepared for the morning hunt, Cecil made sure to stomp around the mobile home as heavily as possible, kind of get the whole floor vibrating. It'd serve her right if she couldn't get back to sleep after he left.

He met up with Beth's brother, Howard, at the ranch gate at five in the A.M., just as planned—plenty of time to reach the blinds before first light. Seeing as how they had a few minutes to spare, Cecil took the opportunity to remind Howard what a lazy, good-for-nothing sister he had. Howard heartily agreed while munching a breakfast taco his own wife had prepared for him. *Sorry, I ain't got but one,* Howard said around a mouthful.

The men split up and Cecil proceeded to his elevated tower blind, a beauty he had ordered from the Cabela's catalog last spring. Once inside, Cecil readied himself for a long, relaxing morning hunt. He loaded his Winchester .270, double-checked the safety, and leaned the rifle in the corner. He pulled out his binoculars and gave the lenses a good cleaning. Then he poured a hot mug of java, added a generous dose of bourbon, and waited for sunrise.

The black night slowly gave way to gray, and then the rolling hills of Central Texas started to take shape. The birds began chirping tentatively and then went into full chorus. Cecil leaned back and soaked it all in. He was sitting twelve feet up, with a view that God Himself would appreciate. Man, this was living! Cecil waited all year for this morning, and he just knew there was a big buck somewhere in the woods with his name all over it.

That's when Cecil heard a car rambling along the gravel county road that paralleled the ranch's eastern fenceline. Weeks ago, Cecil had considered relocating his blind, but the road saw such little traffic, he'd decided to leave everything as is.

Looking through his binoculars, Cecil saw a rusty mustard-yellow Volvo easing down the road. It disappeared behind some trees and then the motor faded away. Cecil had thought the occupants were gone for good. But apparently he was wrong.

Now Cecil was staring slack-jawed at the blonde trespasser, knowing that all his preseason plans and preparations were wasted. He was furious. The woman might as well have erected a flashing neon warning sign—DEER BEWARE!—because no self-respecting buck would come within a thousand yards of so much human scent.

Finally, Cecil managed to get over his astonishment and do something. He stuck his head out the small window of the deer blind and yelled, "Hey, lady! What the hell are you doing? Get your ass away from there!"

The tall blonde casually buttoned her shorts, smiled, and flipped Cecil the bird.

Cecil decided enough was enough, and rose to go give the woman a serious tongue-lashing, maybe escort her back to her damn rattletrap car. But as he stood, he spilled his coffee, dropped his binoculars to the floor, and—*Goddamn it all!*—banged his rifle scope against the side of the blind. Cussing loudly now, Cecil opened the blind door and began to climb down the ladder—only to hear a car door closing and the Volvo gently puttering off into a fine Texas morning.

CHAPTER TWO

At nine A.M. on Saturday, November 5, a thick-chested man with crow's-feet, jowls, and graying hair was throwing a hump into his live-in Guatemalan housekeeper—but his mind was elsewhere and his erection was starting to droop. The distraction was laying right there on her nightstand: the "Travel" section of the newspaper. He could see an ad that read, BARBADOS—FROM $549! CALL YOUR TRAVEL AGENT TODAY!

Shit, if only it were that easy. But Salvatore Mameli—formerly known as Roberto "The Clipper" Ragusa—couldn't just pick up and go like normal people. His life was way too fucked up for that.

A few months back—maybe it was more like a year now—Sal had forced himself to take stock, to figure out how he wanted to spend his golden years. After all, he probably still had a couple of good decades left. He was only fifty-seven—knock wood—way past the average age of most men in his former line of work. *So what is it,* he had asked himself, *that I really want out of life?* It boiled down to this: He wanted to live his life in peace, away from the Feds, in some distant country where he wouldn't have to worry who was waiting around the next corner. He wasn't asking much, really, but it would require a lot of dough.

The irritating thing was, Sal still had plenty of money from the old days—a small fortune that the government couldn't seize because Sal had actually earned those particular assets through legitimate businesses. But those accounts were being eyeballed like a stripper at a bachelor party. If Sal tried to make a sizable withdrawal—especially in cash—red flags would go up and he'd be surrounded before he made it to the airport.

No, what Sal needed was fresh money that could be easily concealed. Lots of it. Then he could make his break.

He could picture the location in his mind: Definitely somewhere tropical, like this Barbados place. Maybe a small island that had no extradition treaty with the United States. Better yet—no rednecks, pickup trucks, or country music. He'd had his fill of that shit.

Sal had lived in Blanco County, Texas, for three years now, which was about thirty-five months more than he could handle. And Johnson City, the county seat? Forget about it. You couldn't find decent Italian food anywhere. You had to own a satellite dish to catch most of the Yankee games. And everyone was so damn friendly, it made his asshole pucker.

For two and a half years, Sal had simply lain low, trying to figure out his next move. Unfortunately, the U.S. Marshals Service always had its eyes on him, so closely he could barely take a crap without a marshal there to offer him toilet paper. *Just a few more trials,* they kept saying, *and then you'll be free to do what you want. Leave the country, we don't care. But for now, you owe us. With your life.* And Sal had to admit that was true. He knew he could be rotting in federal prison right now—assuming some wiseguy didn't shank him in the ribs out in the yard. All of Sal's pull from the old days wouldn't mean shit. Some greaseball would waste him without batting an eye. That's the way it was nowadays: No respect for men like Sal anymore.

So, three years ago, as much as he hated to do it, Sal had

chosen the only alternative. The problem was, the trials could take years to wind their way through the judicial system. After all, the Feds were in no hurry. They were going after some heavy hitters, so they wanted to dot every *i* and cross every *t*. And, of course, there could be mistrials, appeals, and all kinds of delaying tactics that could keep Sal Mameli squarely under the U.S. District Attorney's thumb for years to come. With each day that passed, Sal couldn't help worrying that his former associates were closer to tracking him down.

And he knew the kind of justice they would exact if they found him.

After all, Sal used to be one of the guys in charge of dealing out punishment. That's where he had gotten his nickname, "the Clipper." He had done some nasty things to some nasty men, left bodies in the kind of condition that would make the most hardened medical examiner shudder. Sal knew what the horrifying possibilities were, and that's why he kept a loaded .38 in his nightstand and a sawed-off twelve-gauge under the front seat of his Lincoln. Every noise in the hallway at two A.M. could be a goon with a garrote, instead of his son, Vinnie, making a trip to the john, or his wife, Angela, sitting like a zombie in front of late-night TV, a bottle of vodka by her side.

But then, just six months ago, things had begun to look brighter. Opportunity had pounded firmly on Sal's door, as it had done so many times in the past. For some reason—a drought, a low aquifer, or who the hell knows why—residents all over Blanco County had begun clearing their lands of cedar trees and other brush. At first, Sal had barely glanced at the newspaper articles addressing the situation. Then, on a drive through the country with Angela, Sal noticed the tractorlike machines that were used to clear brush. They seemed to be everywhere, rumbling over ranchland like so many Sherman tanks.

After doing a little research, finding out precisely what this land-clearing was all about, Sal realized there was an enormous amount of money to be made in the brush-removal business. *This,* Sal thought, *could be exactly what I've been looking for.*

Hell, he had run a successful concrete company back in Jersey, and had even taken on several juicy projects here, before the water issue brought new construction to a screeching halt. And this brush-removal business, how hard could it be? The concrete business required large machines; cedar-clearing required large machines. All you needed was some operating capital and some big, dumb guys to run the equipment. Piece of cake.

So Sal had jumped right into the brush-removal business with only two things in mind: Number one—stashing away some serious cash. Number two—buying a one-way ticket to some off-the-map Caribbean island where nobody asked questions, checked for proper papers, or cared who the hell you had been in a past life. Sal could almost smell the salty breeze and the coconut oil. He could picture a tanned, nubile body—definitely not his wife's—lounging in the chair next to him.

Sal had noticed something else in the last few months: The Feds seemed to be loosening their grip a little. He no longer had a team of deputies on his tail every time he left the house, no longer heard strange clicks on the line during every phone call. There was still a plain vanilla sedan outside his home on occasion, government plates, but the fat putz inside was easy to handle.

It made Sal laugh to think they actually trusted him.

On the other hand, he *had* been their star witness half a dozen times already, and they seemed to think he was a man of his word, that he'd stick around to the end. With more freedom than he had had in three years, now was the time to make a break for it. Or at least get the plan in the works.

With his new business in full swing, the money starting to pour in, Sal was consumed around the clock by thoughts of flight. That's why, on this particular morning, as Sal was getting a piece of tail, his heart really wasn't in it. He had too much to think about, including tomorrow's meeting. Sal was getting together with a rich old bastard named Emmett Slaton, Sal's largest brush-removal competitor. Sal was going to offer Slaton twice what his business was worth. *Hell of a deal,* most people would say. Of course, the "deal" consisted of a reasonable down payment now, and a balloon payment next year that, in reality, poor old Emmett would never see. It was the same arrangement Sal had with several other area business owners. Better yet, Sal had secured the down payments via a small-business loan at a local bank, another obligation he had no intention of fulfilling. The idea was to have as much money as possible coming in, and as little as possible going out. Then, when the time was right, he'd skip the country, leaving his creditors holding the bag.

If he tried the same stunt back home, he'd wind up with his throat cut and his body tossed in the Hudson River. But down here? Shit—who was gonna stop him?

At ten o'clock Saturday morning, Susannah Branson, senior reporter for the *Blanco County Record*, wheeled her Toyota into Big Joe's Restaurant in Johnson City. There was a scattering of vehicles in the parking lot, including John Marlin's cruiser—a green Dodge Ram pickup issued by the state.

She checked her makeup in the rearview mirror and fluffed her wavy brunette hair. Susannah had been looking forward to the interview with the county game warden for several days. Rumor had it that John Marlin would soon be back on the singles market, and Susannah had had her eye on him for a long time. Ever since high school, actually. He was just her type: a big, strapping guy, with broad shoulders, dark hair, and dark eyes. *No sense in wasting time,* Susannah thought, and unsnapped one more button on her blouse.

She entered the small café and spotted Marlin at a booth, sipping coffee. He rose to greet her. " 'Morning, Susannah."

"John, thanks so much for meeting me," she said with a smile. She gave him an appraising look. "Have you lost weight?"

"Tapeworm," Marlin replied.

"Oh, uh, well," Susannah stammered, unsure whether to laugh. After all, the man *was* a game warden. Who knew what he might pick up out in the woods? "I know you're busy today, with opening day and everything, so I won't take up much of your time."

"I appreciate that, but this is important stuff. Don't rush on my account." Marlin gestured toward the booth and they took a seat.

A waitress quickly took Susannah's order—coffee only— and scooted away.

Susannah ran her hands through her hair and said, "What we're working on is a piece that addresses the environmental effects of clearing brush. Any possible effects on wildlife, livestock, et cetera. I figured you'd be the best man to talk to—especially with Trey Sweeney in the shape he's in."

Trey Sweeney was the county wildlife biologist—an ace in his field, but somewhat eccentric. Sweeney had recently returned from a vacation in Brazil, where he had contracted a mean case of dengue fever. His health was much better now, but Trey had been acting a little more strangely than usual lately. The previous Saturday night, a deputy had found Trey at the high school football stadium, rooting wildly for the home team. Unfortunately, the football game had been played the night before.

Marlin nodded at Susannah. "I'm glad you called. I think it's important that the ranchers and other landowners hear the other side of the brush-clearing story."

Six months ago, with Blanco County in the middle of a severe drought, county commissioners had recommended that residents remove as much brush from their land as possible. After all, brush—chiefly small scrub cedar trees—consumed an enormous amount of surface and ground water. By removing it, residents hoped to replenish the aquifer and pump life back into sluggish wells.

Residents had responded by conducting an all-out assault on cedar trees. Across the countryside, the buzz of chainsaws became as persistent as the droning of summertime cicadas. Huge mounds of cut cedar waited to be burned on every ranch, deer lease, and rural homesite in the county. To date, officials estimated that ten percent of the cedar had been removed. To John

Marlin and other wildlife officials, this was cause for alarm. They knew that a drastic change to the ecosystem—like clearing every cedar in the county—could have less visible long-term implications.

Susannah removed a small tape recorder from her satchel. "You mind if I tape this?" she asked. "Helps me get all the quotes right."

"Sure. No problem."

"Well, Mr. Marlin," Susannah said with false formality—something she herself found rather charming—"tell me what you think about all this cedar-clearing."

Marlin paused for a moment and took a sip of coffee. "Let me start by saying that it's not necessarily a bad idea. But it might not be a good idea, either. We obviously have a water problem, as we've all known for some time. Seems like every year we hear about how it's getting worse. Wells run dry, springs and creeks quit flowing, and Pedernales Reservoir is at a record low, even though we haven't opened a floodgate since the dam was built. And just looking at the face of it, clearing cedar seems like a good way to attack the problem."

"But . . ." Susannah prompted him.

Marlin shrugged. "I think we're all kind of rushing things. We need to step back, take a look at the bigger picture, and think about how our actions could affect the wildlife. Animals have four basic biological requirements—food, water, space, and cover. Whenever man interferes with any one of those, it can have major consequences. For instance, white-tailed deer need brush cover to survive."

"But the deer don't eat cedar trees, do they?"

"No, but they usually bed down in thick brush. And they use it to move around without being seen. Without all the cedars, they'd be a lot more vulnerable to predators like coyotes, cougars, and bobcats. Especially the fawns."

"I never thought about that."

Marlin shook his head. "Most people don't. But for all the ranch owners who are making good money with deer leases, it's something they should consider. They should be wondering what the deer population will be like in five or ten years.

"It's not just the deer," Marlin continued, speaking with obvious heartfelt intensity. "Wild turkey, rabbits, raccoons—they all need a fair amount of brushy habitat. And people should keep in mind that if you fool around with one link in the food chain, it can cause a domino effect. Let's say—just as an example—we remove all the brush, and rabbits become easy prey. Coyotes will have a field day for a while and their population will explode. Pretty soon, we've got coyotes all over the place, but they've eaten all the rabbits. So what do they go after next? Livestock. Goats, sheep, calves. I *know* the ranchers don't want that.

"Or here's another good example: the beaver. Five hundred years ago, before the Europeans came over, there were maybe three hundred million beavers in North America. Place was crawling with them, from Mexico all the way up to Alaska. But then one of the English kings ruled that only beaver fur could be used to make hats. So beaver fur became big business, and it almost wiped 'em out. Fewer beavers meant fewer beaver dams, and that had a horrible impact on the natural habitat. Suddenly, all the ponds and watering holes the beavers created were disappearing, which had an effect on waterfowl, songbirds, deer and elk, raccoons—the list goes on. Hell, those dams even helped keep the aquifers full back then by slowing down runoff. They limited soil erosion, even helped ease flooding."

Marlin shook his head and smiled thinly. "I know I'm rambling on a little. We're here to talk about cedar-clearing, right?"

"No, that's all right," Susannah said, leaning forward, trying to make eye contact. "Like you say, it all ties together. I can tell this issue means a lot to you. You're a very passionate man, John. I can see that in you."

The game warden held her gaze for a few seconds, smiling, playing the game with her. Then he glanced down at his cup. "I need a little more coffee. You want some?"

Susannah nodded, and Marlin gestured at the waitress.

"Okay, next question," she said. "What about the red-necked sapsucker?"

"I was afraid you were going to ask me that." He thought for a moment. "Yes, it's an endangered species, and yes, it nests almost exclusively in cedar trees in Central Texas. So the official Parks and Wildlife Department position is that we are against most brush-clearing in sapsucker habitat."

"And what's your personal *position*, John?" Susannah asked.

He gave her an appreciative smile, acknowledging the double entendre. Just as he was about to respond, the waitress appeared to refill their coffee cups. After she left, Marlin's face was serious again. Back to business.

"Can we talk off the record?" he asked.

"Sure."

"I think, sometimes, when a species becomes endangered, that's the way nature wants it. Think about it: More than ninety-nine percent of all species that ever existed are now extinct. And man has had little to do with the decline of the majority of them. Hell, with most of them, we couldn't have kept them around if we *wanted* to. They just weren't in Mother Nature's plan anymore, and when that happens, there's not a damn thing we can do about it."

"That's an interesting point." Susannah paused, stirring her coffee, unsure what to ask next.

"You're looking good, Susannah," Marlin said, out of the blue. "Beautiful as ever."

Susannah could feel her face getting warm. She was used to a little back-and-forth flirting, but nothing so direct and sincere. "Why, thank you, John. That's . . . that's very sweet."

He nodded, drank the last of his coffee, then said, "So—we all done here?"

"One more question." Susannah reached down and switched off the tape recorder. "Would you like to have coffee with me sometime?"

The game warden grinned and held up his cup. "We *are* having coffee."

"No," Susannah said. "I mean . . . well, you know what I mean."

For the longest time, Susannah thought he wasn't going to answer.

CHAPTER THREE

At seven o'clock Sunday morning, a dented red Ford truck with a primer-gray hood trundled down the isolated dirt roads of a quiet Blanco County ranch. Dust plumed behind the truck, hanging in the air like fog. The driver, a wiry man named Red O'Brien, was having another frustrating discussion with his passenger, poaching partner, and best friend, Billy Don Craddock.

"All I'm wonderin'," Billy Don said while scratching his massive belly, the impressive centerpiece of his three-hundred-pound physique, "is why they call it the BrushBuster 3000. Last year's model was the BrushBuster 2000, then all of a sudden they come out with the dang BrushBuster 3000. But shit if I can see the difference. Motor looks the same. Body's the same. Even the same damn colors. So what the hell's that '3000' mean, anyhow?"

"Who the hell cares?" Red said, drumming the steering wheel, impatient.

"Don't you ever think about stuff like that, Red? I mean, don't it make you wonder?"

"Well, goddamn, Billy Don, it means it's better by a thousand. What the hell you think it means?"

"But a thousand *what*?"

Red shook his head, hoping to draw the conversation to a close. He took a sip of coffee from a traveler's mug and said, "All I know is, we got plenty of work to do. Mr. Slaton's payin' us by the acre to clear these damn cedars, and the faster we work, the more we rake in. *Comprende?*"

Billy Don plucked at his muttonchop sideburns and stared out the window as the truck progressed into the ranch.

"This is easy money, Billy Don," Red continued. "I mean, people all over the county are practically shittin' themselves tryin' to get rid of all the cedar trees. All because of a few dry wells—which don't make a lot of sense to me because wells do that on occasion. It's just a matter of hydrological semantics."

Billy Don glanced over, but said nothing. Red liked to flaunt his vocabulary now and then, but Billy Don had caught Red making up phrases a couple of times. This time, though, the big man let it go.

"Be that as it were," Red said, "we gotta make hay now, before they all come to their senses. You see, Billy Don, it's what you call a limited marketplace." Red also enjoyed showing off his mastery of economic issues. "They's only so much work to go around, so we need to get what we can, while we can. Plus, if this drought breaks, people are gonna forget all about clearing cedar. You foller me?"

Billy Don nodded and donned a serious expression. "You think it has sumpin' to do with horsepower?"

"What's that?"

"The '3000.' Maybe that's the number of—"

"Will you quit harping about that shit!"

Red pulled around a copse of live oaks and spied the two bulky tree-cutting machines looming in the early dawn. The BrushBuster 3000 was truly an awesome piece of work. It looked a lot like a tractor—except for the ominous steel appendage jutting out in front. It resembled nothing so much as an overgrown lobster claw, with two hydraulic pincers that could shear a twenty-inch tree at ground level in a matter of seconds. Red loved the rush of power he felt when sitting at the Brush-Buster's controls. And the fantastic noises it made! Man, when you got that ol' diesel engine screaming at eight thousand RPMs, and combined that with the wrenching noises the blades made when they bit into a big softwood tree like a cedar . . . goddamn! It sounded like you were beating a pig to death with an accordion. And the amazing thing was, it was *supposed* to sound that way! It sure beat anything Red had ever seen at the monster-truck rallies.

Red pulled up beside the twin machines and cut the truck's engine. "Billy Don, we'll be working in separate areas today. That means I'm not gonna be around to watch after ya, so pay attention to what you're doing. No screwups today, all right?"

Red was referring to a minor flaw in Billy Don's botanical skills that had caused some problems the week before.

Namely, Billy Don could hardly tell a cedar tree from a telephone pole.

They had been working a ranch that was home to the single largest madrone grove in Texas. The madrone was a fairly uncommon tree—now even more rare thanks to Billy Don. He had polished off a six-pack of Busch with lunch, then proceeded to level half of the ten-acre grove before the infuriated rancher shot out both of Billy Don's tires with a twelve-gauge. Mr. Slaton had been boiling mad when he heard about it, but Red talked him out of firing Billy Don. Red had become good friends with the old guy, but boy could he get wound up tight sometimes!

Both men fired up their BrushBusters, and Red watched Billy Don head off toward the northernmost pasture on the ranch. It was a damn big place. They had been working the ranch for three days solid and hadn't laid eyes on the house or even seen another vehicle. Most owners would stop by every so often to check the progress, but not this one. Red figured the owner might live over in Austin or down in San Antonio. Maybe a fancy lawyer or doctor. Those kinds loved owning big ranches: someplace they could bring their buddies and act like a big-shot cowboy.

Red was just about to put his BrushBuster in gear when a Land Rover pulled up beside him. *Speak of the devil,* Red thought. *Must be the owner, finally deciding to take a look.* Out of the vehicle climbed a man in his fifties, hair graying, wearing outdoor gear straight out of some catalog. Red cut his engine and hopped down to introduce himself. It never hurt to get acquainted with these society types. He might get invited to a party . . . or better yet, he could learn the man's schedule and come out and poach a few deer when nobody was around.

" 'Mornin'," Red said. "Red O'Brien."

The man shook Red's hand, but had a strange expression on his otherwise friendly face. "Uh, yeah, I'm Walter Gibbs, the owner. I saw the tracks in here and—well, uh, I'm kinda wondering what you're doing out here."

"Sir?"

"What exactly are you doing on my ranch?"

Red gestured at the BrushBuster. "Clearing cedar, just like you asked."

"But I didn't order any land-clearing. I was thinking about getting it done, same as everyone else, but—"

Red scratched his head. "This is the Leaning X, right?"

Gibbs chuckled. "I hate to tell you this, but no. It's Raven Hill Ranch. The Leaning X is the next gate down."

The man continued talking, but Red didn't hear any of it. His mouth had gone dry, his temperature was rising, and all he could hear was what Billy Don had told him just three days ago: *Aw, hell, this is the place, Red. It's right here on the map. Slaton musta given us the wrong combination to the lock. Let's just cut it off and git to work.*

"So what'd you tell her?" Phil Colby asked.

John Marlin steered his Dodge Ram off the highway onto a gravel-topped county road. He was answering a hunter-harassment call from a man named Cecil Pritchard. It was a low-priority call from the day before, and Marlin had been too busy to respond yesterday. Colby, Marlin's best friend since childhood, was joining him on what the Parks and Wildlife Department called a "ride-along," a chance for civilians to get an up-close look at a game warden's daily activities and responsibilities. Colby joined Marlin several times a year and Marlin always enjoyed the company.

"Well, Susannah Branson is a nice gal, no doubt about it, so I wasn't sure what to say," Marlin said. "And I didn't want to hurt her feelings. So I told her that it might be nice sometime."

Colby nodded. "No harm in that. It's no big deal, just a couple of friends getting together for coffee."

Marlin gave Colby a sideways glance.

"On the other hand," Colby grinned, "she's damn good-lookin'. Hell, if you don't wanna take her out, give her my number." Colby was trying to lighten the mood a little, but Marlin was having none of it. After a pause, Colby said, "Listen, John, you know how sorry I am about this whole deal with Becky. But that's how things work out sometimes. You gotta tell yourself it's for the best."

Marlin didn't reply. He pulled into a dirt driveway and approached a run-down mobile home where a filthy toddler was playing in the barren yard. Marlin recognized Beth Pritchard sitting on the porch steps, in white shorts and a pink tube top, smoking a cigarette. Next to the house was Cecil Pritchard's gray Chevy truck, with a bumper sticker that read: KEEP HONKING. I'M RELOADING.

"'Mornin', Beth," Marlin called as he and Colby stepped out of the cruiser. "I hear Cecil's been doing a little hunting this weekend."

"Wasting time and money is what I call it," Beth sneered. She gestured around her. "What do you think, John? Does it look like we can afford a deer lease?"

Marlin simply shrugged, not wanting to get in the middle of a domestic squabble. He looked over at Colby for help, but Phil was suddenly interested in something on the horizon. A few yards away, wisps of smoke floated out of a barrel, carrying the acrid scent of smoldering garbage. Evidently, Cecil was too chintzy to pay for trash pickup. Marlin considered mentioning that there was a burn ban in effect in Blanco County—due to the drought—but then Cecil Pritchard would probably just toss his trash out on the highway.

"Cecil around?" Marlin asked.

Beth gave a dismissive wave. "He's out in his workshop. Do me a favor and arrest him for somethin', will ya?"

"Thanks, Beth." Marlin eyed the toddler. "Looks like Junior's growing up real good."

Beth grunted.

Near the mobile home sat a small low-slung building slapped together with tar paper and sheet metal. A couple of old tires had been thrown on the roof to keep it secure on windy days. Marlin and Colby entered the shack, where Cecil was sprawled on a torn plaid couch watching a football game on a small black-and-white TV.

The men exchanged greetings and Cecil offered Marlin and Colby a beer from a large galvanized washtub that was currently functioning as an ice chest. They declined.

After a few minutes of small talk, Marlin said, "I got your message on my machine, Cecil. What's up?"

Cecil turned down the TV, hiked up his suspenders, and said, "Y'all ain't *even* gonna believe what happened to me yesterday."

CHAPTER FOUR

Emmett Slaton was a robust seventy-five-year-old rancher who looked like he could still leap from a galloping horse and wrestle a steer to the ground. He was a stereotypical raucous Texan, always sitting at the loudest table at any cafe. Friendly enough, most of the time, but with a legendary stubborn streak and a tendency toward bigotry. Salvatore Mameli had experienced both traits firsthand during his initial phone call to Slaton two weeks ago. At first, the rancher had been polite, if not cordial.

But when Sal had made his proposition, Slaton ladled out a string of obscenities, then summed it all up by saying he'd "rather kiss a sow on the mouth after feeding time than sell my operation to some two-bit Capone."

Apparently, Sal's well-oiled hair and pinkie ring weren't a big hit with the locals.

But Sal had patience—and a remarkable ability to control his temper when needed. He simply thanked the man for his time and wished him a good night.

A week later, Sal felt he was making progress. During the second phone call, the rancher had merely told Sal to "catch the

next train to hell or Houston, it don't matter which." Sal, however, still didn't lose his temper, mostly because he had never
been to Houston. Also, he could tell that being a little blus-
tery—"ornery" was the word they'd use around here—was
merely part of the Texan's act. The truth was, Sal was having a
tough time reading some of these Texans. Sometimes he would
think he was on the verge of a fistfight, only to have the man
clap him on the back, say, "Hell, I was just bullshittin' ya," then
laugh like it was the funniest thing since Grandpa dropped his
dentures into the mashed potatoes. Sal took heart in the fact
that Slaton had seemed to soften a little during the second
phone call, as if he just enjoyed giving people a hard time.

Finally, on the third phone call, the rancher had said, "Aw,
what the hell—I'll hear you out. Come see me at the ranch."

So Sal was practicing his spiel, thinking of the empty prom-
ises he was about to make, when he pulled into the entryway of
Buckhorn Creek Ranch on Sunday morning. Slaton's home, a
limestone-and-granite monstrosity, sat half a mile off the road,
ringed by towering hundred-year-old oak trees.

As Sal parked his new Lincoln, a fearsome-looking Doberman pinscher raced off the front porch, placed both front paws
on Sal's door, and howled at Sal through the glass. Sal instinctively recoiled from the growling beast.

"Heel, Patton!" Slaton yelled as he came out the front door.
The dog immediately retreated to his master's side and plopped
his rear onto the ground.

Sal, feeling somewhat safe now, climbed out of his car.
"Mistuh Slaton?"

"Call me Emmett. With an accent like that, you gotta be Sal
Mameli," Slaton said, extending his hand. "Damn glad to meet
you."

Sal shook Slaton's hand, keeping an eye on the Doberman.

"Don't worry about him," Slaton said. "The growlin' is just
for show. If he really wanted to do ya any damage, you'd never
even hear him comin'."

Sal wondered if that was supposed to make him feel better.
"Patton, huh?"

"Yessir. Named after a great American—and a distant relative of yours truly, I don't mind tellin' ya."

"Dat right?" Sal feigned interest. He had noticed that Texans tended to be long-winded—and he hoped he wasn't in for a story.

"Somethin' like a third cousin on my daddy's side," Slaton said. "But that's neither here nor there. Let's head inside and hear what you've got to say."

The two men entered the house, with the dog following a little too closely in Sal's footsteps. Slaton led Sal to a large den where a rust-colored cowskin rug covered the polished Saltillo tile underneath. It was furnished in a traditional ranch motif, with blocky wooden furniture, wood paneling, and several antique-looking firearms mounted on the walls. Slaton motioned to two chairs beside a large fireplace. "Have a seat. Can I get you something to drink? I know it's early, but the bar's always open 'round here."

"Got any scotch?"

"No sir, fine Kentucky bourbon's the only liquor I keep in my home. And I got some cold beer."

"Beer'd be fine," Sal replied, looking around the room. It was much too gaudy for his tastes, but the room—in its own backwoods way—spoke of money. And a man who understood the value of a dollar was certain to appreciate Sal's generous "offer."

Slaton brought over a couple of drinks and sat in the chair next to Sal. The dog lay obediently beside Slaton's chair.

The men chatted for a minute—polite but meaningless conversation—and then Sal decided to lay it on the table. "Emmett, I know you're a serious man, so I'll be straight wit' ya: I'm interested in buying your land-clearing operation. As you know, I've been in the business a few months myself, and it's treated me well."

Slaton took a sip of bourbon but didn't comment. So Sal continued: "I hope you don't mind—I done a little research, found out how many machines you own, how many employees you got . . ."

Sal removed a pen and a small notepad from his coat pocket and wrote a figure on a page. ". . . and dis is what I'm prepared to offer ya." Sal held the notebook up for Slaton to see. "I'm ready to pay twenty-five percent now, and the rest one year from today."

Slaton remained quiet.

Sal squirmed a little in his seat. He was used to holding the upper hand in negotiations like this. "Whaddaya say, Mistuh Slaton? Can we talk about it?"

"What's there to talk about, son?" He broke into a grin. "The outfit's all yours."

"Seriously?" Sal hadn't expected things to go quite this smoothly.

"Hell, yeah," Slaton said. "I know a good offer when I see it. I'll get my attorney to draw up the contracts on Monday. Until then"—he raised his glass—"I'll wish you luck on your new venture."

Sal raised his beer. *"Te salute."*

Slaton eyed Sal a little suspiciously, probably thrown by the foreign phrase, but he drank anyway.

"So, how you enjoyin' Texas so far?" the rancher asked.

"Fuhget about it," Sal said. He figured he'd make a little small talk, then exit gracefully. "What—we're already into November and it's eighty degrees outside? And the summertime? Place is a goddamn sauna."

"It's not so bad," Slaton said.

"You kidding me? I don't know how you live in dis hellhole."

Right then, Sal knew he'd made a mistake. Slaton stood slowly, and the only sound was the scrape of the chair on the tile floor. Sal felt awkward looking up into the old man's weathered face.

"Son, did you just call the great state of Texas a 'hellhole'?" Slaton asked.

Sal gave a feeble smile. "I was just talking, ya know? Figger of speech."

"Well, the deal's off. You can take your figure of speech and your shiny East Coast suit and get the hell out of my house."

"C'mon, Mistuh Slaton, why ya breakin' my balls? I was just—" Sal heard a growl. The Doberman had risen also, and was now at Sal's right elbow, fixing him with an unsettling stare.

"I think it's time for you to leave, Mameli."

Sal couldn't believe it. What would have been an offhand remark back home was apparently cause for a duel here in Texas. "Aw, fuck it," Sal said. "You're making a mistake here, pal. A big one."

"You're the one who made a mistake, son. Now clear out."

On his way toward the door, Sal pointed a meaty finger at Slaton. "You're gonna regret dis."

Twelve miles away, two twenty-year-old men were smoking a fat joint and slamming Budweisers at Pedernales Reservoir. Terrence Jackson Gibbs—"T.J." to his friends—was lying on top of a picnic table, indifferent to the puddle of old ketchup that was ruining the back of his hundred-dollar polo shirt. His friend, Vinnie Mameli, was sitting on the table's bench seat, shooting a pellet rifle at any bird who made the mistake of lighting in a nearby tree. Vinnie was a tall, well-muscled kid, with dark eyes, close-cropped hair, and a purple birthmark on the left side of his neck. T.J. was smaller, and thick through the middle, like a frat boy who'd been drinking beer all summer.

"I need a new car," T.J. wheezed, propped on an elbow, trying to contain the pot smoke in his lungs. "My fuckin' Porsche sucks." He finally exhaled a large cloud of gray smoke. "It's in the shop half the time, then I have to drive one of my dad's trucks. Feel like a redneck."

"Goddamn, quit yer bitchin' already," Vinnie said. "Just get your old man to buy you something else." He spotted a mourning dove thirty yards away in a Spanish oak. He pumped the rifle five times and let a pellet fly. The bird flapped, then flew away erratically, leaving a few feathers to drift gently to the ground. "You're spoiled rotten anyway," Vinnie said.

T.J. sat up straight. "Look who's talking, you asshole. You're the one who's always packing a wad of hundreds. And you don't even fuckin' work. At least I got a job."

"Assistant manager at Dairy Queen? You're really climbin' the corporate ladder, T.J."

"Hey, work builds character. At least that's what my dad tells me. And anyway, I also got my own place to stay."

Vinnie snorted. "Aw, give me a break. You're livin' in the guest cabin on your parents' ranch. That's really cutting the ol' apron strings, I tell ya."

T.J. thought it over. "Fuck it," he finally said.

"That's what I say. Fuck it. Pass the joint."

T.J. handed it over, and Vinnie took a long hit. "Dude, why don't we go over to the ranch and do a little four-wheelin'?"

Since moving to Texas, Vinnie had discovered—and fallen in love with—this exciting and aimless activity. Guys in jacked-up four-wheel-drive trucks or all-terrain vehicles would take off cross-country, bouncing over culverts, splashing through creeks, trampling the foliage and any animal unfortunate enough to find itself in the vehicle's path. T.J. owned a bright-red Toyota four-by-four with an oversized engine, headers, enormous tires, and a roll bar. Hell on wheels, but too tricked-out to be street-legal.

"Nah, there's a couple of guys over there clearing cedar and shit. My dad musta called 'em. He drove in from Austin yesterday. He's been comin' out more often lately, ever since the party. Like he's checking up on me."

T.J. and Vinnie had thrown a huge celebration three months earlier, for T.J.'s birthday. T.J. had done it up in style, with a dozen kegs, a live band, and enough illicit substances to stock the local drugstore. Naturally, every county resident between the ages of fifteen and twenty-five had attended. It was a fairly typical T.J. Gibbs party, with topless women in the hot tub, minors vomiting behind bushes, and three fistfights. When Walter Gibbs showed up unexpectedly the next morning, what angered him most was the fact that the riding mower—a brand-new John Deere—had somehow ended up in the swimming pool.

"Where is the trust?" Vinnie asked with a smile.

"No shit," T.J. replied, missing Vinnie's sarcasm. "Plus, I gotta be at work at five."

"Better smoke up, then, my man."

As T.J. took another hit, Vinnie's cell phone rang. He slipped it off his belt. "You got Vinnie, talk fast. . . . Oh, hey, Pop."

After a thirty-second conversation, Vinnie hung up and turned to T.J. "My old man on his car phone. He's pissed off about something. I gotta go."

CHAPTER FIVE

Rodney Bauer wiped the sweat from his brow and vowed for the hundredth time to lose about twenty pounds. Forty would probably be a healthier goal, according to his doctor. The weight always had been a bit of a problem, but really became an issue when he was quail-hunting, hiking around in the Texas sun.

His small ranch—like the rest of Blanco County and the Hill Country west of Austin—was poor quail habitat. Too rocky, not enough wide-open grassland, and too many fire ants, which could kill the quail's hatchlings. But there were usually a few coveys scattered about on his acreage, and that's what he was searching for on Sunday afternoon.

Rodney's dog, Honeybee, a one-year-old yellow Lab, had a decent nose, but Labs weren't really meant for quail. Rodney enjoyed running the birds with her just the same.

Honeybee was scampering through tall native grasses about twenty yards ahead of Rodney when she came to a stop. Rodney eased up beside the dog, and then raised his shotgun to his shoulder. "Git 'em," he whispered. The dog bolted straight for a mound of cedar brush—and the air exploded with the sound of flapping wings. A dozen quail took to the air, and Rodney fired two quick booming shots. Honeybee scurried through the grass, picked up a quail gently in her jaws, and delivered it to Rodney.

"Good girl!" Rodney said, stroking the dog's neck. "Now, fetch! Get the other one!" Honeybee started in the direction of the other fallen quail, but suddenly veered to her left and took off at a run, wagging her tail.

Rodney was shouting at Honeybee, calling her back, when he realized he had an unexpected visitor. A woman had emerged from the cedar thicket that bordered the open meadow where Rodney was hunting.

For a moment, Rodney was stunned. The woman was gorgeous: tall, with flowing blonde hair. Trim but curvy. Like something right out of a beer commercial. She was dressed in snug blue shorts and a bikini top that was barely handling its contents. Rodney was suddenly grateful it was unseasonably warm today.

The woman was kneeling down, rubbing Honeybee's head, and that gave Rodney time to regain the powers of speech. "'Mornin'," Rodney said, walking over. "I wasn't expecting a visitor today."

The woman looked up and gave him a smile that made his palms sweat. She said in a soft voice, "Sorry to barge in on you like this, but I was driving by and heard the shots. I've always wanted to learn how to hunt, so I just hopped the fence." The smile again. "I hope you don't mind."

Honeybee was still wagging her tail furiously—and Rodney would have been doing the same thing if he had one. "No ma'am, don't mind at all. My name's Rodney Bauer, and this is my ranch." He stepped forward and offered his hand.

The woman's fingers were slender and smooth. "Inga Mueller."

"Oh, you're German. Same here. *Guten Tag.*"

"Well, German on my father's side. My mother is Swedish."

Praise the Lord you take after your mama, Rodney thought. There was an awkward pause, and Rodney finally said, "So . . . you want to learn how to shoot birds?"

"I'd love to," the woman said in the same sexy voice. "I find guns very . . . exciting." She stepped closer and lightly touched the barrel of Rodney's twelve-gauge. "That's a very nice gun you have there, Rodney."

Rodney visibly gulped. What was going on here? Had someone set this up as a joke? This couldn't possibly be happening. Rodney stole a nervous glance in the direction of his house, imagining the heat of his wife's glare from five hundred yards away. "Why, thank you," Rodney croaked. "I'd be happy to show you a thing or two. I need to grab a little more ammo, so why don't we walk over to my truck?" Actually, Rodney had plenty of shells in his hunting vest. He just wanted to continue this conversation over by his Chevy, tucked in the privacy of the trees.

As they walked, Rodney noticed the hiking boots the woman was wearing, and the way they brought out the fine lines of her sculpted calf muscles. "You sure are lucky to own a ranch," she said. "You do a lot of hunting out here?"

"Oh, yeah, all the time. Shot a twelve-point buck yesterday," Rodney lied. "Gonna mount him for sure."

The woman said, "Do you mount a lot of things, Rodney?"

Rodney's face flushed and he began to feel a little dizzy. He tried to answer, but only managed a few stutters.

The woman looped her arm in his and walked beside him. She leaned and whispered in his ear: "Cat got your tongue?"

Rodney could feel her warm breath on his neck, and desperately wished he could play this game as well as she did. He wanted to think of something clever to say, but was stumped. He managed to blurt, "Ever shot a gun before, Inga?"

"Nope, I'm a virgin." Another suggestive smile.

By now, Rodney was waiting for Allen Funt to step from the brush and tell him he was on *Candid Camera*. "It's really simple," he said. He showed the woman how to load the shotgun, the proper way to hold it, and where the safety catch was. "The main thing is, never aim it at anything you don't intend to shoot." He handed her the weapon.

"Ooh, this feels nice."

"Great," Rodney said. "Let's see if Honeybee can scare us up some quail."

"That would be really fun, Rodney. But first, let me try a few practice shots." Suddenly, the woman turned, shouldered the shotgun, and aimed at Rodney's one-year-old pickup. Before Rodney could react, the woman fired.

The first shot tore through the front grille and loosed the contents of the radiator.

The second shot turned the windshield into a network of cracks with a gaping hole in the center.

The last shot punctured the right front tire. The air whooshed out and the truck bowed like a circus elephant on one knee.

Rodney began to whimper softly.

Honeybee cavorted around the woman with glee.

The woman turned to Rodney and said, "Well, look at that. I think I've already got the hang of it."

"You're about the most stupidest hillbilly I ever met, you know that, Billy Don?" The men were back in Red's truck, driving over to Emmett Slaton's house. Red felt certain they'd both get fired this time. They had wasted a great deal of time chopping cedar on the wrong ranch, and now they had to come clean with their boss.

Over on the passenger's side, Billy was pouting. "It wasn't my fault, Red. All I done was foller the map, and it was wrong."

"The map, huh?"

"You saw it."

"But you're the one who drew the freakin' map!"

"Oh yeah."

"I have to tell ya, I'm impressed, though. I didn't even know you could operate a pencil without an owner's manual."

Billy Don gave Red a harsh glare—kind of a cross-eyed grimace that appeared when he was particularly angry—and Red knew he was walking on thin ice. Billy Don was a three-hundred-pound brute, and Red decided he'd better ease up.

"Well, I'll see what I can do about keeping our jobs. Just leave the talkin' to me."

As Red turned into the gate at Emmett Slaton's ranch, a late-model Lincoln coming the other way barreled through beside him, blasting its horn. Red caught a glimpse of the driver as it passed by. "Hell's bells, what's wrong with that guy?" He glanced in the rearview mirror. "You know, that looked like that Eye-talian who tried to hire us last week."

"Wonder if his offer is still good?" Billy Don whimpered.

Red hissed: "You can go to work for a wop if you want, Billy Don, but not me. Besides, somethin' didn't feel right."

The man had called Red on the phone, offering an employment deal that included complicated incentives and escalating per-acre commissions. *You could make a coupla g's a week if you work hard enough,* the man had said. Red wasn't sure what a "g" was, but he had pulled a few fast ones in his time and he thought it sounded like a scam. He said thanks but no thanks, he was sticking with Slaton.

Red parked the truck and the Doberman bounded off the porch, howling at the visitors.

"Hey there, Patton," Red said, and the dog wagged its docked tail. "Look what we got here." Red pulled a piece of beef jerky from his pocket and Patton gently took it from his hand. "You're just a big ol' pansy, ain't ya? Where's your daddy at?"

As if he understood, the dog ran to the front door and barked.

Emmett Slaton opened the door and ushered the men into his den. "What brings you out here this time of day, boys? You done with the Leaning X already?"

Red held his hat in his hand and told the full story, waiting for Slaton to get angry, tell them they were both idiots. But Slaton didn't get mad, and actually seemed distracted, as if he were hardly listening.

When Red was finished, Slaton simply nodded. Then he pulled a large handgun out of a drawer and laid it on his desk. "Either of you ever shot a forty-five? I want to sight this in, but my eyes ain't quite what they used to be."

Red was startled. "What about the Leaning X, sir? Ain't you gonna fire us?"

"Aw, hell, son, I would never fire you for that. Besides, you wasted your time, not mine. Now help me sight this gun in."

Red stared down at the weapon. "Somethin' got you worried, Mr. Slaton?"

The rancher shrugged. "Aw, not really, son. But a man can't be too careful these days."

Sunday evening, a cold front moved southward into Blanco County, bringing half an inch of much-needed rain, harsh winds, and a twenty-degree drop in temperature. John Marlin was glad to see it. The first week of deer season was always his busiest, and the nasty weather would help put a damper on poaching activities around the county.

He received only one call that evening. Just after sundown, a hunter on a day lease had struck an axis deer with his truck. The landowner was furious, claiming the hunter owed him two thousand dollars for the imported exotic buck. The hunter didn't see it that way, and wanted the landowner to pay for the damages to his Chevy. Marlin knew the law, and sided with neither of them.

Over the phone, he told them the hunter wasn't liable for the cost of the deer and the landowner wasn't liable for the damages to the truck. They each had to take their own lumps. That seemed to satisfy them both, and Marlin hung up, grateful he didn't have to brave the weather for something so petty.

CHAPTER SIX

The rain was long gone by Monday morning, but things were still slow—no calls from the sheriff's dispatcher—so Marlin met Phil Colby for breakfast at a small café attached to the bowling alley in Blanco. He was also expecting to see Rodney Bauer, who had called Marlin's home number early that morning. Bauer wouldn't specify why he wanted to see Marlin, but said it had something to do with an odd incident that happened while he was quail-hunting yesterday.

The diner was quiet, with only a dozen or so customers, all die-hard regulars willing to brave the weather for a hot breakfast. Marlin and Colby were in a booth, drinking coffee, waiting for the waitress to bring their orders.

"You watchin' the Cowboys this afternoon?" Colby asked.

"Probably catch it on the radio," Marlin replied.

"Lookin' like a pretty bad year."

Marlin nodded.

"Their runnin' game has gone to hell," Colby said, "and their defense is a sieve."

Marlin heard the jingle of the bell hanging on the front door of the diner and glanced over, but it wasn't Rodney Bauer.

"Have I told you about my new two-seventy?" Colby asked. "That sucker can hit the same hole twice at a hundred yards. Can't wait to get out hunting next week."

"Yeah, you mentioned it," Marlin said. He knew Colby was trying to draw him into conversation, to help him quit dwelling on other, less pleasant topics. Like the fact that Becky was gone, probably for good.

Unfortunately, in a small town, gossip travels faster than a spooked mare, and Marlin knew the locals were wondering whether he and Becky were still seeing each other. Marlin had no idea why people were so interested in other people's social lives. They were always asking vague, not-so-innocent questions, giving him sympathetic looks, trying to draw information out of him. *What have you been doing lately? Haven't seen you in town much . . . where you been? You still living by yourself out there in the sticks?* Like the other day, when Susannah Branson had asked him if he had lost weight. What Marlin had heard, between the lines, was: *Haven't you been eating? What's bothering you?* That's why he had given her the smart-ass "tapeworm" answer. Because Marlin didn't want to talk about it.

Colby went quiet and focused on the basketball game playing on the TV mounted above the bar.

After a few minutes of silence, the bell jingled again and Rodney Bauer walked in. He spotted Marlin and Colby and strolled casually to their table. "Hey, John—hey, Phil. Y'all mind if I join you?"

"I thought that was the plan," Marlin said, and Rodney sat down.

Rodney signaled the waitress for coffee, then leaned in close over the table. He whispered, "Something really strange happened to me yesterday, John, and I'm pretty pissed off about it." In a quiet voice, Rodney led Marlin through the events of the day before.

"She jammed the muzzle of your gun into the mud?" Marlin repeated. Next to him, Colby let out a small laugh.

Rodney nodded. "That's what I said: She shot the shit outta my truck, and when she was done, she shoved my gun into the mud. Then she said that I should be ashamed of myself. For shootin' birds, of all things."

Colby suppressed a giggle by trying to disguise it as a cough.

"Ain't funny," Rodney said, glaring at Colby. "Took me a solid hour to clean that mess up. And my Chevy is all screwed up."

"She driving an old yellow Volvo?" Marlin asked.

"Never did see what she was drivin'. By the time I came to my senses, she had hopped the fence again and was gone."

"What'd she look like?"

Rodney looked down at the table. "Well, that's why I'm keepin' this kinda quiet." He glanced furtively around the diner. "She's finer than frog hair, boys. Tall and blonde and an absolute knockout. See, I don't want word to get back to Mabel. She may think I've got something going on with this gal."

Colby finally lost it and erupted in laughter. "You been datin' your way through the supermodel circuit, Rodney?" he managed to ask.

Rodney tensed, and Marlin held up a hand to quiet them both. "She look anything like that?" Marlin gestured to the front windows of the diner.

Outside, two people had just arrived in a rusty yellow Volvo. The driver was a short, scruffy guy with ragged curly hair, a wispy beard, and a weathered camouflage jacket. The other was a tall blonde woman who would have looked right at home on the cover of *Cosmopolitan*. She was dressed casually, in a tailored jacket and cream-colored denims.

The residents of Blanco were accustomed to strangers passing through town; after all, Main Street was also U.S. Highway 281. But the majority of visitors looked like they belonged on the streets of Austin or Dallas, whereas this woman looked like a vision from the runways of Milan. When she walked through the front door of the diner, the small crowd went dead quiet.

The couple found a table and, as she prepared to sit down, the woman removed her jacket. She was wearing a tight red turtleneck that hugged a curvy torso. Marlin was embarrassed when one deaf old regular said, a little too loudly, "I'm glad I took my heart medicine this mornin'." The crowd tittered.

The woman turned, found the old man, and gave him a sly wink, which caused a murmur.

"That's her!" Rodney hissed. "She's the one who blasted my truck!"

"You sure about that, Rodney?" Marlin sounded skeptical. "I mean, if I go question her, I won't be making a complete ass of myself?"

"No doubt whatsoever. Look at her, John. You think there's two of her kind runnin' around Blanco County?"

"Good point."

Marlin gave Colby a look that asked, *What am I about to get myself into?*

Colby responded with a shrug. "Duty calls."

Marlin rose and crossed the room to the woman's table. The crowd was silent, enjoying a front-row seat to whatever was about to happen.

"'Mornin', ma'am . . . sir." Marlin nodded to them both.

The woman gave him a poker face. "Good morning, Officer." The woman appeared so Scandinavian, Marlin was expecting an accent, but there was nothing but a Midwestern twang.

"Ma'am, I was wondering if I could speak to you outside for a minute."

"Pardon?"

"Well, I just want to ask you a few questions about an incident. I'm the game warden in Blanco County."

The woman started to reply, but her scruffy companion spoke up, with a bit of an attitude. "We can read the badge on your shirt, sir. Do you mind telling us what this is all about?"

The internal radar Marlin had developed by interviewing thousands of poachers simply said: *Asshole.* Marlin dealt with all types of people in the course of a season. Most were respectable, law-abiding citizens. But some were belligerent, some were drunk, and still others—like this guy—were self-righteous jerks who thought they were above the law.

Marlin responded with a little attitude of his own: "Sir, at the moment I'm speaking to this young lady. If I have any questions for you, I'll be sure to let you know." He kept a firm glare on Mr. Scruffy for a moment. The man gave Marlin a contemptuous sneer, but remained silent.

Marlin turned back to the blonde woman and gestured toward the front door. "Ma'am, if you don't mind . . ."

The woman remained seated. "I believe I'll stay right here, but feel free to ask all the questions you want."

"Fine," Marlin said, taking a breath. "We've received a couple of reports of hunter harassment in the last few days, and you match the description of the woman involved. Now, can you tell me where you were yesterday at about two in the afternoon?"

The woman raised her hand and drummed her fingertips theatrically on her cheek. "Well, let's see. After lunch we stopped at the grocery store and got a few things, then we filled the car with gas. And then, yes, right at about two o'clock, I was teaching good ol' Rodney over there the error of his ways." The woman looked across the room at Rodney and said, in her best cocktail-party voice, "Why, hello, Rodney! Good to see you again, sweetheart."

The crowd turned and stared at Rodney, who blanched and turned toward the wall.

Marlin was taken aback. Most lawbreakers, when questioned, knew how to do three things: Deny it; deny it; and deny it some more. "Ma'am, are you saying that you *were* over at Mr. Bauer's ranch yesterday, and you *are* responsible for the damage to his truck?"

"What I'm saying is that I was saving the lives of quail, dove, deer, and all the other innocent animals he would have murdered with his shotgun."

The crowd had grown tense. Someone murmured, "Take her in, John."

Which was exactly what Marlin was planning to do. "Stand up, please," he said.

The woman crossed her arms. "I will not."

Marlin glanced at Mr. Scruffy, who gave him a smug smile. Inside, Marlin groaned. He had had run-ins with antihunting activists in the past, and it was almost always a messy business.

"Ma'am . . . please . . . stand up."

"Like hell I will. Why are you here bothering me when you should be out arresting guys like Rodney? They're the ones carrying guns, blasting everything that moves. And yet I'm the one who's causing trouble? That's a joke."

Mr. Scruffy began to add something, but Marlin hushed him with a stare.

Marlin took a deep breath. He was determined not to let this situation get out of control. "Miss, I'll ask you once again: Please stand up. Don't make me use the cuffs."

"Go to hell." She grabbed her mug and threw her coffee onto Marlin's chest.

The crowd gasped. *This,* Marlin thought, *isn't going well at all.*

Marlin drove northward on Highway 281 in silence for a few moments, steadily covering the sixteen miles between Blanco and Johnson City. He noticed the sky was clear of clouds now, and the temperature was rapidly climbing. So much for the cold front.

He glanced over at his passenger. He couldn't remember the last time he'd had a handcuffed woman in custody. In fact, in nearly twenty years of enforcing hunting and fishing laws, almost all of his dealings had been with men. Simply put, men would do things women would never dream of. Like shoot deer on the side of the highway at night. Throw dynamite into a lake to kill fish. Blast a hundred doves in one day, instead of the legal limit of fifteen. Then they would spin lie after lie to try to escape punishment. At least this woman had owned up to her behavior. Too easily, Marlin figured. There had to be something behind it.

"You didn't have to throw the coffee on me, you know," Marlin said.

"Pardon me?"

"I was going to arrest you anyway." He looked over, but her face remained expressionless. "That's what you wanted, wasn't it? I mean, my cruiser was sitting right in the parking lot, plain as day. You came in there for a reason."

"What are you, Sherlock Holmes?"

Another mile went by.

"These are really hurting my wrists." The woman shifted in her seat, arching her back to relieve the pressure of the handcuffs behind her. Marlin tried not to notice the way her breasts strained against the front of her turtleneck. He hadn't wanted to cuff her, but after the coffee, he'd wanted to make sure she was restrained, at least until he had a bead on her companion, Mr. Scruffy. That guy had turned out to be the placid one, merely sneering—apparently a trademark of his—while Marlin read the woman, one Inga Karin Mueller from Minnesota, her rights.

Marlin pulled to the shoulder of the highway and put the cruiser in neutral. He held the handcuff key up for Inga to see. "Gonna behave?"

She snorted and rolled her eyes.

Marlin started to put the key back on his belt.

"Okay, okay," she said. "Can't you take a joke?"

She twisted toward the window and Marlin removed the cuffs.

She rubbed her wrists as Marlin pulled the cruiser back onto the road.

"Thank you," she said.

"No problem."

They crossed over Miller Creek, which was barely more than a slow-moving mud puddle despite last night's brief rain.

"What's the deal with your friend, anyway? Did he take a mail-order course on the fine art of sneering?"

Inga laughed. "Oh, that's just Tommy. Not a real happy guy, but he's pretty harmless."

Marlin wasn't sure he agreed. Thomas Collin Peabody had been arrested three times for destruction of property and twice for trespassing. A typical rap sheet for an aggressive activist. Unfortunately, when Marlin had radioed him in, there were no warrants. He had to watch the mousy little guy get back in the Volvo and drive away.

"He's a very intelligent man, actually," Inga continued. "Has a bunch of degrees. Philosophy. Government. History. Went to Harvard for about a zillion years. And now he wants me to marry him." She gave Marlin a sidelong glance, but he just nodded.

"So you're not going to share your secret with me," Marlin said, "tell me why you wanted to get busted?"

Inga gave him a hard stare for several seconds, as if sizing him up. Finally, she said, "Unlike some people, I love nature. When I see people shooting animals, dumping sewage in creeks, destroying forests, I do something about it."

Marlin was tempted to chastise her for putting hunting in the same league with polluting and deforestation, but he held his tongue.

She went on: "When I see a guy like Rodney Bauer blasting away at beautiful, defenseless birds, it just makes me so angry—" She shook her head in frustration.

He gave her a few moments to continue, but she stared out the window at the passing countryside instead.

Marlin said, "Surely you didn't drive two thousand miles to get Rodney Bauer all hot and bothered and then vandalize his truck." He was hoping to make her grin, but had no luck. He was certain she had a wonderful smile.

"Nope. We drove down here for a different reason entirely."

"And that would be—?"

She paused, seeming reluctant to let Marlin into her confidence. But he must have passed some sort of test. "Let me ask you something. Have you ever heard of the red-necked sapsucker?"

The sapsucker again.

"Sure," Marlin replied. "Endangered species."

"And obviously you know about all the brush-clearing that's going on around here. But I don't think most people even realize the effect it's having, that they're wiping out the last of a species. If all the cedars are removed, that's it, end of story, the red-necked sapsucker is gone. I'm here to change that."

"Meaning what?" Marlin had already admitted to himself that he liked the woman, despite the coffee stain on his chest. But if she was going to get out of hand, he knew he'd have to do something about it.

"I'm going to do my damnedest to make sure everyone knows exactly what they're doing. I just can't believe that these ranchers will continue clearing land if they know they're removing an animal from the face of the Earth forever."

Thinking of Thomas Peabody, Marlin said, "Maybe you know birds better than you know men."

Marlin hadn't meant it as an insult, but the woman got red in the face. Marlin could tell that Inga had a temper.

"Oh, I see. You probably agree with them, right? That they can do whatever is best for man regardless of the consequences. Just cut all the trees down, who the hell cares. What's one less bird, anyway?"

Marlin let her finish, then handed her a copy of the *Blanco County Record* that had been resting on his dashboard. It was opened to Susannah Branson's article. The reporter had captured Marlin's thoughts accurately, stating that "our local game warden encourages area residents to consider the impact of brush-clearing on native wildlife."

Inga read it through, then looked at Marlin sheepishly. "Sorry. Guess you're not one of the bad guys. My mistake."

Marlin decided now was not the time to mention that he was an avid hunter. That would surely set off some fireworks.

"Guess this Susannah Branson has the hots for you, huh?" Inga said in a teasing voice.

"What do you mean?"

"Well, God, it's obvious. Listen to her opening line: 'Beneath John Marlin's rugged good looks lies the sensitive soul of a nature lover.' See that? She managed to get 'Beneath John Marlin,' 'rugged good looks,' and 'lover' all in one sentence. The woman is shameless."

Marlin started to speak, but couldn't come up with anything, just sat there with his mouth open.

Inga responded with an impish smile. He saw that his guess was correct; it was a wonderful smile.

CHAPTER SEVEN

At four o'clock on Monday afternoon, a tall, muscular young man with a purple birthmark on his neck walked into the Save-Mart two miles north of Johnson City. He was browsing in the Lawn & Garden section when a clerk approached him.

"Can I help you find anything, sir?"

"Yeah, I need a shitload of rat poison," the young man said with a pronounced East Coast accent.

An elderly woman in the same aisle gave the young man a glare and scurried away with her shopping cart.

"Well, let's see . . . if you'll follow me, I believe that's in the next aisle over. How much do you need, exactly?"

"Enough to kill a small army of those fuckers. We got rats everywhere."

"Indoors or out?"

The young man shrugged. "Some in, some out. What's the diff?"

The clerk picked up a yellow box and read the label. "It's just that some of these poisons are pretty strong, so you have to make sure other animals don't get to it. Yeah, like right here, it says to keep it away from pets and livestock."

"What, so, a cow could accidentally eat that stuff and croak?"

"I believe so, sir. You have to be very careful."

"Gimme a box of that, then. That should do the trick."

"I'm sure it will. Anything else I can help you with?"

The shopper glanced around and said, "Uh, yeah, can you tell me where the saws are at?"

The clerk pointed toward the rear of the store. "Those would be in Hardware. Aisle twelve, I believe."

"Yeah, thanks."

The customer strode away and the clerk thought: *Rat poison and a saw. What a strange young man.*

Marlin was in the kitchen, drinking a beer and eating some cold pizza for dinner, when the phone rang. He was tempted to let the machine get it, but during deer season duty called at all hours.

On the third ring, he grabbed the phone, his mouth full of cheese and pepperoni. "John Marlin."

"Hey, John, it's me."

His heart thumped, as it always did lately when he heard her voice. It was Becky, calling from Dallas.

"Oh, hey, I was just thinking about you." The truth was, he thought about her all the time. "How are you doing?"

"I'm doing okay. How are you? How's deer season so far?"

"Pretty quiet, really. Some bad weather yesterday. . . ." He saw no need to tell her about the woman he had arrested this morning. "How's your mom doing?" It was a question he hated to ask, but it needed asking.

"That's kind of why I'm calling. She's not doing real well and she's back in the hospital. Her white count is sky-high and she has another infection. This one seems much worse and I'm afraid—"

Her voice broke and Marlin knew she was on the verge of tears.

After a moment, she said, "I don't think she has much longer, John."

Marlin wished he could reach out and hold her, wipe her tears away. He wasn't very good over the phone. "Becky, I'm so sorry. Margaret is a tough woman. . . ." His voice trailed off because he didn't know what else to say. Both of them knew Margaret's illness was terminal. It was just a question of how long. "I wish I could be there for you," he finally said.

"I know you do, and I appreciate it. That's sweet. But I'm doing all right, really." She gave a little laugh. "It's just that when I talk to you, my emotions tend to get out of hand a little. I'm sorry."

"You don't need to apologize, Becky. You know I'm here to talk whenever you want. I just wish I could do more. Sometimes I feel like I'm letting you down."

"Don't say that, John. You could never let me down. If anything, it's the other way around."

Marlin assured her this wasn't the case, even as a wave of melancholy washed over his heart. Sometimes, when he was upset, he felt that she was right, that she *was* letting him down. After all, she was the one who had left. Four months ago, when Becky had first learned of her mother's illness, she had packed a few things and headed for Dallas. It was to be a temporary stay, just an extended visit to help her mother through the crisis. But when Becky had discovered the true condition of Margaret's health, she had decided to remain with her until the end. Becky would come home on weekends and as the weeks went by, Marlin began to notice a change in her mood. She continued to be distraught about her mother—but professionally, she seemed to be elated.

She had taken a nursing position, a short-term contract, at a hospital in Dallas, one of the top facilities in the Southwest. *It's so exciting, John,* he remembered her saying. *This hospital is absolutely amazing. It's making me remember why I became a nurse to begin with.* Marlin had known that Becky hadn't been happy with her job at Blanco County Hospital. It was a small, unimpressive facility, where the most challenging case might be a kid getting his tonsils removed, or an elderly person with the flu. The tougher cases went to Austin or San Antonio. Becky had considered returning to her old job in San Antonio, at the hospital where she was working when Marlin had met her. But it was more than an hour's drive each way, a longer commute than she had wanted to make on a daily basis.

The last time Marlin and Becky talked, she'd told him the hospital had made her an offer. They wanted her on the permanent staff. The salary was outstanding, the benefits were excellent, and the career potential was enormous. She would be able to work on the kinds of cases she had always dreamed of. *Have you accepted the offer?* Marlin had asked. She hadn't. She wanted time to think it over. Now, with this phone call, Marlin figured her thinking was done.

"How's the job?" he asked, knowing he wouldn't like the answer.

"It's great," she said and took a deep breath. "And I've decided to take the offer."

Both of them were silent for a moment. Marlin wanted to tell her she was doing the wrong thing, that he loved her and wanted her back by his side. He even considered—as he had in the past—asking her to marry him. But that would never resolve the problem at hand: Becky was an independent, career-minded woman, and Blanco County simply didn't hold anything for her.

Marlin said quietly, "I know it's what you wanted, Becky. Good for you. I'm proud of you."

But Becky was choking up again. "This just isn't fair," she said. "I can't live in Blanco County . . . and you wouldn't be happy anywhere else."

And, of course, she was right. Marlin had considered asking for a transfer to the next available game-warden position anywhere near Dallas. But it was a fleeting thought. There was no way he could ever leave his hometown. His roots were too deep.

"So I guess that's it, then," Marlin said. *No sense in dragging this out,* he thought. It would only make it more painful.

"You know I would do it differently if I could. I love you very much, John."

"I love you, too. Good luck with everything."

"Thanks."

"You take care of yourself. I'm sure I'll see you again sometime. . . ."

"I know you will, John. Oh, what are we saying? I've still got to come back down there and pick up the last of my things. I'll try to do that in the next few weeks."

"That sounds fine." Marlin said. They each said a sad good-bye, and he cradled the phone. The house seemed so quiet and empty. *Hell, it's no big deal,* Marlin thought. He had lived alone for years. It was nice to have a woman like Becky around, but he knew he'd be able to handle her leaving. Just had to get back in the groove of being single again.

He sat in the quiet house for a moment, and then his eye wandered to the bottle of Wild Turkey perched on top of the refrigerator. It had been weeks since he'd had a good stiff drink.

And right now he could use one.

Make people fear you.

Vinnie Mameli could remember his dad telling him that as if it were yesterday.

Actually, though, it was three years ago, when his father took Vinnie out to dinner one night, ordered linguini and clams for the both of them, then calmly revealed what he did for a living. Vinnie always suspected there was more to his dad than the concrete business. But for his dad to take him into his confidence—to lay all the cards on the table—was quite a rush for a seventeen-year-old already buzzing from too much wine. *You're a man now, Vinnie,* Sal Mameli told him. *And a man needs to know certain things to get by in this world.*

On that night, and on many nights since, Sal had done his best to share his wisdom with the boy.

A bribe will almost always get the job done. And if a bribe don't work, a threat will.

Surround yourself with people you can trust. But never completely trust anyone but yourself.

No matter how much you hated the guy, always go to his funeral.

And Vinnie's favorite: *Respect may work for the Pope, but not for you and me. Fear is better. Make people fear you.*

And that's exactly what Vinnie had in mind Monday night when he drove toward Emmett Slaton's house, dressed head to toe in black. He would show the old douche bag that you don't fuck around with the Mamelis. Before Vinnie was done, the old geezer would be begging to sell his business.

Vinnie spotted the entrance to Buckhorn Creek Ranch and slowly idled past. Two hundred yards farther down the road, he found another ranch entrance. He knew the place was a deer lease, not a residence, so nobody would be coming or going at this hour. He pulled into the entrance and killed the engine.

Five minutes later, Vinnie was positioned in a grove of cedar trees a hundred yards from Emmett Slaton's front door. The porch light was on, and the interior lights said Slaton hadn't gone to bed yet. Now it was a waiting game. Vinnie had no problem with that. He'd wait out here all night if it would make his dad happy. Vinnie was proud to be in charge of such an important mission, and equally proud that his dad had left the specifics up to him. *Just do whatever you gotta do to get that bastard to make a deal. But watch your ass. We don't need any heat on us. And let me know when you're gonna pull somethin', so's I can have an alibi.*

Vinnie was enjoying these thoughts when the front door of the home opened and Slaton's Doberman pinscher trotted out. From his hiding spot, Vinnie caught a glimpse of Slaton before the door swung shut.

Vinnie had chosen his location carefully: The wind was in his face to prevent the dog from scenting him.

The dog pranced away from the house, found a small sapling, and took a long leak. Then, nose to the ground, he sniffed a path through the grass, coming in Vinnie's direction.

When the dog was about thirty yards away, Vinnie opened a Ziploc bag, removed the contents, and tossed it toward the mutt. When the projectile hit the ground, the dog stopped abruptly and let out a small, surprised bark. Vinnie shrunk back into the trees.

Vinnie knew this was the moment of truth. In the next few minutes, his plan would either unfold smoothly—or it would fall to pieces.

Finally, after staring intently into the darkness, the dog cautiously approached the interesting object on the ground.

CHAPTER EIGHT

Billy Don said, "*Bunion*'s kind of a funny word. Don't you think so, Red?"

The men were sitting at their regular barstools in the Friendly Bar, drinking a couple of longnecks, listening to the jukebox, Merle Haggard singing about the big city. Moments ago, Billy Don had announced that his mother had had bunion surgery, and he was happily sharing the details with Red and anyone else who would listen.

Red's concentration, however, was elsewhere. He was busy eyeballing Sylvia, the buxom barmaid, as she restocked the beer cooler. It was an event Red eagerly anticipated, because Sylvia tended to wear tight T-shirts without a bra, and the cold air from the cooler always perked things up around the nightclub.

"Watch out there, sugar. You're liable to put somebody's eye out," Red said as Sylvia finished her task. She gave him a *Go to hell* look and walked down the bar to wait on another customer. Red guffawed loudly and took a long swig from his beer bottle. He loved the way Sylvia took his comments, without getting all pissed-off like some women might. He figured Sylvia secretly wanted to get in his pants, and he couldn't blame her. Women loved a good sense of humor.

"Hey, Red, lookee there," Billy Don said, nodding toward the entrance. Across the smoky room, Sal Mameli had removed his overcoat and was hanging it on a peg by the door. The rest of the regulars glanced over. It wasn't often they were visited by a portly Italian dressed in a silk suit. Mameli turned and made his way through the tables to the bar, oblivious to the stares he was receiving from the locals. He plopped down on the barstool next to Red.

"'Evening, boys," Sal said as he waved a hundred-dollar bill at Sylvia and called out, "Scotch and soda."

Billy Don had slipped his boots off and was studying his own feet for podiatric abnormalities. So Red alone returned the Italian's greeting—without much enthusiasm. There was something about this guy that made him uneasy. Mameli reminded Red of one of the characters in *The Godfather*—what was his name? Clementine? Chlamydia? Something like that. Red was tempted to turn his back on Mameli, simply ignore him, but for some reason that didn't seem like a wise thing to do.

Mameli tapped the wristwatch on his arm. "You got the time? Dis piece of shit quit working on me."

Red said, "Clock on the wall right over there."

"Yeah, right. Ten-thirty."

Sylvia brought his drink and Sal said, "Dis is the good stuff, right—not the crap from the lower shelves?" She nodded and he slid the c-note across the bar. He half turned his head to Red and said, "So how's business? Slaton been keeping youse busy?"

"Can't complain," Red said. "But sometimes I still do." A favorite line of his.

Sylvia returned with Mameli's change and he left five bucks on the bar. "Dat's for you, doll."

She smiled and tucked the bill in her jeans. Sal gave her an appreciative leer.

Turning back to Red, he said, "What's the old man cutting—three, maybe four hundred acres a week?"

"Probably more like five or six." Red said, pulling numbers out of the air. "And me and Billy Don is his chief operators."

"Whazzat?" Billy Don asked, snapping to attention like a dog who just heard a doorbell.

"Never mind."

Billy Don leaned forward to catch Mameli's eye. "You got any idea why they call it the 'BrushBuster 3000'?" he slurred. "What the hell is that '3000' all about?"

Mameli scratched his head. "Horsepower? I don't know nuttin' 'bout engines."

Billy Don was crestfallen. If a man who actually owned a couple of BrushBusters couldn't answer the question, nobody could. He turned his attention back to a large callus on his left heel.

"You guys still considering my offer?" Sal asked.

Red gave him an ambiguous head-bob gesture, not wanting to commit to anything. "Mr. Slaton takes care of us real good."

Sal patted him on the back. "I'm sure he does. Hey, looks like youse guys is runnin' on empty. Lemme get the next round." He signaled Sylvia for two more longnecks and another scotch.

Red watched the wad of bills come out from Sal's pocket again. It was a roll a couple of inches thick, mostly hundreds. *Well, maybe this guy ain't so bad after all,* Red thought.

The dog was damn tough, Vinnie had to give him that. It took nearly an hour for the Doberman to quit twitching and moaning and finally take a last gasping breath. Quietly, Vinnie ventured into the clearing and dragged the carcass back into the trees.

He stopped for a breather and . . . he heard a noise. Through the branches, he saw Emmett Slaton emerge from his house.

"Patton!" Slaton shined a weak flashlight in Vinnie's direction. "Patton! Gawdammit dog, git in here."

Vinnie huddled up close to a large cedar. His hand instinctively went to the .38 automatic in his jacket pocket.

"Patton, you old bastard, come to Papa." Slaton was gingerly stepping through the high native grasses now, coming toward the cedar grove.

Damn! Vinnie had worried that something like this might happen. He knew it could end up sloppy, unprofessional . . . and his dad would be mad as hell. But it had been a chance he was willing to take, because the plan had so much potential.

Slaton was about fifty yards away now, and Vinnie could see he was wearing a robe and houseshoes. The old man started whistling and clapping his hands. Vinnie had to grin. *Your dog can't hear you now, old man.*

The beam from the flashlight swept across Vinnie's face and he felt as obvious as a deer in the headlights. But Slaton kept coming.

"Patton! Dammit, I'm losing my patience!"

Slaton was fifteen yards away now . . . then ten. Vinnie switched off the safety on the gun. He noticed he was breathing rapidly now; way too loud, he thought, sure that Slaton would hear him.

No, ol' Sal was all right, Red figured, after the Italian had bought yet another round—the fifth, for anyone who was counting. For a Yankee, the man knew how to have a good time.

Sylvia brought Sal change for a hundred again. Red wondered why Sal always used the big bills instead of the change from earlier rounds.

Sal, evidently feeling the liquor, held up a bill and said, "Hey, Sylvia. Fifty bucks if you show us your tits."

Ears perked up all around the bar.

Sylvia, drying a glass, casually said, "Add a zero to that and you got a deal."

Men hooted and hollered, and Sal looked around at the regulars. "All right, anyone willing to kick in some cash?"

No hands went up.

"How 'bout you, Red? Wanna see her twins?" Sal grinned at his drinking companion.

"Hell, like my daddy always said: If you've seen one, you've seen 'em both." The crowd roared.

After the laughter subsided and it became apparent there wasn't going to be a floor show, Sal said, "Geez, what time is it? Twelve-thirty already? I gotta go." He slurped down the fresh scotch. He laid another hundred on the bar in front of Sylvia. "Get these guys another round, will ya. And the change is for you, sweetheart."

Sylvia nodded and winked.

At twelve forty-five, Maria Consuelo García Rodríguez was awakened by the sound of a garage door creaking as it trundled upward along its tracks. Seconds later, she heard the slamming of a car door and then the groaning of the garage door coming back down. Maria's small one-bedroom cottage was behind the garage, which was attached to the end of the Mamelis' house.

She knew her boss had left a few hours ago, and she assumed it was him returning. His wife, Angela, had already drunk herself into a stupor and gone to bed, a little earlier than usual. Maria knew this was not good. She was afraid she was due for another one of Mr. Mameli's late-night "visits." The thought of it—of his sweaty, flabby body lying on top of her— sent a shudder down her spine. She pulled the covers tightly around her, as if that might help ward off his clumsy advances.

She heard the familiar clicking of his Italian shoes on the concrete driveway, receding toward the house. Tonight, it seemed, she was in luck, and he would not be visiting her. Or maybe he wanted to check on his wife first, to make sure he would not be caught.

Lying there in the dark, feeling empty and lonely and far from home, Maria could not help but remember the first time Mr. Mameli had approached her. Mrs. Mameli was away on a shopping trip, and Mr. Mameli had asked Maria if she would fix a hem in his pants. Sí, she said, happy to help. Then he'd proceeded to take them off right in front of her. Maria blushed and turned away, only to feel his thick hands on her shoulders, then reaching around her to cup her breasts. Maria had resisted, she had pleaded and begged, but Mr. Mameli would not listen.

She pulled away from him, and then she saw a side of him she had never before seen. He grabbed her firmly by the wrists, hard enough to leave a bruise, and told her she had better do what he asked or he would turn her in to the INS. *I'll send you back to your little mud hut in Guatemala,* he had said. Maria wanted to pretend that she didn't understand, but it was too late. The fear already showed in her face. So, with bile in her throat, Maria had given in.

Thinking back on it, Maria began to shake. Her cat, Tuco, jumped up into the bed and nestled beside her, as if to comfort her. Tuco was a beautiful black cat, a stray she had taken in last spring. She glanced over at the corner of the room, where Pablo, her bird, was sleeping in his covered cage. Pablo was also a foundling; one she had nursed back to health after she had discovered him, only a few days old, with a broken wing, in the garden. He was a healthy bird now, black like Tuco, handsome, with a long beak and bright eyes. His wing, however, had not mended properly and he could not fly.

Tuco purred loudly and Maria smiled. She remembered the day last week when Tuco had saved Maria from Mr. Mameli's groping hands. Mr. Mameli had come to Maria's cottage while Mrs. Mameli was taking a bath. He climbed on top of her, but before he could complete his filthy act, Tuco jumped on his back and hissed. Mr. Mameli shrieked like a small girl, pulled on his clothes, and left the cottage, careful to avoid the cat. He appeared to be afraid of Tuco, and that made Maria giggle.

There were times when Maria became so depressed she wanted to return to her home in Quetzaltenango, to forget her dreams and accept the life she had been given. After all, what chance did she have as an illegal alien? She had always hoped to fall in love with a wonderful American man, raise a family, and then, when the time was right, go to college. She wanted to be a doctor. She felt she had a healing heart, and that a career in medicine was her destiny. Her *amigas* back home had laughed when she told them that. Maybe they were right; perhaps it was silly. After all, she had been in the United States for two years now. She was twenty-three years old, and she felt that time was slipping away.

When Maria got this way—a heavy feeling in her heart—she often meditated. She would light candles, play some soothing music, and sit peacefully on the floor.

Weak batteries saved Emmett Slaton's life. He was five yards away from Vinnie, playing the light all around the cedars, but the beam was apparently too faint for the old man to pick Vinnie out through the thick, low branches.

"Aw, to hell with you," Slaton grumbled. "Stay out here all night and see how you like it."

The old rancher retreated toward the house and Vinnie's nerves began to settle down.

After a few moments, he heard the front door close, and he finally released his grip on the cold steel of the automatic.

CHAPTER NINE

When John Marlin woke up Tuesday morning, his brain was pounding against his skull and he felt as if he had little individual sweaters on each of his teeth. Now he remembered why he didn't hit the bourbon too often. It was five A.M., but he just couldn't sleep any longer. So he walked to the end of his driveway and grabbed the newspaper.

Back inside, he was greeted with a front-page headline that blared, ACTIVIST BREWS UP BIG TROUBLE. Marlin chuckled. The story—another piece by Susannah Branson—recounted the coffee-throwing episode of the morning before. It stated that Inga Mueller, a Minnesotan, was being held on a variety of charges, including assaulting an officer.

Near the bottom, Inga was quoted: "I'm just trying to draw attention to the plight of the red-necked sapsucker. It's an endangered species, but nobody seems to care. They live only in cedar trees, so we need to stop cutting the cedars before it's too late." Well, at least Inga was getting the ink she wanted. Marlin was surprised Susannah hadn't called him for a quote. She must have gotten everything she needed from the police report.

Marlin glanced through the rest of the paper, then took a hot shower, swallowed a couple of aspirin, and headed out the door.

He wasn't going anyplace in particular, just cruising. He stopped at a few meat lockers—places that typically opened at sunrise to accommodate hunters—to check the quality of the deer brought in so far. The drought in the spring had been tough on the regional deer population, but they seemed to be rebounding nicely. Marlin saw several nice bucks, with antler spreads hovering around the twenty-inch mark. Couple of nice does, too, much fatter than he had expected. Seeing a healthy deer herd always put Marlin in a good mood. Animals often had to struggle against the cruel whims of Mother Nature, so it was nice to see the deer thriving.

At nine-thirty, Jean, one of the dispatchers from the Sheriff's Department, came over the radio with a report of a poacher at Pedernales Reservoir. The park was closed on selected dates during deer season, to give hunters access, but today the park was open to the public.

Marlin swung his cruiser east and wheeled through the park entrance in less than six minutes. Driving through the camping area, he spotted a young man skinning a five-foot rattlesnake that was hanging from an oak tree. A rifle leaned against a nearby Nissan truck. Marlin asked the young man for his driver's and hunting licenses, and everything came back clean. The man told him the snake had almost bit his dog, and that he was concerned about letting the snake go when there were families around. Marlin sensed he was telling the truth.

"What're you skinning him for? Gonna make a hatband?" Marlin asked.

"Naw, I just want the meat. Might fry it up for lunch. You can have the skin if you want it."

Marlin liked the young man's answer. So he was polite, but firm: He told the offender that firearms were not allowed in the park, and killing any type of animal on the premises was against the law. In the end, Marlin wrote him a citation for possession of a firearm within the park boundaries. He could have been much tougher, arresting the young man and confiscating his rifle, a cheap bolt-action .22.

The remainder of the morning was slow, so Marlin headed back home for lunch at twelve-thirty. While eating a sandwich, he noticed the light blinking on his answering machine. He hit PLAY.

> *"Yeah, John, this is Lester Higgs. I got something out here, and uh, well, I don't want to get into it over the phone, but I really need to see you right away. It's about eleven-thirty and I'll be here at the house for a few minutes. But I've got to head back to the southern property line and you can find me there, near the back pasture. It's urgent, John. You'll understand when you get here."*

Lester Higgs was a Blanco County native, about Marlin's age, now foreman of the Hawley Ranch, a large hunting operation. People called the game warden all the time with "urgent" problems, but Lester's tone told Marlin he'd better return the call right away. Marlin knew Lester to be a man who wasn't easily ruffled. Many years ago, Marlin had seen Lester get kicked in the head by a horse during a rodeo. Lester went to his truck, stitched the wound himself, then rode a bull an hour later. Lester wasn't the type to call the game warden every time he heard a late shot or saw a spotlight in an oat field after dark. Marlin dialed Lester's number but got no answer. He grabbed his sandwich and headed out the door.

Fifteen minutes later, Marlin arrived at the gate of the Hawley Ranch. There were no vehicles at the foreman's quarters, so Marlin navigated the rutted dirt roads to the heavily wooded back pasture. He passed a red late-model SUV on the side of the road, rounded a curve, and spotted Lester's white truck along the fenceline. Marlin parked beside it.

Marlin shut his truck door and immediately heard Lester calling to him from behind a dense curtain of cedars. A tall deer blind loomed over the treetops.

Marlin came through the trees and found Lester just yards away, squatted on his haunches with his dirty Stetson in his hands. In front of him was a body.

Five summers ago, Emmett Slaton had been in the drive-through at the local bank when he'd glanced over at the parking lot of the grocery store next door. He noticed a rough-looking couple sitting on the tailgate of a jacked-up yellow truck. The man was dressed in a leather Harley-Davidson cap and a matching vest with no shirt underneath. The woman wore a green bikini top and greasy blue jeans. On her left biceps was a tattoo of a penis and a caption that read *Born To Ride*. Between them was a cardboard box that read, FREE PUPIES. Apparently, they were down to the last pup in the litter, a wormy-looking black-and-brown runt that lay panting on the hot pavement at their feet.

The biker hoisted the puppy up into the bed of the truck and shoved a bowl of water in front of it. When the puppy went to drink, the man slid the bowl out of its reach. The puppy tried again, and the man moved the bowl once more. After three or four attempts, the puppy lay down with its head between its paws. The man picked up the puppy by the scruff of its neck and gave it a good shake, as if scolding it for giving up so easily. With his free hand, the biker roughly jabbed the puppy's belly.

Slaton had seen all he needed to see. He wheeled his Ford out of the bank line and pulled in next to the yellow truck. He grabbed a tire iron from behind his seat and held it beside his leg as he approached the man in the vest.

"Son," Slaton said, "don't you know you shouldn't treat an animal that way?"

The biker glanced at Slaton, then gave the woman an exaggerated, *I can't believe this shit* expression. "Who the hell are you?"

"I'm Emmett Slaton, and I believe I'll take that dog off your hands."

The biker looked down at the dog. "This'n here? Gonna cost you a hunnert bucks."

"Your box says it's free."

"Yeah, they was free to the general pop'lation, but for ass-holes, they's a hunnert bucks."

Slaton reached down to pick up the dog and the biker grabbed his arm in an alarmingly strong grip.

Slaton brought the tire iron down fast and hard and felt the bones give way in the biker's arm. "Son of a bitch!" The biker yelled and laid down in the bed of the truck, bringing his knees up to protect himself from another blow.

"Now, there," Slaton said. "That's how you treat an animal." He glanced over at the woman, who smiled coolly and exhaled a mouthful of cigarette smoke. She gestured at the dog. "He's all yours."

Sitting on his front porch Tuesday afternoon, Slaton remembered that afternoon as if it were yesterday. He had nursed the puppy to good health, and it became a strong, confident dog. For five years, Patton had been his companion, his best buddy, right there by his side day and night. Slaton loved that ornery old mutt, even if he didn't always come when he was called.

Slaton was heartsick. He had hung around the house all morning, even canceling a doctor's appointment in San Antonio, waiting to hear the familiar yip at the front door. But it never came. If Patton didn't show up by sundown, Emmett Slaton just didn't know what he was going to do.

It was one o'clock now, and Slaton got into his truck to take a slow drive along the county road near his home.

About goddamn time, Vinnie said to himself as Emmett Slaton pulled out of his driveway. Vinnie had been waiting and watching from the same cluster of cedar trees he had hidden in the night before. He grabbed the Hefty bag off the ground and proceeded toward the house. He couldn't help but grin. His dad would love the poetic symbolism of the act Vinnie was planning. It was pure genius, that's what it was.

He tried the back door, found it unlocked, and quickly made his way to the master bedroom.

Emmett Slaton returned from his drive feeling worse than ever. No sign of Patton. That damn dog was going to give him more gray hairs than he already had.

Slaton went to the kitchen, hoping to find new messages on his answering machine. He had left word with area kennels, veterinarians, and the county dogcatcher—asking them all to be on the lookout—but the red light stubbornly refused to blink.

Slaton fixed a bourbon on the rocks and went to his den. He flipped the TV on but couldn't get interested in any of the programs.

He decided to go take a little nap, to give himself plenty of energy to continue his search later that evening.

At his bedroom doorway, he noticed the door was closed. *Strange,* he thought. He never shut that door because the room got too hot if he did.

He swung the door open and cautiously flipped the light switch. Everything looked normal. Nothing out of place. "Getting paranoid," he muttered. "Either that or Alzheimer's."

He sat on the edge of the bed to pull his boots off, then stood and peeled off his shirt and jeans.

He tugged the blanket back and came face-to-face with a bloody nightmare. He didn't even realize he was screaming. There, in his bed, was the severed head of his beloved Patton.

Slaton gingerly picked up the head and clutched it to his chest, his screams now subsided to a low moaning wail. He staggered into the bathroom—he didn't really know why—and placed the head in the sink. He began rinsing it off, watching the blood swirl down the drain.

Even in his grief, the gears in his mind were frantically spinning. *The head in the bed—I've seen this before,* he thought. *What was it? A movie?*

Then he had it. *The Godfather.* The scene where the Hollywood producer wakes up in bed with the head of his prize stallion.

The anger—the pure, unadulterated fury—built in Slaton's heart as it never had before. This was no subtle message. It was designed to taunt him, to tell him exactly who did it. And he received that message loud and clear. Cradling the sopping head of his dog in his arm, Slaton turned to retrieve his .45 automatic from his nightstand.

CHAPTER TEN

"Lester, you all right?" Marlin asked, carefully eyeing the wooded area around him. A man was down, and at this point Marlin didn't know why. Common sense—and law enforcement savvy—told him to approach the situation with caution.

"I'm okay, John," Lester said, standing up. "But this ol' boy ain't doing good at all. I woulda called for an ambulance or somethin', but it's too late for that. I started to wait for your call at the house, but I figured I'd better come on back down here, keep the buzzards away."

Marlin looked for footprints in the area, didn't see any, and carefully stepped up beside Lester. He gazed down at the dead man and saw a familiar face.

The man was on his back, his head tilted to one side, eyes open but unseeing. Marlin noticed lividity—pooled blood—in the cheek closest to the ground, while the other cheek was white as a newborn's butt. No need to even take a pulse; the man was long gone. A rifle lay by his side and the center of his camouflage jacket was dark with blood. His hands, too, were covered with dried blood.

"Bert Gammel," Lester said dryly. "One of my hunters. I figure it was a stray shot that got him. Either that, or he somehow managed to shoot hisself."

Marlin didn't reply, but eyed the apparent entry wound. Dead center in the chest. Very unlikely that it was self-inflicted, even accidentally. Keeping his feet in place, Marlin bent low over Gammel's rifle, trying to catch a scent of cordite, but there was none. It didn't mean the rifle hadn't been fired, but Marlin's intuition told him it hadn't.

"Did you move the body?" Marlin asked.

"Naw, just felt for a pulse. Gave me the willies, to tell the truth."

Marlin stood and said, "Lester, I want you to step over here with me for a minute and answer a few questions. If you can, try to walk back to your truck the same way you walked in." Marlin knew that Lester, even as tough as he was, would think more clearly if he wasn't staring at a corpse. Also, Marlin had to protect what might be a crime scene.

Before questioning Lester, Marlin radioed the dispatcher and asked for assistance. Before long, the area would be swarming with personnel, including the sheriff, deputies, and the medical examiner.

With help on the way, Marlin grabbed a pen and notepad and turned to Lester, but the ranch foreman didn't have much to tell. Lester said that he kept a spiral notebook at his house; hunters were supposed to sign in and out when coming and going from the ranch. Lester said that Gammel had hunted yesterday afternoon but had never signed out. It happened all the time. Hunters simply forgot, or didn't want to bother with stopping at the foreman's quarters on the way out.

When Lester came down this morning to repair a hole in the southern fence, he saw Gammel's vehicle. He scouted the area, found the body, and immediately called Marlin. "I didn't want to call the sheriff's office just yet, John. Small town, you know, and I didn't want to start a bunch of rumors. I knew you'd handle it right."

Gammel was an employee with the county Public Works

Department, a well-known figure around town. If word got out that he was found dead, the entire population would know by the end of the day.

"Did you hear any shots yesterday afternoon?" Marlin asked.

"A couple."

"Can you remember what time?"

"I think there was one at about four o'clock, another at around five or five-fifteen, and then one more right before dark."

"A little after six?"

"Yeah, I guess. Thereabouts."

"Did any of the shots sound like they came from this direction?"

"The last one did. I figured it was probably Gammel, but I checked the notebooks and they didn't show that he had killed anything." The foreman was required to keep a second notebook that listed the date and time when all deer were killed on the ranch. "That's when I noticed that he hadn't signed out. Figured he forgot."

"What time did he sign in yesterday afternoon?"

"Three o'clock."

"Did you see him come in?"

"Yeah, he waved at me over at the barn. I was feeding the horses." The ranch owners, the Hawleys, kept several quarter-horses on the property, coming out occasionally on weekends to ride. But they rarely showed during deer season.

"Was there anybody with him?"

"Nope."

"Were any of the other hunters out here yesterday?"

"Jack Corey was here. Signed in at three-twenty; out at six-thirty. Didn't shoot nothin'. But I never saw him, just what it says in the notebooks."

Marlin gestured toward the neighboring property across the fenceline. "That's the Bar T. They doing any hunting over there nowadays?"

"Not that I've heard of. Hasn't been hunted in ten years."

"You haven't heard any shots from over there, or seen any hunters?"

"Not a one. I see the foreman on occasion. Sometimes we shoot the breeze over the fence for a while. Saw him a week or ten days ago. He didn't say nothin' about opening it to hunters this year. And if they had, I'm sure me or you woulda heard about it."

Marlin paused for a moment and scribbled a few notes. Then he asked another question, trying to keep his tone casual: "Lester, have you ever heard or seen any kind of disagreement between Gammel and any of the other hunters? You know how a deer lease can get—guys get kind of possessive of their favorite hunting spots, or they don't want anybody shooting does, things like that. Ever have any problems out here?"

Lester removed his Stetson and rubbed the back of his free hand across his brow. "I've had a few of them come to me over the years and ask me about a couple of things, wanting me to settle a disagreement or somethin'. But nothin' that would lead to somethin' like this."

Marlin nodded.

"Let me back up for a minute," Lester said. "I should say that I'm in charge of the lease and everything. I collect the money, lay down the rules, and get the hunters' signatures on the leases. But as far as how they divvy up the ranch or whose blind goes where, I leave that all up to them. So there coulda been some disagreements I ain't never heard about. But there is one thing that seems to have caused some trouble over the years. Mind you, when I say trouble, it really hasn't been that big of a deal."

Marlin waited patiently.

"It's been about spikes," Lester continued, referring to bucks who have two nonforking antlers, rather than the multipointed antlers most deer carry. Many hunters consider spikes to be inferior deer, and insist they should be culled from the herd to prevent them from passing along their genes. "Can we talk off the record for a second, John?"

Marlin knew he was about to hear about some hunting violations—minor considerations when investigating a hunter's death—so he told Lester to tell him anything he needed to.

Lester glanced over at the body. "Bert was big on shooting any spike that came along. He'd just shoot it and throw it in the ravine. Probably shot three or four every year. He wasn't being an asshole or anything, just thought it was the right thing to do."

Marlin nodded. Each time Gammel had done this, he was committing two game violations: one for failing to tag the deer, and the second for wasting the meat.

"And some of the other hunters wanted him to ease off?" Marlin asked.

"Yeah, there was a couple. The one time I saw it come to a head, Gammel almost got in a fight up at the barn where they butcher their deer."

"With who?"

"Jack Corey."

"What happened?"

"I arrived in the middle of it all, but I guess they had a few words and Gammel popped Jack in the jaw. Ol' Jack was in the middle of gutting a doe, so he had a knife in his hands. It looked to me like he was thinkin' of using it. But I stepped between them and it cooled off real quick. Bert said that he shouldn't have lost his temper, and then he just left. Most of the guys seemed to side with Jack and had a few things to say about Bert after he took off."

"When did this happen?"

"Middle of last season."

"Anything else happen since then?"

"Not that I know of."

Marlin knew a deputy would want to cover all this ground with Lester again, maybe in front of a tape recorder, but it was good to get everything down on paper now. Marlin asked several more questions, but nothing of relevance came up.

"Lester, do me a favor. I'm gonna take a quick look around for a minute. I need you to just wait in your truck, grab some coffee. We don't want to make more footprints around the body than we need to."

"Sure, John. No problem."

Marlin followed the same path toward the body that he had originally taken, careful to watch for footprints, tire tracks, or any other type of evidence. He saw none.

Standing over the corpse, Marlin tried to re-create the shooting in his mind. He could picture Gammel climbing down the ladder from his blind, taking a few steps in the haze of twilight, then—*Boom!*—a high-powered slug rips through his chest.

Television viewers often think that a body is thrown back violently when a person is shot with a rifle, but this is rarely the case. Depending on where the victim is hit, the bullet often passes through quickly and cleanly, hardly swaying the victim at all. Deer hunters can attest to this, as whitetails rarely ever fall when struck through the lungs, but instead race off in a frenzied sprint until the oxygen is depleted from their system.

Marlin could envision Gammel dropping the rifle, clutching at his chest, then falling to the ground in a heap, his heart a shredded, useless clump of muscle.

Looking beyond the corpse toward the blind, Marlin could see the spray of Gammel's blood and small bits of tissue from the exit wound. Marlin carefully stepped around the body and sighted back down these lines of blood. He found himself staring down a long, alleylike opening through the heavily wooded area. The alley dead-ended at a clump of cedars just across the fenceline.

Rather than walking directly down the natural alley, Marlin worked his way through the dense surrounding cedars until he came to the barbed-wire fence. He eased his way over the wire and approached the massive cedar tree at the end of the alley. Once again, he was careful to watch for shoeprints, shell casings, or any other signs of recent activity.

Marlin knew that in such a heavily treed area, a bullet could not have traveled far in a parallel path to the ground. Of course, the bullet might have been a stray, coming from a great distance in a large arc. They'd know if that was a possibility later, when the body was in the hands of the medical examiner, Lem Tucker. But Marlin had a hunch the bullet had traveled right down the alley, which was, in essence, a perfect shooting lane for a hunter. Regardless of what was being hunted.

Marlin peered through the low-hanging limbs of the bush-like cedar and noticed a partially broken, inch-thick limb dangling downward. Looking more closely, Marlin saw several smaller limbs and twigs on the ground a few inches below the tree's lower branches.

At this point, Marlin donned a pair of latex gloves from his jacket. He gingerly reached underneath the branches and grabbed one of the fallen twigs. It appeared to be cleanly cut—as with a small set of hand snippers. In a month or so, these cuttings would turn brown and be easily visible. But for now, they were hardly noticeable, blending in with the rest of the tree. Marlin never would have seen them if he hadn't first spotted the broken branch.

Marlin had cut and snapped his share of cedar branches before. Actually, you couldn't really snap them because they were too resilient. You just bent them until they gave way and stayed where you wanted them. Or you brought along a pair of snippers. In any case, Marlin could think of only one reason he had ever bent or cut cedar limbs. To create a "window" through the limbs—so he could get a better shot. Hill Country hunters commonly used cedars as makeshift blinds because the trees provided such good concealment.

Marlin looked past the canopy of the tree to the base of the trunk. There, he saw a recently disturbed area of soil. Marlin could see exactly where the man had sat, the impression of his butt, the troughs where his heels had scraped through the cedar mulch.

Then Marlin spotted a dark brown stain on the ground a foot or so from where the man had reclined. Marlin recognized this as the remnants of a puddle of tobacco spit.

Marlin gingerly made his way behind the cedar tree and peered through the canopy, giving himself the same view as the man who had used this little hideaway. Looking through the small window the man had created, Marlin couldn't see much. But he could sure as hell see the ladder to Bert Gammel's deer blind.

CHAPTER ELEVEN

Sal Mameli was enjoying a leisurely afternoon, sipping a scotch, thumbing through the local newspaper. He noticed an article about some tree-hugger causing all kinds of trouble with local hunters, throwing coffee on the game warden and shit like that. Reading further, he saw that she was calling for a halt to cedar-cutting. *Just great,* he thought. First he had Emmett Slaton to deal with—hopefully, Vinnie was on top of that situation—and now he had a crazy broad badmouthing his business.

Sal tossed the paper aside and gulped the last of his scotch. Up to now, he had been enjoying his time alone in an empty house. Vinnie was off doing something, and Angela had thrown something into a Crock-Pot for dinner, then gone shopping with Maria, the housekeeper.

Maria.

Now, there was a broad that was starting to give Sal the willies. More and more, she reminded Sal of his mother's aunt Sofia—and that was not a good thing. Thinking about Aunt Sofia gave Sal a tremor.

She had died when Sal was only ten, maybe eleven years

old, but he still had sharp memories of her. She was a Gypsy. Not just a woman who liked to dress in scarves, skirts, and funky jewelry, but an honest-to-fuck Gypsy. She had powers, this woman, and everybody in the village knew it.

Sal remembered a time, sitting on the front porch of their ramshackle home, maybe two years before his family immigrated to America. A neighbor walked by, the father of a large family that lived down the hill. He and Aunt Sofia didn't get along too good, always exchanging sneers, maybe a rough word here and there. Sal had no idea what had started the bad blood.

On this particular day, the man had two goats with him, herding them along the country road, taking them to market in town. The man saw Sofia and muttered, *"Fattucchiera,"* under his breath. "Witch"—that's what it meant. Sofia said nothing, and the man continued down the lane, not looking back. But then Aunt Sofia raised her left hand, pointing in the man's direction, her eyes fluttering in their sockets, and she chanted something Sal didn't understand.

The goats dropped dead. Fell like stones, the both of them. Sal wouldn't have believed it if he hadn't seen it.

Another time, a beautiful young woman in town had tried to seduce Sal's father, a virile, good-looking man. Sal's mother heard about it and, in tears, complained to Aunt Sofia. The old Gypsy just held her tight, shushed her, told her that the woman would get what was coming to her.

The next day, Sal saw the young woman in town. Her face was covered in warts—large, scaly warts—from the top of her forehead to the collar of her blouse. The rumor was that the warts continued down her chest onto her breasts. People pointed and whispered, and the young woman skulked away in shame and embarrassment.

There were dozens of episodes like this, occurrences that ultimately caused the villagers to shrink away in fear whenever they saw Aunt Sofia.

And now there was Maria.

Sal was beginning to believe that Maria had the same powers as Aunt Sofia. Okay, maybe not Gypsy powers, but black magic or voodoo or something. Whatever the hell they practiced down in Guatemala.

For starters, there were Maria's pets—that damn cat and that pathetic lame bird. Sal had often seen the cat out in the garden, stalking songbirds, dropping little dead sparrows and wrens at Maria's front door. So, a couple of months ago during breakfast, Sal had asked Maria how she managed to keep the cat from trying to eat her own bird. It took a few tries before Maria understood his question because her English wasn't so good. But she finally got what he was asking, and, in her broken English, said she had put a spell on the cat, made it think the bird was just another cat. Then she had laughed like it was only a joke.

But Sal had seen the look in Maria's eyes. That gleam, like Aunt Sofia used to have.

Just last week, Sal had slipped out to Maria's cottage one night to play a little "Hide the Salami." Maria pretended to resist his visits on occasion, as a good girl would, but Sal figured she secretly enjoyed them, that she craved the attention. After all, she was thousands of miles from home, had no boyfriend, and Sal was no slouch. He knew a few tricks in the sack. But on this particular night, Maria seemed kind of depressed. Sal noticed her staring into the corner of her darkened bedroom. Seconds later, the cat jumped on his back like some demon from hell— left claw marks down his back. Almost as if Maria had sent some sort of voodoo message to the cat, telling it what to do.

A couple of other times, Sal had walked in on Maria in the middle of what appeared to a black-magic ceremony. She had candles burning all around the room, some kind of freaky music playing, and she was sitting cross-legged on the floor. And chanting . . . the woman was chanting. Low, indecipherable words, the same as Aunt Sofia did. The cat was always perched on the bed watching her, blinking its black, soulless eyes. Gave Sal the friggin' creeps.

Maria also wore all kinds of weird little necklaces and bracelets she made out of cheap trash that she found. Broken glass with the edges sanded down. Little bits of polished rock and metal. Aunt Sofia wore cheap crap like that, too—to ward off spirits, she said. Who knew why Maria wore her jewelry, but it had to be something evil.

Sal was staring into space, thinking about Maria, when the doorbell rang and he flinched, dropping his empty scotch glass on the floor.

Goddamn, just like someone to come along and ruin his peace and quiet. He started to ignore the visitor, but then figured it might be one of the guys from his work crews. They stopped by sometimes when they finished a job, looking for more work. That was the amazing thing: These jamooks were eager to bust their balls all day long for a lousy twelve bucks an hour when Sal was making twenty times that without breaking a sweat. *Gotta keep those crews working,* Sal thought, as he made his way down the hallway.

Sal peered through the peephole—something that always made him feel a little cowardly—and there was Emmett Slaton standing on his front porch.

"Hey, *paisan!*" Sal said with a self-satisfied smile as he opened the door. "Finally come to your senses?"

But something was all wrong. Emmett Slaton appeared to have blood all over his shirt, on his forearms, even up his neck and on his face. He emitted a low, threatening growl, a rumble from deep in his chest, and launched himself onto Sal.

Sal tumbled backward, his legs buckling under him, his head banging smartly off the tile, a jolt of pain running down his spine. He could feel Slaton groping, trying to get a grip with both hands around his neck. Sal brought a knee up hard into the rancher's chest and felt something give, maybe a rib. Then he brought an elbow down onto Slaton's collarbone, then again on the crown of his head, and managed to drag himself away from the old bastard. But Slaton seemed unfazed. He sprang to his feet and rushed Sal again, wrapping him in a bear hug. The men went spinning wildly down the hall, sending a lamp crashing to the floor, and ended up in Sal's den. There were no words exchanged, only grunts and groans as both men jockeyed for an advantage, gripping, grabbing, throwing an occasional short punch. Finally Sal broke free again, but then Slaton landed a tremendous right cross to his chin.

"That's for Patton, you wop sumbitch!" Slaton yelled.

Sal was confused, staggering, feeling the impact of the blow, a couple of teeth loosened. *What the hell does Slaton's damn dog have to do with this?* he wondered. Before Sal could clear his head, Slaton grabbed a poker from beside the fireplace. He lunged, swinging wildly, the hum of the steel rod whistling past Sal's ear. Another swing, this one catching Sal hard on the left wrist.

Sal screamed in anguish, getting nervous now, frustrated, wracked with pain. This old geezer was kicking his ass and meant to kill him, Sal had no doubt. If he could only get to the .38 in his nightstand . . .

Slaton took another swipe, the pronged end of the poker scraping across Sal's torso, Sal feeling the blood begin to flow.

Then he remembered the .35-caliber in his desk drawer. It was an old collectible, a family heirloom. But like every gun in Sal Mameli's house, it was loaded and ready for action.

Sal feigned left then went right, Slaton stumbling, not able to keep up. Sal scurried behind his desk and ducked as Slaton hurled the poker inches from his skull, leaving it embedded in the wall like a spear.

Sal yanked open the top drawer, fumbling for the small gun in the back—so close to ending this fiasco—only to glance up and see Slaton aiming a .45 directly at his face. He must have had it in the waistband of his pants.

"You lowlife piece of shit," Slaton croaked, out of breath, cradling his arm against his wounded ribs. "Bring your hands up . . . slowly!"

Sal did as he was told, the .35 hanging in his hand. Now the room was cloaked in an eerie calm, both men gasping for air, eyeing each other carefully, Sal feeling the blood pound in his ears, the ache in his arm, the warm stickiness of blood on his belly.

"Toss that piece over here," Slaton demanded.

Sal pitched the gun at Slaton's feet.

"What the fuck is this?" Sal shouted, trying to show a little bravado, maybe back Slaton down a little. "Have you lost your freakin' mind?"

"Shut up! Just shut your goddamn mouth!"

Sal stared Slaton directly in the eyes, refusing to look away, knowing that would only make him look guilty. Whatever Vinnie had done, he had pushed it too far. Or he hadn't pushed it far enough, gone ahead and clipped the guy. And now Sal was the one paying the price.

CHAPTER TWELVE

Slaton just stood there, his pupils large as dimes, boring his eyes into Sal's skull. Sal knew that look, and he didn't like it at all. He had seen it on plenty of faces back East, wiseguys looking to make their bones, trying to work up the courage to kill another human being. In a matter of seconds Slaton would either pull the trigger or lose his nerve.

Sal had owned a .45 just like the one Slaton was holding, knew the damage it could do, the softball-sized hole it would leave in the back of his head. His brains would be all over the wall behind him. Sal stared down the barrel of the weapon, feebly holding his hands in front of him, waiting to hear the roar that would cast him into another world.

Then he noticed that the safety was still on.

The old fucker was so worked-up he'd forgotten about the safety. It was Sal's only chance, but he had to act quickly, before Slaton tried to pull the trigger and realized his mistake.

This time, it was Sal who leaped forward, literally vaulting himself over the desk, wrapping his arms around Slaton as the rancher pulled frantically on the trigger. Both men crashed to the ground, Slaton grunting as he landed on his back, a stream of frothy blood rolling from the corner of his mouth. Sal felt a new cut open on his scalp as Slaton slammed the butt of the gun against the crown of Sal's head with surprising force. Sal grabbed Slaton's right wrist, shook the gun loose, then gripped the left wrist. Now he had both of Slaton's wrists pinned to the floor. Before the rancher could begin to struggle, Sal crashed his head against Slaton's, a classic head-butt, and the rancher was out cold.

Sal rolled off of him and sat, breathing heavily, on the floor, one leg still arching over Slaton's knees. "What the fuck!" Sal said to himself. He had never been in a brawl like that. Back home, you pop a guy one time in the chin and he's ready to call it quits. But this old bastard fought like he was possessed by the devil.

Sal worked his way to his feet, got a head rush, and almost fell back to the floor. He squatted there a moment, hands on his knees, and regained his composure.

Finally, he picked up both guns and turned to go clean himself up. *Maybe I should call the law,* he thought. *Wouldn't that be a switch? The cops coming to* my *rescue?*

Then he heard a noise behind him, the growl again. Sal turned to see Slaton standing, a bloody mess, ready to come at him once more.

"Don't even think about it," Sal hissed. He raised his .35 and pointed it.

But Sal saw another familiar look on Slaton's face. A look that said, *Sure, I might die today, but I'm gonna take you with me.*

With a bone-chilling scream, Slaton lumbered forward.

Sal shot him in the center of the chest—and Slaton stopped in his tracks. Sal fired again. And a third time. For a moment, both men were frozen, motionless, the rancher standing bolt upright, confusion on his face, his eyes staring into space somewhere above Sal's head.

Then he crumpled to the ground like a house of cards.

Seconds later, Vinnie came bursting into the room, eyes wild, ready to act. "What the hell? Pop! What's going on?"

Sal collapsed into a chair, giving Vinnie a clear view of the body on the floor.

"Jesus," Vinnie said, going pale. "Jesus Christ. What the hell is he doin' here?"

Sal gave his son a harsh glare. "I was gonna ask you the same fuckin' thing."

Bobby Garza, a rugged, handsome man in his mid-thirties, had held the office of Blanco County sheriff for just more than a year. He had won the appointment by default when the previous sheriff, a corrupt, greedy ape of a man, was implicated in a drug-smuggling ring. A collective sigh of relief could be heard around the county when Garza was selected, because he was the only available deputy with the right combination of experience, intelligence, and honesty. Later, John Marlin had been one of Garza's chief supporters in the general election in the spring, and Garza had held the office by an overwhelming margin.

Thirty minutes after Marlin had radioed the dispatcher to request assistance with the death of Bert Gammel, Garza's patrol car crunched down the gravel road of the Hawley Ranch and pulled in next to Marlin's truck.

Marlin's relief at seeing Garza, who had become a close friend over the years, was tempered by the presence of a skinny, red-faced man with a crew cut in the passenger seat. Wylie Smith had been hired to fill Garza's deputy position when Garza rose to sheriff, and the new man hadn't made many friends since. Before coming to Blanco County, Wylie had been stationed in Houston with the Harris County Sheriff's Department, and he had brought along the cynicism, sarcasm, and attitude of superiority that so many big-city residents seem to pack with them when they come to the country. But Marlin had to admit that the forensic training Wylie had received in Houston would be valuable to the case.

"What we got, John?" Bobby Garza asked, shaking Marlin's hand. Wylie surveyed the landscape and offered no greeting.

"Lester found one of his hunters dead near his blind this

morning," Marlin replied, picking a careful path toward the body. "It's Bert Gammel."

Garza and Wylie both nodded somberly as they stared at the corpse.

Marlin said, "Took a round right in the chest. Plus, he's hunting with a two-seventy automatic. I didn't find a shell casing, so I guess we can assume he didn't fire."

"Do me a favor, will ya, and don't assume what we know at this point," Wylie said. "Leave that to us to figure out."

Marlin gave Wylie a cold stare, but before he could reply, Garza spoke up: "Well, it doesn't hurt to go into this with a fresh eye, but Marlin was first on the scene, so let's hear what he has to say." Marlin wished Garza had added *asshole* to the end of that last sentence.

Marlin checked his notes and quickly ran through Lester's report, then summarized what he himself had discovered so far. He discussed the narrow alley between the trees and ended with the likely-looking hiding spot where the killer had carried off the ambush.

"So you just took it on yourself to begin the investigation?" Wylie asked. "Decided to start without us?"

"Well, it wasn't what I'd call a real thorough bit of detective work, Wylie. I saw what I saw and decided to give the area a look. Anyone could have figured it out. Even you."

Wylie's face turned a vivid red.

Garza spoke up again: "Cool it, both of you. I don't need you at each other's throats right now." He turned to Marlin. "John, it sounds like you did what any of us would have done. Now let's see what you found."

Marlin led them to the fenceline and the three men crossed the barbed wire. Marlin pointed out the makeshift blind under the cedar tree, drawing their attention to the puddle of tobacco spit.

"There's our DNA," Garza said, giving Marlin an approving smile. "Hell of a job. Anything else?"

"I saw a partial boot print over there between a couple of

cedars. That's all, so far." He looked at Wylie. "I decided to leave the area and wait for reinforcements."

"Great," Garza said. "Good work." He turned to Wylie. "Wylie, you're the lead dog on this one. You've got the most experience in this area, and I'm hoping we can all learn a couple of things. So, how do you want to proceed?"

Wylie looked around and made an exaggerated gesture with his hands. "My first question is, where is Lester Higgs?"

Marlin said, "Took off about twenty minutes ago. Said he had some ranch work to do. I think he went back up to the barn for some supplies. I told him a deputy would be in touch."

Wylie snorted. "You let our first witness just wander off? He could be on the phone right now, telling half the county what happened."

Marlin swallowed the anger that was rising in his throat. "Listen, I asked him not to discuss—"

"Yeah, right," Wylie interrupted. "I'm sure that'll stop him. Smart move."

Marlin opened his mouth, but once more Garza interceded: "Wylie, would you just back off a minute? Lester's a good man. If John asked him to keep it under his hat, that's what he'll do. We can stop and interview him again if we need to on the way out."

Marlin could tell that Wylie didn't like it. "All right, the first thing I need to do is a more thorough search," Wylie said. He looked at Marlin. "I'd prefer it if everyone just stayed out of my way."

Wylie turned and made his way back toward the fence, returning to Garza's patrol car for equipment.

After he was gone, Marlin looked at Garza and said, "That boy needs his cinch tightened a little."

"We gotta clean dis shit up and quick, before your mother gets home," Sal said, placing the handgun on his desk.

"But, Pop, what the hell happened?"

"Never mind dat shit now. Go out to the garage, grab dat tarp on the shelf above the washer. Bring a bucket and a bunch of rags. We don't got much time," Sal said, glancing at his wrist-watch. It was three-twenty. Angela had said she and Maria would be home by six at the latest, when her Crock-Pot dinner would be ready.

Vinnie hustled to gather the items, and both men went to work cleaning up the scene.

First they wrapped Slaton in the tarp, bound it tightly with duct tape, and dragged him into the garage. Vinnie hopped into his Camaro in the driveway and backed it into the garage, park-ing in his mother's usual spot. Fortunately, the Mameli home sat on five acres, and this provided plenty of privacy. Vinnie easily hefted the corpse and plopped it into his trunk.

For the next hour, the men attacked the grotesque residue in Sal's den. They scrubbed, washed, wiped, and sponged, and the evidence was quickly disappearing—except for a large oval bloodstain on the carpet where Slaton's body had fallen.

"Dis ain't workin'," Sal muttered, rubbing the rust-tinted carpet. "Fuck! *Dis ain't workin'!*"

"Want some more water?" Vinnie asked, holding the bucket.

Sal pondered the situation for a moment. "Naw, we'd be here all night. Look, what you gotta do is run down to the Super S and rent a carpet cleaner, one-a dose portable jobs. Take my Lincoln, and get your ass back here *pronto!*"

"What about his truck, Pop?"

Damn it to hell! Sal had forgotten about Slaton's Ford out front. "Why didn't you remind me!" he shouted, Vinnie shrink-ing back. Sal thought things through, gears spinning. "Okay, listen. I'll take my Lincoln, you follow in his Ford and we'll ditch it somewhere along the way."

He turned and grabbed something off the shelf behind him. "Put on dese gloves. We don't need your fuckin' prints all over the place."

CHAPTER THIRTEEN

By five-thirty, U.S. Marshal Smedley Allen Poindexter was wolfing down his fifth Twinkie, sitting in his nondescript sedan, bored out of his mind. That was the thing about this job—there were times when you sat for hours doing nothing but watching and waiting.

Unfortunately, Smedley had a habit of combating the tedium by eating; there was always an assortment of packaged cookies, donuts, chips, and salty snacks on the passenger seat beside him. Sometimes a quart or two of Big Red soda, which tasted just fine to Smedley even when it was warm. In the past eleven years, he had packed a total of seventy disgusting, blubbery pounds onto his already pudgy body. He now tipped the scales at a whopping 280, way too much for his five-ten frame.

The worst part of it all was that he shared a name with a certain cereal-loving pachyderm. When the Cap'n Crunch folks had come out with Smedley the Elephant decades ago, Smedley Poindexter had been a skinny boy of thirteen. Sure, he had gotten razzed because of the name, but it would have been much worse if he had been overweight. He had had other problems to deal with—acne, shyness, a mild stutter—but thank God he hadn't been fat!

Now, however, he *was* fat. Way too fat. And when you're an overweight guy walking around with a name like Smedley— well, plenty of people can't resist a setup like that. In Smedley's office, there was this marshal named Todd—a *GQ*-looking jerk—who would press his cheek to his shoulder, toss his arm in the air like a trunk, and make a trumpeting noise when Smedley walked by. Everybody just laughed and laughed at that. Including Smedley. He pretended it didn't bother him, but he secretly envisioned bitch-slapping Todd into early next week. Smedley just couldn't assert himself enough to tell those guys to shut the hell up. He daydreamed about it, though. A lot.

What the hell, Smedley thought, as he crammed the remainder of the cream-filled delight into his mouth. Maybe he'd start a diet next week. It was never too late, right?

With his hands free now, he twirled the radio dial. He preferred talk radio. Rush Limbaugh, Dr. Laura Schlessinger, even those two goobers who yakked on and on about car repair. Those guys were pretty funny, even if they did have weird accents. Smedley found some sort of program about horticulture and sat back in his seat.

A car came bouncing down the rutted street in front of the Mamelis' house. Could be a Mercedes. It looked kind of gray, too. Kind of hard to tell yet. . . nope, it was a Lexus, and it kept on going down the road.

Smedley had knocked on the door when he first arrived, but nobody was home. Looking through the garage windows, all he saw was the kid's Camaro. So Smedley parked out on the road, a hundred yards down, waiting. A few minutes later, Sal's Lincoln came ripping along with Sal and the kid inside, returning from who-knows-where.

It was Smedley's job to drop in on the Mamelis on occasion, maybe a couple of times a month. Kind of keep an eye on them, make sure everything was kosher. Granted, Sal didn't have a lot to gain by running at this point, but with some of these guys, you never knew what they'd do.

Smedley remembered Gino Riccotto, a wiseguy who had turned federal witness. Late in the game, Riccotto decided he'd made a mistake, he wasn't a rat, and it was time to kiss and make up with the men he was going to send to prison. So, the day before the trial, Gino slipped away from the safe house while Smedley was asleep on the sofa. *Not much you can do for him now,* Smedley's boss had said. *He'll turn up eventually.* Three days later, a security guard found what was left of Gino oozing out of a bus-station locker. *Maybe that's how Sal will end up,* Smedley thought. Then he realized he was smiling.

Angela and Maria drove along in silence in Angela's gray Mercedes, the only sound the hum of the tires and the soft classical music on the stereo.

There were times when Angela could hardly stand to look at her housekeeper. She didn't hate Maria, exactly; in fact she didn't hate her at all. After all, deep down, Angela knew it wasn't Maria's fault. If something was going on between Maria and Sal, Angela felt certain it was all Sal's doing. It wouldn't be the first time.

Sal's infidelity had left Angela plodding through life in a state of despair and regret for twenty years. She didn't love her husband, and wasn't sure if she ever would again. Sure, she had loved him at one time, back when they first met. Those days seemed like a fairy tale compared to the last two decades.

Sal had swept Angela off her feet in 1983. She was a secretary working for the New York building inspector's office, leading a dreary life, living in a dreary apartment, hanging out with dreary friends.

Then one day, in walked a good-looking young man with thick black hair, playful eyes, and a beautiful smile. Tall. Charismatic. In an expensive suit. He had an appointment, he said, and his name was Roberto Ragusa. (Angela couldn't get used to his new name, Sal. She still slipped sometimes and called him Bobby. Sal always looked around nervously and said, *What, you trying to get me killed? It's Sal, goddammit—Sal!*)

While Sal had waited for his meeting, he flipped through magazines and flirted with Angela. She played coy, but inside, she ate it up. He seemed so lively and fun, so different than anybody she had ever met.

They had their first date that night and were married six months later.

They were the toast of the town, attending Broadway premieres, rubbing elbows with important politicians and captains of industry, going to the hottest clubs and dancing till dawn.

Then, fourteen months after the wedding, Vinnie was born.

That's when things changed.

Angela knew, with a newborn, that she and Sal couldn't do the things they had done when they were courting. The wild, exciting ride was fun while it lasted, but now it was time to settle down and raise a nice family.

Sal had other things in mind.

While Angela stayed home with the baby, Sal still caroused until all hours of the night, often coming home drunk, sometimes with the lingering scent of perfume woven into his clothing.

He always claimed she was imagining things—but he had affairs, the bastard, and she knew it. He was cold to her, treating her like a nanny and a maid. Their sex life vanished.

But what was she to do? Disgrace herself by divorcing the son of a bitch? Her mother would simply die if that happened. Her new friends—wives of men with money and power— would pity her at first, then slowly stop calling. She'd be out of the loop, dropped from the inner circle, and the extravagant lifestyle she had grown accustomed to would slip away.

There was also the baby to consider. She could never support herself and a child if she returned to her job as a secretary. Also, Vinnie deserved a father—and Sal, Angela bitterly admitted, was a good father. Hell, he spent more time with the boy than he did with Angela.

It was also about this time when Angela reluctantly admitted to herself that her husband wasn't a mere businessman. Despite his claims to the contrary, Sal was nothing more than a thug. He ran a concrete business, but from snippets she heard while Sal was on the phone, the business was far from legit. There appeared to be kickbacks, strong-arm tactics, and laundering involved. Not to mention the way some of Sal's associates tended to disappear suddenly. Here one day, gone the next, never to be seen again. She always wondered if Sal had anything to do with those disappearances.

So, for twenty years, Angela had resigned herself to a lonely, bleak existence, the wife of a common criminal.

Then, three years ago, Sal had finally come clean. The federal investigations and upcoming trials forced his hand, and he told her everything. Or at least he said he did. The newspapers referred to Sal as a hit man, but he never confessed to that, despite the mounds of evidence against him. *I bent a few tax rules,* Sal would say, *but kill somebody? Never.*

Now she thought Sal was screwing the housekeeper.

It made Angela furious.

When their family had been relocated, Angela, oddly, had been elated. She looked at it as a fresh start, an opportunity to wipe the slate clean and begin a whole new life. A chance to gain respectability, make up for Sal's evil deeds in the past. And maybe now, away from the circles that had turned Sal into a corrupt, heartless man, they could fix their broken marriage.

But it wasn't working out that way at all.

Sal, so far as Angela knew, was staying inside the law, even with his new brush-clearing business. But his womanizing—the thing that hurt her most—had returned.

Wheeling into the driveway now, Angela was on the verge of tears. She shouldn't let her mind wander like that, because it always made her upset. And angry . . . oh, so angry.

Twenty yards from the garage, a black cat ran out in front of the Mercedes and froze. Angela's foot immediately rose from the gas pedal, and lingered over the brake.

In a split second, though, something dark and macabre in Angela's psyche took over. It was Maria's cat, she knew, and here, finally, was a way for Angela to spread a little of the pain around, to share some of the misery. It was nonsense, of course.

Sal was the one Angela wanted to hurt, not Maria. But Angela wasn't thinking clearly; she was merely looking for a way to release some of the torment in her soul.

She lightly pushed the accelerator. The fine German engine responded, and the cat seemed to be swallowed up like a piece of lint in front of a vacuum cleaner.

"Mi gato!" Maria cried, as they both heard the thump beneath the wheels.

CHAPTER FOURTEEN

Another thirty minutes went by and Smedley was dozing off behind the wheel, his head bobbing to his chest every twenty seconds or so. Then, just as he was reaching for the bottle of Big Red, needing a caffeine jolt, he saw Angela Mameli's car glide into her driveway. He thought he could see the pretty housekeeper—Maria was her name—in the passenger seat.

Finally. Smedley preferred to drop in when Angela and Maria were home. Angela was much nicer than the Mameli men. Sal Mameli could be a real bastard, and that smart-ass son of his wasn't much better. They always brought up that tired bit about how their taxes paid Smedley's salary, looking smug about it. But both men seemed to behave a little better when Angela was around. And she sometimes invited him to stay for dinner.

Smedley decided to give Angela a few minutes to get settled before he paid a visit.

Maria sprang from the car in a panic. She was dumbfounded. It almost seemed as if Mrs. Mameli had hit her cat on purpose.

Maria knew Mrs. Mameli was a sad, angry woman, but surely she would not take out her emotions on a defenseless animal.

Behind the car, Tuco lay broken and bloody. Maria went to one knee and cradled the cat's head, but it was obvious there was no life left in him.

"Maria, I'm so sorry!" Mrs. Mameli was behind her, looking over her shoulder. "I meant to hit the brake but I hit the gas. I don't know what happened. It was all so quick."

A tear ran down Maria's cheek.

"You poor thing," Mrs. Mameli said. "I know that cat meant a lot to you. I feel just awful." Mrs. Mameli patted Maria's shoulder, then returned to her car and continued up the driveway.

Alone now, Maria gently lifted the mangled body—and saw something that surprised her: a small tuft of white hair on the cat's chest. Tuco had no such patch. It was not Tuco!

Maria was momentarily elated, then was washed over with guilt for feeling happy while this innocent animal lay dead in her hands.

Sal placed the steam cleaner in the trunk of his Lincoln and slammed the lid just as the gears of the garage-door opener groaned and the door began to lift. *Jeez, that was close,* he thought.

The door open now, Sal could see Angela sitting out there in her Mercedes. She made an impatient gesture that said, *What's Vinnie's car doing in my spot?* then killed the engine and climbed out.

Sal planted a fake smile on his face and walked over to greet her, trying to gauge her mood; she had been such a bitch lately. He could already hear her carping about having to park in the driveway, asking why Vinnie had parked in the garage. Sal had a good lie ready: *Vinnie was vacuuming the inside of his car and needed to be close to an outlet.*

But Angela let him off the hook by speaking first. "What a goddamn day!" she moaned. "Poor Maria, I just ran over her cat."

Sal looked down the driveway. "You hit her cat?" As far as

he was concerned, that was good news. He wondered why he had never thought of that himself.

Angela jerked a thumb over her shoulder. "Not to mention, we got company again out on the road."

Sal's heart fluttered and his balls shrank to about half their normal size. She was talking about that damn marshal! Even between trials, the Feds still dropped in now and then—usually a whale of a guy named Smedley, who always seemed to show up around dinnertime. Angela would usually ask him to stay for a bite, despite Sal's whispered protests. Did it to piss him off, he figured.

Angela was grabbing shopping bags out of the trunk, asking Sal to give her a hand, but Sal turned and raced into the house. Vinnie had to get his car the hell out of there.

When Smedley pulled up to the house, Mrs. Mameli wasn't in sight. But Maria was standing in the middle of the driveway, down a ways from the house, looking disoriented. Wait a minute—was that blood on her blouse? Had something happened to Sal, right here under Smedley's nose? Panic gripped him.

Smedley shoved it into PARK and struggled out of the sedan, his hand fumbling for his revolver under his coat. Then he saw the dead cat at Maria's feet. What a relief—just a dead cat.

Smedley looked at Maria, who was wiping the tears off her cheeks. "You okay?" he asked.

Maria nodded, wrapping her arms around her torso as if she were cold.

Smedley glanced around for help, maybe Angela or even Sal. Somebody to step in and take care of this poor gal. But they were all alone, standing in silence. Meanwhile, Maria continued to look miserable. Smedley knew he should do what a real man would do: Step up, be gallant, console the damsel in distress. But the problem was, he had always been so awkward around women. Especially beautiful women. He became klutzy and tongue-tied and sweaty and . . . and, oddly, none of that was happening right now.

Whatever it was, Maria was somehow different. She didn't look at him with disdain or mockery, as American women did. Her eyes held compassion, even now, with her dead pet lying in front of her. So Smedley swallowed his doubts and walked over to Maria. He gently wrapped an arm around her, this woman he barely knew. She surprised him by pressing her head against his chest and accepting his comfort.

She looked up into his eyes and Smedley felt his heart flutter. She was so vulnerable and beautiful, with soulful brown eyes, high, sculpted cheekbones, and skin as smooth and creamy as a Hershey bar.

Maria said something to him in Spanish. He didn't understand a word, so he just said, "There, there, everything will be all right." It sounded corny to him, but she placed her head back on his chest.

Smedley's heart was beginning to race. It had been—what?—three years since he had held a woman close. He had forgotten how good it felt. He could feel the warmth of her cheek on his chest, the rhythmic cadence of her breathing. And, wait a minute, he could also feel her large breasts pressing against his belly. Oh, God. How could he be such a cad? This woman was in emotional pain and he was thinking about her hooters.

He made a hushing noise, trying to provide solace and take his mind off her anatomy.

Then he realized, with incredible embarrassment, that the little federal agent in his pants had decided that now was a good time for an interrogation.

Maria pulled away from him, and he was waiting for a fierce tongue-lashing, maybe even a slap, certain that she had taken offense at the hardness in his crotch.

But she simply walked around the side of the house and came back a few moments later with a shovel. Jesus—this was worse than he thought. She was going to attack him with a gardening implement! But instead, she asked him a question in Spanish.

Smedley didn't understand, but at the same time, he knew exactly what she wanted. He nodded, then grabbed the deceased feline by the tail and followed her to the rear of the property.

•   •   •

Sal poked his head out of the garage and saw the agent's sedan sitting in the middle of the driveway. But no sign of Smedley.

He gave a thumbs-up to Vinnie, who fired up his Camaro, raced out of the garage, whipped around the sedan, and drove off into the dusk.

"Where's he going in such a hurry?"

Sal jumped. Smedley was standing right beside him now, holding a shovel.

Sal licked his lips nervously. "He's, ah, just heading into town, gonna see a coupla friends, to . . ."

He noticed Smedley sniffing the air, catching a whiff of Angela's dinner.

"Whaddaya say?" Sal chirped. "You gonna stay for supper?"

The sunlight was fading as Marlin watched Wylie fashion a small, shallow frame out of cardboard and duct tape. The deputy placed it gently around the footprint, then produced a can of hairspray from the canvas bag he had retrieved from Garza's patrol car.

"Having a bad hair day?" Marlin grinned, making a genuine attempt to be friendly. *Maybe Wylie could be a decent guy if anyone took the time to get to know him,* Marlin was thinking. Nobody had given the man much of a welcome, so far.

Wylie shook his head as if he were dealing with a three-year-old. "This helps the plaster hold together better. Something I'm sure they don't teach at game-warden school."

Or maybe Wylie is an absolute prick, Marlin thought, revising his theory.

Several other deputies had arrived, along with the county medical examiner, Lem Tucker. Earlier, Wylie had conducted a painstakingly slow search of the area, starting in wide circles that got tighter and tighter. He had found a few tire tracks in a dirt road about three hundred yards from the cedar tree where the killer had sat. The tracks could have been left by the ranch foreman, but Wylie would take casts and compare them to the tires on the foreman's vehicle.

After Wylie had taken numerous photos, Garza had flipped the body over, revealing an exit wound in the center of Gammel's back. This seemed to indicate that the bullet had traveled in a line parallel to the ground, rather than in an arc from a long distance. Marlin's theory that there had been a shooter in the cedar tree looked better every minute.

After the body had been loaded into the M.E.'s van, Garza called Marlin and Wylie aside.

"We'll wait and see what Lem can tell us, but Wylie, you can get started on other things. We'll need to talk to the other hunters on the ranch, do some background on Gammel, the usual." He paused for a moment. "I don't think I'm going out on a limb here to say that someone ambushed Gammel. And they did it with a rifle. That says 'deer hunter' to me. That's why I want you to keep Marlin in the loop on this investigation."

Inwardly, Marlin smiled. It was always up to the chief investigating officer to decide how much involvement a game warden had in a case like this. Garza was asking Wylie to keep Marlin in the inner circles, whether Wylie wanted to or not.

"But Bobby," Wylie said, "I'm sure I can handle everything—"

"I know you can, Wylie," Garza cut him off. "You're an ace with forensics and questioning, and that's what we need. But you're new to the area, and Marlin's been here all his life. He knows every deer hunter in this county and he might be able to turn something up. I'm not saying I want him actively working the case—that's not his job—but when you approach some of the hunters on the ranch, I want you to take Marlin with you when you can."

Wylie glared at Marlin. Marlin gave him his best *Eat shit* smile.

CHAPTER FIFTEEN

Vinnie drove around for an hour, thinking, trying to come up with a plan. He had picked up a twelve-pack of beer in Johnson City, and was now on his fifth can, desperately trying to steady his nerves. This shit was out of control. He knew his dad was in a rough line of work, but tooling around with a corpse in your trunk?

Vinnie took a long swig of beer.

To be honest, it was kind of exciting. This was way beyond any rush he got from Ecstasy or cocaine. Pure adrenaline, pumping through his heart like water through a hose.

Now, if he could just think of a way to get rid of the body. Man, he wished he'd had time to talk it over with his dad! But that goddamn marshal had showed up. *Fat prick, always invading our home, sticking his nose into our business. And he has to pick today of all days?*

But back to the business at hand. Vinnie knew he had to think clearly. He couldn't afford to do something stupid, like toss the body on the side of the road. No, there'd be fibers from inside their home on the corpse, maybe some blood leaking through the tarp into his trunk.

So he had to make the body disappear for good, put it somewhere it would never be found.

He considered burning it. Just find a dead-end county road, drench it with gas, and let the evidence drift away in the wind. Sounded okay at first, but there would probably be bones left. Vinnie wasn't sure, but the Feds could probably get a DNA sample from one little shard. And the teeth, too, could give it away.

He could bury the corpse. Find a large, isolated ranch, cut the lock on the gate, and plant it out in the middle of nowhere. But that had flaws, too. Animals might dig it up. Plus, it was hunting season, and you never knew who might come along. You were always hearing in the news about hunters finding corpses out in the fucking boonies. Anyway, the ground around here was full of big rocks. Vinnie remembered T.J. griping one day about having to dig some fence posts.

T.J.

Vinnie mulled it over, and something came to him now: a good, workable plan. A way to dispose of the old fucker for good—and T.J. could help, without even knowing it. That was the beauty of it. Vinnie thought it through for a few minutes, trying to find the flaws in his scheme, the little screwups that would come back later to bite him in the ass.

But there weren't any. The more he thought about, the more perfect it seemed.

He aimed his Camaro back toward Johnson City, ready to find a pay phone. This was one call he wasn't going to make on his cell.

Vinnie had been glad that T.J. was already stoned when he got him on the phone. Vinnie had planned on getting T.J. high before he sprung the idea on him, but he had been able to skip that step.

Now, cruising in the Camaro, Vinnie whipped out a joint and

passed it to T.J. wanting to keep him good and loaded so he wouldn't back out. T.J. had been kind of lukewarm to it at first, then seemed to get excited as they talked.

They had already completed step one of "Operation Porsche," as Vinnie had called it; they had driven T.J.'s sports car over to Pedernales Reservoir, near the boat ramp, and parked it.

Now Vinnie was driving T.J. to the marina where the Gibbs family kept their boat.

"Man, this is crazy!" T.J. said, but he was smiling, getting off on this wild scheme. "What if something goes wrong?"

"Trust me," Vinnie replied, trying to sound confident. "I've done this a coupla times. Works like a fuckin' charm. All you gotta do is call it in stolen, then get ready to pick out your new wheels." He passed T.J. a lighter. "Smoke up, dude."

T.J.'s face was briefly illuminated as he took a long hit.

"You don't want to keep driving that dog, do ya?" Vinnie asked. "Thing's a piece of crap, like ya said."

"Yeah, you're right. Won't run for shit."

"Then relax and leave it to ol' Vinnie."

Five minutes later, Vinnie punched in the security code at the gate and pulled into the marina. He drove down by the dock and let T.J. out. "Now, remember, we gotta use the strongest ski-rope ya got," Vinnie said.

T.J. giggled, thoroughly stoned by now. "No prob. I'll meet you in ten." He reached in through the window. "Pass me that joint, man. I wanna get the full effect when that turd goes bye-bye."

"That Sue Ellen is one fine piece of tail," Billy Don stated, wallowing on Red's sofa, his feet propped on the cable-spool coffee table. He and Red were watching a rerun of *Dallas* on cable. "If I had as much money as J.R., I'd be launching my love rocket with women like that all the time."

Red wasn't paying much attention. His mind was on the deerskin coat he was wearing, a fine piece of craftsmanship he had finished making for himself a few weeks earlier.

Damn thing was making him itchy.

He had read an article about tanning hides. Now Red was wondering whether he had made a mistake by skipping the step that had to do with exterminating parasites. Seemed like a lot of trouble to soak the hide in alum, whatever the hell that was. He slipped the coat off and tossed it over the back of a chair.

Billy Don said, "Which would you rather bang, Red—Sue Ellen or Miss Ellie?"

Now, *that* caught Red's attention. "You moron, Miss Ellie is the old one, J.R.'s mama. You must mean one of the younger ones, one of the babes."

"Hell if I do," Billy Don said, his eyes locked on the screen.

Red shivered at the thought of Billy Don groping the matriarch of the Ewing clan. He rose to grab a fresh beer from the fridge.

He popped the top and walked over to the TV set, an old wood-laden console he had picked up for fifty bucks at the pawn shop. "Billy Don, you ever think it should be me and you riding around in Cadillacs, drinking champagne, and all that high-society shit?"

Billy Don nodded eagerly, as Ellie Ewing brushed her gray hair while seated in front of a vanity. "Hell yes."

Red took a long drink, then wiped his mouth with his sleeve. "I've been thinking about something. Sure, we've had a few minor setbacks working for Mr. Slaton. But overall, I'd say we're doing pretty damn good. Wouldn't you?"

Billy Don didn't respond. Jock Ewing had come up behind his wife and was caressing her neck.

"I mean, hell, who's clearing more land than me and you?" Red continued. "We're working harder and longer than anybody else out there. I like Mr. Slaton and all—he's giving us a fair shake and everything—but I'd say we deserve a raise. I think we oughta stop by tomorrow and discuss it with him."

Red glanced down at the set, and now ol' Jock was nibbling Ellie's ear. Really putting the moves on her. Red looked over at Billy Don, who was off in his own little world now, rubbing a pillow against his crotch in a very unappealing manner.

"Aw, man." Red shook his head. "Guess I'll leave you three alone."

By the time Vinnie got back to Pedernales Reservoir, he could already see T.J. idling out on the water.

Vinnie parked next to the Porsche, a good hundred yards from shore, and quickly transferred the tarp-wrapped corpse to the Porshe's passenger seat. It was good and dark now, and there wasn't anyone around anyway. Then Vinnie used a boxcutter to slice through the tarp and remove it from around Slaton's body. The corpse would decompose more quickly that way.

When he was done, Vinnie hopped into the Porsche, fired the engine, and followed the dirt road down to the boat ramp. The park featured a gentle, grassy slope down to the reservoir, making it easy to navigate even the low-slung Porsche over the terrain.

Here at the park, just a quarter of a mile from the dam, Vinnie knew the water would be plenty deep, especially out in the middle.

Vinnie stopped ten yards shy of the water and T.J. idled the boat close to shore.

"You ready?" Vinnie hissed, standing at the water's edge.

He could hear T.J. giggling in reply. Then he saw the end of the joint glow red as T.J. took another hit.

"Throw the rope!"

T.J. tossed the coiled line and Vinnie snagged it in midair.

Vinnie lay down and shimmied underneath the front end of the car. He found a good, solid piece of the framework—maybe the axle, he couldn't see very well—and looped the rope through it. He couldn't tie the rope to the car, because he had to be able to pull it loose later. He'd need both ends in the boat.

He got onto his feet and tossed the end of the rope back to T.J. Vinnie whispered, "Remember, not too fast! Just good and firm. You don't want to break the rope. Take me all the way out to the middle if you can."

He could see T.J. nodding in the moonlight. "Let's do it!"

Vinnie folded himself into the small interior of the Porsche, and gunned the engine. A moment later, he felt a small bump as T.J. pulled the rope taut.

The whine of the boat's engine began to climb as T.J. increased the throttle, pulling harder and harder, just waiting for Vinnie.

Vinnie raced the car's engine, released the brake, and shot down the ramp into the water.

It worked like a charm.

The small car began to float immediately, and T.J. quickly towed it away from the bank.

Slowly the water was climbing higher on the body of the car. Vinnie could feel his feet getting wet now.

But they were fifty yards from shore now. Then seventy-five . . . and one hundred.

Finally, about a hundred and fifty yards out, the resistance was too much and the car could go no farther. Vinnie eased himself out of the driver's window just seconds before the water came rushing in.

Vinnie swam quickly through the cool water to the boat, the engine quiet now.

Laughing hysterically, T.J. pulled Vinnie onboard. "Man, did you see that fucker sink? That was great!"

Vinnie smiled, wishing his dad could be here to praise his creativity. "Always glad to help my friends out of a jam," he said. "I'm freezing my balls off. Pull that rope into the boat and let's get the hell out of here."

CHAPTER SIXTEEN

At eleven o'clock on Wednesday morning, John Marlin stripped off his warden's uniform, pulled on some work clothes, and rolled a large toolbox out of the shed in his backyard. He stood in the sunlight and surveyed the framework of the room he was adding on to his house.

Last night, after writing his report on the death of Bert Gammel, he had gone on patrol until three in the morning. Chased down a couple of idiots spotlighting deer, but he couldn't find a rifle in their truck. The men were out-of-towners, so Marlin had sent them on their way with a stern warning to watch their asses in Blanco County. Other than that, it had been pretty quiet. After a few hours of sleep, he had hit the roads again this morning, but it was a typically slow weekday. Most of the hunting camps were empty, except for a few retirees or serious hunters who had taken off work for the first week of the season.

Also, as Marlin had expected, Wylie Smith had not contacted him. It was likely Wylie was in the process of interviewing the other hunters on the Hawley Ranch, but Marlin hadn't heard a word from the deputy. *Fine,* Marlin thought. *Let him wade through that mess himself.*

Now, in the midday lull, he could afford a little time to himself, a chance to indulge in the primitive therapy that carpentry seemed to offer. Something about working with his hands, seeing a structure slowly take shape from his own backbreaking labor, gave Marlin a release he found nowhere else, not even hunting. Over the years, he had built a large covered deck, a sunroom, and a carport for his state-issued Dodge truck.

But Marlin had more of an emotional investment in this particular project. Or, he used to. Last year, after Becky had moved in, she had commented that his place was awfully small. It was a casual remark, but it forced Marlin to do a little long-term thinking. His place was a simple ranch-style cabin. Two bedrooms, one bath. Small living room. Barely more than a thousand square feet, total. It had always been fine for him alone. But he realized that a man and a woman should have a little more space than his house provided.

So last spring he had begun adding a sixteen-by-twenty room to the back of his house. *More than three hundred square feet,* he had told Becky. *That'll open things up quite a bit, give us plenty of room.*

His secret plan—something he had shared only with Phil Colby—was to propose to Becky as soon as he finished the addition.

But then Becky had gone to stay with her mother, and Marlin had put the project on hold for a while. He had been lonely when she was gone, and his heart simply wasn't in it.

And now she was gone for good.

Oddly, though, now that he knew where things stood, Marlin had the urge to get back to it, to keep himself busy with some honest physical labor. He figured it would be better than moping around all day, thinking himself into a funk.

Marlin eyed the work he had done in the spring. The walls were framed. Now it was time to get the roof up before the weather took too much of a toll on the plywood subflooring he had installed five months ago.

Marlin strapped on a tool belt, pulled a tarp off a stack of two-by-eights, and got busy. Using his circular saw, he notched each rafter to rest on the top plate of the outer wall. Then he began hauling the rafters up the ladder and nailing them in place.

After two hours, the roof line was beginning to take shape. Marlin felt invigorated, his mind fresh, thinking of nothing but the task at hand. He took a break for a large tumbler of iced tea, then pulled his shirt off. Sixty degrees outside, but Marlin had worked up a good sweat wrestling those planks up the ladder.

At two-thirty, he hammered the last rafter into place and remained on the ladder for a moment, catching his breath.

Then he heard a female voice say, "Ooo-whee! Check out the beefcake."

He looked down and saw Inga Mueller grinning up at him. She was wearing jeans and a long-sleeved T-shirt, her hair in a ponytail. Marlin thought he had heard a car pull up. She must have heard the hammering and come around the side of the house.

Inga fanned herself with one hand and attempted a Southern accent, saying, "My, my, I do believe I'm getting weak in the knees," then faked a swoon, leaning against the framework of the new room.

Marlin had to laugh. "You're a real bashful one, aren't you?" he said, climbing down the ladder.

She tapped on one of the wall supports. "Well, at least there was a stud around to catch me."

Marlin grabbed a rag and began wiping some of the grime off his hands. "So, you out of jail already?" he asked, arching an eyebrow at her.

She smiled. "Sure. Got out yesterday. Seems nobody's pressing charges. Not Rodney Bauer, not Cecil Pritchard . . . and not you."

The district attorney had called yesterday, a chuckle in his voice as he read the report and asked Marlin if he wanted to proceed with an assaulting-an-officer case against her. Marlin had declined.

"What about Rodney's truck?" Marlin asked. "Don't tell me his insurance is going to cover it?"

She folded her arms and cocked a hip, like a young girl pouting. "Well, no. Those heartless ghouls said they would sue me for the damages."

"Can you blame them?"

"No, not really. I'm going to pay Rodney back myself. In fact, I already did. Met him in Johnson City and wrote him a check. He told me where you live."

Marlin nodded as he pulled his shirt on. "I was wondering about that."

He stood there a moment, uncertain what to say, thinking Inga would announce the reason for her visit. Instead, she looked up at the roof joists and said, "What're you building?"

Marlin hesitated for a second. "Aw, I'm just adding on another room. Wanted a little more space."

"What is this, a two-bedroom? Three? What's a single guy like you need all that space for?"

Marlin wondered how she knew he was single. There was the obvious sign that he didn't wear a wedding ring, but not all married men did. Who had she been talking to?

Marlin simply shrugged, then grabbed his glass. "You want some tea?"

"You got any beer?"

"I do. What kind you like?"

"Cold."

"My favorite flavor. Think you can refrain from throwing it on me?"

She put her hands up in an *I surrender* gesture. "I come in peace."

Thomas Collin Peabody simply didn't understand women. Not this one, anyway, this wild sprite, this forest nymph named Inga. Ah, what a fiasco. Here she was, mooning over a common man—a redneck, a hick, a yokel. Meanwhile, a man who truly loved her—a man of substance and values and compassion and humanity—sat outside in her rusting Volvo.

She had asked him: Did he want to come inside? Hell no, he didn't. He just couldn't stand watching her make eyes at the man, like she did with all the others. But she always said it didn't mean anything. *Just my way of doing things,* she'd say. *Gets them on my side.* Sure, it got them on her side because they wanted to get her on her back. It gave Thomas Peabody a big knot in his stomach just thinking about it.

Who was this Marlin guy, anyway? A game warden. Not even a real police officer. Peabody was surprised they were even allowed to carry guns. And now this guy—this high-and-mighty *game warden*—was in *there*, chatting with Inga, probably having a good laugh about the incident at the coffee shop, then checking out her breasts when she wasn't looking. Or maybe even when she was.

From the moment Peabody had met Inga at a logging protest, where he had chained himself nude to a massive redwood, Peabody had loved her with a feverish intensity. She was truly a vision, more beautiful than the loveliest Rodin, more haunting than the most provocative Picasso. She seemed to share so many of Peabody's qualities, too: a love of nature and its delicate ecosystem, an affinity for the animals that graced the Earth, and a strong moral compass that dictated the actions necessary to defend both.

They had been fighting the good fight together for two years now, traveling the country when necessary. Living off Thomas's trust fund, doing their best to right wrongs wherever they found them. When Inga had spotted an article in *Birdwatcher* about the plight of the red-necked sapsucker, Thomas had said, *Certainly, by all means, let's see what we can do about it. Let's mosey on down to Texas and have us a look-see.* That had elicited a smile, but not the kind of smile Peabody wanted. More like a smile you'd get from your sister.

Then, when he had humbly asked for her hand in marriage, he had received that same smile again. *Oh, Tommy,* she had said. *I don't know what to say. You're so sweet to ask.* So sweet to ask. What kind of comment was that? That's the kind of remark you make when a friend inquires about your sickly aunt.

That's when he realized she wasn't just going to *give* him her heart. He was going to have to win it. He was going to have to prove just what kind of man he was. A good man. A gentle man. A compassionate man. And if he had to vandalize a few backhoes or slander a couple of developers along the way, so be it.

Inside, sitting at the small kitchen table, Inga sipped her beer and gazed around the room. "I like your place. Kind of rustic, all the wood and rock, nice and comfortable. Makes me feel right at home."

"Thanks. I enjoy it out here, away from town."

"God, from what I've seen, even when you're in town you're not exactly bumping elbows with people on the sidewalk. I think I've got more people living on my block in Minneapolis than you guys do in the entire county."

"Well, a small town like this, it's not for everybody, that's for sure," Marlin said, thinking of Becky.

Inga gave him a curious glance, started to say something, then let it pass.

"Want another beer?" Marlin had noticed her bottle was empty.

"Sure."

As Marlin went to the fridge, Inga said, "Listen, I came out here because I wanted to tell you about something. Tomorrow evening, I'm holding an assembly, sort of a town-hall meeting, at the high school gymnasium. I want to address this brush-clearing business, see if I can talk some sense into some of these people. I think if they heard the facts, some of them would think twice about what they're doing."

Marlin set two fresh beers down and stared at her for a few seconds. He said patiently, "I can tell you right now, you want to be careful how you phrase things. Like, 'talk some sense into these people.' You start making them feel stupid or ignorant, they won't listen to a word you say."

She gave him a surprised look. "Oh, I know that. I wouldn't say that in the meeting. . . ."

Marlin looked up at the clock. Almost time to get back on patrol.

Inga sighed. "Now you think I'm kind of a bitch, don't you? That I think everyone around here is a hick."

Marlin shrugged.

Inga said, "The truth is, I *don't* think 'these people' are stupid or ignorant. Maybe a little uninformed, a little desperate, that's all. They're looking to solve a tough problem, and they're going about it the best way they know how."

Marlin gave her a small smile. "Okay, now you're sounding reasonable."

"Anyway, this assembly, it's at seven o'clock, and I was wondering whether you'd join us."

Marlin didn't want to get in the middle of this.

"Please," she said, reaching across to lightly touch her fingers to his forearm. "It would help out a lot, and I know people would listen to any comments you wanted to make."

Marlin hesitated. "How do you know anyone's even gonna be there? I mean, this is the first I've heard of it, and—"

"There's going to be a notice in tomorrow's paper, right on the front page. I talked to Susannah Branson, the reporter."

Ah, there it was. That's how Inga knew Marlin was single. Probably knew a lot more than that.

"Will you come, John? Help me out a little?"

He tried to avoid her eyes, but she tilted her head, used body language to draw his gaze to hers.

He wanted to say, *Thanks but no thanks, I've got enough issues to deal with at the moment.* But staring into those blue eyes, Marlin knew he didn't stand a chance.

CHAPTER SEVENTEEN

While doing a little light cleaning Wednesday afternoon, Maria noticed that a lamp was missing—the one that normally sat on the table at the end of the hallway, where the Mamelis placed their mail. Maria thought perhaps Mrs. Mameli had moved it into the living room or one of the bedrooms, but she could not spot it anywhere. *Very strange.*

Then, while dusting in Mr. Mameli's den, she realized that some of the art on the walls had been rearranged. Three oil paintings that had been displayed in various places throughout the room were now clustered on one wall. It seemed an odd grouping to Maria, giving the room a lopsided feel, but she was not an art expert.

She rolled the Hoover upright into the den from the hallway and switched it on. Despite the noise—maybe because of it— vacuuming always had a calming effect on Maria. The persistent droning of the motor, the rhythmic pushing-and-pulling motion: it was almost hypnotic. Maria often found her mind wandering when she vacuumed, usually back to her homeland or someplace equally pleasant.

Today she found herself thinking about that nice man from yesterday. *Smedley*. He had visited the Mameli household many times, sometimes staying for dinner. But yesterday was the first time he and Maria had spent any time alone.

She wondered about the name "Smedley," whether it was as regal-sounding to American ears as it was to hers. The man had a kind heart, she was sure of that. After all, he had helped her bury the cat in the backyard. How many men would be willing to do that? Certainly not Mr. Mameli or his strange son.

Maria was not sure of Smedley's relationship with the Mamelis. Maybe he was a friend of the family, or possibly a co-worker of some sort. She knew that Mr. Mameli seemed to get uptight when Smedley came around, so he must be a friend of the *señora*'s.

Maria shook her head and chided herself for being so foolish. Thinking these thoughts about an American man would lead nowhere. What possible interest could he have in a housekeeper, especially a humble foreigner such as herself.

Maria slid the nose of the vacuum underneath Mr. Mameli's couch and was startled by a loud clacking sound. Something was caught in the vacuum, perhaps a coin.

She leaned the Hoover backward and rested it on its neck, exposing the brushes that swept the floor.

She peered inside—and there, in the small mouth of the vacuum, was a short cylindrical tube made of brass. She reached in with her slender fingers and extracted it. Maria was fairly certain she had seen one of these objects before, and she thought it was part of the ammunition for a handgun. Something called a shell. But she was not certain, because she was not familiar with handguns at all. Whatever it was, it was quite pretty, in a way. She slipped it into the pocket of her apron.

Sal slipped into Maria's cottage while she was in the house getting dinner ready.

Earlier, Vinnie had said he had taken care of Slaton's corpse. *Got rid of everything, including the guns and the two shells.*

Vinnie had said it, plain as day. But it wasn't until a few minutes ago that Sal realized what Vinnie had said. *Two shells?* Sal thought. *There shoulda been three.*

Cleaning up yesterday, they had been in a rush and they must have missed one. Just the kind of small thing that can really screw you over good. So he had gotten down on his hands and knees and given his den a thorough search.

Nothing.

Except fresh vacuum tracks.

So he had taken the bag out of the Hoover and sifted through it. Came up empty there, too.

That left Maria's cottage. She had probably found the shell and thought it was some sort of magic trinket. Like the goddamn Indians who sold Manhattan for a handful of baubles and beads. Sal always remembered that phrase from his high-school textbook. *Baubles and beads.*

Sal was going to ask Vinnie to search Maria's small house, but the kid had wandered off somewhere again. That meant Sal would have to do it himself, because this was the kind of thing that needed to be taken care of quickly.

So Sal eased Maria's bedroom door open and stepped inside. In the dim light, it took a moment for his eyes to adjust. Then, he pawed through the drawers of her bedside table. Nothing there but Spanish-language women's magazines and various types of lotions and hand creams.

So he turned to her dresser. He sifted through her clothes, spending a little extra time in her lingerie drawer. *Where the fuck did all this good stuff come from?* he wondered. She had never worn any of this lacy stuff for him. He spied several jewelry boxes on top of her dresser and sorted through those. Nothing but cheap knickknacks.

He turned, looking for another likely place to search. Then he saw something that made his heart thump. It couldn't be, but it was! Maria's cat! It was peering out from under the bed, eyeing Sal wickedly. This simply wasn't possible. Angela had flattened that fucker with her car.

But Sal remembered Aunt Sofia. If she could make goats drop dead, maybe Maria could make a cat come back to life.

Sal whispered, "Good kitty," and eased backward toward the door, sweat breaking out on his forehead. Had to move slowly now. One wrong move and that cat might spring at him, rip his goddamn throat out. "Good kitty. Uncle Sal is leaving now."

The cat squirmed out from under the bed and hissed at Sal.

Mary, Mother of God! It was coming for him!

Sal took another step backward—and the evil creature took a stealthy step forward.

Sal's heart was jackhammering now, slamming against his rib cage. All the deadly men Sal had faced, and now he was about to be slaughtered by a house cat. The devil's house cat.

"Stay right there, kitty." Sal could hear his own voice trembling. He fumbled for the doorknob behind him, his palm slick on the brass.

The cat took another small step forward and hissed once more.

Sal jerked the door open, quickly stepped outside, and slammed the door behind him, leaving the horrible beast on the other side.

Oh, Jesus, that was close! Sal leaned against the outside of the door, waiting for his breathing to slow.

Fuck it, he thought. *That shell's not in there—and if it is, that damn cat can have it.*

Red kept one hand on the steering wheel, the other on the cold beer between his legs. It had been another long hard day driving the BrushBusters, and the ice-cold Keystone tasted like some kind of elixir from the gods.

Red drained the can, admired the scenic landscape printed on the label, then tossed it out the window at a speed-limit sign. He grabbed a dirty rag off the seat and wiped some grime off his neck.

"So," Red said, turning slightly toward Billy Don. "What ya think I oughta say to him?"

Billy Don finished a long slurp of his own beer and belched out, "Who?"

That was one of Billy Don's favorite conversational tactics: belching words. Red had never been able to master that particular trick himself, so he condemned it as juvenile.

"Slaton, goddammit," Red said. "Remember? We was gonna swing by his house, talk to him about a raise. I wanna get my geese in a row, lay everything out for him. Question is, should I mention the screwups, maybe make up some good excuses, or just let 'em slide?"

"Hell's bells, Red. He knows all about them anyway, which is why he ain't gonna give us no raise. The other day, you thought he was gonna fire us. Now you wanna ask for a raise? Sounds like a shit-brained idea to me."

Red thought of a handful of good replies, but let them all pass. He drove in silence for a few miles.

"Guess what I'll do, then," Red finally said, "is go in there, tell him how much land *I've* cleared in the past few months, mention how many hours *I've* been working, and point out that *I* haven't taken a single goddamn sick day yet. Then I'll say, 'Sir, considering my commitment to your company, I sure would be appreciable if you could consider giving me a raise. On the other hand, I don't know about ol' Billy Don. I don't think he really wants any extra dough. In fact, he seems to be perfectly happy with the generous garnishments he is now receiving.'"

Billy Don let out a huff, but Red could tell his words had hit home.

A mile later, Billy Don pawed through the ice chest on the floorboard and came out with two dripping beers. He passed one to Red and said, "Well, hell, don't leave me out."

Five minutes later, Red wheeled into the entryway of Buckhorn Creek Ranch and parked in front of Emmett Slaton's massive home. Slaton's truck wasn't parked in its usual spot and the porch light was dark.

Damn, Red thought. *Got my nerve all worked up and he ain't even home.*

"What we gonna do now?" Billy Don asked.

Red scrounged in his glove box and came up with a match-book from Chester's, a topless club in Austin. He scribbled a note on the inside and said, "Tell you what, go stick this in the door and I'll talk to him about it tonight. Do it over the phone."

"Go do it yourself," Billy Don said in a rapid-fire staccato of gastric releases.

"Hell, it was my idea," Red said. "When you come up with the ideas, you can be the one who's in charge of things. Now, you want a raise or don't ya?"

Billy Don grumbled, but climbed out of the truck and proceeded toward the house.

He lumbered up the stairs, took one step on the porch, and his feet shot out from under him. He came crashing back down on the stairs, accompanied by the sound of splintering wood.

Red stuck his head out the window and giggled. "God-damn—you all right, Billy Don?"

He heard cursing and grunting, then: "I'm stuck like a sumbitch, Red. Come help me outta here."

Red grabbed a flashlight, walked over, and found Billy Don's sizable rump wedged in a hole in the staircase.

"I hit something slick as goat shit," Billy Don groaned. "My back feels like crap. Get me loose, will ya?"

Red stuck out both hands and hauled Billy Don to his feet.

"What the hell did I slip on?" Billy Don whined. "Shine the light up there."

Red swept the light over the front porch and saw a smeared red streak where Billy Don had lost his footing. There were several other dark-red drops between the stairs and the front door.

"Billy Don said, "That looks like blood."

"I can see it." Red stepped around the drops and knocked firmly on the door. They waited, but there was no answer.

Billy Don said, "Could be anything. Maybe he shot a deer and hauled it in through here."

Red stooped and shined the light directly on one of the drops. Definitely blood. "Billy Don, if you shot a deer, would you drag it right into your goddamn living room?"

Billy Don started to answer, but Red cut him off, saying, "Forget I asked. Stupid question."

Vinnie drove to a pay phone in Johnson City and made a call.

"Yo, T.J. what's up?"

"Nothing, man. I been meaning to call you, but I was at work. I just got home."

"Everything cool?"

"Man, I was so wasted last night, I can't believe we did that." T.J.'s voice sounded shaky.

Vinnie licked his lips, getting a little nervous. "Don't turn into a pussy now, dude. Everything will be solid. Did you call the cops yet, report it stolen?"

"That's the thing, man. I started thinking about it, and I remembered something. The deal is, I got LoJack."

The word meant nothing to Vinnie. "Shit, bring it over and we'll smoke it." He forced a laugh, but T.J. didn't join in.

"Nah, man, I'm talking about one of those anti-theft deals, you know?"

"What, like a burglar alarm? Fuck, that's no big deal. Your car is fifty feet underwater. If the thing goes off, it won't bother nobody but the friggin' fish."

"Not an alarm system, it's worse than that. Goddamn, I was so blitzed, I completely spaced. You're gonna hate this."

"What the hell're you talking about, dude? Just fuckin' say it."

T.J. took a breath. "It's a trackin' device, you know, like a chip, with satellites and all that shit. So when a car gets stolen, the cops can just log on to a computer or something, and they know exactly where the goddamn car is. Soon as I call it in, they'll find my car in about two seconds."

Oh-my-fucking-Jesus-Mary-Mother-of-God! Vinnie was suddenly very hot. His heart began to pound, and his palms became damp. The earth began to shimmy and he grabbed the pay phone for support.

"You there, man?" T.J. was talking, but to Vinnie, the voice sounded distant, fuzzy, like a poor signal on an A.M. radio station.

"Yeah, yeah, I'm here. Be cool . . . gotta think for a second."
Bowel-loosening fear was squirming into Vinnie's guts, and he
tried desperately to ignore it, to stay cool and think clearly.
There had to be a way out of this fucking mess. There always
was. "Did you call the cops yet?"

"No, man, you already asked me that."

"Oh, yeah. Oh, yeah. Good. Whatever you do, don't call
them yet!"

"Goddamn, Vinnie, I ain't stupid."

Vinnie felt a throbbing in his temples. He took a large
breath, all that his lungs could hold. "It's underwater, man.
Gotta be fifty feet. You think it's still working?"

"Yeah, dude. I checked the brochure that came with it.
Fuckin' thing's watertight."

"Okay, okay, no big deal. Where's your old man?"

"Back in Austin. He left Monday."

"Good. That means we've got some time. Nobody knows
your car is gone but us."

"Man, I been thinking. Even if they found the car in the lake,
how would they know we did it? It coulda still been stolen and
dumped there, you know? Cops'd think maybe some punks
nabbed it, took it for a joyride, and just sunk it for kicks."

Vinnie thought it over. T.J. was pretty smart, and he was
probably right. But Vinnie had to convince him otherwise because of Slaton's corpse. "Yeah, but all it would take is one goddamn witness to say he saw you in your boat last night, or saw
me drivin' the Porsche into the park. Then we'd be screwed,
man, totally screwed. And what about fingerprints? If some kids
stole it and dumped it, the cops would expect to find prints. No,
we gotta make sure they don't find it. It's the only way to cover
our asses for sure."

"Yeah, I guess. . . ."

"Listen to me, T.J. Don't even think about callin' it in. You
don't want to go to fuckin' jail, do you?"

"Hell no!"

"Then just give me a little time, goddammit. I'll think of
something."

CHAPTER EIGHTEEN

Thursday morning, Marlin was on patrol when he heard Wylie Smith calling for him over the radio. The deputy wanted to meet "to talk a few things over." Fifteen minutes later, Marlin was waiting in the empty parking lot of a dance hall called the River Palace when Wylie wheeled up beside him, his driver's door next to Marlin's.

The first thing Marlin noticed was that Wylie had a black eye.

Marlin gave him a nod and Wylie, without a greeting, said, "D'you hear about the mess from last night?"

"No, what's up?"

"Got a call from a man named Red O'Brien, said he worked for this old guy Emmett Slaton. Cutting down cedar. Anyway, so him and this other guy, Billy Don Craddock, stop by Slaton's house last night and find blood all over the front porch." Wylie gave Marlin a serious look, like, *Welcome to the big city, boy.* "Slaton's truck's gone, nobody's home. The front door was unlocked, so O'Brien walks right into the house—all over my goddamn crime scene—and dials nine-one-one. What a dick."

"And?" Marlin wondered why the deputy was telling him all this. It wasn't like they were buddies.

Wylie shook his head. "More blood inside. All over the bed, inside the goddamn bathroom sink, on the carpet, a trail leading right out the front door. And by the time we get there, these two backward assholes have been tromping all over the place. They had plenty of their own wild theories about what had happened, too, like they were gonna solve the whole damn thing for me. I could barely shut this guy Red up. I swear, if being a redneck was against the law, those guys would get a life sentence."

Marlin knew Wylie was expecting a smile on that line, but he didn't give him one. The deputy was awfully talkative all of a sudden—with sort of a *We're in this thing together* attitude.

"Anyway, Slaton's nowhere in sight," Wylie continued, "so I seal the house off and get to work. But other than the blood, I can't find shit. No forced entry, no signs of struggle. I was up all night and didn't get anywhere. The old man just vanished. The only thing: Curtis was on patrol last night and spotted Slaton's truck in the Save-Mart parking lot, locked up tight. More blood in there, too, but nothing else to go on."

Marlin had gotten to know Emmett Slaton over the years and had chalked him up as one of the good guys. Ornery old coot, but likable. And, of course, Marlin knew Red O'Brien and Billy Don Craddock well. Two of the worst poachers Marlin had ever come across: *Worst*—meaning not only did the two rednecks poach whenever they got a chance, but they were also exceedingly bad at it. No wits about them whatsoever. "Sounds like you've got your hands full," Marlin said. It was obvious Wylie had a request to make, and Marlin wasn't going to be the one to extend the olive branch.

"Yeah, which brings me around to this other thing—Bert Gammel from Tuesday." Wylie bit his lip and stared out his windshield for a moment. "I talked to all the other hunters on the lease, and they all come across legit, except Jack Corey. Went out to his place first thing yesterday morning. Right off the bat he was giving me lip, telling me all kinds of stories but not really saying anything at all, you know? Guy's got an anger-management problem, too."

Marlin pointed at his own eye. "That where you got the shiner?"

Wylie nodded and spit on the ground beneath his window. "I started poking around a little too close to home and the son of a bitch took a jab at me. I'll tell you what, he won't be doing that again."

Marlin raised his eyebrows, giving a quizzical look.

Wylie said, "He's in lockup right now. I was wondering whether you could stop by, have a nice little chat with him. I've been thinking: Maybe it's true, he'll open up a little more to a local boy like you."

Local boy. *Damn,* Marlin thought, *Wylie's an offensive jerk even when he's trying to call a truce.* Marlin let it slide. "What's Corey told you so far?"

"Not much. He hunted Monday evening, just like the log-books say. Didn't shoot, didn't see anybody else. Heard some shots at about the same time the foreman said. Thought one of them—the one around sundown—came from Gammel's direction. But man, when I asked him about his run-ins with Gammel, he sure got tight-lipped fast. Said something like, 'I didn't do nothin'. You ain't makin' me the fall guy.' Boy's been watching too much *NYPD Blue.*"

"He didn't ask for a lawyer?"

Wylie absently drummed on the steering wheel and stared into the horizon. "Well, now, he mighta said he should probably get a lawyer, but he never specifically asked for one, no."

Marlin thought: *Great. You've muddied up the waters and now you want me to clean it up.*

Marlin had known Jack Corey since grade school, and they had been on the football team together in high school. Corey was a large, quiet guy, a plumber by trade. As far as Marlin could recall, Corey had never gotten on the wrong side of the law, outside of a few speeding tickets. Just a big guy who liked to drink beer on Saturday night and hunt deer on Sunday.

Marlin remembered something. "After I left, did y'all have any luck finding the slug?"

Wylie grimaced. "No, but not for lack of trying. Damn place is so wooded, it could have ricocheted or fragmented and ended up just about anywhere. From what Lester says, Corey hunts with a thirty-thirty. So I estimated the trajectory based on the drop of that big ol' heavy bullet and we scoured the area for about two hours. Even went fifty yards further out than my calculations gave me. Nothing. But talk about your needle in a haystack. It's damn near impossible to find a slug in these kinds of situations. Give me a shoot-out in a building any day, then I'll find your slug for ya."

Marlin nodded. A lot was riding on that bullet, and they both knew it.

Wylie slipped his cruiser back into DRIVE. "So, if you could talk to Corey this morning, uh, I would appreciate it."

Marlin noticed that Wylie wouldn't meet his eyes and seemed almost embarrassed to ask this small favor.

"I'm not expecting you to get a full confession out of him or anything," Wylie continued. "Just talk to him, see if you can get him to loosen up a little. Otherwise, that boy's setting himself up as the prime suspect."

"Did you mention the evidence from the scene?"

"I didn't get specific yet, because I'm trying to get a warrant to search his truck and his house."

"How's that going?"

"I wrote it up last night and left it for Judge Hilton, but it could go either way. It's all circumstantial, I know, but everything points toward Corey. If I can come up with something on the search, then I'll go for a blood sample. Get some DNA evidence that will nail him good."

"Unless he's innocent."

"What's that?"

"Unless he's innocent."

"Well, yeah," Wylie said. "Of course."

•   •   •

On the way to the jail, Marlin stopped at a convenience store and made a quick purchase.

Three minutes later, he was checking in with the jailer, leaving his .357 revolver at the desk.

Marlin went into the visitation room, sat at the small, scarred pine table, and waited. Five minutes later, the door leading to the cells opened and Jack Corey walked in, wearing blue jailhouse clothes. His left arm was in a cast.

"Come on in, Jack," Marlin said. "Grab a chair."

Corey mumbled a greeting and took a seat. The man looked awful. Dark bags under his eyes. Greasy, unwashed hair. A couple of days' worth of beard.

After Corey got settled, Marlin asked, "You doing all right, Jack? What happened to your arm?"

Corey eyed him skeptically. "You didn't hear?"

Marlin shook his head.

"That asshole Wylie nailed me with his nightstick. Fractured my wrist."

"Before or after you popped him in the eye?"

"After," Corey admitted grudgingly, staring at the floor. "He deserved it though."

"You wanna tell me what happened?"

Corey raised his left arm and set it down on the table with a loud *plonk*. "He was all over me, telling me how he knew what I did and I was gonna end up in Huntsville. Kept describin' how the needle would feel going into my arm, tryin' to rattle me. But he wouldn't listen to a goddamn word I had to say." Corey lifted his head and met Marlin's eyes. "John, I had nothin' to do with Gammel gettin' shot. I swear to God. Man, you've known me for, what, nearly forty years? You know I wouldn't do somethin' like that, right?"

Marlin took a deep breath and leaned forward. "Jack, I have to say, it doesn't sound like something you'd do. And if you're not involved, all I can tell you is to sit tight and wait, because we've found some things that should help us clear this up. But Jack, if something *did* happen between you and Bert Gammel, that same evidence is going to tell Wylie the complete story. There won't be any getting out of it, because science doesn't lie."

Marlin noticed that Corey was still steadily meeting his gaze, a good sign.

"What I'm saying, Jack, is that if something pissed you off enough to lose your head, to do something stupid, now's the time to come clean and tell us. You know how the prosecutor is. He's willing to take a plea when a guy owns up to what he did. On the other hand, when a guy clams up and the deputies have to follow the case all the way to the end, for a crime like this . . . well, things can get kind of rough."

Corey shook his head. "John, I'm tellin' ya—you can give me one of those lie-detector tests or whatever, but all it will ever show is that I didn't do it. I don't give a damn what Wylie says or what he believes, he's got the wrong guy. And there ain't no way I'm gonna confess to something I didn't do."

Marlin's intuition, honed from dealing with hundreds of poachers over the years, told him Corey was telling the truth. Of course, Marlin remembered all too well the times he had been fooled by a good lie.

"Tell me a little bit about your problems with Gammel, the arguments you had at the deer lease." As he spoke, Marlin pulled an item out of his hip pocket. It was the pouch of Red Man chewing tobacco he had purchased earlier at the store.

"Aw, man, it wasn't nothin', really. He shot spikes all the time and threw 'em in the ditch. I thought it was a goddamn waste, and almost called you a couple of times."

Marlin opened the package and stuffed a small amount of tobacco in his jaw.

"The only time it was really a problem," Corey said, "was this one time we got into an argument and he took a swing at me. But all the guys were there and can tell you it was his fault, not mine. Even Lester showed up and can tell you what happened."

Marlin laid the tobacco pouch on the table and noticed Corey eyeing it.

"How come you won't let Wylie search your house and truck?"

Corey looked confused. "Hell, he can search all he wants. He never asked."

Marlin was stunned. "He didn't ask permission?"

"No, but I woulda told him to go right ahead. I ain't got nothin' to hide."

Marlin figured Wylie probably had been afraid to show his hand, to let Corey know a search was coming.

"Well, I'll let him know you said it was okay, then," Marlin said. He paused and looked around the drab room. "Not exactly the Hyatt, is it? They treating you all right?"

Corey shrugged. "Yeah, no problem. But I need to get back to work. I'm self-employed, and when I don't work, I don't get paid."

"You want anything? Maybe a Coke . . ." Marlin slid the Red Man toward Corey. Time for the test. Was Corey a tobacco user or not? "Or a chew?"

Corey glanced at the package. "Naw, not right now. Maybe later."

"All right, Jack," Marlin said.

CHAPTER NINETEEN

Marlin had finished dinner and was headed out the door when Bobby Garza called. The sheriff said, "Listen, if you've got a minute, I wanted to talk to you about Jack Corey."

Marlin glanced at the clock. Six forty-five. Inga's assembly started in fifteen minutes. "What's up?"

"Well, Wylie is right in the middle of this thing, but I just wanted to hear your thoughts. You talked to Corey this morning?"

"For about fifteen minutes. Went over it with Wylie on the phone."

"Well, you know how he is. He didn't share much with me. What was your impression?"

"Corey seemed a little nervous about being arrested, and damn pissed off at Wylie. But to be straight up with you, I think he's wrong for it. Gut feeling, but I've known him for a long time."

"Yeah, me too, but I never really got close with the guy. You probably know him better since y'all were in the same class."

"Could be. Anyway, he said that he was more than ready to have his truck and home searched and I told Wylie—"

"That's where he is as we speak," Garza cut in. "First thing he did—just a couple of hours ago—was compare the tire prints to Corey's truck. If you can believe it, Corey had four different brands of tires on that old heap. And one of them looked like a pretty good match. So then Wylie started going though the house, looking through all of Corey's work boots and hunting boots. He found a pair of Red Wings on the back porch, covered with mud. I hate to say it, but those look like a match, too."

"That's a pretty common brand of boot."

"That's true," Garza conceded. "Anyway, we'll know more when we get the results back from DPS." The Texas Department of Public Safety performed most of the forensic testing and analysis for smaller law-enforcement agencies throughout the state. Garza said, "We sent the tire, the boots, and the plaster casts down there. Asked 'em to put a rush on it, but we'll see about that. Those guys are up to their eyeballs around the clock nowadays."

"What about a DNA test? That would be the clincher."

"Yeah, I almost forgot. He went for that, too. We took some blood and a buccal swab and sent it all to the lab. I imagine that'll take a couple weeks. By the way, if I haven't said it already: Thanks for talking to Corey. He sure got a lot more cooperative when you were done with him."

Marlin looked through the kitchen window at a passing bluejay. "It must be my charming personality. Plus the fact that I didn't hit him with a nightstick."

"Ouch," Garza said. "Low blow, and Wylie isn't even here to defend himself."

"Which brings up another thing," Marlin said. "How come Wylie didn't just ask Corey for permission to search?"

"Judgment call. He didn't want to make Corey jittery, give him a chance to destroy evidence. Hey, he had a hard enough time just asking you to talk to Corey. You know how proud he can be sometimes."

"Pigheaded is more like it."

Garza chuckled. "And that's what makes him such a good cop. If nothing else, give him that. But we're getting off-topic, aren't we?"

"All I'm saying is that he's always the last to admit when he's wrong. So if Corey comes back clean, you know I'm gonna have to ride him a little about it."

"Yeah, yeah. But right now, that's looking like a pretty big 'if.'" He lightened his tone. "You know, I'm glad we had this little chat, John. You've got a sharp mind, even for a redneck. You sure you don't want to come work with me at the sheriff's office?" Garza had asked Marlin that question several times in the last year.

"I prefer hanging around with animals," Marlin deadpanned. "They're much nicer than people."

"This is insane, you know that?" T.J. asked, killing the engine on his boat. Darkness was settling over the water now, the surface of the lake as smooth as glass. "You know how deep this water is? And besides—you've never even scuba dived."

"How hard can it be to find a fuckin' car?" Vinnie replied as he pulled on the wetsuit.

T.J. took a hit from his ever-present joint. "Speaking of cars, I hear there's catfish as big as Volkswagens down there. Swallow you whole. Better watch your ass."

"Just shut the fuck up, will ya? I don't need you psychin' me out with that shit."

Vinnie was feeling a little nervous, on edge, his guts tumbling around inside him. He had never scuba dived before. But when he had stolen the gear from the scuba shop—a little mom-and-pop operation up by Lake Buchanan—he had found a brochure with a checklist for scuba beginners. It said something about remembering to breath normally, especially on your way back up. And you were supposed to come up slower than your slowest bubble. Sounded pretty easy.

"Gimme the rope."

T.J. handed him the end of a hundred-foot line, which Vinnie cinched around his waist.

Vinnie said, "Keep it tight, but don't yank on it, for chrissakes. Might be the only way I'll know which way is up."

"Gotcha."

Vinnie pulled the scuba mask on and adjusted it for comfort. A few seconds later, he tugged his flippers on, gave T.J. a thumbs-up, and dropped backward off the boat into the cold water.

Marlin slipped through the side door of the gymnasium just as Inga Mueller was taking the microphone, standing on a small stage underneath one of the basketball goals. There was a much larger crowd than Marlin had expected—probably close to three hundred.

"Ladies and gentleman, I want to thank you for coming to-night."

Marlin spotted Phil Colby waving at him from the lower row of bleachers and took a seat next to him.

"Howdy, stranger," Marlin said.

"I figured you'd show up," Colby replied. "She's just getting started."

Marlin turned his attention to the stage. Inga was wearing a short black skirt, low-heeled boots, and a clingy gray turtle-neck. *Man, if her goal is to get attention, she'll definitely succeed,* Marlin thought. It was like dropping a supermodel into the middle of a PTA meeting.

Inga strolled slowly around the stage as she spoke into the handheld microphone. "I would like to talk to all of you tonight about a sensitive topic, one that requires serious thought from every citizen in Blanco County. Now, I know that many of you don't know me, and that's because"—she slipped into a Texas accent for a moment—"I'm not from 'round these parts."

Mild laughter rippled through the audience.

"I wish I was, though, because Texas looks like a beautiful place to live. The people are so friendly, and proud, too. I met a man yesterday who showed me a picture of his new baby. He told me the baby weighed ten pounds, but he used to weigh twenty. I asked him what happened, and the man said he had him circumcised."

Marlin smiled. He hadn't even seen that joke coming. For a brief moment, the crowd was silent, maybe a little startled, as if everyone was taking a moment, waiting to see if it was okay to laugh at such an off-color joke. Like: *Did she really just say that?* Then the chuckles began and rolled quickly through the crowd. Some guy yelled "Everything's bigger in Texas, honey!"—which produced another round of laughter.

"That's what I've heard," Inga replied with a coy smile, letting the laughter slowly fade away. "And I can see that when you do something around here, you do it in a *big* way. Like all the cedar-clearing that's taking place in Blanco County . . . which is what we're here to talk about tonight. The cedar tree, and its effect on the water supply . . . among other things."

Inga knelt at the front of the stage and flipped the switch on a slide projector. A large square of light appeared on the wall behind her.

She pulled a device from her skirt pocket and punched a button. "This," she said melodramatically, "is the evil cedar tree."

A scrubby Ashe juniper—commonly called a cedar in Texas—appeared on the screen. Inga playfully gave the tree a thumbs-down sign and hissed loudly. The audience chuckled, and many members joined in with a chorus of boos.

Marlin shook his head and smiled. Yesterday, he'd figured Inga would offend the audience—either by not being very tactful or simply by being an outsider. But now she had them in the palm of her hand. Clever gal.

"Now we all know what a pain in the, uh, derriere these things can be. They choke out all the hardwood trees, ruin your pastures, and hog all the water. I've read that an average-sized cedar uses about thirty-five gallons of water a day. And that seems to be the biggest complaint around here."

For the next ten minutes, Inga went on to discuss the water shortage in Blanco County, and the continuously low level of the aquifer. Marlin thought she was doing a great job; she obviously had a knack for keeping the interest of large groups, and her looks certainly didn't hurt.

As Inga continued, Marlin glanced around and saw a mixed

crowd of people he knew: rural residents and city dwellers, schoolteachers and day laborers, Realtors and ranchers, young and old alike. Everyone appeared to be listening intently.

". . . so I understand the need for brush-clearing," Inga was saying. "I mean, protecting the aquifer just seems like a smart move. But I wanted to talk to you about the impact the brush removal is having on the wildlife in the area."

She turned toward the screen as she punched a button. A rather unattractive black bird appeared on the screen.

"Can anyone tell me what this is?" she asked the audience.

Someone shouted that it was a crow. Someone else said a raven.

"Not quite." She flipped to the next photo. The same bird, but photographed from behind. Now you could see a faint ruby-colored half-band on the back of its neck. "Does that help?"

In the front row, a young girl—probably a student, Marlin guessed—said, "Red-necked sapsucker?"

"Exactly right!" Inga said. "Take a good look, because it may be the only time you'll ever see one. These birds used to be found throughout the Southwest, but now they are found mostly in Central Texas, especially in Blanco County, and they are extremely rare. Nobody knows exactly how many are left, but the latest studies show there could be as few as just a couple hundred. Even more of a problem, the last dozen or so sightings have all been females. For whatever reason, the male population seems to be dwindling more rapidly than the females. Right now, biologists are hoping to locate and trap a male so they can try to breed the birds in captivity. So far, no luck. See, the females don't need a male in order to lay eggs. But they do need a male to lay a *fertilized* egg—that is, one that can hatch a young bird. The women in the audience might say that's all the males are good for."

Once again, the audience chuckled.

"But here's the biggest problem the red-necked sapsucker is facing: Unlike most birds, they are extremely picky when it comes to the materials they use for building nests. In fact, they chiefly use the long, stringy bark from cedar trees. It's one of those unfortunate cases when nothing else will do. They have to have cedar bark or they can't make nests, they can't produce offspring, and the species will gradually fade away. In other words, without plenty of cedar trees around, the red-necked sapsucker will become extinct—it's that simple."

Marlin thought: *Here's where the audience either sides with her or against her.*

"My question is," Inga said, "is it worth it? Is the water situation serious enough to justify wiping out an entire species? I'd like to make this a group discussion, so would anyone care to comment?"

Heads turned and looked at neighbors, and a woman holding a toddler meekly raised her hand. "What are we supposed to do for water? I mean, if we don't clear the brush."

"Well, I'd like to suggest a combination of two things: conservation and rainwater collection. Now, by 'conservation,' I don't mean anything drastic. Just take shorter showers. Cut the water off when you're brushing your teeth or shaving. Water your lawn by hand instead of with a sprinkler. Stuff like that. It's amazing how fast the gallons you save can add up.

"And secondly, harvesting rainwater. Some residents in this county already have elaborate systems that provide all the household water they need. I saw one home over off Miller Creek Loop that had two enormous cisterns that probably hold ten thousand gallons each. That'll last a pretty long time between rainshowers."

A middle-aged man held up his hand and remarked that that kind of system was very expensive.

Inga nodded her head slowly. "Yeah, you're right, they can be pricey. Most systems pay for themselves in the long run, though. And you don't necessarily have to do anything that elaborate. You could simply attach a hundred-gallon barrel to your rain gutter and use it to water your garden. You don't need a pump, a filter, anything like that."

An elderly woman—Marlin recognized her as a retired biology teacher from the high school—stood up. "What are this bird's chances if we quit cutting cedar? Won't it die out anyway? If they're already having a rough go of it with plenty of cedars still around, it sounds like they'll be in pretty bad shape regardless of what we do."

Inga nodded. "The only answer is, nobody knows for sure. Sometimes, it's easy to pinpoint the reason why a species becomes endangered. It's usually something like hunting pressure or habitat destruction. But here, the red-necked sapsucker is almost extinct and that's regardless of the brush-clearing. But what we do know for sure is, if all the cedar is cleared, they will definitely vanish. And in my opinion—"

She was interrupted by a muttered comment from another person in the crowd.

"I'm sorry, I didn't catch that. Please stand up and join the discussion."

A large dark-haired man in a well-tailored suit stood up. "I don't see what the problem is," he said, waving his hands emphatically. "I mean, one little bird? Fuhget about it. How important is dat? We gonna hold up progress for dat?"

Marlin couldn't remember the man's name, but he had seen him around town. A new guy, only in Johnson City for a couple of years. The guy had a thick accent, something like Robert De Niro's in his gangster pictures.

"I appreciate your comment, sir." Inga said. She cocked her head and gave him a momentary stare. "I believe we've met before. May I have your name?"

The man looked around warily, then said, "Salvatore Mameli."

Now Marlin remembered. He had caught a Vinnie Mameli—no doubt this guy's son—four-wheeling in the park a few months back. Had given him and his friend, T.J. Gibbs, a citation.

"Thank you, Mr. Mameli. I understand your attitude, but it's not really a matter of progress. We're not holding up something as important as a housing development or a shopping center."

Marlin wasn't sure if anybody caught Inga's sarcasm in that last remark. She seemed to have her hackles up a little now.

"Ya don't think it's holding up progress, huh?" Mameli said. "Let me ask ya somethin'. Without water, how's the county gonna grow? How we gonna build homes for our families, hospitals, new schools for our kids, things like dat? Gotta have water for all dese things. Don't tell me you think dis bird, dis sapsucker, is more important than our kids' futures?"

The crowd waited silently for Inga's reply, some people nodding their heads in agreement with Mameli. She gave a patient smile and said, "No, of course I don't think that. I just believe there's a sensible answer that will allow us to do both—to live comfortably *and* save the sapsucker."

"Yeah, like collecting *rainwater*," Mameli said, plenty of mockery in his voice. "So you got a guy like dis here . . ." He placed his hand on a man next to him in the audience. "He's spent maybe five, six grand digging a well, building a pumphouse, but you want him to forget all dat and catch the few measly drops dat happen to fall out of the sky instead. What's he supposed to do when summer rolls around? Say it's July, August, and dere ain't been any rain in weeks. He's suppose to go outside and, what, do a rain dance every time he wants to take a shower?" The guy actually started doing a jig, patting his hand over his mouth, doing an Indian chant that was straight out of a 1950s B movie. People chuckled right along with him.

Marlin felt the momentum starting to shift, the audience starting to get behind this obnoxious clown.

CHAPTER TWENTY

The weight belt around Vinnie's waist took him down nice and slow—and Vinnie descended into a world he had never experienced before. All sounds disappeared, except for his own rhythmic breathing, loud in his ears. Sounded like goddamn Darth Vader or something. It was an eerie world down here, almost claustrophobic.

Using a waterproof spotlight, Vinnie could see much better than he had expected, maybe seventy or eighty feet. There wasn't much to see at first. Just water and more water, with millions of tiny particles floating in it, reflecting the light. Vinnie wondered if all that stuff was maybe fish crap. *Fuckin' gross.* He'd have to take a nice long shower when he got home.

After half a minute, Vinnie was no longer sure he was going any deeper. There was no way to tell, no landmarks to gauge his descent. Then his light swept the skeletal remains of trees reaching up from the lake bottom. Damn, he hadn't counted on any trees! He used the flippers to kick gently, to stop his descent, while he untied the line around his waist. Last thing he needed was to get tangled around a bunch of branches, get stuck down there in a panic, air running out. T.J. might freak out a little when the rope went slack, but screw him, he'd have to deal with it.

Free of the line now, Vinnie swam parallel to the treetops and began his search for the sunken Porsche. He and T.J. had agreed that they were damn close to the original location. But it could be fifty or a hundred feet off in any direction. This could take awhile.

In the stands, Marlin saw another man rise to his feet, not far from Mameli. Marlin had no problem remembering this guy, because his sneer was operating at full strength.

"There's no reason to be a jackass." Tommy Peabody spat the words out with venom, and Mameli halted his clumsy Indian dance. The room went silent except for a few hushed murmurs.

The two men locked eyes for a moment and the audience watched with rapt attention.

Finally, Mameli smirked, put his hand against his chest, and said, "Me? You callin' me a jackass?"

"If the horseshoe fits."

That got several nervous giggles, the crowd treating it as a good-natured joke, like: *Okay, you boys have had your fun, now let's settle down and get back to business*. But Peabody was standing up straighter now, looking a little more confident, ready for action.

Phil Colby leaned over to Marlin and said, "Interesting little show." Marlin nodded, glancing around for a cop. Surely a couple of the deputies must be here, but he didn't see any. With Bert Gammel murdered and Emmett Slaton missing, maybe they couldn't spare the manpower.

Mameli straightened his tie and said, "Well, you're a tree-hugging hump—whaddaya think of dat?"

Marlin was on the edge of his seat now, ready to wade in and break this thing up if it got physical. He could practically smell the testosterone in the air, could feel the cloak of embarrassment that settles over a crowd when two grown men behave like schoolchildren.

Peabody furrowed his brow, an exaggerated look of confusion. "I'd be offended, but frankly, I'm not even sure what that means," he said, a few diehards still laughing, egging on this sneering little man. Several people in the bleachers, though, were rising, starting to leave.

"Uh, gentlemen . . ." It was Inga, still on the microphone, holding her hands up in a placating gesture, trying to rein this thing in. "There's no reason to—"

But Mameli pointed at her and spoke over her amplified words. "She's the jackass, if ya want my opinion. Her and all her bird-loving friends, including you. Oh yeah, I seen youse two runnin' around town together. I know you're in dis thing together. Well, screw both of you," he said, pointing back at Peabody now.

As soon as Mameli had made the remark about Inga, Marlin could see people throughout the crowd reacting with distaste, shaking their heads. Using body language to say, *Pardner, you just crossed the line.* Now Sal's coarse language brought glares and angry mutterings.

When the crowd quieted down, Peabody spoke again: "You, sir, are not only a ridiculous boor, you are a rapist of the Earth."

Mameli spread his hands wide. "Yeah? Well, what the hell ya gonna do about it?"

Peabody's voice rose. "I'm gonna shut you down. One way or another, I'm going to stop your carnage!"

Mameli grabbed his crotch with both hands and said, "I got your carnage right here!"

Peabody cocked his head toward the ceiling, hands on his hips, muttering to himself, as if he were trying to summon his patience. Mameli defiantly glared his way. Marlin rose now, with the sense that it was about to get messy. He could hear Phil saying something to him, but Marlin was making his way toward the floor, keeping an eye on the two men.

Before Marlin's feet hit the tiles, Peabody let out a growl and rushed along the bleachers toward the large Italian.

Women screamed.

People piled out of the bleachers, tumbling, jumping, to get out of the way.

. . .

Vinnie got lucky. After only six or seven minutes, he spotted the Porsche, already coated with a thin layer of brown goo. Give it another month or so and the car would be practically invisible, blending right in with the bottom of the lake, tucked between a couple of oaks.

Vinnie let the weight belt pull him down to the car, just a small kick here and there, until he felt his flippers sink into the muck beside the driver's door.

Bending low, flooding the interior of the car with light, Vinnie saw Emmett Slaton staring back at him, his face green and bloated. Slaton was floating off the seat, his arms levitating in front of him, reaching for the dashboard, as if the Porsche had just gone over a large bump in the road.

Vinnie eased the driver's door open, keeping an eye on the corpse. Couldn't have ol' Emmett floating past him, rising to the surface. That would sure kill T.J.'s buzz quick.

Now the important thing: finding the LoJack. T.J. had said it was small, about the size of a deck of cards, Velcroed under the dash, right below the steering wheel.

Vinnie reached under, fumbled around for a few seconds, and . . . *Hell yes! There it was!* He grabbed the LoJack firmly and tugged it loose from the Velcro. He examined it under the light. Damn thing looked harmless, but it would have sent him to fucking Huntsville, sitting in a cold, dirty prison cell. He unzipped a pocket in his wetsuit and shoved the LoJack inside.

Inside his mask, Vinnie grinned. *See there? Every problem has a solution. All you gotta do is think it through, use your goddamn brains. And your balls sometimes, too.* His father would be proud—if only Vinnie could tell him how his son had risen to meet this challenge.

Now there was only one more detail to take care of. He hated to do it, but this whole LoJack mess had made him realize it was a necessary step. Vinnie had wrestled with the idea for a while, trying to think of other options, but he had decided it was for the best. A smart man leaves no witnesses behind.

·   ·   ·

The love of a good woman was worth doing battle over. At least
that's how Thomas Peabody had felt thirty seconds ago, defend-
ing Inga's honor, trading verbal barbs with Salvatore Mameli.
Inga and Peabody had done their research and knew exactly
who this Mameli character was: a land-clearer, a rabid destroyer
of wildlife habitat, the kind of man who made Peabody fighting
mad. But now, as he charged toward Mameli—who was looking
larger and meaner as Peabody got closer—Peabody wondered
about the wisdom of it all.

Would this be the act that finally drew Inga to him?

Would this gesture force her to recognize his integrity, his
loyalty to the cause, his bravery in the face of daunting odds?

Would she become infatuated with his courage, his willing-
ness to defend the defenseless?

Or would she simply think he was a moron?

Peabody realized he would have to ponder these issues later,
because right now, Mameli's meaty right fist was coming toward his face.

Vinnie finally emerged to the surface twenty yards from the
boat.

As he swam the short distance, he could see T.J. rise to his
feet. "Goddamn, dude, what happened down there?" T.J.
hissed, trying to keep his voice quiet on the windless lake. "The
rope went slack and I nearly had a damn heart attack!"

Vinnie grabbed the transom and pulled himself over. "Trees at
the bottom of the lake. I had to untie it so I wouldn't get tangled."

"Oh, man, you had me freakin'. Did you get the LoJack?"

"Hell no," Vinnie said, his voice thick with mock anger. "I
don't know what the fuck you were talking about, 'right under
the dashboard.' It wasn't there, man."

T.J. groaned. "Aw, man. It's right under the steering column,
plain as day."

Vinnie put his hand to his brow and shook his head, going

for a look of frustration. "The steering column? I can't believe this shit. Man, you told me it was under the passenger's side."

"Dude, I told you three times, it's right under the driver's side. Just stuck there with Velcro."

Vinnie slumped in one of the seats and let the silence hang in the air for a moment. Then he tossed the scuba mask to Vinnie. "Your turn."

"What? What are you talkin' about?"

"It's your turn. You know exactly where it is, so you go down and get it."

"But I don't know how to work the scuba gear," T.J. said, his voice shaky.

"I'll show you. It's no big deal. And you'll have the spotlight. You're not scared, are you?"

"Hell, no, gimme a break." T.J. grabbed the stub of a joint and took a hit. "Hand me those damn flippers," he said, smoke curling around his face. "I'll go do it myself."

Peabody ducked under Sal's first punch and wrapped himself around the beefy Italian's torso. Mameli responded by thumping Peabody several times on the back of his head, a sound Marlin could hear from ten yards away. Mameli then yanked Peabody's head back by the hair with his left hand and was preparing to land a blow with his right, but his foot slipped between the plank he was standing on and the next bleacher down. Both men collapsed onto the bleacher seats now, Peabody howling in anguish as his hair was pulled tight. Mameli was moaning in agony, too, his right leg dangling unnaturally beneath the bleachers.

Marlin vaulted up the bleacher steps and started grabbing arms, trying to pry each man loose, hoping to situate himself between the two of them. "Let go! Both of you!" But both men continued grunting and cursing, taking short punches at each other when they got the chance.

Marlin couldn't find an opening between them, with Mameli more or less lying on top of Peabody now. So Marlin got behind Mameli and reached around, attempting to loosen Mameli's grip on Peabody's stringy hair. That's when he felt teeth—he wasn't sure whose—clamping down on the meat of his left forearm. "Son of a bitch!" he yelled, feeling the warm blood begin to flow. With his right hand, he fumbled for the pepper spray on his belt. He found the small canister and popped the cap with his thumb. He couldn't see around Mameli's bulky torso, so he just sprayed a powerful blast between the two men, swiveling his wrist back and forth, likely hitting each man squarely in the face.

The brawl ended immediately as both men cried out and covered their faces.

Marlin pushed off of Mameli's back and sat down on the bleachers, winded, cradling his wounded arm.

Peabody, wiping furiously at his eyes, managed to slither out from under Mameli.

Mameli propped himself on his elbows, prone on the plank floorboard, trying to see through squinted eyes. "My fuckin' leg! The bastard broke my fuckin' leg. I can feel it."

"You deserved it, you cretin," Peabody replied, tears streaming down his cheeks from the pepper spray. "You think you can just rape the land and get away with it?"

"Quiet!" Marlin yelled. He faced the crowd that was gathered below the bleachers, watching. He noticed Inga standing there silently, looking rattled, one hand over her mouth. "Anyone have a cell phone?" Marlin asked. A man Marlin recognized—the uncle of one of the sheriff's dispatchers—raised his hand. "Mr. Briggs, please call nine-one-one, let 'em know we need an ambulance over here." The man nodded and began to dial.

Marlin turned and glared at Peabody, who likely would have sneered if his face hadn't been contorted from the spray. Marlin could see a bloody circle around Peabody's mouth. Marlin's blood.

Marlin stood, got behind Peabody, and grabbed his right arm. The handcuff locked in place with a satisfying click.

"Hey!" Peabody yelled. "What the hell? You're arresting *me*?"

"You're damn right," Marlin growled. "Assault."

Peabody gestured toward Mameli, who was sprawled on the bleachers now, his face pasty-white, his lower leg bent at an odd angle. "He hasn't even said he wants to press charges. And he assaulted me right back."

"Not assault on *him* you little . . ." Marlin struggled to keep his temper. "Assault on *me*."

Never trust anyone but yourself.

Vinnie was sad that it had to turn out this way, but he knew he had to follow his father's words of wisdom.

After all, could he really trust T.J.? Someday the kid might be hanging out with some friends, get a buzz going, and brag about their little adventure together, how they had cheated the insurance company and gotten away with it. *We sunk a god-damn Porsche in the lake!* he'd say. *What a fuckin' rush!*

Eventually word would make it back to the cops, they'd do a little sniffing around, put the pressure on T.J., and it would lead straight to hell from there.

No, this was the smart move—but Vinnie still kind of wished he'd never gotten T.J. involved at all.

He could picture his friend right now, slowly making his way down to the car. Vinnie had told him exactly where it was, so it'd be easy for him to find. Getting back up would be another story.

Vinnie hadn't told T.J. the most important thing the scuba brochure had said: *Come up slower than your slowest bubble.* It had something to do with the oxygen in your bloodstream, how you could end up with a fatal embolism—whatever *that* was—in your lungs.

And what would T.J.'s natural reaction be when he stared into Emmett Slaton's bloated face? He'd panic, gasp for air, and shoot to the surface as fast as he could. No doubt about it. Hell, Vinnie had almost felt that urge himself.

He hoped that it would be quick and easy. He didn't want T.J. in a lot of pain, screaming, begging for help, that kind of mess. If T.J. didn't die quickly, Vinnie would have to get inventive, figure out something on the fly, maybe drown the poor bastard. But that embolism thing sounded pretty nasty. Probably wouldn't take too long.

After that, Vinnie would just leave T.J. and the boat floating on the reservoir. Cops'd be thinking, *What the hell happened here? Something don't look right.* But what the fuck did Vinnie care? Nothing would point to him because he wasn't actually murdering T.J. T.J. would be killing himself, without even knowing it.

Yeah, it was much easier this way, not having to do the deed. Not having to put a gun to the back of T.J.'s head and pull the trigger.

Sitting there on the boat, in the dark, Vinnie smiled. It was pretty clever, really.

Peabody was locked securely in Marlin's truck, and now Marlin was tending to Sal Mameli, trying to keep him comfortable. It was a pretty bad fracture, and Mameli appeared to be slipping into a mild shock.

Mr. Briggs appeared at Marlin's elbow. "Just got hold of Jean," he said, referring to his niece, the dispatcher. "There's an ambulance on the way, but it sounds like they're having a little excitement over at the sheriff's office."

"Oh yeah? What do you mean?"

Mr. Briggs gave him a small jerk of the head, pulling him aside. In hushed tones, the elderly man said, "The details are a little rough right now, and Jean's not really supposed to share this stuff with me anyway . . ."

Marlin nodded. "Between you and me."

Mr. Briggs' expression was grave. "Apparently, Jack Corey just shot Wylie Smith."

CHAPTER TWENTY-ONE

The small building that housed the Sheriff's Department and the county jail was surrounded by vehicles and people, mostly deputies and other personnel who worked inside the building. Marlin saw two black-and-whites from the Texas Department of Public Safety, and he spotted a couple of staff members from the newspaper office across the street. The rest of the crowd was composed of curious bystanders, locals who had been eating or shopping in the small downtown area. An ambulance idled out front.

Marlin backed up and found a spot as close as he could get, a block away. He turned to Peabody, whose eyes were still puffy and wet. "Stay put," Marlin said. "I'll be right back." He didn't wait for a sneer, but then again, Peabody hadn't seemed too lively on the trip over.

Marlin jogged toward the building, swerving through the milling crowd.

"John! Over here!" It was Bobby Garza, a few paces outside the front door, huddled in a conference with the DPS troopers and a couple of deputies. As Marlin approached, Garza stepped toward him and steered him against the outside wall of the building. "Here's the situation. Corey . . . Jesus, John—what happened to your arm?"

"Guy bit me. Long story."

Garza nodded and continued, speaking quietly and quickly with his back to the crowd. "Wylie came back from Corey's house and decided to have another go at him. He felt pretty good about the evidence he has so far, and wanted to see if Corey would cop to it." Garza took a breath. Marlin couldn't remember the sheriff ever looking so grim. "Next thing we know, there's a shot from inside the interview room. I don't know if Wylie went in there with his weapon or what, but Corey's barricaded in there, he says Wylie's been shot, and he's not coming out."

"Any word from Wylie?"

"Yeah, he hollered that he was wounded but okay before we evacuated the building. There's nobody in there now but Corey, Wylie, and Darrell." Darrell Bridges was one of the night dispatchers. "Corey insisted that we clear the building, and the damn place is so small, he'd know if we tried to keep a couple of guys inside. But Corey said it was okay for Darrell to stay when I told him that we had to have a dispatcher in there, otherwise nine-one-one would be down. I got Darrell wearing a vest. Jean was still in there at first, right when this thing got started, but Darrell's shift started at eight and he insisted on relieving her. Acted like it was no big deal, but man, in my book, that makes him pretty brave."

Marlin appreciated the information, but wondered why Garza had called him aside. After all, Marlin was a game warden—an employee of the state, not of the Sheriff's Department.

Garza gave him a quiet stare. "We tried talking to him earlier on Wylie's cell phone," Garza said, "but he wouldn't listen. Said he'd only talk to you. Then he hung up. We've called back a dozen times, but all he says is, 'I want Marlin.' "

"Oh, you've gotta be kidding me."

"No, sir. Not a good time to kid."

Marlin glanced around the crowd, noting the worried looks on the deputies' faces, the excitement in the civilians' eyes.

He looked back at Garza. "You know I'm not trained for

this. I don't know the first thing about negotiation."

"I know. But I'm not sure we have any other options."

Marlin batted the idea around in his head, wondering how much guilt he'd feel if the deal went sour. On the other hand, what if he refused to act, and Wylie—or Corey, for that matter—wound up dead? Either way, he was taking a gamble. "Well, hell," he finally said. "Where's the phone?"

"That's the other thing," Garza said, giving Marlin a smile that said, *Don't kill me when you hear this.* "He kinda wants a face-to-face."

Marlin opened his mouth, but Garza shook his head and said, "I know . . . one of the first rules of hostage negotiation is, don't send in other potential hostages. You should know that straight-out. I'm not gonna lie to you. But you seem to have a pretty good rapport with Corey, and since Wylie might be wounded in there, I thought I'd at least run it past you. I'm willing to give it a try."

"*You're* willing to give it a try?"

Garza shrugged. "You know what I mean." He lowered his voice. "Look, John, don't get me wrong here. I'll understand completely if you tell me to screw off. It's not your job, and the guy's probably killed one man already. . . ."

Marlin let out a snort. "Boy, that's a pep talk. You and Knute Rockne, two of a kind."

Garza grinned at him, but there wasn't much behind it.

"No weapons, right?" Marlin asked.

"No, you leave your belt out here. We can get you a vest."

Marlin rubbed the nape of his neck, feeling the sweat back there. He made his decision quickly, because he knew if he mulled it over too long, he'd never go in. "Wylie is gonna owe me a damn six-pack for this one."

Garza placed a hand on Marlin's shoulder, an attempt at emotional support. "I hear ya."

The office of the Sheriff's Department occupied roughly two thousand square feet, and that included a recent expansion. The county jail occupied the other half of the stone building, with no interior doorway leading between the two sides. It was a hassle for officers to shuttle prisoners back and forth, but in this instance it made things simpler. There was only one way in and one way out, and that was through the glass door on which Marlin's hand currently rested.

Looking through the door, Marlin saw that everything looked quiet inside. Plenty of lights on. Desks stacked high with paperwork. But it looked odd without any people in it. Down the left wall—what used to be an exterior wall—Marlin could see two wooden doors. The first was a small coffee room, and that door stood open. The second was the door to the interview room, which was closed. The small eye-level window was dark. Marlin eased the glass door open and yelled, "Corey? Can you hear me? It's Marlin. I'm coming in." He waited, but there was no answer.

He glanced back at the crowd, which had been pushed back now by about fifty yards. Marlin could see a couple of newsstation vans from Austin or San Antonio already setting up shop, bright lights shining on reporters who were covering the breaking story.

Garza, a handful of deputies, and the two DPS troopers stood about thirty yards away.

Marlin took a step into the office and let the glass door close behind him. He glanced toward the dispatcher's cubicle, a small partitioned area in the right-hand rear corner of the large main room. "Darrell, you back there?" he called out.

"I'm here."

"Just stay put, you hear me?"

"Ten-four."

A little louder, Marlin repeated, "Corey! Can you hear me?"

After a beat, a muffled response: "I hear you."

"I'm coming in, Jack. I have no weapon and I'm all alone."

"I've been waitin' on ya, John. Come on back and join the party!" Corey sounded on edge, kind of hyped-up. Not a good sign.

Marlin walked slowly down the left side of the room past a

row of desks until he was outside the closed door to the interview room. In a softer voice, Marlin said, "Okay, I'm here, Corey. All alone, like you asked. Everybody doing all right in there?"

"Oh yeah, we're all just dandy." Corey sounded like he was just on the other side of the door.

"Jack, we need to talk. I need to see Wylie, make sure he's okay."

"Sure, we can do that. But no bullshit, all right? I mean, we're friends and all, but . . ."

"You got my word. It's just me out here, and I only came to talk."

Marlin saw a crack of light appear at the bottom of the door as Corey turned the interior light on. He heard Corey's voice again, addressing Wylie: "You don't move a damn muscle, you hear me?"

Then the door opened about an inch and Marlin could see Corey eyeing him through the vertical crack. *You're lucky I'm telling the truth,* Marlin thought. *You'd be easy pickings right now if I was armed.*

Corey said, "Grab a roll of tape offa one of those desks."

Marlin found a Scotch-tape dispenser and slipped it to Corey.

The door swung open and Corey stood to the side, Wylie's handgun held at his hip. "Hurry up, now."

Marlin entered the room and Corey quickly closed the door. The small table that normally sat in the middle of the room had been pushed against one wall, along with the four chairs that went with it. Along the opposite wall was the only other piece of furniture in the room—a ratty sofa one of the deputies had hauled to the station one weekend. On that sofa sat Wylie Smith, looking embarrassed and uncomfortable. He was clutching his bloody right hand, which looked like any other hand—except that the thumb had been blown off by a high-powered handgun. There was nothing left but a mangled stump.

"Oh, Jesus," Marlin said. Judging from the front of Wylie's uniform, the thumb had bled a great deal. But the bleeding appeared to have stopped.

"Yeah," Corey said. "Wylie won't be hitching rides anytime soon."

The deputy's face was extremely pale, either from fright or blood loss. "Wylie, you all right?"

Wylie began to speak, but Corey interrupted. "No! You don't say a word," waving the gun in Wylie's direction. "That's our only rule in here, John. He can't speak. Nothing but horseshit comes outta his mouth anyway. Now, you go have a seat along that wall."

Marlin eased himself to the floor opposite the door. He wasn't sure what the experts would advise in a situation like this. Was he supposed to comply with Corey's every demand? Do exactly what he said? Or try to resist, dole out the commands himself? He decided he needed to control the room as best he could. "All right, so tell me: What the hell happened in here, Jack?"

Corey was busy taping a few pages of newspaper over the small window in the door. Marlin noticed that Corey had already jammed one of the sofa cushions in the frame of the exterior window, blocking the view from the outside. Corey got the newspaper in place, then leaned with his back against the door. Marlin thought: *Careful, Jack. One good shotgun blast and this whole thing will be over before you know it.* And the truth was, Marlin had no idea what Garza might be organizing out there. It wouldn't be all that difficult for an armed officer or two to station themselves outside the door, waiting for an opportunity.

Corey glared at Wylie. "It's all his fault. He pulled me from my cell and drug me in here again. Started in with the same ol' shit—how I was gonna end up on Death Row, him tryin' to be all big and mean. I told him he could go to hell, and that's when he pulled his gun and jammed it against the back of my head."

Marlin was mortified. Could Wylie possibly be that stupid? He looked at the deputy, who gave a slight shake of his head.

Corey exploded toward him. "Don't goddamn lie! At least be a man, own up to what you done!" Corey made a gesture with the gun, as if he was tempted to aim it at Wylie, but he pointed it back at the floor. Corey continued, his words nearly sobs now. "I thought it was all over, man! He was gonna shoot me and say I was tryin' to escape or somethin'. So I spun around, grabbed for the gun, and it went off."

Marlin held both hands up, palms out. "Take it easy, Corey. Settle down. I believe you." That wasn't exactly the truth, though. Marlin wasn't sure what to believe at this point. It seemed to appease Corey, however, and he returned to the door.

"Now, I can see you're awfully pissed off, Jack. And hell, I don't blame you. You've really been through the wringer in the last twenty-four hours. But I gotta tell you, Wylie is gonna need some medical attention real soon."

"Screw *him*."

Marlin tried a small laugh. "I've felt that way many times myself. Let's face it: The guy can be a real asshole."

Corey nodded, wiping his sleeve across his nose.

Marlin said, "But are you gonna let an asshole ruin the rest of your life for you? You're not in too deep yet, Jack. I mean, most people could understand what you've done so far. You've been under a lot of stress, you're scared . . . and then, to have a gun at your head? Most people would do the same thing. And, like you say, if you had nothing to do with Bert Gammel, you could still come out of this okay." Corey seemed to be listening, relieved that someone was finally taking his side. Now Marlin had to go for the big payoff. "But Jack, listen to me, man. You gotta let Wylie go. He needs a doctor."

"Forget it."

"But—"

"*Forget* it! If I let him go, I'm screwed, end of story. They'll burn this place down with me in it. You know that."

On that point, Marlin couldn't lie. It would be too obvious. Marlin reached into his shirt pocket and removed the package of Red Man he had been carrying. "Want that chew now?" He slid the package across the floor to Corey's feet.

Corey eyed Marlin for a second, then slumped to a sitting position on the floor, his back still against the door. He opened the package and stuffed a wad into his mouth.

Corey chewed in silence for a few minutes, the ritual seeming to calm his nerves somewhat. He spat in the corner behind the door and said, "I didn't call you in here to see about Wylie anyway. I asked for you because you're the only one who seems to believe that I didn't shoot Bert Gammel."

Marlin tried to sound sincere. "If you say you didn't do it, then as far as I'm concerned, you didn't."

"That's why I need you to find out who did."

"Do what?" Marlin was taken aback.

"Forget Wylie and the other deputies—I want *you* to work on it. To figure out what happened."

Marlin wrestled with his answer for a moment, wanting to choose the right words. "Jack, I appreciate your faith in me. I really do. But it's not that easy. See, I'm not trained for this kind of investigation. But Wylie—"

"Forget Wylie! He's the one who got me in this mess to begin with. He's not leaving until we get this straightened out." Both men glanced at Wylie, who glared back in contempt.

"Well, then," Marlin said, "what about Bobby Garza? You trust him, don't you? He's a good man."

Corey fidgeted with the package of Red Man. "Yeah, I guess he's all right. But even he said that the evidence don't look good." He closed his eyes for a moment, then opened them again, staring at the floor. He looked sad, defeated. In a quiet voice, he pleaded: "John, you gotta help me, man. You're the only one who can do it. You're like me, born around here. You know everybody, and you can find the guy who done it."

Corey was giving Marlin an opening here, some leverage to negotiate. And Marlin intended to use it, even though he'd have to lie. "Tell you what. If you'll let me come back in with some medical supplies, to fix Wylie up a little . . ."

Corey raised his eyes to meet Marlin's. "Then you'll do it? You'll help me out?"

Marlin nodded. "I'll do everything I can."

CHAPTER TWENTY-TWO

Raccoon meat was a lot tastier than most people gave it credit for; Red knew that firsthand. Most people were just too uppity to try that kind of thing, though. Hell, back when Red was a boy, he'd wander the hills late at night, just him, a spotlight, and his rusty single-shot .22. If he was lucky, he'd come home with a couple of fat coons and his mother would make a big pot of stew the next day. Nowadays, Red liked his raccoon barbecued or chicken-fried.

He wasn't quite the all-out hunter he used to be, either, preferring instead to let the coons come to him. He and Billy Don had worked out a pretty good system. They had a deer feeder set up in the oak trees about thirty yards behind Red's mobile home, and the raccoons just couldn't resist such an easy meal. They'd come ambling along just after dark and eat all the corn they could stuff into their greedy little faces.

So Red and Billy Don would sit on the back porch, an ice chest full of beer between them, Billy Don working the spotlight, Red doing the shooting because he was a much better shot, even if Billy Don wouldn't admit it. They couldn't do this more than once or twice a month, because the coons got gun-shy pretty darn quick. Plus, after you shot up the local popula-tion, it took awhile for other neighbor coons to come along and fill the gap.

On this particular evening, the hunting was pretty bad. They had seen only one coon, a big, fat bastard, and Red had missed it. They had resigned themselves to the fact that they'd have to eat store-bought food for dinner—Red wanting a frozen pizza, Billy Don arguing for burritos—when the phone rang inside.

Red rose to answer it. "Don't be shining that light all over creation while I'm gone or you'll scare 'em all away," he said, as he opened the screen door. He always forgot that he didn't need to open the door—the mesh screen had been missing for several months and he could just step right through the frame—but old habits die hard.

Red answered the phone as he always did: "Barney's Whore-house, home of the two-for-one special."

There was a moment of silence on the other end, and then: "Uh, Red O'Brien, please."

"You got him. Who's this?"

"Yes, Mr. O'Brien, my name is Harold Cannon. I'm an at-torney in Austin."

"An attorney? Zat the same as a lawyer?"

"Yes. Yes, it is."

"Well, then, whatever she's sayin', the kid ain't mine."

"Pardon me?"

Red chuckled. Some people just didn't know a joke when they heard one. "I'm just funnin' with ya, Harold."

"Yes, I see. Sorry about that. Anyway, the reason I'm calling concerns Emmett Slaton, who is one of my clients."

With that, Red's smile slowly disappeared. It had been a full day now, and Mr. Slaton was still missing. Red had called the Sheriff's Department earlier that afternoon, but they said there had been no progress on the case. It was the darnedest thing: Ever since last night, Red had had this strange feeling in his gut, something he couldn't identify and had never experienced before. He wasn't sure, but he thought it might actually be concern for a fellow human being—or maybe gas pains.

"I've been trying to reach Mr. Slaton for the last twenty-four hours," Cannon continued, "regarding some routine matters. But when my calls went unreturned, I got a little worried. See . . . how can I put this delicately? . . . Mr. Slaton has a medical condition, and I was afraid he might be having some trouble, all alone at his residence. This afternoon, I called the local police, just to have them stop by and make sure everything was okay. Unfortunately, as you are no doubt aware, they informed me that Mr. Slaton is missing."

"Yessir, I was the one that discovered the problem. Called it in last night."

"I see. In any case, in a situation such as this, I've been instructed to contact you regarding Mr. Slaton's brush-removal business."

Just then, there was a shot outside.

"Uh, everything all right over there? Was that a gunshot?" Cannon asked.

"Just the TV," Red said. "Go on with what you were sayin'."

"Well, Mr. Slaton had—or has, rather—confidence in your abilities to run the business. Several months ago, he instructed me, in the event that he is incapacitated, to appoint you as vice president of operations of the company."

Red's throat went dry. He reached for a beer on the bar and took a large swig.

"Are you there, Mr. O'Brien?"

"I'm here," Red croaked.

"I know this is rather sudden, but I do have all the proper papers here in front of me. I can have them couriered out to you tomorrow, if you'd like. That is, if you're interested in the position."

Red's mind was racing so fast, he could barely hear the voice on the other end. *Me? Vice president of something? Vice presidents drove Cadillacs and smoked big cigars!*

"Mr. O'Brien?"

"Well, hell yeah, I'm interested," Red managed to blurt. "Now, what does that mean, exactly?"

"It means you'd be responsible for lining up new customers, assigning projects to the work crews . . . just managing the day-to-day operations of the company in general."

Red thought that over for a minute. "You mean I wouldn't be runnin' a BrushBuster myself?"

Cannon chuckled. "No, not as a vice president. I should also mention that the position includes a fifty-percent salary increase."

Red's knees buckled and he had to grab the bar for support. *Fifty percent! That was nearly one and a half times what he was making now!* "That sounds fair," Red said.

"Further, he has instructed me to inform you that, in the event of his demise, he has bequeathed the company to you."

Now Red slumped to the floor, pulling the phone with him. He was having a hard time catching his breath. Suddenly, that fifty-percent raise seemed like small potatoes. He'd have to look up the word *bequeath*, but he was pretty sure it meant Mr. Slaton had left the company to Red in his will.

"Are you okay, Mr. O'Brien?"

"Yeah, yeah, I'm fine," Red panted. "It's just, with Mr. Slaton missin' and all . . ."

"Yes, I understand. It's a very difficult and sad time for us all."

Red was thinking fast now, his mind buzzing. This all seemed too easy. Things didn't just fall into your lap like this.

"Of course, for now, we all just have to wait and see what develops," Cannon said.

There it was. Red knew there had to be a catch. "You mean, like, they haven't declared him dead yet—"

"Well, no. Probably not until they find . . . well, to be direct, not until they find a body. Until they do, this matter could be tied up for months. Maybe even years."

Red's spirits dropped for a moment, but he consoled himself with the whopping promotion and raise he had just received.

Cannon said he would make arrangements to have the paperwork delivered to Red's home, and then wished Red a good night.

Red hung up the phone, still sitting on the floor.

Billy Don stepped through the screen-door frame carrying a large raccoon by the tail. "I got one, Red! A big sumbitch!"

Red rose from the floor and took the dead animal out of Billy Don's hands. "Screw that coon," Red said, tossing it back out the door. "Tonight we're doin' it right."

Billy Don's eye grew large. "You mean . . . ?"

"Hell, yeah," Red said proudly. "We're eatin' at Dairy Queen."

Marlin was slumped in a chair in front of his television set, exhausted by the events at the sheriff's office. The adrenaline rush had finally subsided and left a bone-weary void in its place. He had stopped at Blanco County Hospital on the way home to have his bite wound treated, and now he was ready for a quiet night.

Marlin had the TV tuned to KHIL, a station that covered half a dozen counties in the Hill Country west of Austin. The situation at the sheriff's office was, of course, the big story, and they had preempted regular programming to carry live coverage.

As the reporter droned on, Marlin wondered how long it would be before Garza decided to take action. Would he wait Corey out, or make a move of his own? Marlin had no idea what the experts advised in hostage situations. But he did know that it would be a fairly simple matter to knock down the wooden door and take Jack Corey out for good. Theoretically, Wylie would have sense enough to know something like that might be coming, and he'd stay hunkered on the floor, out of the line of fire.

If only Corey would give it up—just let Wylie walk out of there before things got even more out of hand—Marlin might feel a little better about it all. As it stood, Corey was under the impression that Marlin was planning to launch his own investigation into the murder of Bert Gammel. *I flat-out lied to the guy,* Marlin thought. *But what the hell was I supposed to do?* Bobby Garza had agreed that Marlin had handled it just right. When Marlin had told Garza what Corey wanted, Garza had simply shaken his head and said, *I'd say we've got our man already, right in there.* The thing was, Marlin was inclined to agree. He wanted to believe in Corey's innocence, but there were just too many things stacked against him. The tire tracks. The muddy boots. The motive. If the DNA came back against him, it was Corey's one-way ticket to Huntsville.

Marlin shook his head and tried to drive it all from his mind. *Why the hell should I feel bad about all this?* After all, the lie had gotten the results everyone wanted: They now knew that Wylie was stable, not in need of immediate medical attention. The deputy would probably need surgery on his hand, but there wasn't any hope of reattaching the thumb because there wasn't any thumb left to reattach.

Marlin fetched a beer from the fridge and settled back into the chair. Then the reporter—standing in a harsh circle of light, the sheriff's office in the distant background—reminded Marlin of the other big screwup that was bothering him tonight. Glowering into the camera, the reporter said,

> "As we mentioned earlier in our broadcast, the events at the sheriff's station aren't the only problems facing the local law-enforcement community tonight. We also have reports of a fugitive on the loose here in Blanco County. Earlier this evening, the area game warden arrested a man for assault and was transporting him to the jail for booking. According to Sheriff Bobby Garza, in the turmoil resulting from the hostage situation, the current fugitive—Thomas Collin Peabody—managed to free himself from the game warden's vehicle and escape on foot. He is, however, handcuffed, and authorities do not consider him a danger to the community."

Just great, Marlin thought, feeling like an idiot. While he had been inside the sheriff's office with Corey, Marlin had completely forgotten about Peabody. He should have asked Garza to put a deputy on Peabody, but it had slipped his mind.

He hadn't figured the guy as a flight risk—and on top of that, his hands were cuffed *behind* him. But the little scumbag had slipped away, probably just to spite Marlin. Normally, Marlin would have expected some good-natured ribbing from the deputies, but nobody had said a word. Probably because Marlin had just successfully negotiated with an armed gunman, a probable murderer.

Oh, well, Marlin thought. *Too late to do anything about Peabody now. At least the damn reporter didn't mention me by name.*

> "*We have been unable to reach Game Warden John Marlin for comment. . . .*"

Marlin groaned and changed the channel. A rerun of *Andy Griffith*, with Barney doing something idiotic, as usual. Marlin could relate.

The ringing of the phone pulled him out of Mayberry. *Answer it or no? Probably a reporter.* He let the machine get it.

> "*This is Marlin. Leave a message.*"

After a pause: "John, you there? It's Becky."

His heart leaped at the familiar voice and he rose to pick up the handset. "Hey, I'm here."

"God, John, what in the world is going on down there?" she asked, concern in her voice. She said that Vicky—a nurse she had worked with at Blanco County Hospital—had been watching the news, including the earlier report of Peabody's escape. Vicky had heard Marlin's name and called Becky to let her know.

Marlin shook his head in disgust. "I can nail a dozen poachers in one night, but does that ever make the news?"

"You're okay, though?"

"Yeah, I'm fine." He told her a little about the murder of Bert Gammel and the hostage situation. From what Marlin had seen, the news report didn't mention that he had been inside with Corey. He decided not to worry Becky with it. The conversation swung back around to Thomas Peabody. "Little bastard's runnin' around with cuffs on," Marlin said, "so how far can he get?"

Becky giggled. "I remember those cuffs."

Marlin smiled, but felt sad at the same time.

Becky noticed the silence and said, "I'm sorry. I shouldn't have said that."

"Hey, no big deal. How are things going up there? How's Margaret?"

"About the same. She hates the chemo, and I think she's wondering whether it's worth it at this point."

"What do *you* think?"

"If she wants to stop treatment, that's what we'll do."

"I'm sure y'all will make the right decision."

"Thanks, John. Listen, I better go. I'm calling from work right now. I just wanted to make sure you were okay."

"A bruised ego, as they say, but fine otherwise. Give your mom a hug for me."

"I'll do it. Talk to you later."

The first thing Vinnie did when he got home was strip off all his clothes, including his shoes, and put them in a garbage bag. He'd get rid of it all tomorrow, maybe dump it in a trash barrel out on the highway. Couldn't be too careful about shit like that. Sure, if it came down to it, he could argue that he had been in T.J.'s boat dozens of times, and that was why the fibers were there. But why let them find a specific shirt or pair of jeans that matches a specific fiber? Say maybe one of his fibers was wrapped up with one of the fibers from the clothes T.J. was wearing today. Then maybe they could link him to being in the boat when T.J. died.

And he *had* died, just like Vinnie thought he would.

Poor guy came sputtering to the surface, frothy blood spilling out of his mouth, trying to speak. Vinnie had had to stifle a fucking giggle, he was so pleased with himself, how his plan had worked out. A few minutes later, T.J.'s eyes rolled back and he floated facedown.

Now the Gibbs family boat was floating unmanned, T.J. bobbing in the water nearby, waiting to be discovered. Could be days, though. The reservoir wasn't busy this time of year.

Vinnie had swum to shore in the chilly water, hopped in his car, then crushed the LoJack and scattered it along the roadside.

CHAPTER TWENTY-THREE

"It's your own fault, ya know. You're always pissing people off with your smart mouth. Why ya have to piss people off like that?"

Angela had been going on like that for about ten minutes. Or maybe it just seemed that way—who the hell knew? Sal was so stoned on painkillers, he really didn't give a fuck about Angela, the doctors, the hospital, or his damn broken leg. The only thing he really felt—the one emotion that was eating away at the tattered edge of his slippery consciousness—was rage. That fucking tree-hugger. Smart-ass little bastard thought he was gonna shut Sal Mameli down? That'd be the day. Son of a bitch was lucky Sal hadn't gotten a good hold of him. Goddamn cop—what was he, a game warden or some shit?—had stuck his nose in the middle of it.

Where the hell did that little tree-hugging jamook come from, anyway?—and that blonde broad, the one stirring up all the trouble. What a pain in the ass those two were. How's a man supposed to go about his business with people like that breaking your balls all the time?

"You listening to me?" Angela whined. "Can you even hear me, Sal? Sal?" She leaned over his hospital bed to peer into his half-open eyes.

Well, if they wanted to play hardball, then Sal'd show 'em the heat, the ninety-mile-per-hour fastball right under their chins. Nobody fucks with Roberto Ragusa . . . oh, wait, that's not the right name. Sal something. Boy, these drugs really sneak up on ya. Sal Mameli, that's it. Nobody fucks with Sal Mameli and gets away with it. That old rancher—Emmett something—he had tried, and look where it got him.

"Are you asleep? Because if you're asleep, I'm going home."

Christ, why won't she shut the hell up? Let a guy have a little peace and quiet for once. Sal had important things to figure out and he had to concentrate. What had he been thinking about? Yeah, the old man. Sal had taken care of that little problem, him and Vinnie. Vinnie was a good boy. Learning quick. It was a good thing, too, because Vinnie would have to take care of this situation, too.

"Okay, I'm going home." Angela stood and grabbed her purse off the floor. In a surprisingly gentle voice, she said, "You get some rest now, Sal. The doctors'll take good care of ya." She leaned and gave Sal a light kiss on the forehead, then left the room.

Yeah, Vinnie was turning into quite a soldier. Sal would have a long talk with him tomorrow, when he had a clearer head. Vinnie could handle it.

Marlin must have dozed off for a few minutes, and now something was nagging at him, telling him to wake up. He lifted his heavy eyelids and looked around in a daze, wondering why his bedroom looked so much like his living room. The phone rang again, and he pulled himself out of the chair in front of the television. He noticed that KHIL was still broadcasting live from the courthouse. Apparently, the standoff was ongoing, and Marlin figured it might be Bobby Garza calling.

"This is Marlin."

It wasn't the sheriff. It was a man who lived off Sandy Road, a photographer who had bought a couple hundred acres west of Johnson City a few years ago. According to the man, there had been half a dozen shots in the last half hour on the place east of his. He suspected poachers and wanted Marlin to check it out. Marlin glanced at his watch. Two-seventeen A.M. He told the caller he was on his way.

Normally, Marlin wasn't thrilled with middle-of-the-night phone calls. Half the time, there was a reasonable explanation for the gunfire: someone shooting raccoons or scaring a fox away from their chickens. The rest of the time, the shooters were gone before Marlin arrived.

But tonight, Marlin was kind of glad the call had come in. This was just a plain old "shots fired" call, no dead bodies lying in cedar thickets, no suspected murderers to negotiate with. Now he could forget about the Jack Corey mess and get back to business as usual.

Ten minutes later, he was pulling through an open gate off Sandy Road. He quickly came to a large pasture, where he saw a truck with its tailgate down, three men standing behind it. Marlin gave the truck a quick blast with his spotlight, letting the hunters know who he was, then bounced across the pasture toward the truck.

As he parked, he aimed his headlights at the three men: all locals, men he recognized, each with a beer in hand.

Marlin climbed out and said, " 'Evenin', Joe."

The owner of the property was Joe Biggs—a tall, slender man with black hair, an insurance agent in Johnson City. Joe said, "Hey, John. Soon as I saw your truck, I figured somebody musta called in."

"One of your neighbors."

Joe grimaced. "Sorry about that. We woulda called and let you know we were huntin', but it was kinda late and it was a spur-of-the-moment kind of deal."

Marlin played his flashlight across the truck bed. Three dead hogs lay inside. Due to their devastating impact on the environment, feral hogs could be legally hunted at night in Texas, but hunters were encouraged to contact the game warden first and make their intentions known.

"No big deal. Looks like you had some luck."

"Hell yeah. I been seeing about a dozen every night. Figured it was time to thin 'em out a little. They been runnin' all the deer away from my feeders."

The men chatted for a few minutes about the current deer season. One of the men had taken a ten-point on opening day.

"All right, then," Marlin said. "Guess you're done for the night? I'm sure your neighbors could use a break."

Joe gave an embarrassed smile. "Yeah, sorry 'bout that. Didn't think the shots'd bother 'em. We're all done."

Marlin waved and turned to leave.

"Hey," Joe called out. "Heard you were the big hero tonight."

Marlin was always amazed at how fast news traveled through the county. "I wouldn't say 'hero' is the right word," Marlin replied.

"Well, hell, you walked right in there with Corey holding a gun. Pretty damn brave, if you ask me. So what do you think, John? Think Corey done it? Killed Bert?"

"Can't really talk about that, Joe." Marlin said, opening the door to his cruiser. "He'll get his day in court."

"Well, tell me this, then: Have the deputies figured out where Bert got all that cash?"

Marlin paused for a moment, then closed his truck door and walked back over to Joe.

"What cash are you talking about?"

Marlin and Joe were in the cab of the cruiser now, out of earshot of the other two hunters.

Joe's eyes were wide. "I figured y'all knew all about that. You hadn't heard?"

"Why don't you tell me?"

Joe rubbed his chin. "Well, I didn't know Bert real well, but he was a friend of Virgil Talkington's, and Virgil is a friend of mine. Virgil has this poker game every Friday night, and Bert would sometimes show up over there. Anyway, he was always a penny-ante kind of guy. Never brought much money with him, usually just a big jar of change, and he'd fold every hand unless he knew for sure he had a winner. Man, I've seen him throw away three of kind, if you can believe it. To hear Virgil tell it, Bert didn't have much money to spare. Barely made his mortgage."

"When did he first join the game?"

"Oh, I don't know. Coupla years ago. And he didn't play every time, maybe once every month or two. But then, maybe a year ago, he started showing up with a lot more cash. He'd pull out this big roll of bills and flash it all around, and man, would that get our attention! See, he wasn't that good of a player and, well . . ."

Marlin smiled. "Y'all would try to separate him from his money."

"Well, yeah. He seemed to have plenty of it all of a sudden. Brought expensive cigars for everybody, too. Lots of liquor."

This didn't sound like much to Marlin. Maybe Bert got a raise, or an inheritance, or won a few bucks on scratch-off lottery cards. Could be anything.

"But then here's the other thing," Joe continued. "One day I was over at Kyle's place"—Kyle Parker owned a small car lot next to Joe's office—"and Bert comes in to pick up that Explorer he's been driving for the last eight or ten months. So I'm sitting there eating lunch, shootin' the shit with Kyle, while Bert fills out the paperwork. Finally, Bert gets done with the forms, Kyle totals up the price on the car, and—get this—Bert hands it all over in cash. Kyle didn't even bat an eye, like they had already talked about it or something. Sure, that Explorer was three or four years old, but the price was still something like twelve grand. I mean, shee-yit. You know anybody who carries around that kind of cash?"

Marlin agreed that he didn't—but, thinking it through, he wasn't sure it meant anything. Some people have strange saving habits, tucking cash away in a Mason jar or, literally, under the mattress. He'd heard about one little old lady in Blanco who lived as if she were one step above the poorhouse. Then the lady died and the heirs discovered she had been a millionaire, hiding huge sums of cash in coffee cans in her attic.

"Did Bert ever say anything about the money—like where he got it? I mean, you're all sitting around, drinking a few cold ones, somebody's bound to ask, right?"

Joe nodded his head vigorously. "Damn right, we asked, but he was all tight-lipped about it. One time, he said he made it on one of those dot-com companies, but he wouldn't never name which one. None of us believed him. Shoot, Bert didn't know nothing about no stock that wasn't runnin' around on four legs."

Marlin sat in silence for moment, pondering this new information. Joe tipped his beer can and sucked out the last few drops. "Think that'll help you any?" he asked.

Marlin had no idea. "I don't know, Joe. I really don't know."

CHAPTER TWENTY-FOUR

Marlin headed back to Johnson City, his dashboard clock telling him it was nearly four A.M. Driving through the cool night air, his window down, Marlin contemplated what Joe Biggs had told him.

Okay, so Bert Gammel had been throwing a lot of money around. Big deal. Didn't necessarily have anything to do with the murder. And if it did, it didn't rule out Jack Corey. Hell, it might implicate him even more. Corey was already at odds with Gammel. The cash could have pushed him over the edge. On the other hand, if Corey had been after the money, why would he ambush Gammel out at the deer lease? Didn't make a lot of sense. In fact, why even murder him? It seemed only natural that Corey would have tried breaking into Gammel's house to find the cash.

Another strange thing: Wylie hadn't said anything about Gammel's surplus of cash—or if he had, word hadn't reached Marlin. The likely answer was that Wylie had been so focused on investigating Corey, he hadn't done much digging into Gammel's affairs. Wylie had seemed convinced of Corey's guilt from the beginning, so he probably hadn't questioned enough people in Gammel's circles. The spotlight had been on Corey right from the beginning—because of Lester Higgs's account of the troubles between Corey and Gammel. Something like that could easily send an overzealous detective off in the wrong direction.

The long and short of it: Marlin wanted to talk to Garza about Joe's story. Maybe Garza and the deputies already knew about the cash and had followed that trail to a logical conclusion. There could be a perfectly reasonable explanation. Marlin was wide-awake now, so he figured he might as well swing by the sheriff's office and see what was going on. Maybe Corey had come to his senses by now. Or he could have fallen asleep, allowing Wylie to sneak out. This thing couldn't go on forever.

Marlin tuned his stereo to an all-news AM station out of Austin.

> "... at a press conference earlier this evening outside the sheriff's office. Blanco County sheriff Bobby Garza cautioned local citizens not to expect a quick resolution to the standoff."

Marlin recognized Garza's voice:

> "We're doing everything we can to ensure the safety of the officer involved, but the truth is, this could take some time. It's a delicate situation and we intend to handle it with the greatest of care."

The reporter continued:

> "At this point, the man involved in the standoff has been identified as Jack Albert Corey, a resident of Johnson City arrested yesterday evening for assaulting the very officer now held hostage. Stay tuned to KNOW for further updates."

Marlin found Sheriff Bobby Garza sitting in his patrol car, eyes closed, a cup of steaming coffee perched on the dashboard.

Marlin looked through the passenger-side window. "Wake up, cowboy."

Garza swiveled his head Marlin's way. "Wake up, my ass. I've got a headache that would floor a mule."

"And eyes like two pissholes in a snowbank." Marlin said. "You know, I hear four out of five doctors recommend Excedrin for hostage situations." He climbed inside and nodded toward the squat building forty yards away. "What's the latest?"

Garza shook his head and took a sip of coffee. "Corey told Darrell to get the hell out about an hour ago." Darrell Bridges was the dispatcher who had remained inside the sheriff's office. "That was fine with me," Garza said, "because by then I had a couple of the phone guys tapping into the lines from outside. So now we can take calls without interrupting nine-one-one service. And we don't really need the radio at this point. We can still talk car to car."

"So Corey has the run of the entire office now?"

"Yep, and he's covered up all the windows so we can't see inside. Pretty smart move, really. But at least he's talking to us now."

"Yeah?"

"I've got Tatum acting as negotiator. He's doing a pretty fair job. Taking things one step at a time." Bill Tatum was one of the deputies—a man Marlin liked and respected. Hopefully, Jack Corey felt the same way. "Corey damn sure isn't talkin' about coming out yet, though. All Tatum's managed to do is twist his arm a little. Corey wants some food in there but we're refusing it until he gives us something in return."

"Like what?"

"Well, we know he ain't gonna give up Wylie, so I asked him for Wylie's gun belt. I want to take away that extra ammo. Later on, he'll want something else, and I'll ask for a bullet out of the gun. You just keep picking away at what they've got. I've read that sometimes you can get them down to just a bullet or two that way."

Marlin grinned. "Pretty smart. But why is Tatum negotiating instead of you?"

"For starters, he's taken a couple of courses on hostage situations. I've only taken one. Never thought I'd need it. I mean, how often do we come up against something like this? Shit like this just doesn't happen out here. It'd be like asking the folks in Kansas to have emergency plans for a hurricane.

"And the other thing; one of the few things I do know—the top cop is never supposed to be the negotiator. Otherwise, Corey would expect immediate answers to his demands. He'd be like, 'Why can't you do this for me? You're the sheriff.' This way, Tatum can string things along, tell Corey he needs to check with me and get back to him."

"Not to be ignorant, but what does that accomplish?"

Garza stopped for a moment to listen to some radio traffic. One of the deputies at the door wanted a bathroom break.

"You're supposed to drag these things out as long as you can," he said. "Supposedly, the longer it lasts, the less chance there is of someone getting hurt. The perp is supposed to come to his senses, so they tell you to stall all you can. Unless someone's in immediate danger. Then all bets are off."

The men sat in silence for a moment, and Marlin noticed the scene was eerily quiet. It was amazing, really. The better part of the Blanco County Sheriff's Department was figuratively handcuffed, held at bay by the whims of the hapless redneck inside.

Marlin spoke up: "What about the DNA test? Can't the lab speed it up, let us know if Corey's a match or not?"

"You'd think so, but I guess they got cops all over the state asking for rush jobs. That's just business as usual. They told me six days."

Marlin sighed in frustration. "But, Christ, we've got a real situation here."

"You don't have to tell me. Oh, speaking of test results, did you hear? The blood all over Emmett Slaton's house wasn't human."

Marlin had forgotten—for the last few hours anyway—about

the disappearance of the old rancher. "Then what the hell was it?"

"Animal of some sort, but the tests don't tell us which. They just show that the blood's not human."

"What do you make of that?"

Garza made a passive, palms-up gesture. "Got me. But I'm taking it as a good sign, for now. We never found his dog, so maybe it ran off injured and Slaton's been looking for it. 'Course, that doesn't explain Slaton's truck at the Save-Mart. Anyway, we'll see what the boys can come up with. All the deputies who aren't here are either working on Slaton or looking for your boy Peabody."

Marlin waited for a gibe that didn't come.

"I'm pushing everybody to the limit as it is," Garza said. "Everyone's on the clock, and most of them have been on duty since yesterday morning. If something doesn't shake loose pretty soon on that Slaton mess—and this one here—I'm gonna have to call in the Rangers."

The Texas Rangers, a division of the Texas Department of Public Safety, were available to smaller law-enforcement entities on an as-needed basis. But Marlin knew Garza prided himself on running an independent department.

Marlin mentioned what he'd just learned from Joe Biggs about Bert Gammel. When he was done, Garza tilted his head to one side and blew out a breath. "That's the first I've heard of that. A lot of cash, huh?"

"Enough to buy a Ford Explorer a couple years old, according to Joe."

Garza gave Marlin a sidelong glance. "You up for playing detective a little longer?"

Marlin didn't really know how he felt about it, but he knew the Sheriff's Department already had its hands full. He'd have to make a few calls to game wardens in neighboring counties, asking them to help pick up the slack on poaching calls in Blanco County. "What the hell," he finally said.

"That's my boy," Garza smiled.

They talked it over and agreed that Garza would secure subpoenas first thing in the morning so Marlin could check into Gammel's financial affairs at the local banks. Apparently, a couple of deputies had already searched Gammel's home—including the only financial records they could find: his checkbook—and nothing had raised a red flag. Marlin would have to look a little deeper.

"After the banks, you might want to talk to his friends and coworkers," Garza said, with a pained look on his face. "Wylie obviously didn't cover those bases very good."

Marlin nodded.

Garza grinned and said, "Man, it would look so good." He waved a hand across Marlin's left biceps, as if reading an imaginary patch on his arm. "Blanco County Sheriff's Department."

"Here we go again," Marlin said as he climbed out of the car.

CHAPTER TWENTY-FIVE

Handcuffs were nothing new to Thomas Peabody. He had been shackled several times before, and had even managed to extricate himself from the infernal devices on a couple of occasions. Those were pleasant memories. It was always amusing to see the puzzled expressions on the officers' faces (oppressive pigs!) when Peabody managed to slip his delicate hands free.

But this time, the cuffs were just too restrictive. Yes, he had been successful at "walking through" the cuffs backwards (the benefits of yoga were wonderful, indeed), so now his hands were cuffed in front of him. But there was simply no hope of slipping his hands through the metal manacles. The game warden had been too perturbed when he had clamped them on Peabody's wrists, and Peabody could feel them biting into his skin ever since. Therefore, Peabody would have to be a bit more resourceful. In time, he'd find a way out of this puzzle, and then he could proceed with the more urgent task of shutting down Sal Mameli, just as he had threatened to do. In truth, Peabody regretted making such a bold statement in front of Inga. But he had, and now he must live up to it.

He surveyed his surroundings and wrinkled his nose in disgust. He was in a stable, complete with a gassy old horse. The hayloft where he had slept last night was fairly comfortable, but the foul—and quite audible—emissions from the horse's hind end had wreaked havoc with his sinuses. All things considered, however, he had been fortunate to stumble across a structure this accommodating. After all, he was a fugitive now. A wanted man. An escapee. He thought it sounded quite romantic, actually, and wondered if Inga, wherever she was at the moment, was impressed with his new status. Perhaps he would become a man of some renown, like Robin Hood or one of the Three Musketeers. A hero for the common man; a strident force for good in the battle against evil.

He let loose a violent sneeze, which brought him back to reality. He'd have to contemplate his place in folklore later, after he found a way out of his current predicament. He was filthy and hungry, a forlorn soul straight out of a Dickens novel.

Peabody carefully descended the ladder from the hayloft. The horse stared from its stall with unconcerned eyes and broke wind. Peabody scowled at the horse, got no noticeable response, and was thankful the neighboring stall was empty: Twice the gas would certainly make the stable uninhabitable.

The only other structure in the stable was a small closet in one corner. Peeking in, Peabody saw a saddle hanging on the wall and a pair of rough-woven blankets on a shelf. There were also a couple of brushes and several oddly shaped metal implements—items that had something to do with riding this malodorous beast, Peabody assumed. No hand tools to be seen.

Even if he found some sort of useful tool, how was he to operate it? This quandary would require quite a bit of thought, he knew. But never fear: The brain is the most powerful tool of all, and he owned a dexterous one.

Weighing his options, Peabody turned to the peculiar contraption squatting just inside the stable doors. It looked like a golf cart on steroids, with four large knobby tires and HONDA painted on what seemed to be the gas tank. Not quite a motorcycle, but related to one. Peabody had no experience with such vehicles. Unfortunately, it appeared that he would have to look elsewhere for salvation.

Peabody strode to the wooden double doors of the stable and peered outside. Just a few minutes past sunrise, he surmised. Forty yards away stood a shambling old house with a rusty truck parked in front.

Then he heard a noise, the low growl of a motor. A few seconds later, another truck, a newer model, bounced its way up the driveway and stopped next to the first. A lanky gentleman in overalls and no undershirt climbed out and proceeded into the house.

Peabody was nervous now. He eased the door closed and focused on the decision at hand: Should he try to slip away undetected, or wait until the occupants of the house left the vicinity? Peabody was pondering the possibilities when the choice was made for him.

He heard two voices coming his way—a man and a woman, giggling. Peabody quickly scrambled back up the ladder into the hayloft, finding refuge just as the door to the stable swung open.

"—and we could get caught," the woman said. "Frank is sleeping right on the couch."

"I got news for ya, sugar. He ain't sleepin', he's passed out."

"Well, we gotta be quiet, you hear?"

More giggling followed, finally replaced by a lustful moaning. Peabody chanced a cautious peek over a bale of hay and saw two figures—the man in overalls and a brunette in a long nightshirt—kissing passionately. Peabody watched as the man clumsily fondled the woman's breasts through her nightshirt.

The woman pulled free, gave a coy smile, then tugged the shirt over her head. *Well.* She was quite naked now, and Peabody couldn't help admiring the woman's sturdy physique. She had the solid build of a Midwestern girl. Large hips, ample bosom.

Ogling the woman with all the subtlety of a dog eyeing a pork chop, the man let his overalls fall to his feet. "Come to Daddy," he said.

Peabody almost chuckled out loud. Surely the woman would be offended by such a crass come-on.

The woman responded by jumping into the man's arms, her legs wrapped around his torso.

My lord, what type of woman is this? Peabody wondered. She had no more couth than a common . . . a common . . . He lost his train of thought for a moment.

The man shuffled toward a wall, the woman slid into place, and now they were coupling with remarkable vigor.

Peabody noticed that his own breathing had become rapid and shallow. Well, that was understandable. He was on the run and these people could possibly catch him. That's what accounted for the changes in his respiratory patterns. It certainly wasn't due to the tawdry scene unfolding before him. He was of too high a moral fiber to be seduced by the sight of two rednecks copulating like barnyard animals.

Peabody decided it was beneath his dignity to watch the whole sordid affair, so he quietly eased back and settled into the hay. A few grunts later, an idea struck him. These frolicking fornicators could be his ticket to freedom!

He peeked at the couple again, and it appeared they would be at it for quite some time. The woman's eyes were closed and the man was facing the wall. Perfect. Ever so stealthily, Peabody made his way to the ladder and began a painstakingly slow descent. This was the vulnerable point. If the woman opened her eyes now, she would scream in terror and all would be lost. But she continued with her moaning, calling out, "Bubba, oh, Bubba."

Peabody reached the ground, tiptoed over to her nightshirt, scooped it up, and scampered back up the ladder. The handcuffs rattled against the ladder a few times, but that was irrelevant at this point. He already had what he needed, and besides, the couple was still oblivious to his presence.

After ten more minutes, the couple finally reached a grunting, squealing crescendo. Peabody had decided letting them finish was merely the polite thing to do; he certainly had no voyeuristic interest in the event. The man—named Bubba, apparently—sagged forehead-first against the wall as the woman lowered her feet and stood on her own. She glanced over Bubba's shoulder and said, "Where's my nightgown?"

Bubba, in his postcoital bliss, didn't reply.

The woman smacked him on the arm and asked him again.

"Right up here," Peabody called.

He had never seen two people so startled. The man quickly tugged his overalls back up his torso while the woman cowered behind him. "Who the hell are you?" Bubba growled, glaring up at Peabody.

"There's no time for that," Peabody replied. "I'm afraid I'm in need of some assistance."

They both gaped at him for a moment with all the intelligence of sheep suffering from heatstroke. Finally, Bubba said, "Mister, are you plumb out of your mind? What the hell are you doing hidin' up in that loft?"

Peabody summoned his patience. "As I said, I'm in need of a favor." He raised his arms so they could see the handcuffs. "Once you've helped me out of my current difficulties, I'll gladly return the nightshirt."

Bubba stared at Peabody as if he had just landed a spaceship on Main Street. "What the hell? You kidding me? Throw that goddamn nightgown down here or I'll whup your ass for ya."

Typical, Peabody thought. He had noticed these Texans were quite bossy. Always ordering you around like an old schoolmaster. "Sir, I'm afraid you've miscalculated your leverage in this situation. Now, if you'll just—"

But Bubba wasn't listening anymore, he was moving toward the ladder, muttering obscenities along way.

Before Bubba's feet hit the first rung, Peabody called out, "Frank! Hey, Frank!"

Bubba froze. "Shut the hell up, will ya! Goddamn, you tryin' to get us all kilt?"

Peabody smiled. "No, actually, I had something quite different in mind. But it will require some sort of cutting implement."

•   •   •

Five minutes later, Bubba returned with a pair of ratchet-action bolt cutters, scavenged from the cuckolded Frank's toolshed. Peabody instructed the woman to climb up to the loft with the tool. Bubba started to object, but by then all the fight had gone out of him. He was nervously looking over his shoulder, just wishing to bring the ordeal to an end.

The woman did as she was told, bashfully climbing the ladder stark naked while trying to maintain some semblance of dignity. She failed miserably.

While Peabody attempted to conceal his perusal of her body, she pumped the handles of the bolt cutter and snipped the linked chain between the two handcuffs. "Thank you. You are quite kind," Peabody said. Regardless of the circumstances, it was only proper to extend his courtesies.

After Peabody reminded Bubba that Frank was still within earshot, the woman climbed back down the ladder. Peabody followed.

Just as his feet touched the ground, there was a loud *crack*—the slamming of a screen door—followed by: "Sally Ann? You out here?"

Sally Ann grabbed the nightshirt out of Peabody's hand and pulled it over her head.

Bubba peeked out the door. "Oh, shit! Frank's headed this way! He's got a shotgun!"

Peabody had not counted on this development, and was struck with panic. There was only the one door, and Frank was rapidly approaching it. Certain death was closing in, but for some inane reason, Peabody had only one thought: *What would D'Artagnan do in such a situation?* An idea took root. The obvious solution squatted near the doorway. That bizarre vehicle, the Honda. Yes, D'Artagnan would ride that modern-day steed to freedom.

Peabody raced over to it, hopped on, and spotted a set of keys dangling in the ignition. Bubba and Sally Ann retreated to the rear of the stable.

The door of the stable swung open, and there stood a mountain of a man. The shotgun in his hand looked like a child's toy. Small mammals could have gotten lost in his beard. With his brow furrowed, Frank surveyed the stable. When he saw Sally Ann, his eyes seemed to glow with fire. "Sally Ann? Bubba? Either of you care to tell me what the hell's going on out here?" He glared at Peabody. "Who the hell is this guy?"

Before the two dimwits could respond, Peabody said, "I'm Jay Gatsby, with the Agriculture Department, here to inspect your barn."

Frank appeared momentarily perplexed. But suspicion quickly clouded his face once again. "And what exactly are you doing in my stable with my wife?"

"I'm sorry, that's out of my jurisdiction," Peabody responded. "However, I will need to take this vehicle for a test drive." With that, he turned the key. Amazingly, the vehicle jumped to life.

"Now hold it right there!" Frank shouted over the engine noise. "You ain't going nowhere!"

Peabody spoke loudly. "Just a quick trip around the property, sir. Bear with me. You *are* aware that the ozone output on these vehicles can't exceed 'E equals MC squared,' aren't you?"

"I . . . I don't . . . what the hell are you talkin' about?" Frank frowned and took a step forward. Peabody noticed that the man's finger was tightening around the trigger of the shotgun.

"Don't thank me, sir," Peabody yelled back. "Just your tax dollars at work!" Peabody started pulling on various levers, stomping on various pedals . . . and the vehicle shot forward—directly at the wall of the stable.

With Frank shouting angrily, Peabody braced for the impact, then busted cleanly through the dry cedar siding, and ducked low as the shotgun roared behind him.

CHAPTER TWENTY-SIX

"How far back you wanna go?" José Sanchez asked over his shoulder. Sanchez was the branch manager of First County Bank in Johnson City. Marlin was standing behind Sanchez's chair, both men eyeing the computer on the manager's desk.

"I'm not sure," Marlin said. "How about a year?"

"No problem. Why don't we go back two, just to be sure?"

Marlin nodded. He had spent half an hour on the phone this morning, calling employees of various banks in Blanco County. It appeared that Bert Gammel did all of his banking at First County. It wasn't much, though—only a single checking account. No savings account or CDs or any other type of deposit account.

The banker brought up Gammel's most recent bank statement. There was remarkably little activity, mostly small checks written to pay utilities, plus a small mortgage note written to a bank in Austin. There were only two deposits, identical amounts transferred electronically from a county account.

"That's his paycheck," Sanchez said, anticipating Marlin's question. "Direct deposit, twice a month."

"Not much of a balance, really."

The banker quickly navigated through several months of statements, none showing anything out of the ordinary.

"Can you tell me specifically what you're looking for?" Sanchez asked.

"Just any large deposit, probably in cash, in the last year or so." Marlin thought about the Ford Explorer Gammel had purchased with cash. A call to Kyle Parker, the owner of the car lot, had revealed that Gammel had purchased the car nine months ago. "Especially in the springtime," Marlin added.

But the statements showed nothing. According to the paper trail, nothing unusual had happened to Gammel's financial condition in the past two years. Just the same deposits made by the county like clockwork, the same checks written monthly to the same creditors.

Marlin was disappointed, but not really surprised, since Gammel seemed to have an affinity for carrying cash. He thanked Sanchez for his time and went outside to his truck. Next stop: a meeting with Maynard Clements, the county employee who worked most closely with Bert Gammel.

Red figured he could get used to this vice president stuff real quick. Here it was ten o'clock—a time when he'd normally be working his ass off in the brush—but instead, he was back at the Dairy Queen enjoying a couple of breakfast tacos.

He'd already spoken to most of the men on the work crews and told them what's what: that Slaton was gone and Red was ramrodding this operation now. Most of them hadn't even batted an eye. Of course, the majority of them were illegals and couldn't speak good English, so Red wasn't sure they had understood. But the important thing was, they were off doing the work while Red and Billy Don were sitting in air-conditioned comfort.

Last night, Red had told Billy Don everything the Austin lawyer had said. But he hadn't sprung the Big Idea on Billy Don yet—the major brainstorm that Red had had while lying in bed.

With Billy Don, you had to take things kind of slow or the big man would flip out. He wasn't a big-picture kind of guy like Red was. You had to work up to important stuff one step at a time. Hell, half the battle was just getting the man's attention, getting him to focus for even just a few minutes. It was like he had that attention-defecate disorder or something.

"I used to work here, ya know," Red said. "Back when I was a kid."

Billy Don nodded, unhearing, as he peeled back the foil from his fourth taco. The man could demolish a taco in two bites.

"I was the cook," Red continued. "Man, I only earned a couple bucks an hour, but I bet I ate twenty bucks' worth of food during every shift."

That caught Billy Don's attention, pulling his eyes from his taco for a second. "What, you just grabbed whatever you wanted?"

"Hell, yeah. A burger or two, a big order of onion rings, maybe a couple of corny dogs. And that was just the appetizer."

Billy Don searched Red's face for a lie. "Shee-yit."

"The God's truth. Hell, the owner was never around. He always left his twin daughters in charge." Red let out a whistle. "Good-lookin', too. I wonder whatever happened to those two. I used to call one Beltbuster and the other Hungerbuster." Red chuckled. Yep, those were the times.

Billy Don didn't respond.

"Don't you get it?" Red said. "That's what the hamburgers are called."

Billy Don glanced at the menu above the serving counter. "What'd they call you? DQ Dude?" Billy Don grinned, chunks of sausage caught between his teeth.

"Har-de-har-har," Red said. He watched an elderly couple trudge out the door to a waiting RV. Snowbirds, probably—Yankees carrying their tired asses down to the warm Rio Grande Valley for the winter.

Red waited until Billy Don had a mouthful of taco before he said, "Listen, we need to talk a little more 'bout that lawyer what called last night. See, there's somethin' that's gotta happen before the company is all mine."

"Like what?"

"Well," Red looked around the room, checking for eavesdroppers, "they gotta find the body," he whispered.

A confused expression crossed Billy Don's face and he set his taco down on a napkin.

"Relax, it's no big deal," Red said. "They just need to make sure Mr. Slaton ain't still alive. That lawyer would look like a reg'lar moron if he signed the company over to me and then Slaton showed up again, wouldn't he? On the other hand, it's a real pisser if you think about it. For instance, what if they don't never find the body? That's entirely possible, you know. Then where would we be? This thing could drag out for years—buncha lawsuits and torts and expositions. Now, that's something we'd all love to avoid, wouldn't we?"

Billy Don belched, loosing a torrent of noxious air in Red's direction. "What do you mean, 'we'? You got a mouse in your pocket? I don't see how this affects me none."

Red could tell from Billy Don's tone that the giant man was pouting a little. Hell, Red couldn't blame him. If the positions were reversed—with Billy Don owning the company—Red would fully expect Billy Don to share a little of his good fortune. More important, Red knew he would need Billy Don at his side in the days to come.

"Aw, now, you don't think I'm forgettin' about my best buddy, do ya?"

Billy Don stuck his bottom lip out a little but didn't reply.

"Well, hell, Billy Don, I was gettin' to that." Red stood up beside the booth and cleared his throat. "Ladies and gentleman, may I have your attention, please?"

There were only three other occupied tables in the restaurant: two sets of gray hairs and a trio of young punks who were likely skipping school. Red waved his arms with an elaborate flourish. "I'm pleased to present to you the new office management supervisor of Slaton Brush Removal, Incorporated." The retirees were happy to provide an arthritic round of applause. One of the schoolkids simply muttered, "Dorks."

Red could see that Billy Don was trying to stifle a grin, but it broke through anyway. "Come on, Red, sit down. You're 'barrasin' me."

Red sat back down and patted Billy Don on the shoulder. "Congratulations, big man. You deserve it. Now, for your first official act as office management supervisor . . ."

Billy Don had already gone back to his food.

". . . you're gonna help me look for Mr. Slaton's body."

Billy Don stopped assaulting his taco.

"And," Red said, "I got a pretty good idea how we're gonna go about it."

Sitting in his sedan near the sheriff's office, far enough away to be discreet, Smedley Poindexter munched a king-sized bag of potato chips and pondered recent events in Blanco County. The hostage situation had made the Austin newscast last night. Smedley had done a little checking into it, and had then stumbled upon a new missing-persons case: a rancher named Emmett Slaton. That was enough to put him back into his car early this morning, heading for Blanco County.

On the surface, there was no indication that Salvatore Mameli had had anything to do with the standoff or the disappearance of Slaton. But Smedley had to wonder. Too often, things seemed to "just happen" in the vicinity of guys like Mameli.

Smedley was proud to be a federal deputy marshal, but there were times when he felt somewhat guilty being involved with the witness protection program. Of course, some participants in the program were simply that: witnesses. Good people who were willing to stand up and do what's right, even though it meant placing themselves at risk.

But plenty of people in the program were criminals—evil, brutal, coldhearted men like Mameli—who had turned on their own kind and had no choice but to go underground.

And what does the federal government decide to do with men like that? Give them total immunity for their crimes, then relocate them to peaceful, suburban neighborhoods. So all of a sudden, the Joneses—a nice hard-working family with cute kids, a Labrador retriever, and a barbecue grill in the back-yard—have a murderer or drug dealer living next door. Worse yet, they have no idea who they're dealing with, and Smedley can't even warn them.

This wouldn't be so bad if the program worked the way it was supposed to. But too often, the recently relocated scumbag continues living the way he always has. He sets up shop, earn-ing a living the only way he knows how. Smedley often won-dered: Was the attorney general's office putting a dent into organized crime, or were they really just helping the mob set up branch offices around the country instead?

He'd discussed this with a couple of fellow marshals on one occasion. One of them was that asshole Todd. Todd listened to what Smedley had to say, then said, "God, quit your worrying. Go eat a Twinkie or something." He threw his arm in the air and made that familiar elephant-trumpeting sound. Everybody laughed, and Smedley even tried to join in.

But inside, Smedley was upset. So upset that he didn't go eat a Twinkie as Todd had suggested. He might have had a Ding Dong or two, but no, not a Twinkie.

"We clear on what I need you to do?" Sal asked, his speech slurred by the painkillers. He was home now, in his own bed, fading in and out of sleep.

Vinnie nodded, almost too excited to speak. He was seeing way more action than he ever had back in Jersey. This was fucking awesome. With his dad laid up, Vinnie was now more in charge of things than ever before. It was a rush.

"Yeah, yeah, Pop. Trust me, I won't let you down."

"I know you won't, Vinnie. You're a good kid." He patted Vinnie's hand, and Vinnie felt like he had just been blessed by the Pope.

As Sal nodded off, Vinnie's mind was racing. Oh man, the possibilities were just too goddamn cool.

The Blanco County Public Works Department consisted of eleven employees, but only two were project managers. One was Bert Gammel, the other was Maynard Clements. When Marlin entered the PWD offices in the courthouse, he found Clements—a gangly, bald man in his forties—sitting at his desk in a corner office, on the phone. Clements waved toward a chair, and Marlin took a seat. Clements appeared to be speaking to someone about road construction somewhere in the county. After a few minutes, he wrapped up the conversation and turned to Marlin. "John, good to see you. You doing all right?"

"Just fine, Maynard. How's the family?" Marlin remembered that Clements's wife had recently given birth to their third child.

"Oh, doing great," Clements said. "Have you seen the newest one yet?" He turned a framed photo on his desk in Marlin's direction. "Henry Stanton Clements."

"Good-lookin' boy," Marlin said.

Clements made a little more small talk, mostly about the lack of sleep in his household. "But I wouldn't change a thing," Clements said. "He's my first boy, and he's worth the four A.M. feedings. There's nothing quite like being a daddy, John. You oughta give it a try."

Marlin forced a smile, wondering if Clements was fishing for information about Becky. Clements had tried to set Marlin up with one of his sisters a few years back, a date that hadn't worked out too well. "I'm glad you're enjoying it, Maynard," Marlin said, deflecting the comment.

"Well, anyway." Clements took the hint and changed the subject. "What can I do for you? You still lobbying for more boat ramps out at the reservoir? I tell ya, I wish we had the budget for it."

Marlin leaned in a little closer, keeping his voice down. "No, actually I wanted to talk to you about Bert Gammel."

Clements looked confused. "Uh, no offense, but isn't that being handled by the Sheriff's Department? And I figured, with Jack Corey and this thing down at the courthouse . . ."

"Garza asked me to give him a hand. I'm just looking into a few things."

Clements nodded. "Hmm. That's interesting. Well, I'll help if I can, but I'm not promising much." He opened one of his desk drawers and came out with a pack of cigarettes. "You mind if we talk outside so I can grab a smoke? I'm trying to quit, but I haven't had much luck yet."

CHAPTER TWENTY-SEVEN

"Yeah, we're both project managers," Clements said, "but we really don't work together—uh, *didn't* work together—that often. See, most of the projects that come through our office can be handled by just one of us. I take care of most of the road-work, and Bert handled structures. Like when they expanded the sheriff's office last year, that was all Bert."

Marlin wiped his brow. It was humid as hell today, the temperature in the low eighties. Not a cloud in the sky. "But I'm sure you had a lot more interaction with Bert than the rest of the staff."

"Yeah, I guess I did."

"Then let me ask you: Did you notice anything unusual about Bert's behavior in the last few months? Any changes in his lifestyle?"

Clements's eyebrows climbed his forehead. "How do you mean?"

"Ever see Gammel with any large amounts of cash? Maybe whipping out a roll of bills to pay for lunch?"

Clements took a long drag on his cigarette and stared at the horizon. He finally exhaled and said, "You know, he did seem to have a little more money lately. Not that he was rolling in it or anything, from what I saw, but I know he wasn't griping about bills as much as he used to. And he bought that Explorer a while back."

"Any idea where he would have gotten the money?"

Clements rubbed a hand over his scalp. "No idea. Sorry."

Marlin felt as if he were groping in the dark. It was obvious that something strange had been going on with Gammel, but the facts remained elusive. Marlin was used to questioning poachers, who were relatively easy to figure out. Their motives were clear and their methods of operation rarely changed. This murder investigation, on the other hand, was like trying to grab a wisp of smoke.

Marlin tried a new tack. "Did he ever mention any run-ins with anybody? Maybe some bad blood with somebody else in town?"

"All that comes to mind about that is his feud with Jack Corey. He mentioned it a few times to a bunch of us in the coffee room." Clements sucked on his cigarette again. "I know Corey seems all easygoing and everything, but if you ask me, Corey's got a temper. At least from the things Bert told us. He said Corey pulled a knife on him once, out at the deer lease."

Marlin remembered what Lester Higgs had said about that incident: that Corey hadn't actually pulled a knife, but had been using it to field-dress a deer.

"And now with this thing at the Sheriff's Department . . ." Clements continued. "This whole mess is a damn shame. Bert Gammel was a good man."

There was a bright yellow sticker on Bert Gammel's front door:

STOP!
CRIME SCENE SEARCH AREA
ENTRY PROHIBITED
**Premises sealed by Blanco County Sheriff's Department
Violators will be prosecuted to the fullest extent of the law**

It was a run-down two-bedroom house, maybe forty years old, with cedar siding and a sagging roof. Marlin used the key Garza had given him and stepped inside. The front door opened into the living room, a small area with nothing but a ratty couch, a worn end table, and an old console TV—the big wooden kind they used to make. Nearly as old as the house, Marlin guessed.

Marlin stood for a moment, just looking and listening. He could hear water dripping somewhere, the refrigerator humming in the kitchen. The place smelled kind of funny.

He wasn't sure what he was hoping to find, so he began with a casual tour through the house. He discovered something right off the bat: Bert Gammel was a world-class slob. Crusty dishes were piled in the kitchen sink, the bathtub was pocked with mildew, and the sheets on his bed looked like they might just crawl away. Beer cans and fast-food wrappers were strewn on stained carpets throughout the house. The tiny spare bedroom looked to be a makeshift office, with a rusty metal desk against the wall, but clutter had taken over. Two old bicycles. A disassembled lawnmower that was leaking oil. A dozen boxes filled with old clothes. Six boxes of *Playboy* magazines, some from as far back as the 1970s. Everything had been opened and rooted through by the deputies. Marlin figured there were probably fewer *Playboy*s now than before the search.

Marlin was no neat freak, but he had no idea how a man could live like this. Coming home to a hovel like this would be depressing. And what about bringing a woman over? Either Gammel never did, or the kind of woman he brought home didn't care.

Marlin checked his watch—ten fifteen—then began a slow, methodical search of the contents of the house. He knew he was covering ground the deputies had already covered. But maybe they had missed something. By the time they searched, their minds already had been on Jack Corey. They had their man, and they had plenty of evidence to back it up. So they might have gotten a little sloppy.

As two hours passed, Marlin's optimism faded. He had

found some financial records in the metal desk, including a few
months' worth of bank statements, but nothing that shed any
light on Gammel's windfall. Marlin had spotted a pull-down
ladder that led to the attic. Nothing up there but spiderwebs and
rat droppings.

This just wasn't adding up. Gammel, according to witnesses,
had always lived from paycheck to paycheck. Then, suddenly,
he was rolling in dough. Surely there would be some kind of
records—if the money was legitimate. And if the money wasn't
legitimate, Gammel must have been dealing drugs or burglariz-
ing houses or something.

Or bribes. Maybe he was taking bribes.

The thought struck Marlin out of nowhere. Gammel super-
vised large building projects for the county. Plenty of private
contractors would want that kind of business, enough to pony
up some cash to secure the contract. It was nothing new: People
in Gammel's position were bribed all the time. But Marlin had
never heard of it happening in Blanco County. That was the
kind of thing that happened on the East Coast, where mob
bosses ruled the building industries with an iron fist. Try to
bribe someone in Blanco County and they'd look at you like
you were naked in church.

But still, it was worth checking into.

The standoff was seventeen hours old now, and Bobby Garza
was starting to get nervous. Jack Corey's behavior was becoming somewhat erratic, probably due to lack of sleep. Early this
morning, they'd heard him in there shouting, apparently at
Wylie; none of the deputies could make out what he was saying.
But when they called him on the phone, he seemed reasonably
collected. Not friendly, but not delusional or irrational, either.

Garza figured Corey's exhaustion was both a blessing and a
curse. If he nodded off, Wylie might be able to slip away or get
control of the gun. On the other hand, Corey might become ag-
itated, excitable, or violent. Garza decided to stick with the current plan, which was simply to wait. Sooner or later, Corey

would realize it was hopeless and give up. That was the optimist in Garza talking. The other side of his brain knew that Corey could kill Wylie—or turn the gun on himself. And the blood would be on Garza's hands. People would question his choices for the rest of his career.

At sunrise, some of the local volunteer firefighters had shown up with big thermoses of coffee, breakfast rolls, even hot eggs and bacon. Then they had erected a large canopy to give Garza and the deputies some shade. It was going to be a hot one for November. Texas weather could sneak up on you: cool and balmy one day, warm and muggy the next.

Most of the deputies were dozing in their cars or patrolling the perimeter, keeping curious locals and reporters away from the building. Garza was sitting in a chair under the canopy, his eyelids drooping, when he heard: "Sheriff Garza?"

He looked up to see an obese, friendly-looking man wearing a rumpled tan-colored suit. Garza figured him for media—probably radio, based on his looks. "I'm sorry, I have no comment at the moment," Garza said, rising. "And you're not supposed to be back here—"

The man surprised him by flipping open a badge. A U.S. marshal. "Smedley Poindexter," the man said, extending his hand.

Garza shook it. Pudgy, but firm. "Sheriff Bobby Garza. How can I help you? I hadn't heard the Feds were coming."

"Oh, this isn't official, Sheriff," the man said, his accent identifying him as a Central Texas native. "I work out of Austin, but I was in the area and decided to stop by and offer moral support. Tough situation you got here."

It struck Garza as a little odd that a U.S. marshal would drop by, especially since the standoff was not the type of thing that would ever fall under federal jurisdiction.

Garza gave Poindexter a quick recap of the events of the previous three days, starting with the discovery of Bert Gammel's body and the evidence that pointed toward Jack Corey. He noted that the man nodded approvingly when Garza described his strategy to wait Corey out.

"So you think Corey's good for it, then?" Poindexter asked, meaning the murder of Gammel.

"We're still waiting on the results from the DPS lab, but yeah, that's the way it looks. And I know I shouldn't infer anything from Corey's actions in there"—he gestured toward the building—"but it sure doesn't help his case."

Poindexter stared at the sheriff's office for a few moments. "You know Corey well?"

"Sure. He grew up a few years ahead of me."

"Any previous record?"

"None at all." Garza eyed Poindexter, who returned his gaze calmly.

"What about this missing-persons report? Man named Emmett Slaton?"

"What about him?"

"Any leads on that?"

Garza hesitated, feeling that he was being probed. These questions seemed like more than casual interest. "Nothing so far. Blood at the scene, but it was animal blood."

Poindexter raised his eyebrows.

"Slaton had a dog," Garza explained. "We're wondering if the dog might have been injured. There's nothing to indicate that anything happened to Slaton, other than the fact that we can't find him."

The marshal frowned, but remained silent.

"Look, Marshal Poindexter—"

"Call me Smedley."

"All right, Smedley. Is something going on here that I need to know about? I appreciate you dropping by and all, but it seems kind of strange. . . ."

The big man opened his mouth to reply, then seemed to reconsider. After a moment, he said, "I'm just checking into something, Sheriff. I'm working a confidential federal case and . . ." Poindexter appeared to choose his words carefully. "I just wanted to make sure it had no connection to all the excitement you're having around here."

"And?"

Poindexter shook his head. "I don't see any connection at all."

"Let me ask you something, Maynard. . . ." Marlin was back in Clements's office, just after lunchtime, Maynard sucking the last few drops out of a soft drink from Burger King. Marlin leaned in close again. "Anyone ever try to bribe you?"

Clements chuckled, then realized it was a serious question. "Not once in twenty-three years on the job. Nobody ever even hinted around it. I got a plate of chocolate-chip cookies from an old lady once," he smiled. "After we patched up the road in front of her house. That's about as close to a bribe as I ever got." Clements smacked his lips as if he was thinking about those cookies.

Marlin felt a little foolish. "Then I guess you never heard Bert Gammel mention anything along those lines."

"No, never. And, see, John, there wouldn't be any use in trying to bribe me or Bert anyway. We go out and solicit bids, but we're not in charge of awarding the actual contracts—the county commissioners are. Then we manage the projects after they've been awarded." Clements kicked his boots up onto his desk. "Hell, I wish someone *would* offer me a bribe. A big one. I got my eye on a new boat."

"You know, this is all your fault," Jack Corey said, rousing Wylie Smith from his nap. The deputy was stretched out on the couch, wrists still cuffed, his wounded hand heavily bandaged. Corey was back to his usual position: sitting on the floor, his back against the door.

Corey glared at Wylie, who didn't reply. In fact, the deputy hadn't spoken since Corey had imposed the "no-talking rule." Corey wondered whether he could get Wylie talking now.

"You just had to keep pushin' me, didn't you?" Corey continued. "But the thing you don't understand is, how can I confess to somethin' I didn't do?"

Wylie swung his legs around and sat upright. He stared into space, apparently groggy from the painkillers Marlin had brought in.

Corey tried to sound reasonable, tried to keep the threatening edge out of his voice. "You kept talkin' to me about tire marks and boot prints, but come on, that's pretty shitty evidence, ain't it? I'm not the only guy around the county with a Firestone tire and Red Wing boots."

Finally, Wylie spoke in a raspy voice: "Don't forget the tobacco spit. If you didn't do it, then the smartest thing to do is give up. The DNA evidence will clear you."

Corey snorted. "Yeah, right. I know what you're capable of. Hell, you pointed a gun at my head, threatened me with Death Row. Planting evidence would be no big deal for a guy like you."

Wylie shook his head, like he was talking to a slow child. That made Corey angry, but he swallowed it down.

Wylie said, "Now, tell me, where would I get a puddle of your saliva?"

Corey had an answer ready. "I done some thinkin' about that, and you coulda stolen a spitcan out of my truck."

"But I didn't even find the spit," Wylie said, his voice rising. "Marlin found it. I hadn't even gotten to the scene yet. Can't you understand that?"

"You coulda put it there earlier."

Wylie leaned back against the couch. Quietly, he said, "What you're talking about is crazy, Jack. If I framed you for Bert Gammel's murder, that would mean I probably killed him myself."

"How do I know you didn't?"

"You gotta be kidding me." Wylie shook his head. "I had no motive, for starters. I didn't even know the guy. And secondly, on the day Gammel was killed, I was in Austin with my wife. It was my day off. We spent the night with her sister. You're really grasping at straws here, Jack."

Both men fell silent. Corey felt so tired, so ready to give in. If he could just sleep for a few minutes . . . but he had to keep

Wylie talking. "At least tell me why you pointed your gun at my head. Don't you know a man can't think straight in a position like that?"

Wylie sighed. A few heartbeats passed and Corey thought the deputy wasn't going to respond.

"Well?" Corey said.

Wylie licked his lips and said, "Okay, I'm sorry about that. I really am. But when I'm investigating a guy for murder, and I feel like I have some solid evidence, I tend to go at him pretty hard. It's just my style. Let's say, worst-case scenario, you confess to the murder but you didn't really do it. We'd *know* that, because you wouldn't be able to tell us specifics about the crime scene. And if you *did* do it"—Wylie shrugged—"the gun is just my way of speeding things up a little."

Corey smiled at Wylie and rose off the floor. He walked to the table and stared down at the tape recorder that had been sitting there all along. Such an innocent-looking device. Last night, before this whole ordeal started, Wylie had wanted to record Corey's confession.

"Thanks, Wylie," Corey said. He reached down and pushed the STOP button.

Wylie was staring at him now, eyes bulging, mouth agape. Then his jaw snapped shut, like a dog trying to catch a passing fly.

CHAPTER TWENTY-EIGHT

"Feel like taking a ride?" Marlin asked. He was at a pay phone in Johnson City. One of these days, he'd break down and buy a cell phone. But for now, the department didn't require it and he didn't want one. What was the point? If something was really urgent, they could reach him on the radio. If it wasn't important, he'd rather not take the call anyway.

"Where to?" Phil Colby replied.

"The Hawley place."

"Swing on by," Colby said and hung up. Marlin smiled. His best friend was like that: always up for an impromptu ride in the country, no questions asked. Sheriff Garza wouldn't be too thrilled if he knew Colby was tagging along, but Marlin was feeling lost and needed someone to brainstorm with.

Thirty minutes later, Marlin and Colby found the gate unlocked, as Lester Higgs had said it would be, and Marlin steered his truck onto the Hawley Ranch.

On the ride over, Marlin had brought Colby up to date on the Jack Corey fiasco, including Marlin's reluctant entry into the world of homicide investigation. He described Gammel's mysterious supply of cash, then detailed his search of Gammel's house and his discussions with José Sanchez and Maynard Clements. This, Marlin said, would be his final effort: One last visit to the crime scene, a search for anything the deputies might have overlooked. After that, Marlin would have to pack it in, because there was really nothing more he could do for Jack Corey. Marlin was feeling a little silly, actually, like he was wasting his own time. Here he was, trying to find evidence that would clear Corey, when it was becoming more and more obvious that Corey was guilty.

But that's up to a jury to decide, Marlin reminded himself. *An investigation is only about finding evidence.* It was up to the district attorney, and then the jury, to decide what the evidence showed.

Marlin followed the dirt road to the southern end of the property and stopped his cruiser in the same place he had parked three days ago. Gammel's Ford Explorer was gone now, probably at the crime lab in Austin.

Marlin killed the engine and both men climbed out. It was quiet here, only a few birds chirping in the trees, no wind to rustle the leaves in nearby Spanish oaks. A few weeks from now, those leaves would turn a brilliant ruby-red and begin to drop from their branches. For now, they merely sagged in the unseasonable heat.

Colby surveyed the wooded area. "So . . . what exactly are we looking for?"

Marlin shrugged. "Hell if I know."

Colby smiled in return. "That's what I figured."

Marlin decided they should do another ground search, starting at the killer's hiding spot in the cedar trees. Native grasses, dry from the drought, crunched under their feet as they tramped through the brush. After fifteen minutes, they tried the same thing around Gammel's deer blind. All they found were the footprints of the dozen or so men who had reported to the crime scene on Tuesday.

"Strike one," Colby said. "Nothing doing on the ground search. What's next, Mannix?"

Marlin thought it over for a few minutes, then said: "Corey hunts with a thirty-thirty . . . and the deputies looked for a heavy bullet that drops quickly. Wylie says they even looked beyond where a thirty-thirty might drop, but . . ."

"They mighta been slackin' a little?" Colby interjected.

Marlin nodded. "Let's take a look around, thinking in terms of, say, a two-seventy. Something with a fast bullet and a much flatter trajectory."

Marlin led Colby to the cedar trees where the killer had hidden himself. They crouched down and got a clear view of the ladder to the blind, giving themselves a visual line-of-flight for the fatal round.

Colby spoke up. "See that one small tree back there, directly behind the ladder?—I think it's a mountain laurel. About a hundred yards past the blind?"

"Yep."

"That looks like the right path to me."

Marlin agreed, and they hiked to the mountain laurel. From there, they proceeded farther back into the brush, attempting to follow the path the bullet might have taken. It quickly became obvious that what Wylie had said was true: The area was just too heavily treed to expect success, no matter how accurately you calculated the trajectory. And, of course, the bullet had passed through Bert Gammel's body, and there was no telling how that might have affected its flight.

Still, the men combed the woods for thirty minutes, but to no avail. No telltale sign of splintered wood or any gouge in the underlying soil.

"Strike two," Colby muttered.

Marlin gave him a glare. "You're doing wonderful things for my confidence."

Colby shrugged. "Sorry, but it'd be a damn miracle if we found that round out here. Anyone tried a metal detector?"

Marlin blew out a heavy sigh. "Won't find lead. The brass casing, sure, but not the round itself."

"Okay, then. What's next?"

Marlin nodded toward Gammel's deer blind, and they

walked to the towering structure. Like most blinds, it was simply a wooden box on metal legs, with a welded ladder that led to a small door on one side.

"Cover me, hoss, I'm going in," Marlin deadpanned, and made his way up the twelve-foot ladder. He popped the eyehook on the door and swung it open. He had expected to see at least a few of the items typically found in a deer blind: a chair, for starters, along with some empty soft-drink cans, a jug of water, perhaps some food wrappers, or maybe a couple of hunting magazines. But it was completely empty. *Of course it is,* Marlin thought, realizing his oversight. Everything that had been in there would have been taken to the crime lab, too. It appeared the deputies had even stripped the carpet from the floor of the blind, leaving a rough coat of dried adhesive on the plywood subfloor. Marlin didn't even bother climbing into the blind, because there was simply nothing to inspect.

"See anything?" Colby called from below.

"Yeah, I got a severed head up here. Go get me a plastic bag, will ya?"

Colby chuckled. "I take that to mean 'strike three.'"

"Would you shut up with the—"

"Okay, okay. We'll call it a foul ball."

Marlin descended, and they retreated to his truck, where they pulled soft drinks from a small ice chest Marlin had filled earlier in the morning. They lowered the tailgate and took a seat.

"This po-leece work sure gives a man a powerful thirst," Colby said, and guzzled from a Dr Pepper.

"Don't it?" Marlin replied. He sipped from his own drink and surveyed the woods around him. "You got any bright ideas?"

Colby cocked his head to one side, thinking. "You could always beat a confession out of him. That's how some of those big-city cops do it on TV."

"What if he didn't do it?"

"Well, I guess you'd figure that out by the time you were finished, huh?"

Marlin rolled his eyes.

"Hey, man, I'm just kiddin'," Colby said. "This thing sure has you uptight."

"Something just isn't right with all this," Marlin said. "But I can't figure out what the hell it is." He finished his drink in silence, then stood and tossed the can into the interior of his truck. "Well, so much for this, then. You ready to head back?" he asked. Marlin had given it his best shot, tried to spot something that had eluded the deputies, but had come up with nothing. Probably because there was nothing to find. Jack Corey had shot Bert Gammel and was desperately trying to convince someone—anyone, really—that he hadn't done it. It was typical behavior for a lawbreaker. No matter what the evidence suggested, guilty men would profess their innocence until the end. It was as if they believed their sacred word should override the forensic science that pointed an accusing finger their way.

Strangely, Marlin felt a sense of closure. He could report to Garza now, tell him that all avenues had been investigated, and then put all this bullshit behind him.

"Ready when you are," Colby said, draining the last of his drink.

Both men were in the truck, Marlin about to turn the key, when they heard a familiar sound. It was the clattering of a deer feeder as it slung dried corn for three or four seconds, then went silent.

Marlin looked at Colby, who simply grinned. "You thinkin' what I'm thinkin'?" Marlin asked.

"That a cold beer sounds good?"

Marlin swatted Colby across the arm. "No, you dumb-ass. That nobody checked inside Gammel's deer feeder."

"Damn, I bet you're right."

Marlin maneuvered his truck through the brush and found the feeder in a small clearing fifty yards from Gammel's deer blind. The ground beneath it had been worn grassless from the hooves, paws, and claws of all types of wildlife looking for an easy meal.

It was a fairly typical feeder: a battery-operated motor and spinning plate attached to the bottom of a 55-gallon barrel that rested on three metal legs. Eight feet tall, from top to bottom. A drum like that could hold six bags of deer corn weighing a total of three hundred pounds.

Marlin backed his truck up to the barrel, donned a pair of latex gloves, then stood on the rail of his truck bed. Judging by the dust on the feeder lid, Marlin guessed that it hadn't been disturbed in quite some time. He removed the O-shaped locking ring that clamped the lid to the barrel, then removed the lid itself. He peered down into the feeder.

Deer corn has to be kept dry. If a little moisture builds up inside the feeder, a crusty cake of corn plugs the funnel at the bottom of the barrel. The spinning plate will rotate, but no corn will be thrown. That's why feeders are designed to be watertight. The corn—and anything else in there—is fairly safe from the weather.

And there was more in this feeder than just corn. Looking down into the barrel, Marlin could see a small bit of clear plastic jutting out of the feed.

"I've got something here."

He reached down, grabbed the edge of the plastic, and gently pulled. Up came a large Ziploc bag. Inside the plastic bag was a lumpy manila envelope, a small one, maybe six inches by nine. On it, in ink, were the initials *B.G.*

Marlin hopped down onto the bed of his truck, went to one knee, and placed the plastic bag on the floor. As Colby watched over his shoulder, Marlin eased the Ziploc open, slid the envelope out, and lifted the unsealed flap. The envelope was filled with cash.

Marlin felt invigorated by his discovery—for about ten seconds. Then he realized it didn't really change anything. They had an envelope with nearly three thousand dollars in it, but it didn't tell Marlin where Bert Gammel had gotten the money or why he had been so secretive about it. And it didn't bring Marlin any closer to proving—or disproving—Jack Corey's guilt.

Back in the truck now, driving off the ranch, Colby said, "What ya think Garza's gonna say?"

"I imagine he'll be glad we found the cash . . . but we already knew it had to be tucked away somewhere. For all we know, Corey mighta known that Gammel kept his stash somewhere on the deer lease, but he just couldn't find it after he killed him."

"It was still pretty smart of you, if you want my opinion. You figured out something that nobody else had. Not Wylie Smith, that's for sure."

Marlin gazed out the window at the passing scenery, gently sloping hills thick with cedars, elms, and half a dozen different types of oak trees. "On the other hand," Marlin added, buoyed by Colby's remarks, "I can at least send this stuff to the lab in Austin and see if they can tell us anything. You never know—" Marlin stopped speaking in midsentence. Something on his police radio had caught his ear.

He turned up the volume and was startled to hear the voice of Jack Corey. Marlin remembered that Corey had the run of the sheriff's office now, and was apparently broadcasting from the dispatcher's radio. Marlin pulled to the side of the road as Corey's plaintive drawl came over the airwaves:

> ". . . and I understand why you might think it was me. But you gotta remember that things aren't always what they look like. Take your boy Wylie here, for instance. I told y'all he held a gun to my head, but did anyone believe me? Hell, no. Well, screw it. . . . just listen to this goddamn tape before y'all make up your minds."

Marlin heard Corey fumbling with the microphone, and then the hiss of an audiotape. Corey's voice came on first:

> "At least tell me why you pointed your gun at my head. Don't you know a man can't think straight in a position like that? . . . Well?"

Then Wylie's answer . . .

> *"Okay, I'm sorry about that. I really am. But when I'm investigating a guy for murder, and I feel like I have some solid evidence, I tend to go at him pretty hard. It's just my style. Let's say, worst-case scenario, you confess to the murder but you didn't really do it. We'd know that, because you wouldn't be able to tell us specifics about the crime scene. And if you did do it—the gun is just my way of speeding things up a little."*

The radio went silent, and all Marlin could think to say was: "Way to go, Corey."

Phil Colby gave a low whistle. "Now, that's an interesting development, wouldn't you say?"

CHAPTER TWENTY-NINE

On Friday evening, Sal was sitting in the living room, his bum leg in front of him on an ottoman. Twenty-four hours since that skinny little tree-hugging bastard had broken Sal's leg, and he was finally figuring out how to manage the pain. This codeine was pretty good stuff—you just had to watch out how much you took, that's all. Sal had figured that out real fucking quick. It took the edge off the pain, but if you got a little too aggressive with it—say, like popping three pills instead of one—you'd find yourself in la-la land, chasing imaginary wildebeests, wearing a loincloth, all from the comfort of your own bed.

But a pill and a half worked just right, holding the pain at bay without putting Sal into a stupor. Last night had been a wild ride, one weird-ass dream after another. Stranger than any of the trips he experienced as a young punk, when he had occasionally indulged in a few of the drugs that members of his crew were selling. Kind of fun, but you had to keep a handle on that shit. Couldn't overdo it. Sal sometimes wondered if Vinnie ever took any drugs, but he figured Vinnie was smarter than that.

Speaking of Vinnie, Sal vaguely remembered talking to him earlier in the day, asking him to take care of some things. Sal couldn't remember exactly what he had asked him to do, but what the hell. Vinnie knew what to do. Didn't have to spell things out for him anymore. That was the good thing about having a son. You could teach him things, help him learn a few of the basics in life. Like throwing a curveball. Changing the oil in your car. Busting a guy's kneecaps.

Sal and the family had already eaten dinner, and Angela was doing something in the bedroom now. That's the way it was: If Sal was in his den, Angela would be in the living room. If Sal came into the living room, Angela would find a reason to go to the bedroom. Sal knew that Angela was pissed off at him about the whole Maria thing (who, by the way, he hadn't humped in several days, thank you very much), but he was noticing lately that she didn't even want to be in the same room with him. That's one angry woman, who can't stand the sight of her own husband. What the fuck were you gonna do?

Sal was flipping through the channels, not a goddamn thing to watch on TV, when the phone rang.

"Angela, you got dat?" he yelled.

No answer. The phone rang again.

"Angela! Maria!" Where the hell was everybody?

It rang again.

"Well, fuck." Sal leaned toward the end table and grabbed the cordless phone off its charging base. "Yeah?"

"Sal?"

"Who's dis?"

"Is this Sal Mameli?"

Sal paused. He didn't like unidentified callers. If one of his former colleagues ever managed to track him down, Sal figured he might receive a call like this one. And this guy here sounded like he was speaking carefully, trying to disguise his voice. But he didn't sound like a Jersey boy; more like some local yokel. "Maybe it is, maybe it isn't," Sal said. "Depends on what you want."

There was no answer, and Sal began to hang up. Then the caller finally responded. "I saw what you did with the body."

Sal's jaw dropped and his heart flopped like a fish on a dock gasping for air. He let a few seconds pass while he tried to get his shit together. Then he spoke again, trying to sound casual—and a little angry. "What the hell are you talking about? Who is dis?"

"I saw it, Sal. I saw where you put the body."

Sal managed to give a small laugh, one that he thought sounded believable. "Yeah, you keep saying dat, but which fucking body are you talking about? Jimmy Hoffa? Amelia Earhart? Who?"

Sal heard the caller take a breath, as if he were about to answer, but then the line went dead. Sal stared at the receiver, as if he could look through miles of telephone line and get a clear view of the man who had just called.

"Think it'll work?" Billy Don asked around a mouthful of beef jerky.

Red had just climbed back into his battered red truck after using a pay phone. Damn right, a pay phone. Red had seen enough of those criminal-type shows on TV to know better than to use his own phone. Never knew who might be listening in, who might trace the call. Plus there was regular old Caller ID. "He sounded pretty shook up," Red said. "Acted like he wasn't, but I could hear it in his voice. Guy was about to drop a load in his britches."

"So you still think it was him?"

Red nodded and scowled. "That's what I been tellin' ya, ain't it? Now pass me a beer." Billy Don dug into the ice chest on the floorboard and came up with a cold one. They had stopped by the grocery store earlier and stocked up on drinks, jerky, chips, donuts, and other snacks. Red figured it might be a long night, so he wanted to be prepared.

Red was kind of pissed that Billy Don kept asking him that question: *So, you think it was him?* Well, damn, of course he did, and he had already listed all the reasons why.

First, Sal Mameli had what the cops called a *motive*. That

meant he had a reason to kill Mr. Slaton. Mameli had been trying to buy up all the brush-clearing businesses in Blanco
County, Slaton's included. But ol' Emmett—from what Red
had gathered—wasn't playing ball. Red imagined that had
pissed Sal off pretty good.

Second, Red and Billy Don had seen Sal Mameli driving
away from Slaton's house in a huff, just a couple of days before Slaton disappeared. Coincidence? Hell no. So not only did
Mameli have a motive, he seemed to be hacked off at Mr. Slaton, too. Red had mentioned all of this to that deputy named
Wylie, the cocky son of a bitch, but the guy didn't pay much
attention.

And fourth, Mameli just *seemed* like one of those . . .
whatyamacallits—a *wiseguy.* A man that's connected to the
mob. No telling whether Mameli really was in the mob—and
Red doubted it since the guy lived in Blanco County, about as
far from mafia country as you can get. But that didn't mean
Mameli couldn't be just one of your garden-variety criminals.
And hell, everybody knew that your average Eye-talian American was nothing but a street thug. From what Red could tell,
watching cable TV shows, the wops who made it into the mafia
were just the ones with the biggest balls, the ones willing to
take the biggest chances. But none of them—whether they were
in the mob or not—could be trusted. Oh, sure, you had a few
exceptions to the rule. Real Italian heroes, like Sylvester Stal-
lone and Arnold Schwarzenegger. But Sal Mameli wasn't so-
phisticated like those guys. No, Mameli was a greaseball, and
he practically had *murderer* written on his face. But it seemed
like Red was the only person who had figured that out.

Red cranked the ignition and looked over at Billy Don, who
had already made a sizable dent in their food supply. "Goddamn, Billy Don, take it easy, will ya? That stuff might have to
last awhile."

Billy Don belched and blew the expelled gas in Red's direction. "What now, Red?"

Red rolled down the window as he steered his truck out onto
Highway 281. "Now we play a little cat and mouse."

Billy Don nodded seriously.

Red said, "Hey, Billy Don. Who the hell is Jimmy Hoffa?"

Sal Mameli had nothing to do with the death of the deer hunter, Bert Gammel. Smedley kept telling himself that as he munched a bag of honey-roasted peanuts. The sheriff had seemed confident that he had the right man, and that's why the suspect had taken a hostage. It all made perfect sense. Right?

Likewise, there was nothing to indicate that Mameli had anything to do with Emmett Slaton's disappearance, either. But Smedley was having a tough time convincing himself of that, too. A quick background check had shown that Slaton owned a number of businesses, including the largest brush-clearing company in the county. And it wasn't long ago that Sal had gone into that business himself. Way too much of a coincidence. It gave Smedley an uneasy feeling in his gut, worse than a large pizza with extra jalapeños.

That's why Smedley was once again sitting in his unmarked sedan, staking out the Mameli house. And that's why he was considering talking to the higher-ups in Austin, asking for a wiretap. That would be a big step, but Smedley thought it was warranted. In spite of what Sal Mameli had accused the U.S. Marshals Service of in the past (mostly because he was a paranoid son of a bitch), they had never tapped his phone since he had joined the program. They had had no legal reason to do so. But now . . .

Smedley's train of thought was broken as he saw a flashlight bobbing down the Mameli driveway. It might be Angela coming to get the mail or something. He had seen her and Maria pull in about an hour ago, right at sunset. As the figure crossed the street and approached his car, Smedley got a lump in his throat. It was Maria! Smedley quickly ran his tongue over his teeth to remove the peanut residue.

Maria leaned down to his window and said, *"Hola."*

"Hola, Maria," Smedley replied, feeling like a freshman in Spanish class.

Maria said something else that Smedley couldn't understand, but he was pretty sure he heard the word *comida* in there
somewhere. He shrugged and said, *"No comprendo."*

In the moonlight, he could see Maria's beautiful smile. She
said, "You like dinner?"

Ah, now he got it. Angela must have sent Maria out to invite
Smedley to supper. Smedley nodded and extracted himself
from the sedan.

Unexpectedly, Maria grabbed his hand and began walking
back up the driveway. Smedley tried not to read anything into
it. Maybe hand-holding was just a common courtesy in
Guatemala. He tried to focus instead on the wonderful evening.
Crickets were chirping, there were plenty of stars in the sky, the
temperature was in the upper sixties. But when Maria strolled
right past the Mamelis' house and continued to her small cottage behind the garage, Smedley broke into a sweat.

Marlin picked up a hamburger in Dripping Springs on the way
home from the lab in Austin. The lab technician, a quiet man
named Richard Fanick, had promised to work overtime on the
evidence Marlin had found. Fanick had said he might be able to
pick up some latent prints on the plastic bag, but the manila envelope was a little more iffy because it had been sealed within
the plastic bag. The humidity in the bag might have degraded
any existing prints.

Now all Marlin could do was wait.

He had stopped by the sheriff's office on the way out of town
and nothing had changed: Jack Corey was still holed up with
Wylie Smith and wasn't coming out anytime soon. Garza had
frowned when Marlin mentioned Corey's on-air announcement
earlier in the day. Marlin felt it was a clear indication that Wylie
was to blame for the standoff; Garza wasn't so sure.

"For all we know, Corey might have been holding a gun to
Wylie's head this time," Garza had said. "So that recording he
made doesn't prove anything."

Also, as Marlin had expected, Garza didn't say much

about the new evidence from Gammel's deer feeder. "Helluva job, John," Garza said. "Let's just wait and see if it tells us anything."

Driving in the dark now, Marlin continued west on Highway 290 and turned right on 281. Six miles to the north, he approached the edges of Johnson City, where a sign proudly proclaimed: HOME TOWN OF LYNDON B. JOHNSON.

A few hundred yards past the sign he passed a convenience store, where he saw a rusty yellow Volvo with its hood up. With all the hectic events in the past twenty-four hours, Marlin had nearly forgotten about Inga Mueller. He pulled in next to her car and saw Inga elbow-deep in the engine compartment. She was wearing snug blue jeans and a clingy green blouse. Marlin was surprised half the male population of Blanco County hadn't already arrived to offer assistance.

Marlin stuck his head out the window. "You need any help?"

She looked his way and grinned. There was a streak of oil across her forehead. "Can I borrow your gun? I want to put this damn thing out of its misery."

Marlin hopped out of the truck and walked to the front of her car. He couldn't remember ever seeing an engine actually appear *tired*, but this one was pulling it off. "I'm not sure we should waste a perfectly good bullet," he replied.

"Think they'd be mad if I just left it here? Maybe as a little gift from me to the county?"

"Cops might write you up for littering."

Inga shook her head in frustration. "One minute it runs just fine, then it won't start at all. Won't even turn over."

"Let me hear it."

Inga climbed into the vehicle and turned the key. Marlin didn't even hear a click from the starter. "You're not getting any juice at all from the battery," Marlin said. The symptoms reminded him of the problem he'd had with his truck the previous spring. He jiggled the Volvo's battery cables and, sure enough, found one of the clamps to be loose. "Hold on a second." Marlin retrieved a wrench from his truck and tightened the nuts on both clamps. "Try it now."

She turned the key and the car sputtered to life. "Wow," she said over the engine noise. "You're good."

"Lucky guess," Marlin said. "You just want to keep an eye on those nuts and don't let them get loose like that."

Inga killed the engine and stepped out of the car, wiping her hands on a rag. "Speaking of loose nuts, I want you to know that I'm really sorry about what Tommy did last night at my assembly. Getting in that fight . . . and then biting you like that . . ."

"And then escaping from custody," Marlin reminded her.

"Yeah, that too. It's just Tommy, you know? He gets all worked up about things and does some stupid stuff sometimes. He doesn't mean any harm."

Marlin tried to hold his tongue, but couldn't. "Inga, I'm not gonna sit here and debate his good and bad points with you, but when it comes down to it, he's a criminal. In a way, he's even worse, because he breaks the law and pretends it's okay since it's all for a worthwhile cause. He hides behind this false nobility, and I think that's total bullshit. He may have some sort of philosophical message he wants to deliver to the world, but he's going about it the wrong way. Tommy's taking the coward's way out. Anyone can vandalize a bunch of tractors or drive spikes into trees that are marked for logging. But it takes someone with real dedication to try and change things through the proper channels."

When Marlin was done, Inga stared at him but didn't reply.

He eyed the sparse traffic passing on the highway and leaned against the fender of his truck. After a moment, he said, "I'm sorry, I shouldn't have unloaded that on you. It's Tommy that needs a lecture, not you."

"No, you're right," she said. "Tommy takes things a little too far. And the thing is, it can be contagious. Like me shooting Rodney Bauer's truck. A few years ago, I never would have behaved that way. But Tommy has this way of getting *me* all worked up, of making me indignant about all the crappy ways people are mistreating our environment. But the other thing is, it's gotten where I'm not sure Tommy even does all these things

for"—she made quotation marks in the air with her fingers—
" 'the cause.' I think he does them at least partly because he
thinks it'll impress me. That makes me feel somewhat responsible for the things he's done." She reached out and caressed his
bandaged forearm. "And I wanted to apologize for that."

Marlin nodded, feeling like he may have come down on her
a little harshly. He also felt somewhat guilty for enjoying the
touch of her hand on his arm. "Don't suppose you've seen
him?" he asked.

"No, and I'm getting a little worried. After I heard the news
about him escaping, I went straight to the motel and waited for
him to show up. He never did." She tilted her head to catch
Marlin's eye. "I *was* going to call the police if he showed up,
you know."

Marlin held her gaze a moment longer than he meant to.
"Maybe we can reform you yet."

CHAPTER THIRTY

Red woke with a start, and it took a moment for him to remember where he was: in the darkened cab of his truck, parked on an isolated county road fifty yards down from the Mamelis' driveway. Next to him in the moonlight, Billy Don was snoring like a bloodhound with a sinus condition.

So far, the plan wasn't working. Here it was nearly two A.M. and there had been no activity whatsoever at the Mameli house. Nobody had come, nobody had gone. Maybe Red's phone call hadn't rattled Mameli as much as it had seemed. Or maybe Red's theory was all wrong and Sal Mameli had nothing to hide. *Shit. Depressing thought.*

The only strange thing Red had noticed was a gray sedan sitting on the gravel shoulder across from the Mamelis' mailbox. Maybe they had houseguests. Odd, though, because behind the trees that lined the street, it looked like the Mamelis owned four or five acres. Plenty of room for guests to park. The next driveway was another hundred yards beyond where Red was parked, so Red doubted the sedan belonged to neighbors.

Red amused himself for a few minutes by toying with his

Colt Python. It was a huge handgun . . . forty-five caliber. Would stop everything but a crazed elephant in its tracks. He popped the cylinder open and gave it a spin. Fully loaded with hollow-point bullets. He shuddered to think what a round like that could do to a human being.

After a while, though, he got bored. So he reached over and jostled Billy Don. "Wake up, goddammit."

A snore caught in Billy Don's throat and he produced a couple of phlegmy coughs. "What the hell? Time to eat?" he muttered, half asleep. A string of drool hung from his lips to the front of his shirt.

"You're nappin' on the job again," Red snapped. "You 'spect me to stay up all night while you get your beauty sleep? Though I won't say you don't need it."

Billy Don stretched his thick arms and yawned. "Anything?" he asked.

"Couple of trucks come by earlier. Probably poachers."

"Hell, that's what we should be doin', Red. Not wastin' our time on this wild-goose chase. Besides, I've gotta take a big dump."

Red sighed, trying to remain patient. Billy Don was always so shortsighted. *That's the difference,* Red thought. *Why I'm vice president material, whereas guys like Billy Don end up digging ditches for a living.* Red thought maybe Billy Don could learn something from this experience.

"You ever hear of a guy named Garwin?" Red asked.

"Steve Garwin? First baseman for the Dodgers back in the seventies?"

Red shook his head. "Naw, Charles Garwin. The guy what come up with the theory of revolution. See, his theory was pretty simple. Say you got two caveman hunters livin' on the savannas of Asia. One of 'em can run real fast, and he's good at chasin' down antelope. He can throw his spear real hard and he hits anything he aims at, because he practices a lot. But now, the second guy, he's kind of a slacker. He runs real slow and he don't practice with his spear. He's a damn lousy hunter, and he never tries to get any better. So tell me, which one of those guys is most likely to get eaten by bears?"

"Shut up, Red!" Billy Don growled, looking out the window.

Obviously, Billy Don didn't enjoy being compared to a dumb, slow hunter. "Don't get your panties in a wad," Red shot back. "I was just askin'—"

"Hush, I said! I heard something. Sounded like a car door."

Both men fell silent. In the distance, they heard the sound of a large engine roaring to life.

Maria was sleeping, but Smedley was awake. A wide-eyed, heart-fluttering, spirit-soaring, I'll-never-sleep-again kind of awake. He turned his head on the pillow and studied Maria's tender face in the candlelight. Such a gentle, caring soul. Smedley had never dared imagine that such a woman existed. And yet, somehow, he had chanced upon an angel. He had found a woman who overlooked the flaws—both in his physique and his character—or perhaps didn't see them at all.

Dinner had been fantastic. An authentic south-of-the-border dish, similar to the enchiladas from Smedley's favorite East Austin Mexican diner.

Dessert was even better.

She had taken his hand and led him to her bedroom. There, they joined together as naturally and seamlessly as a creek and the banks that it hugs. At first, she had seemed to understand his hesitance, his lack of confidence. And so she showed him the way. She guided his hands as he unbuttoned her dress, stroked his hair as he slipped her panties down her thighs. She then re-moved his clothes, slowly, with Smedley expecting her to pull back in disgust at any moment. But she never did.

Naked, Smedley feeling a remarkable lack of self-consciousness, they moved as one. She eased back onto the bed, and he followed, his body just inches from hers, like a shadow.

And Smedley was overcome with ecstasy as they began to make love.

For Smedley, the first stage was over abruptly, as soon as he entered her. But he was amazed at his own endurance. He never lost his stiffness, but continued, unabated, for . . . for what seemed like an eternity. Finally, Maria clenched his biceps with urgency, growled something beautiful in Spanish into his ear, moaned deeply, and then collapsed back onto the bedspread in exhaustion.

Just before she had fallen off to sleep, she had said, "You are very sweet man."

Smedley had discovered that she spoke some English, though not much. He had hardly heard her speak more than a few words during his visits to the Mamelis' house. As he lay in the dark, he was elated with the idea of learning Spanish. This wonderful creature was captivating enough, but imagine how close their bond could become when they could converse freely! It was almost more intoxicating than Smedley could bear.

He glanced at the clock on her wall. Nearly two in the morning. Thankfully, tomorrow was Saturday, and he could lounge in bed with Maria for as long as she would allow him to stay.

Smedley laid an arm across Maria's breast, and she murmured approval in her sleep. He stroked the hollow of her throat, and then gently lifted and studied the necklace around her neck. Angela Mameli had once mentioned that Maria made her own jewelry and sold some of it to small boutiques in Blanco and Johnson City. *Kitschy stuff,* Angela had said. *She takes all these throwaway items and makes them into something beautiful.* This particular necklace featured a strand of stones, what appeared to be granite or marble. Maria had probably picked the stones up on trips around the Hill Country, then painstakingly ground and polished each nugget into a gem.

There was something else hanging from the necklace, an object that had caught Smedley's eye earlier in the evening. But the light had been dim, and he had been understandably preoccupied. Now, leaning for a closer look, he saw what it was.

A spent shell from a handgun. That seemed odd.

Squinting, he could see the inscription on the butt of the shell: .35 AUTO S&W. Smedley had never even seen a .35-caliber handgun before, but he seemed to remember that Sal owned one, an old family heirloom. Sal had mentioned it over dinner one night: His grandfather had bought it when he immigrated to the United States, his way of saying, *There. Now I am an American.* Maybe Maria had found an old shell lying around. He'd have to ask her about it in the morning. Or *attempt* to ask her about it, anyway. With her poor English, she might not—

Smedley's train of thought was broken by a noise outside. Sounded like a car door, but he couldn't be sure. Then he heard the rumble of Vinnie's Camaro, and there was no doubt.

Where in the hell was Vinnie going at this hour of the night? Sure, Smedley might expect Vinnie to be *coming home* this late, but not leaving. With the recent events in Blanco County, Smedley realized he had no choice. He'd have to tail Vinnie and see what was up.

In bed, Sal Mameli could barely open his eyes. Was that Vinnie's car he heard? Could be. The kid was probably getting down to business, just like Sal had asked. Sal didn't want to know *how* the kid took care of the problems, just as long as he took care of them. It was nice to have someone he could rely on, someone who didn't question his orders.

Sal hadn't told Vinnie about the caller earlier in the evening, but wondered if he should have. Nah, probably better this way. He didn't want Vinnie to think he was totally whacked-out on painkillers—or losing his edge, getting senile.

I saw what you did with the body. What the fuck was that supposed to mean? Sal himself hadn't done anything with any body. Probably some asshole's lame idea of a practical joke. Nothing new. Sal had received some weird looks and some occasional muttered comments over the years in Blanco County. Even gotten a couple of prank calls, someone whistling the theme to *The Godfather*. Jerk-offs. Fuck 'em. They didn't know nothing. Sal had always been known for his nerves of steel, and he wasn't about to freak out over a little harassment.

Or what if I dreamed it all? Sal wondered as he fell back into a deep slumber.

CHAPTER THIRTY-ONE

Red had to make a decision. Would Sal Mameli be driving a souped-up black Camaro? Didn't seem likely, but that was what had just pulled out of the driveway. A real nice car, sleek and shiny, with tricked-out rims and a throaty-sounding exhaust. Red remembered that Sal had mentioned a son named Vinnie a couple of times. Seemed a lot more like the kind of car a kid named Vinnie would drive. Then again, maybe the son was in on the murder and would lead them straight to Mr. Slaton's body. Or it could be a trick. He and Billy Don would go high-tailing after Vinnie, then Sal would take off a few minutes later, free to do his dirty business without any onlookers.

"So what we gonna do, Red?" Billy Don asked as the Camaro's taillights faded in the distance.

"Let me think, dammit!" Red said, fidgeting with his keys. He needed a moment to think. His entire future came down to this moment. He could wind up as a local hero by helping the cops find the corpse. And that, in turn, would make him the owner of Slaton Brush Removal, Incorporated. If there ever was a time when he needed to think like a vice president, this was it.

"Better git if we're gonna git," Billy Don said.

Red peered down the Mameli driveway, trying to see lights at the house. Was Sal waiting down there somewhere, watching to see if Red took the bait? All Red saw was darkness.

He cranked the truck's big engine and took off after the Camaro.

Panting and already starting to sweat, Smedley trundled down the driveway as fast as he could, which really amounted to more of a fast walk. He could hear Vinnie's car rumbling down the county road, and he knew he'd have a tough time catching him. Two miles to the west, the county road teed into Highway 281. If Smedley didn't catch up before Vinnie reached that intersection, the kid would be long gone.

Smedley struggled to slip his jacket on as he walked, his ample gut jiggling, wishing he hadn't eaten so many of Maria's enchiladas.

Then he paused for a moment. What the hell was that? He thought he heard another engine. For a second he wondered if Vinnie was returning to the house. But no, he could tell it wasn't Vinnie's Camaro. It was a different vehicle, with an engine that sounded every bit as powerful—except that it needed a tune-up.

Vinnie could already feel the fucking adrenaline pumping through his system. That was something he had discovered about being a stone-cold killer. You could control the rush. You could shape it and mold it and make it work for you. He'd done it when dealing with Emmett Slaton, and he'd done it when he'd handled T.J. That was what made him different from some of the *cugines* back home, weaklings who didn't have the balls to do what needed to be done.

Prowling in the night like this, dressed in black, mentally prepping himself for action—it excited Vinnie, and his crotch stiffened as he contemplated his plan.

Then he noticed headlights in his rearview mirror, another vehicle maybe a quarter-mile back, coming on quickly. Oh, shit, it was probably that damn Smedley. When Vinnie had pulled out of the driveway, he had seen the marshal's car sitting on the shoulder of the road. But it had been empty when Vinnie's headlights swept over it. Or maybe Smedley had been napping in the backseat. Who the hell knows? The marshals were pretty strange fuckers, showing up when you least expected it, just hanging around, watching. They said they were guarding their precious witness; but wasting tax dollars, that's what it really was.

Normally, Vinnie didn't give a rat's ass what Smedley did. Hell, he could follow Vinnie around for days, who gives a shit? But not tonight.

Red caught up with the Camaro about a mile before it reached Highway 281, but now he had another concern on his mind. Headlights were bouncing along on the road behind him, gaining fast. Could that possibly be Sal? If sending Vinnie out first had been a trick, Sal would be stupid to show himself like that.

Smedley was pushing the cheap little sedan as fast as it would go, and now he had to ease up on the gas. He was forty yards behind an old Ford truck now, and he could see the taillights of Vinnie's Camaro about fifty yards ahead of the truck. The highway was seconds away.

Vinnie reached the highway and had to come to a stop as an eighteen-wheeler roared past. There was no need to rush now. Whoever was behind him—and it wasn't Smedley—was right on his damn bumper. Nothing to worry about, just some redneck's truck. Old and red and ugly. Vinnie thought he recognized it from around town, but he didn't know who owned it. Vinnie sat at the stop sign, idling, glaring into his rearview mirror. Looked like two guys back there, lurking in the dark.

Probably just some teenagers out for a cruise. Or it might be poachers. Hillbillies in Texas seemed to enjoy that sort of thing.

Then he saw Smedley's sedan pull up behind the truck. Oh, fuckin' great! So the marshal *had* been sitting in his sedan. The question was, was Smedley following Vinnie, or was the dumb-fuck simply heading back to Austin?

There was one way to find out.

"He's just sittin' there, Red."

"I can see that, doofus. What do you want me to do? Get out and knock on his window? Ask him where the body is?"

"Hell, I was just sayin' . . ."

A car pulled up behind Red's truck. "Shit, we got company," Red yelped.

Billy Don craned his head around. "It's that sedan from outside the Mamelis'."

Red peered into his mirrors and saw nothing but headlights. "Can you see who's in it? Is it Mameli?"

Billy Don twisted around in his seat. "Naw, it's just some fat guy in a suitcoat. He's—"

The Camaro gunned it and laid rubber out onto the highway, fishtailing left, then gaining traction and zooming off into the darkness.

Well, shit. Red's well-planned surveillance operation had obviously come to an end. Time to get serious. He popped the clutch, the truck's big engine gulping gasoline, and took off after the Camaro.

Smedley watched the two vehicles scream away and tried to steady himself. Who *were* those men in the truck? They might be Vinnie's friends, and they were all just heading out for a little late-night carousing. Could be as simple as that. But something nagged at him. The kind of friends Vinnie had wouldn't be driving a truck like that. He had another idea that spooked him, something almost unthinkable.

It was a long shot, but could those two guys be button men for the mob, trying to pass as locals? After all, a couple of hitters would stand out—well, as much as Sal did—if they arrived driving a Lincoln, wearing double-breasted suits.

They might have come to whack Sal, saw Smedley's car on the road, and decided to follow Vinnie instead. If they could manage to abduct Vinnie, Sal would do anything they asked, including having a sudden memory loss at the next trial.

Smedley gulped. It could all be happening right under his nose. Todd the Asshole would never let him live it down. Smedley could almost see his supervisor's report now: "The suspects initiated their operation while Agent Poindexter was having intercourse with the Mamelis' Guatemalan housekeeper."

Smedley stomped the accelerator—and the sedan lurched to a stall.

Creeping up to 110 miles per hour now, Highway 281 as straight as a ribbon in front of him, Vinnie was leaving the truck in his dust. And he couldn't even see Smedley's headlights behind the truck. Yeah, like either of those assholes ever had a chance against his Camaro. Another mile or two and he'd be long gone. The rednecks had surprised Vinnie by chasing after him, but the teenagers living out in the boondocks liked to get out on the roads and raise hell on weekends. Nothing else to do around this fucking county.

Two minutes later, Vinnie smiled as the truck's headlights faded from his mirror. A couple miles farther ahead he'd take a right on Miller Creek Loop, a narrow, curvy blacktop that wound north, back to Johnson City.

Red was pretty sure if he pushed his old truck any harder it might just come apart around him. It had been years since he had taken it up to a hundred miles per hour, and the thirty-year-old vehicle groaned in disapproval. Up ahead, the taillights of the Camaro were becoming two faint specks on the horizon. Red slapped the steering wheel in frustration, then eased up on the gas, dropping his speed to ninety.

He was feeling miserable. His first full day as a vice president, and already he was a failure. God, what a screwup.

Then it struck him. At first, it was merely a germ of a thought. Then, unlike many of his other thoughts, it sprouted into a full-blown idea. Hot damn, he had it all figured out!

A bodyguard! The guy in the sedan was Sal Mameli's bodyguard!

And when you're a thug like Mameli, who would be more likely to take care of simple tasks for you—things like disposing of a corpse—than your hired muscle?

"We got the wrong guy," Red muttered.

"We what?" Billy Don wailed, his arms still braced on the dashboard.

"We got the wrong guy!"

Smedley figured it was a lost cause. He had the gas pedal floored, but the sedan barely reached eighty-five. He crested a small rise and could now see a mile of highway before him. Nothing. Not another vehicle in sight.

But he pushed on anyway. The men in the truck—if they *were* wiseguys—might have Vinnie pulled over a few miles up the road. There might still be time for Smedley to catch them before they abducted Vinnie and took off again.

He covered the mile ahead and came to another small crest. He topped it—and what he saw next sent a thunderbolt of fear through his colon.

There, maybe forty yards ahead of him, was the red truck. It was parked broadside in the middle of the highway, a huge, steel, Detroit-made roadblock. It all happened so quickly, Smedley barely had time to react. He slammed on the brakes with both feet. From the corner of his eye he saw two shadowy figures standing on the median, waiting.

The men from the truck. They had outsmarted him.

Maybe that's why they called them *wise*guys.

Smedley closed his eyes and waited for the impact.

CHAPTER THIRTY-TWO

Inga lay in bed and watched the digital clock on the nightstand. She was certain more than sixty seconds had passed, yet the clock still read 2:59. It was kind of stuffy in her hotel room. She considered turning on the air conditioner to help her sleep. Finally, anticlimactically, the clock flipped to 3:00.

She was worried about Tommy. Somewhere out in the darkness, he was roaming the Texas Hill Country in handcuffs. Poor little guy probably hadn't had a meal since before the town assembly on Thursday evening. Now it was almost dawn on Saturday.

And there were coyotes in this part of the country, right? She was pretty sure there were, because—my god—they even had them in New York City now. She could almost picture Tommy unconscious at the bottom of a ravine, curious coyotes nearby sniffing the air, drawing closer and closer.

She had a thought that made her smile: If one of the coyotes bit Tommy, he'd probably bite it right back. Send it yelping into the night with its tail between its legs.

Tommy, for all his faults, had a fierce determination about

him. He was unwaveringly committed to what he thought was right. Yes, part of his motivation was his love for Inga, she knew that much. Inga felt certain, though, that he'd still be pursuing the same causes even if she weren't by his side.

The truth was, he was a good man.

That's why she felt guilty that her mind kept wandering away from Tommy and his predicament. For a few moments, she would lie in the dark, trying to focus on Tommy—and whether or not he might fit into her long-term plans for life. But then her mind would slip off in another direction and she would find herself thinking about the game warden, John Marlin.

She found herself wanting to be in his company, to have deep meaningful conversations well into the night. And yes, she found herself wanting him on the most basic level. It wasn't because of his looks: Sure, he was handsome, but not in a leading-man kind of way. It was something beyond that. Maybe it was his sense of confidence, or the honest, straightforward way he dealt with the world around him.

Really, who knew what caused one person to be attracted to another? If someone had said, *Inga, you're going to meet a game warden in Texas and want to rip his clothes off, then make him dinner afterwards,* she would have laughed. Inga Mueller dating a law enforcement officer from Texas? Wanting to feel his big, strong arms around her, making her feel safe and loved and adored? Sounded like some corny movie. The kind that sets the women's movement back with every showing. Gag.

She decided to take her mind off things by watching TV. As she reached for the remote control, she heard a noise outside her room. Kind of a scratching, like tree limbs across a window. Not the window by the front door, but from the window in the adjacent wall.

Chuck's Motel was a long concrete-block building with six units in a row. Inga was at the end of the line—room 6—at the opposite end from the office. She had requested it for privacy, which was a waste of time, really, because the only other lodgers were a friendly retired couple in room 1—Mel and Lydia from Detroit, whom she had met briefly a few days ago.

The motel was several blocks off Highway 281, away from the well-lit town square. Back here on the side streets, with Tommy gone, it was easy to get lonely. And a little spooked.

The scratching came again.

"Tommy, is that you?" she called out.

No answer. Inga thought Tommy might be trying to get her attention without going to the door. Deputies still cruised the parking lot every few hours, hoping to catch Tommy coming back to the motel. Where else could he go?

But the truth was, you could hardly go anywhere in Johnson City without seeing a cop right now. The small town was like a beehive, with city, county, and state units coming and going all the time. All because of the hostage situation at the sheriff's office only four or five blocks away. Then again, everything in Johnson City was only a few blocks away. When Inga had first arrived in town, she couldn't believe how small the—

She heard it again. Another scratch at the window.

Inga slipped out of bed and stepped over to the wall. "Tommy, dammit, is that you? You're scaring me. Just come to the front door."

Maybe there *was* a tree or bush just outside the window swaying in the wind. But she knew it was too dark on that side of the building to see anything . . . and, to be honest, she didn't really want to open the curtains to take a peek.

She stood in silence, her ear pressed against the wall, waiting for another scratch. She watched the digital clock as one full minute passed, then two more. She breathed a little easier. It was obviously nothing. She was acting like a schoolgirl.

Then another noise came, an urgent rattling and slapping of aluminum against glass. Inga stifled an urge to scream. Somebody was just outside the window, removing the screen.

"Tommy!" she yelled. "Dammit, answer me!"

The noises ceased, but there was no reply. Clearly, whoever was outside, it wasn't Tommy.

Inga turned to call 911—and remembered with a sudden

panic that the room had no phone. When they had checked in a week ago, the stooped, gray-haired owner had said, *There's a pay phone just outside the office if you need to make any calls. Ice machine right 'round the corner.*

Inga suddenly felt extremely vulnerable wearing nothing but panties, so she quickly donned a T-shirt and jeans. Then she surveyed the sparsely furnished room for anything she could use as a weapon. There were a couple of wooden clotheshangers in the closet. The drinking glasses in the bathroom were, unfortunately, made of plastic instead of real glass. Then she remembered she had a can of pepper spray in her purse. Wasn't much, but it was better than nothing.

She dumped the contents of her purse on the bed and quickly sifted through the pile—when she heard a gentle knock on the door. From the other side came a whisper: "Hey, it's me. Let me in."

Inga blew out a sigh of relief and walked to the door. "Tommy, you jerk, why didn't you answer me earlier?" Her hand went to the dead-bolt lock, but she waited for Tommy to reply. Silence. "Tommy?"

Then, in a barely audible voice: "Yeah, it's me. Open the door!"

The voice was faint, but it *sounded* like Tommy. Who else would it be? She felt silly for letting herself get worked up. Just to be sure, she put her eye to the peephole—and saw nothing but the parking lot. She moved to the window and parted the curtain slightly. Nobody out there. "Tommy! Where'd you go?"

Once again, silence.

Boy, he must really be worried about getting caught. Probably hiding behind a car. She slid the chain off its track, slowly turned the knob, and eased the door open. She poked her head outside and, in a louder voice, said, "Tommy, quit screwing around. Get in here!"

She saw a shadow move. Across the parking lot, behind a tree. She stepped out onto the concrete walkway in front of the room. "Very funny. Would you stop with the bullshit?" She

glanced left and right, then took a few steps and stood beside
her Volvo. The shadow seemed to have vanished. Or was that
someone peeking out at her?

"Tommy?"

Right behind her, a voice said, "Expecting someone?"

Smedley could tell that he was lying on something hard, like a
floor, rather than a bed. It felt like there was a wet cloth across
his forehead, and his head was throbbing with each heartbeat.
He had a hell of a headache. He got those sometimes, from too
much sugar. Almost enough to make him cut down on the
Twinkies.

He heard voices, far off, maybe in another room. He wanted
to speak up, ask somebody where he was, but he didn't have the
energy. He couldn't open his eyes, either; he seemed to have
forgotten how. One of the voices was speculating that "Maybe
the guy needs stitches," with the other saying, "Naw, he'll be all
right." Smedley wondered who they were talking about. Some
poor guy had gotten injured. But he couldn't worry about that
now. He had to go back to sleep.

Smedley awoke again, maybe five minutes or five hours later,
and this time he seemed to remember a car wreck. Had he been
involved in a collision? He tensed for a moment. Had Maria
been with him when it happened? He couldn't remember. . . .
probably not. Where would they have been going? No, most
likely he had been alone. He recalled lying in Maria's bed, then
leaving for some reason. What was it? Something to do with
Vinnie—having to follow Vinnie.

With a massive effort, he managed to lift his eyelids. He was
staring at a pair of fluorescent lights on the ceiling. Everything
was foggy, but the lights were bright enough to make him
squint. He tried to lift a hand to rub his eyes clear, but his arms
were immobile.

He drifted again. . . .

· · ·

He had hit that red truck, that's what it was. He remembered that now. The wiseguys had tricked him, parking right in the middle of Highway 281. Shit, they had almost killed him. His head was pounding and he figured he must have slammed it against the steering wheel. What the hell had happened with the airbag?

He groaned and opened his eyes. Still a little muddy, but much clearer than before. He tilted his head to the left and saw two desks against a wall, with several filing cabinets between them. To the right he saw a leather sofa. Above the sofa, on the wall, were several plaques and certificates, one of which read, BETTER BUSINESS BUREAU.

Two figures stepped up and loomed over him. The hit men. One was a big guy, maybe six and a half feet tall, built like a nose tackle. Smedley could relate. The other guy was of average height—slim. Both with four or five days' worth of facial hair, wearing ballcaps with logos on them, work shirts, and blue jeans. Smedley instinctively noted all of this in about two seconds, and he felt reassured that his skills of observation were intact. His vision was blurry, but his thinking was fairly clear.

He tried to lift a hand to probe the injury on his forehead, but his wrists were bound together. He raised both arms and saw that they were lashed with duct tape. He attempted to reach a sitting position, which was futile, because he hadn't done a sit-up since the elder Bush was president.

"Easy there, pardner," the slender man said. "You ain't goin' nowheres anyhow."

Smedley eased his head back onto the floor. "Water?" he croaked. His mouth felt like someone had swabbed it dry with cotton.

The smaller man nodded at the big man, who left the room and returned with a small Styrofoam cup. He bent down and helped Smedley take a few small sips at a time. Eventually, the cup was empty.

"Want some more?" the big man asked.

Smedley shook his head slightly, wary of worsening the pain in his skull.

"Okay," the smaller man said, obviously the leader of the two. "Now that we got that out of the way, let's get down to business."

Smedley was surprised by the two men's accents. He had expected them to sound like typical East Coast thugs, but their drawls were as Southern as his own. Maybe they were Texans. Could be freelancers.

The leader put his hands on his knees and leaned over Smedley. "Now, ladies and gentlemen, here comes the sixty-four-hundred–dollar question: Where is it?"

"Where is *what*?" Smedley replied, immediately regretting it. Better not to answer so quickly, until he got a feel for the situation.

The man shook his head and flashed a smile. "I just knew you were gonna say that. But see, we're all prepared for that. My friend here . . ." He jerked a thumb in the direction of the nose tackle. ". . . he's an expert in subtracting information from people."

This was news to the big guy, judging from the fact that he looked around for whomever the smaller guy was referring to, then gave a *Who me?* gesture.

"So," the leader said. "We can do this the easy way or the hard way. But either way, we're gonna find out what you did with the corpse."

Now Smedley was really confused. Had something happened that he was forgetting about? Maybe he had taken a worse blow to the head than he thought. Was he suffering from amnesia?

He didn't know what else to say, so he said, "What corpse?"

The leader slowly shook his head back and forth. "So that's how you want to play it, huh?"

But Smedley couldn't reply. He felt himself losing consciousness once again.

CHAPTER THIRTY-THREE

Inga gasped as she turned—and found herself staring into Tommy's smiling face. She threw her arms around him in relief, then chastised him for giving her a scare: "Why didn't you answer me when I called out your name?"

He gave her a peculiar look. "What are you talking about? I just got here."

Inga smiled. "Very funny, but I'm not falling for it."

"I swear, Inga."

She shook her head. "Whatever. You've already freaked me out enough tonight. Now we'd better get inside before someone spots you."

Tommy shrugged and followed her into the motel room. She closed the door, and neither of them was prepared for what happened next.

A dark figure wearing a ski mask and gloves emerged from the bathroom carrying a baseball bat. "We having a little party here?"

Tommy looked at Inga, who had grasped his arm in alarm.

With amazing quickness, the man stepped forward and slammed Tommy over the head with the bat. Without so much as a whimper, Tommy collapsed to the floor.

Inga screamed, but the sound was choked off as the man sprang on her and wrestled her to the bed. He placed a hand over her mouth, and she could see his dark-brown eyes gleaming inside the mask.

"You got a lot of balls, you know that?" the man grunted on top of her. "You and your friend there. How come you gotta cause so much trouble?"

Inga struggled to break free, but the man held both her wrists with one viselike hand. He squirmed until he had her legs apart. "I'm real good at taking care of bad little girls like you," the man said.

Horror gripped Inga's gut as he pressed his crotch against hers and she felt his hardness.

"What we gonna do now, Red?"

They were in the kitchen of the small mobile home on Emmett Slaton's property, the official headquarters of Slaton Brush Removal, Incorporated. Red had a clear view of their chunky prisoner lying on the floor in the adjoining room. The guy was still sleeping like a coonhound after an all-night hunt.

Red took a sip of coffee. Setting up here had been a good idea. Almost as cozy as home. Except he had forgotten to bring a bottle of booze, maybe some Wild Turkey or something. Other than that, Red had prepared himself for a long night. Tough guys—like hit men and bodyguards—they don't just talk when you tell 'em to. You gotta put the squeeze on 'em a little. At least, that's the way they did it on *The Sopranos*. That was Red's favorite show, ever since he had run a wire from his unsuspecting neighbor's satellite dish. "He'll talk," he said. "Just give it time."

Billy Don removed his cap and ran a hand through his matted hair. "I don't know, he seems pretty out of it."

"Aw, hell, he just got himself a small percussion when he

whacked his head. He'll come 'round. What choice does he got? We'll just hold on to him till he spills the beans. Then we'll turn him over to the cops. Be heroes, that's what we'll be. Get a big write-up in the newspaper and all. They might just give us a goddamn parade before it's all over."

Billy Don's eyes lit up. Red knew Billy Don was a sucker for parades, because parades were the adult version of playtime—with beer-drinking to boot.

The prisoner—they had no name for him yet because he hadn't been carrying an ID—stirred on the floor. Red and Billy Don walked back into the office and stood over the prone figure.

"Wake up, sleepyhead," Red said. "Time to tell us all your little secrets."

The man glared up at Red. "Where am I?"

"That's not important," Red said. "What's important is that you start cooperating. Believe me, it'll be better for you in the long run."

The man groaned and his eyes fluttered. Red knew he had to keep talking to keep the man awake. "So, hey," Red said, "we'll start with something easy. Like your name."

The man said something Red couldn't understand. Sounded like gibberish. "Come again?"

"Smedley Poindexter. That's my name."

Red looked at Billy Don, and they both grinned.

"Like the elephant," Billy Don said with confidence.

Red frowned, puzzled.

"You know. On the Cap'n Crunch cereal boxes—Smedley."

Red dismissed Billy Don with a wave of his hand and turned back to the prisoner. "But seriously," he said. "Your real name."

"That *is* my real name, you asshole."

Red fluttered his hands with sarcasm. "Ooh, gettin' a little feisty, ain't we? All right, then . . . Smedley. Tell us what you do for Sal Mameli. What would you say is your basic job description?"

After a pause, the man said, "I don't work for Sal Mameli. I'm . . . I'm a United States deputy marshal."

Red and Billy Don exchanged glances again and Red let out

a snort. "Yeah, and I'm ol' . . . what's'ername . . . Reno? The big, tough-looking broad?"

"She used to be my boss, kind of," the man said. ". . . . Er, one of my bosses, anyway." Red leaned over the man calling himself Smedley and could see that his eyes were clearer now. He was slowly regaining his senses.

Red decided to play along. "Tell me something, Smedley. Did Miss Reno ever cop a feel from you when you was working late one night? Anything like that? Because I always had the feelin' she swung the other way, if you know what I mean."

"I never met her directly. She was the attorney general, so she oversaw certain divisions of the U.S. Marshals Service. She worked out of D.C., I worked out of Austin. I never even saw her."

Red wasn't sure what to say to that. The guy sounded pretty read-up about how all that political crap worked.

Billy Don pulled Red to the side and spoke quietly. "Uh, Red. You know, he sounds pretty damn convincing."

"Yeah, so?"

Billy Don held his hands in front of him, palms out. "Well, don't call me stupid or anything, and I know this sounds crazy . . . but what if he's tellin' the truth? Seems like we might could get in a little trouble for all this."

Red rolled his eyes. "Jesus, Billy Don! Don't be a dumb-ass. If he's a gen-yoo-ine U.S. marshal, then where the hell's his badge?"

They turned and looked at their prisoner for a response. "I . . . uh . . . think I left it somewhere. It must have fallen out of my pants."

Red placed his hands on his knees and leaned over the man. "Well, then, I'll make you a deal, Smedley. You tell us where your badge is, then we'll go get it and clear all this mess right up. How's that sound?"

The man didn't reply.

Red cupped an ear. "I can't hear you, Mr. U.S. Marshal, sir. Cat got your tongue?"

"I can't . . . tell you where it is. I can't."

Red stood up straight again. "That's what I thought."

•   •   •

Inga Mueller had always considered herself a tough customer, an independent woman who could handle herself in tight situations. Whenever she heard about a woman being assaulted, she would always visualize how she would respond: with a knee to the groin, a sharp fingernail in the eye, or a good strong bite to any part of his anatomy where she could plant her teeth.

But now she was about to become the victim, and she could feel herself surrendering, mentally withdrawing—as if she could retreat into a quiet place inside herself, away from the horrid violation that was about to take place.

With his free hand, the attacker ripped the front of her T-shirt open and began to paw roughly at her breasts. Inga thrashed and struggled, but it was useless. He was simply too overpowering.

She began to sob, and she hated herself for it.

The man fumbled with her jeans but couldn't get them unsnapped. Inga knew he would have to use two hands to unclothe her, and when he released her wrists, she might have a chance to fight back. For a moment, Inga clung to that small fragile hope. But then the man produced a knife from one of his pockets—a switchblade—and the sharp steel sprang from the handle. He held it at her throat, pressing firmly. Inga was afraid to even breathe, fearing she would draw her own blood.

"Don't move a goddamn muscle," the man said. He rolled to a position next to her on the bed and ordered her to remove her jeans. Inga closed her eyes and ignored his command—but then felt the edge of the blade digging deeper into her throat. "Take off your pants! Now!"

Inga did as she was told, her mind spinning, desperately searching for a way out of this nightmare. She had an impulse to scream, but was afraid it would only anger her attacker—and nobody would hear her anyway. Likewise, there was nothing nearby that could serve as a weapon. She had no options at all.

She slid her jeans down to her ankles and the attacker yanked them the rest of the way off, holding the knife in place.

Then he slid the blade up the outside of her right hip and sliced the waistband of her panties. He did the same thing on her left hip and Inga was now totally vulnerable.

The man forced himself between her legs again and kneeled upright before her, the knife just inches from her torso. "Now, unbutton my fly," he said.

Inga hesitated and the man growled at her: "Unbutton it!"

With trembling fingers, Inga reached and unsnapped the man's black pants. The man began to slide his pants down his hips, and Inga closed her eyes again.

"Grab it."

For a millisecond, Inga thought she had misunderstood him. Had he just said, *Grab it?* That couldn't be right. He couldn't possibly be that stupid. Sure, he had a knife, but if she had a hand in the right place, there was no telling what kind of damage she could do.

Using her left hand, her weaker one, she reached up and—with the greatest disgust she had ever felt in her life—grabbed his stiffened penis.

"There now, that's not so bad, is it?" he whispered.

Inga gave it a small stroke, and the man moaned approvingly. "Okay, good. You're getting into it now. I thought you'd come along."

Inga glanced at the knife in his left hand. He was holding it a little more loosely now, the tip no longer pointing in her direction.

Gritting her teeth, she gave the man another stroke. He moaned again, and his jaw slackened. She looked through the slits in the ski mask and could see that his eyes were closed.

Inga knew it was now or never, that this would be her only chance. If she didn't take this opportunity, she would never forgive herself.

She moved both hands quickly. She shot her right hand out and clasped his left wrist as tightly as possible, hoping to keep the knife away from her.

Simultaneously, she slipped her left hand around the man's testicles—and gave them the hardest, most vicious squeeze she was capable of. Not just a firm squeeze, but a *milking Uncle Bill's most stubborn cow back in Minnesota* type of squeeze.

The howl that erupted from the man's belly was amazing.

The knife dropped to the bed beside her, forgotten. Both of his hands circled her left wrist, trying to get her to release his family jewels. But the more he pulled at her arm, the more she tightened her grasp.

His screams of anguish were earsplitting now, bouncing off the walls of the small hotel room.

Then something happened that left Inga momentarily confused. She heard a tremendous crashing sound, and then felt several small stinging sensations on her face and torso. The attacker collapsed on top of her, then rolled off the bed, wailing in agony, arms wrapped around his head.

At the foot of the bed was Tommy. Staggering, but on his feet. Holding the remains of the ceramic lamp he had just smashed over the attacker's head. A mask of blood coated his face.

The attacker struggled to his feet, pulling up his pants, and the men squared off in the center of the room. Both were hunkered low, exhausted and in pain, like two bone-weary boxers in the final round.

Tommy threw a looping right hand and missed, and the masked man got him in a headlock. But Tommy drove an elbow into the man's sternum, and Inga could hear the air whoosh out of his lungs.

Inga grabbed the knife and vaulted off the bed, preparing to drive the knife deep into the man's back.

That's when there was a loud pounding at the door.

"You okay in there? I called the cops!" It sounded like Mel, the elderly man from room 1.

Now the attacker moved quickly, shoving Tommy out of the way and yanking the door open. Inga saw Mel standing outside, eyes wide. The would-be rapist sprinted past him into the darkness.

Tommy quickly grabbed the blanket off the bed and wrapped

Inga in it. She blubbered a thank-you over and over, and Tommy whispered quietly in her ear and tried to console her.

"It's all right now. . . ." Tommy said to Mel, who was standing in the doorway: "Thanks for your help."

"You sure?" Mel asked, looking suspicious.

Inga nodded. "Thanks, Mel. I'll be okay.

Mel shook his head and said, "Came to Texas, thought we'd be getting away from all the crime." Then he shuffled back to his room.

"Are you okay?" Tommy asked, surveying Inga at arm's length.

She nodded. "Scared the pee out of me."

"Any idea who it was?"

"None whatsoever. But the things he said . . . he knew who I was. It wasn't random."

Tommy cocked his head. "Sirens! I have to get out of here."

"Tommy, you're kidding me. It's time to call this off. Let's get your problems cleared up and get out of town."

"After this? But then they'd win, Inga. That was obviously someone trying to dissuade us from protesting."

"And he did a damn good job of it! I'm ready to go home, Tommy."

The sirens were coming closer.

Tommy leaned in and gave Inga a kiss. "Don't stay here, Inga. Go with the police. They'll take care of you. I'll be in touch when our work is done."

"But, Tommy . . ."

He was already out the door.

CHAPTER THIRTY-FOUR

Marlin was up and out of the house by five Saturday morning. It was deer season, after all, and he was determined to get back to his regular routine. He would patrol for several hours, then call Austin to see if Richard Fanick, the lab technician, had anything for him.

Marlin made a large loop around the county, stopping at hunting camps and deer leases along the way. He cruised north on Highway 281 to Round Mountain, west on 962, south through Sandy, and on down to Blanco. Then northeast through Henly and up to Pedernales Reservoir.

He wanted to check in with Bobby Garza to see if there had been any progress made with Jack Corey, but he decided to swing by his house first and make a call. Almost eight o'clock. Maybe Fanick would be in his office by now.

Back at home, Marlin poured himself a to-go mug of coffee and tried calling Fanick. He got routed into voice mail and left a message. It was the weekend—Fanick might not even go into his office today, despite Marlin's pleadings for a quick turn-around. All he could do was hope.

He stepped outside and saw Inga Mueller's yellow Volvo bouncing up the driveway. She pulled in behind his truck and killed the engine. Marlin waited on the porch for her, but she simply sat in her car, staring at the windshield. Marlin trotted down the steps and walked over to her window. Before he could even say anything, he knew something was wrong. Her face was clenched, fighting back tears.

"You all right?" Marlin asked.

A small shake of the head.

"What happened?" Marlin asked.

She turned and looked him in the eye. "I almost got raped last night."

"Oh, Jesus. When? Where?"

Inga stepped out of the car and told Marlin the horror story from early that morning. A masked intruder, a knife at her throat, Tommy Peabody coming along and saving the day, then taking off just as quickly.

Marlin wanted to reach out and grip her arm, reassure her—but he didn't know if she was ready for any male contact. "I'm so sorry. Did you report it?"

She nodded.

"Which deputy took the call?"

"I think her name was Cowan."

Rachel Cowan was a young, fairly new addition to the department, but she was smart and hardworking. She had spent six years with the Austin Police Department, and had learned plenty in that time.

"I just got through with her about an hour ago. Drove around for awhile, trying to decide what to do next . . . then I came over here."

"It's probably best that you don't stay in town anymore. Johnson City is so small, the guy could spot your Volvo in no time." Marlin was going to suggest that she find a place to stay in Blanco, fifteen miles to the south.

"That's kind of what I was leading up to, John. I had an idea—and please tell me straight-out if you think it's a bad one—but I was wondering whether I might be able to stay with you for a few days?"

The request surprised Marlin, and it must have shown on his face. Inga waved her hand in the air as if she was erasing the idea off a chalkboard. "I'm sorry, that was a stupid thought. Forget I even asked."

"No, it was just a little unexpected, is all." Marlin tried to sound enthusiastic, but he wasn't sure how he felt about it himself. "I've got plenty of space, an extra bed, it's no trouble at all."

"But I don't want to put you out, or—"

"Hey, I wouldn't offer if I didn't mean it. Seriously."

She gave him a weak smile. "I sure would feel a lot safer. And I can't leave town until Tommy—"

"I understand. No problem."

She leaned in and gave him a hug. For a few seconds, he felt awkward, wondering whether he should hug back. But she pulled away before he could decide. "I'll grab my things out of the trunk."

Marlin led her inside, gave her a quick tour, then found a spare key in a kitchen drawer. "This opens both doors, front and back." He glanced around the kitchen. "Help yourself to anything in the pantry or the fridge. And you know where the bathroom is and everything. . . ."

She smiled, and Marlin found it difficult to hold her gaze. She already appeared less distressed by the attack, more like her usual, confident self. "You're helping me out so much, John. I really appreciate it."

"It's no trouble."

She held up three fingers, making an oath. "I'll be a perfect roommate, I promise. Won't even hang my panties on the shower rod."

Marlin felt his face getting warm, so he told her he had to go see the sheriff and would probably be gone for several hours. He walked out of the house and took a breath of fresh air.

.   .   .

Marlin drove into Johnson City and made his way toward the sheriff's office. It was just after nine o'clock, a bright, cloudless morning with remarkably little humidity.

He parked behind the traffic barriers that circled the sheriff's office. Most of the curious onlookers were gone now, and only one news van—from KHIL—sat hunkered nearby.

Just inside the barriers, Deputy Ernie Turpin was sitting in a lawn chair reading a magazine, glancing up now and then to make sure no civilians ventured too close.

Marlin asked him what the situation was, and the deputy said nothing had changed. "Damn guy's stubborn as a mule," the deputy said. "But hell, Garza's sent food in a couple of times, ain't put any pressure on him, so why *should* he come out, you know?"

Marlin had known Turpin for fifteen years, and knew the deputy was a take-action kind of guy. If Turpin were calling the shots, the building would have been raided just hours after Corey had taken Wylie hostage. Several men could be dead. On the other hand, Wylie might be free.

Marlin nodded at Bobby Garza's cruiser in the distance. "Sheriff around?"

"Yeah, he ain't hardly left since this thing began. Took a break early this morning for a coupla hours, but that's it. Guy needs some sleep, if you want my opinion."

Marlin didn't, but he nodded thanks anyway, and walked over to Garza's car. The sheriff was stretched out in the backseat, but Marlin could see that his body was too tense for him to be sleeping.

"Damn," Marlin said through the window, "every time I drop by, you're catching some z's. Being sheriff looks awful damn easy."

Garza kept his eyes closed. "Aw, man, I'm having that same nightmare again. The one with that pain-in-the-ass game warden."

Marlin chuckled and climbed into the front seat, leaving his left foot on the pavement. Both men remained silent for several minutes, Marlin drinking from the traveler's mug of coffee he had brought along. Garza's police radio squawked on occasion.

Finally, Garza groaned and sat up in the backseat. Marlin eyed the sheriff's haggard face in the rearview mirror. "Don't you have a brother named Bobby? Looks like you, but a lot younger?"

Garza rolled his eyes. "You're lucky I'm too worn-out to whip your ass for that. Pass me that thermos beside you, will ya?"

Marlin opened the thermos and poured Garza a cup of coffee. He let the sheriff drink in silence for a few moments, then said, "No change, I guess?"

Garza ran a hand over a stubbled cheek. "No, he's still in there, eating eggs and sausage courtesy of Blanco County. Had some pepperoni pizza for dinner last night. But I'm screwed, 'cause if I don't send food in, Wylie goes hungry, too. Meanwhile, certain people are starting to get uptight."

Marlin raised his eyebrows.

"The mayor, for one," Garza said. "He was griping at me last night, saying this thing would ruin business for the weekend. Like it's my fault we had to rope off some of the little shops along the sidewalk. Says we should shrink our perimeter a little, give people a little more access to the surrounding area." Garza's teeth were clenched now. "But if Corey decides to let a few bullets fly, maybe a tourist gets hit by a stray, guess who everybody would blame? Not the mayor, I can tell you that much."

Marlin nodded in agreement, hoping to cool Garza down a little. "You're doing the right thing, Bobby. Forget what they're saying. Just go with your gut."

"I know, I know. I just want to get Wylie out of there, but it keeps dragging on. Corey's still thinking you're gonna pin it on someone else. Speaking of which, have you heard anything from the lab?"

"Not yet." Marlin glanced at his wristwatch. "I need to head back to the house and give them a call."

"Use my cell phone." Garza slid the phone off his belt and passed it to Marlin. "The lab's phone number's in there if you scroll through the memory."

Marlin stared at the phone as if it were a Rubik's cube. "Uh . . ."

"Oh yeah, I forgot. You haven't joined the age of technology yet." Garza found the number, dialed it, and passed the phone to Marlin. Ten seconds later, Marlin had Richard Fanick on the line.

"Glad you called. I just tried you at home," the technician said. "Got some early results for you. I pulled one set of prints off the plastic bag, then the same guy on the manila envelope, plus two other individuals. Got matches on all three. I would have had them for you late last night, but AFIS was tied up."

Marlin pulled a small spiral notebook and a pen from his breast pocket. "No, this is fantastic. I appreciate you getting on it so fast. Tell me what you got."

"First off, Bert Gammel. But then, you expected that. His prints were on both the plastic and the paper. I haven't fooled around with the bills yet, but I imagine we'll find his prints there, too. Plus probably a dozen others—people who've handled the bills while they were in circulation."

"Yeah, I imagine you're right."

"But I'll start on the bills shortly, mainly looking for the same prints as the three on the envelope. Anyway, sorry to get sidetracked, but print number two . . ." Marlin heard rustling papers at the other end of the line. "It's . . . a guy named Salvatore Mameli."

Marlin sat up a little straighter and caught Garza's eye in the rearview. "Salvatore Mameli?" Garza leaned over the back of the seat.

Fanick continued: "Affirmative. He's in the system from drunk driving last year. Pled it down to a public intoxication. Name ring a bell?"

"You bet it does." Marlin said. "A very loud bell." Suddenly, Marlin's bribery theory was making a lot more sense. "And number three?"

"A guy who got nailed on a simple assault a couple of years ago. Looks like a bar fight." Fanick said the name—and Marlin almost dropped the phone.

Maynard Clements.

•   •   •

Marlin and Garza agreed that it would be best to ride out to Salvatore Mameli's house together in the sheriff's car. Along the way, Marlin relayed his bribery theory and detailed his conversations with Maynard Clements.

Garza was obviously excited about the possibilities. He said, "This guy Mameli, if I remember right, was in the concrete business a couple years back. Right after he moved to town."

"Yep, and now he's into brush removal," Marlin said. "I've seen his rigs on a couple of deer leases."

Garza gave Marlin a strange glance. "I didn't know that. For how long?"

"Six months, maybe a year. What are you thinking?"

Garza tilted his head to the side, as if he were trying to look at the facts from a different angle. "Emmett Slaton owns the biggest brush-removal company in the county, right? Or he used to. And now one of his competitor's names comes up in a murder investigation. Meanwhile, Slaton is nowhere to be found."

Marlin hadn't even considered that fact. He had been too focused on the Gammel case. So, they threw some ideas around, trying to work Slaton into the bribery scenario. They agreed that—regardless of what Maynard Clements said—Mameli could have bribed Gammel in connection with a county project, maybe to ensure that Mameli had the lowest bid.

But they couldn't work Slaton into the mix. It just didn't make sense. "Maybe Mameli paid Gammel off to get the contract on some brush removal for the county," Marlin said. "Then Slaton somehow found out and threatened to expose it all. So Mameli says, 'What the hell, I don't need this grief,' and takes 'em both out."

"But I thought Gammel handled structures, not roads. And if there was a lot of brush to be cleared, you'd think it would be for roadwork."

"No, you're right," Marlin replied. "But . . . Maynard Clements is in charge of roadwork contracts, and his fingerprints were on the envelope, too."

They were a mile from Mameli's house now, so Garza stopped for a few moments on the shoulder. "Interesting, but I wouldn't get too worked up about that yet. There could be a simple reason for Maynard handling that envelope, since he and Gammel worked in the same office. And you'd have to wonder . . . if Mameli bribed Clements instead of Gammel, why is Gammel the one who's dead?"

Marlin had to admit that it weakened the theory. Then he remembered something Clements had said. "You know, Gammel and Clements could have been working a project together. He said they did that sometimes, if the project was large enough."

"So maybe Mameli bribed both Clements and Gammel?"

"Could be."

"Once again: Why is Clements still breathing?"

They batted it around for a few more minutes, but couldn't come up with any possible answers. They knew that Slaton would have needed rock solid, undeniable evidence of bribery—something that would have been very difficult to come by. And even then, they wondered, would it be enough to push a man to murder?

"What kind of man is Mameli, anyway?" Garza asked.

Marlin shrugged. "No idea. Never met him until that brawl last night at the gym."

Garza drummed on the steering wheel, thinking. "Hold on a sec." Garza grabbed the radio mike and contacted Darrell Bridges. "Darrell, I need you to run a background check on a man for me. You'll have to call the DPS office in Austin. Guy's name is Salvatore Mameli. I need it ASAP."

Garza replaced the mike and said, "Worth a shot."

Bridges radioed back in ten minutes. Just as Richard Fanick had said, Mameli had a conviction for public intoxication. But other than that, his record was clean.

"All right, then," Garza said, starting his cruiser. "Guess we'll just have to go see what Mr. Mameli has to say."

CHAPTER THIRTY-FIVE

The Mamelis lived in a rambling ranch-style home, built from native limestone and cedar. It reminded Marlin of his own home, but on a much larger scale. Apparently, Sal Mameli's businesses did quite well. They parked behind a Lincoln and climbed out. Walking to the front door, Marlin could see into a window a couple of rooms down. The younger Mameli—Vinnie—was working out with weights, doing French curls, bare-chested. Kid was pretty well sculpted. Marlin made eye contact and nodded. Vinnie set the weights on the floor and glared back at Marlin. Probably still pissed about that four-wheeling ticket Marlin had given him this summer.

Garza knocked and the door was answered by a pretty Hispanic woman. She led them into a den, where Sal Mameli was stretched out on a sofa, his leg in a cast. Marlin noticed that Mameli's eyes widened for just an instant when he saw the two officers.

"Mr. Mameli, I'm Bobby Garza, sheriff of Blanco County. And I believe you know John Marlin."

Mameli nodded and offered a smile, which came out more

as a wince. "Excuse me for not getting up. With this leg, you know . . ."

"No problem, sir. We were wondering if we could chat with you for a few minutes."

"Sure, have a seat. Youse want somethin' to drink? Coffee?" Both men declined.

Mameli shook his head. "I guess you're out here about Vinnie's four-wheeling. I told dat kid to stay outta the parks, but—"

"Actually, that's not why we're here." Garza interrupted. "We wanted to ask you about a couple of other things."

Mameli gave a look of surprise, one that appeared exaggerated to Marlin. "All right," he said tentatively. "What's up?"

"Well, sir, we were wondering what you can tell us about Bert Gammel. Specifically, what kind of relationship you had with him."

"Bert Gammel? Name's familiar, but I can't place it."

"An employee with the Public Works Department," Garza said evenly. "He was murdered earlier this week."

Mameli snapped his fingers. "Dat's right, I remember now. Poor guy. Wasn't he shot or something? Out on a deer lease?"

Marlin spoke up: "That's right. Did you know him?"

"Well, lessee. I think I mighta met him a time or two. Probably out at a work site. It's kinda hard to remember."

Vinnie Mameli appeared in the doorway, still shirtless. His father made no move to introduce him.

Garza said, "Do you remember having any direct dealings with him? Maybe you met with him to go over some specifics on a job?"

Mameli leaned his head back and appeared to be thinking. "Nope. Never met with the man. Not as far as I can remember."

Garza asked a few more questions, and Mameli continued to answer coolly, using several *I don't know*s and *I can't remember*s. To Marlin, the conversation seemed almost scripted, as if Mameli had prepared for this little discussion in advance.

Finally, Garza took a more direct approach: "Mr. Mameli, I'm going to be frank with you . . ."

Mameli offered a canned smile. "By all means."

Vinnie Mameli strutted over to the wet bar and removed a soft drink from the small built-in refrigerator.

Garza cleared his throat. "We found an envelope of Bert Gammel's—and in that envelope was a large sum of cash. He had it tucked away pretty well."

Sal Mameli nodded and furrowed his brow. His son took a position behind the sofa. "Yeah?" Sal grunted.

"When we find something like that in the possession of a county employee—especially a guy like Gammel, who takes bids for large construction projects—it raises a lot of questions."

"I'm sure it does," Sal said. He gave a sudden raucous laugh. "Sure glad I never met wit' the guy, otherwise I'd think youse was lookin' at me for dis." It was a comment intended to elicit a response from Garza, maybe a *No, Mr. Mameli, that's not the case*. But Garza remained silent. Mameli looked from Garza to Marlin, then back to Garza. "Oh, you gotta be kiddin' me."

"What's going on here, Pop?" Vinnie asked.

Mameli held up a hand to silence the boy. He sneered at Garza. "Where the fuck do you get off, comin' in here with bullshit like dat?"

Garza remained unruffled. "Can you tell us why we found your fingerprints on that envelope?"

Mameli waved his hand dismissively, as if he were making a backhanded swat at a mosquito. "Dat's it, I want you outta my house!"

"Mr. Mameli," Garza said quietly, "if there's an explanation, we'd like to hear it."

Vinnie walked around the sofa and stood to the side of Marlin's chair.

"Outta here, I said!" Mameli shouted. "You got any more goddamn questions, you can ask my lawyer! I got nothin' more to say!"

Garza didn't move. "How well did you know Emmett Slaton?" he asked.

Mameli's face contorted in rage, but before he could answer, Vinnie spoke up harshly. "You got a lot of balls, you know that? Now it's time for both of youse to leave."

Marlin's head snapped toward Vinnie and they locked eyes. Marlin could feel the anger boiling in his chest. Earlier, when Inga had told Marlin about the attempted rape, she'd told him everything the attacker had said. And one phrase matched what Vinnie had just said. Word for word: *You got a lot of balls, you know that?*

Marlin rose slowly, flexing his hands to keep from clenching them into fists. He faced Vinnie, their noses six inches apart. "What did you just say?"

Vinnie stood his ground, a chiding smile on his lips. "I said it was time for youse to leave. Otherwise, you're trespassing, and I got every right to throw you out."

Marlin could feel a spasm ripple across his cheek. He wanted nothing more than to drive his fist into Vinnie's mocking face—and he slowly, discreetly drew his arm back to throw a punch.

It had been a long night. Smedley's bones and joints burned. He was hungry. He had to go to the bathroom. And both his captors could benefit from switching to a new brand of deodorant. But the thing that bothered him most was the fact that *GQ* Todd would have a field day when he found out about all this. Smedley Allen Poindexter, U.S. Deputy Marshal, had been bushwhacked by a couple of rednecks.

Now it was obvious these guys weren't hit men any more than Smedley was a fashion model. The shorter, skinny one—named Red, if they were using their real names—had told Smedley they were employees of Emmett Slaton's, and they needed to find the body so the will could be read. *I promise, just tell us where the body is. We'll let ya go and won't never say how we found it. Ya got my word.* Sounded legitimate to Smedley. Unfortunately, Smedley didn't have the answer. And it was obvious that Red was starting to lose patience. He had taken off in a huff earlier, leaving the big guy, Billy Don, in charge. Maybe Red wasn't a hit man, but he didn't necessarily seem like a choirboy, either. Who knew what he might do?

Smedley cursed himself for thinking that thought, because he heard Red's truck pull up outside—almost as if the redneck had been drawn back to the trailer by Smedley's ruminations. The truck door slammed, and a moment later Red stomped into the room, moving quickly and deliberately. He was carrying what looked like a DVD player, which he set on one of the desks. The big guy—Billy Don—followed with a large TV set. They started hooking the two components together.

Red glared at Smedley as he fumbled with some cables. "We got a sayin' out here in the country, mister. 'If you cain't run with the big dogs, you better stay on the porch.' Well, bubba, get ready, 'cause we're 'bout to find out if you're a big dog or a little dog."

After Red and Billy Don had the electronics in place, they grabbed a chair from one of the desks and hoisted Smedley into it, three feet from the television. Red produced another roll of duct tape and made several loops around Smedley's torso and legs, securing him to the chair. Then he slipped some headphones over Smedley's ears and ran a few lengths of tape under his chin and over the crown of his head. Lastly, he placed one long strip over Smedley's mouth.

Red stepped back and smiled at his handiwork. "Yessir, we're gonna find out 'zackly what kind of man you are." He turned and pushed the POWER button on the DVD. A freeze-frame image came onto the TV screen, one Smedley instantly recognized, even though he hadn't seen it for at least twenty years. It was a scene from *Hee Haw*—a couple of hicks dressed in overalls, preparing to sing a song.

Red gave Smedley one last glance, a look of pure evil on his face. Then he pushed the PLAY button. The bumpkins on the screen began their little ditty.

"Where, oh where, are you tonight?"

Smedley thought this was very strange.

"Why did you leave me here all alone?"

Why on earth were they showing him this old clip?

*"I searched the world over and thought I'd found
true love."*

Hell, watching *Hee Haw* would be better than enduring
Red's questions for another eight agonizing hours.

"You met another and—pffft—you was gone."

Might be kind of fun, actually. A way to break up the tedium.

Then something happened to the image on the screen. It
froze for a moment, then returned to the starting point. The two
men began singing again, wailing about lost love.

Smedley was hoping it was a malfunction with the DVD . . .
but it happened again. The song ended, the disc backed up, then
began again.

And again.

"Whaddaya think?" Billy Don asked.

Red removed his baseball cap and scratched his head. He
could see Smedley reclining in the chair in the next room.
"Hell, it *should* work. The CIA boys use this kind of technique
all the time. Gets so where a song—even a great song like that
one—can plumb drive a man crazy."

Just as Marlin was about to come around with a surprise hay-
maker, he felt Bobby Garza's hand on his shoulder. "Let's go,
John." Marlin stood firmly for a moment, locking eyes with
Vinnie, then allowed Garza to steer him out of the door to the
den and down the hallway.

Outside, back in the cruiser, Garza asked, "What the hell
was that all about? Some bad blood between you and that kid?"

Marlin asked Garza if he had heard about the assault on Inga earlier that morning. Garza had, of course, but he wasn't clear on the specifics since he hadn't seen the report yet.

Marlin said, "The guy that attacked Inga. He used the exact same phrase as our friend Vinnie in there: 'You got a lot of balls.' "

"You sure about that?"

Marlin gave him a look that said he was sure. "You ever hear anybody using that phrase around here?"

Garza didn't answer, just fired up the cruiser and left the Mameli property. Finally, he said, "You and this Inga . . . ?"

Marlin knew what Garza was asking. "Just friends."

Someone other than Garza might have given Marlin a smirk, a *Come on, you can tell me* look, but the sheriff concentrated on the road ahead. "Didn't the perp take a pretty good whack in the head, with a lamp or something?"

Marlin nodded. "Yes, but he was wearing a ski mask, which might've softened the blow a little, or at least kept him from getting cut. Could've walked out of there with nothing more than a lump."

Garza pointed toward the glove compartment. "Notepad in there. You better start writing an incident report. Jot down everything the Mamelis said. The entire conversation."

Sal turned to Vinnie and growled, "They got nothin' on us, right?" His son nodded at him.

"That's right, Pop. They got dick."

Sal trusted Vinnie, but this was no small thing. "You sure of dat? I mean abso-fuckin'-lutely, *we're not all going to prison for life* sure?"

Vinnie smiled—a killer's smile, like the one Sal used to have when he was young. "Yeah, Pop. If you only knew what—"

"I don't wanna hear it! Just so long as everything's taken care of."

"We got nothing to worry about, Pop. Trust me."

Sal wanted to. But what made him nervous was that he *had* to.

CHAPTER THIRTY-SIX

Hank Middleton had been hunting buddies with Frank Ross for twenty-five years. They were so inseparable during deer season, their names would run together when people referred to them. It would be: "I hear Hankenfrank got a nice ten-pointer this morning." Or, "Looks like Hankenfrank are gonna win the big-buck contest again this year." And it was true—not a season went by that one of them didn't bag a fairly respectable trophy, and they always hauled the deer back to Frank's house on the ATV. Hank knew every detail of that four-wheeler, from the dent in the gas tank down to the Dallas Cowboys sticker on the left rear mudguard. Now, as he exited the convenience store in Johnson City with a twelve-pack of Miller Lite, Hank saw a stranger at the gas pumps refueling Frank's ATV. A scruffy-looking guy, who kept glancing around nervously. The man was wearing a camo jacket, but it didn't sit on him right. Like one of those city boys who would come out to a deer lease and try to act country. Sizing him up a little more, Hank figured this guy wasn't anybody that Frank would associate with. No sir.

So he sauntered casually over to the pumps and said, "Howdy."

The man smiled back. He had finished with the ATV and was now filling a one-gallon gas can.

"Nice-looking ATV you got there," Hank said.

"Thank you," the scruffy guy murmured, watching the traffic pass on Highway 281.

"Funny thing is," Hank continued, "it looks just like the one my friend Frank owns. You got any idear why that is?"

The man bobbed his head several times, without making eye contact. "I purchased this vehicle from Frank just this morning. I can understand your confusion."

Hank was stunned for a moment. Frank hadn't said anything about selling his ATV—and Hank told the stranger as much.

"It was a spontaneous transaction on his part," the stranger said. "I happened to see him riding it and realized it was the exact model I've been looking for. I made an offer that your friend was generous enough to accept."

Now Hank was pretty certain something squirrelly was going on. He and Frank had bagged an eight-pointer on Thursday evening, and had celebrated by drinking late into the night at Frank's place. Hank hadn't seen Frank since then, because Frank had to work this weekend. That meant Frank would have been out at the job site since sunup this morning, installing some cabinets. He wouldn't have been out riding his ATV.

Hank wasn't sure what to say. He wasn't the type for confrontation, but he couldn't just let the guy go without checking it out, could he? "You happen to have the title on ya? Maybe a receipt?" Hank asked.

"No, I'm afraid I don't." The stranger lifted the gas nozzle out of the can and went to place it back into the slot in the pump. That's when his sleeve slid down far enough for Hank to see the handcuff on his wrist. In an instant, Hank knew exactly who this guy was: the fellow who had escaped from John Marlin, the game warden.

The men locked eyes for a moment, both of them knowing

the pretense was over. Hank was about to make a lunge for the keys in the ignition, when the stranger aimed the nozzle at Hank and hosed his chest down with gas. Hank dropped his twelve-pack onto the concrete.

"I advise you to remain quite civil," the stranger said. In his hand he now held a disposable lighter. "At least until I've made my departure."

Hank suddenly realized that Frank's ATV wasn't really that important. They could haul deer just as easily in the back of Hank's truck. Hell, if Frank was caught in the same situation, Hank would say, *Man, just let it go.*

"Kindly take a few steps back," the stranger said.

Hank did what he was told, keeping an eye on the lighter.

The scruffy guy strapped the gas can to the back of the ATV and straddled the seat. He turned the key and the motor sputtered to life.

"Please tell your friend I apologize for any inconvenience," the stranger said. Then he put the ATV in gear and roared out of the parking lot.

"What next? Maynard Clements's place?"

Garza nodded. "I guess so. Until we can find a way to get at Mameli. It's gonna be tough if we have to go through his lawyer."

Garza proceeded down Ladybird Lane and came to a wood-and-stone entryway that said RANCHER'S ESTATES. They found Maynard's place—a well-kept home on Pitchfork Lane—and pulled in behind Clements's dusty brown Jeep Cherokee. Maynard answered the door wearing sweatpants and a Texas A&M T-shirt.

"Hey, guys," Maynard said. "What are y'all doing here?" Before they could answer, he gestured over his shoulder. "Game's about to start. Come on in."

Marlin and Garza followed Maynard in and took a seat on a vinyl sofa, while Maynard sank back into a worn recliner. Next to the recliner, a pitcher of orange juice and a large Big Gulp cup sat on a small table. Marlin thought he could smell some kind of liquor. Not even noon yet.

"Playing Oklahoma State today," Maynard said. "Should be a good one. Can I get y'all anything?"

"No, that's all right, Maynard," Marlin said. "Sorry to interrupt . . ."

"Aw, no big deal. It's nice to have company." He looked at them suspiciously. "Y'all *are* Aggie fans, ain't ya?"

On the screen, the Aggie band built to a crescendo as A&M kicked off.

"I just wanted to talk to you a little bit more about Bert Gammel," Marlin said.

Maynard turned the volume down a tad, but kept his eyes on the set. "Figured as much, but I'm not sure what else I can tell ya."

"Well," Garza chimed in, "we were just wondering what you know about Salvatore Mameli. I believe he's had some dealings with your department."

"Oh, sure, I know Sal," Maynard said. "Nice guy—for a Yankee." Maynard chuckled, then got distracted by the happenings on the field. "Aw, damn! What the hell was the defensive end doing on that play? You see him miss that tackle?"

Oklahoma State was marching downfield.

"You ever know Mameli to do anything dishonest, like maybe try to pass some cash under the table?" Garza asked.

Maynard shook his head, but remained focused on the game. "Hate to shoot you down, but me and John been through this already. Seriously, that kinda thing just doesn't go on out here. At least not in my experience. I can't speak for Bert, but he was about as honest as they come. I'm tellin' ya, there ain't no way he'd take a bribe. And if someone offered one, he'd tell me about it. I guarantee it."

Garza and Marlin both asked a few more questions, but discovered nothing new. Finally Marlin described finding Gammel's cash supply in the deer feeder.

"Well, yeah," Clements said, "that does seem like a strange

place to keep your cash, but that doesn't mean it was dirty money."

"No, I guess you're right," Garza said. "The odd thing was, we found *your* fingerprints on the envelope."

Maynard narrowed his eyes, but didn't seem rattled. "What kinda envelope?"

"Standard manila."

The project manager smiled. "Like you'd find in an office, I guess?"

Marlin nodded.

Maynard stood and walked over to a small hutch that was buried with paperwork. He extracted several manila envelopes from the pile. "Look like these?"

Marlin said that it did.

"Come on down to my office if you want. We got hundreds of these lying around. Betcha that's where Bert got it. Hell, he mighta grabbed one off my desk."

Garza stood. "Yeah, that's what we were thinking, Maynard. Just had to check it out."

But Clements wasn't listening. The Oklahoma State quarterback had found a wide-open receiver in the end zone. Clements groaned and let loose with a string of profanities. He grinned at the two men. "Could be another rebuilding year, I guess."

"He seem nervous at all to you?" Garza asked, back in the cruiser.

"Not at all," Marlin replied, wondering whether he should be disappointed or encouraged. "Actually, I guess that makes things easier. Now we can concentrate on Mameli."

"Right now, I say we concentrate on lunch. You hungry?"

Marlin was surprised. He figured Garza would have wanted to go straight back to the sheriff's office to monitor the stand-off. "Lead the way."

Garza radioed Darrell Bridges and told the dispatcher where he and Marlin would be for the next hour. Back in Johnson City, Garza pulled into Big Joe's Restaurant, and the men found a quiet booth in the back. Over chicken-fried steak, they went through the Bert Gammel and Emmett Slaton cases from the beginning, analyzing every detail.

"Still thinking the cases are tied together somehow?" Marlin asked.

"Mameli's face sure got red when I mentioned Slaton, and he seems to have links to both Slaton and Gammel. Problem is, we're awful short on motive for either case at the moment. Yeah, the bribery thing seems like a strong possibility, but we need to keep digging."

"Where?"

Garza gulped some iced tea, then offered a plan. "I'd say we need to reinterview all of the men on the work crews, both Mameli's and Slaton's. Especially Red O'Brien and Billy Don Craddock. They work for Slaton, and they were first at the scene at Slaton's house. Plus, Wylie said they were offering some wild theories about Sal Mameli."

"Yeah, and Wylie blew 'em off," Marlin reminded him.

"I know, I know," Garza said. "Don't get started on Wylie again. Poor guy's in bad enough shape as it is." Garza grabbed the check and glanced at his wristwatch. "Let's start with Red and see where it gets us. Meanwhile, I'll send a couple of deputies out to interview some of the others."

Smedley was slowly going insane. He was sure of it. And if he managed to come out of this with a few marbles still intact, he knew he'd have nightmares about singing farmers for years to come.

Earlier, he'd made an attempt to free himself, but all he'd done was topple the chair with him in it. Now he was lying on his right side, still facing the TV, the headphones still cradling his head. The two rednecks had come in, laughed at his predicament, and left him where he was.

He wondered about his car. Surely it was too damaged to drive. These two goobers must have left it where it was, and, if Smedley had *any* kind of luck, a cop would spot it and start nosing around.

Smedley was aware of a figure standing over him. It was Red, eating a hamburger. Burger King wrapper. Smedley tried to fight it, but his mouth began salivating and drool ran down his cheek. Red was saying something now, holding the burger out, taunting him. Smedley didn't have to read lips to know what he was saying: *Tell us where the body is, and you'll get a burger of your own.* Smedley eyed the burger, stomach growling, and was afraid he was going to cry.

Suddenly, Red's expression changed and he set the burger on a desk. He glanced through a window and his eyes got wide.

Garza pulled through the gate to Emmett Slaton's ranch and followed the driveway toward the house.

"Over there, to the right." Marlin had spotted a small mobile home tucked in a cedar grove, with a small fleet of brush-clearing machines squatting nearby. Headquarters for Slaton's business.

Garza steered off the paved driveway and followed a dirt road to the shiny single-wide.

As they stepped out of the cruiser, Red O'Brien emerged from the trailer and stood on the steps to the door.

"How you doing, Red?" Garza called.

"Hey there, Sheriff. What brings you out here? Hey, John."

Marlin nodded a greeting.

Garza squinted into the sun and told Red they were re-interviewing some of the witnesses in the Slaton case. "We'd like to ask you some more questions about Emmett's disappearance, if you've got a few minutes. Wylie mentioned that you had some theories, and I'd like to hear them personally."

Red was pretty sure he could feel his balls lodged firmly up in his throat. *Something* was in there in the form of a big lump. His hands had started shaking, so he slipped them into the pockets of his jeans. Now, if he could just control his voice, keep it from wavering all over the place like it normally did when he got shook up. Otherwise, the game warden would spot his nervousness in a heartbeat, because Marlin had seen it firsthand plenty of times.

Red took a quick peek at Smedley's car, twenty yards away under a large tarp. Sweet Jesus, he was glad they'd decided to cover it up last night. With it being all smashed up, Garza and Marlin would likely be kind of curious.

"Well, yeah, I tol' your deputy all about it," Red said, trying to keep it brief. "Sal Mameli really had a hard-on to buy Mr. Slaton's business, but Mr. Slaton didn't wanna sell. Then one day—I think it was last Sunday—we seen Mameli driving outta here like a bat out of hell."

Garza nodded. "Tell you what, why don't we go inside and sit down? So John and I can take a few notes."

Red felt faint, and his knees almost buckled.

"You all right?" Marlin asked.

Red tried to respond with a grin. "Little bit light-headed. We're doing some paintin' in there, and the fumes been gettin' to me. You mind if we stay out here so I can get some fresh air?"

Someone was outside! Smedley craned his head and could see Billy Don peeking through the blinds. Red was out there talking to whoever it was.

Smedley tried to pull his wrists apart, but they were bound too tightly. He attempted to straighten his body, to break the tape that was securing him to the chair. No luck. Finally, in desperation, he began slamming his head against the floor of the trailer.

"What was that?" Garza asked.

They all could hear some sort of thumping or banging inside the trailer.

Red giggled. "Oh, that? Just Billy Don movin' some furniture 'round in there. Boy's clumsy. See, Mr. Slaton asked us to fix the place up a little. I figure, with him gone, it's the least we can do. You know . . . in his memory."

Marlin was fairly certain it wasn't paint fumes that were affecting Red's brain. The poacher was obviously nervous— the signs were easy to recognize—and Marlin figured Red and Billy Don had been smoking pot in the trailer. But Marlin didn't care, as long as Red was willing to talk.

Garza asked a couple of questions about Sal Mameli: Had Red ever met him personally? What was he like? Had he ever heard Mameli threaten Emmett Slaton?

Red didn't have much to say. Sure, he'd seen Mameli around a few of the bars in town, but he didn't really know the guy. No—no threats, as far as he knew. Quick, short answers, with plenty of hemming and hawing in between.

Marlin decided to put him at ease. "Red, I'm not sure what y'all are doing in the trailer there, but we need you to concentrate on these questions. Whatever y'all are up to, don't worry about it."

Red gestured to himself with one hand, like, *Who, me?*

Marlin smiled. "We're not here to break up the party. Tell us what you know, then we'll be gone and you can get back to your drinking or smoking or whatever you've been doing."

Red glanced from Marlin to Garza. The sheriff nodded in agreement and opened a small notepad.

"I appreciate that," Red said, and took a deep breath of relief. Suddenly, they saw a more confident, composed Red O'Brien. "The way I figger it," he whispered, as if eavesdroppers were lurking nearby, "Mameli was pissed that Mr. Slaton wouldn't sell, so he offed him. You ever met the guy? He's kind of greasy, if you know what I mean."

"How so?" Marlin asked.

"Seems like kind of a con man. Always talkin' fast, tryin' to get an edge."

"But is there anything you can tell us, beyond just a hunch?" Garza asked.

Red looked puzzled. "You mean, like, uh, hard evidence?"

"Exactly."

Red mulled it over. "Can't think of nothin'."

Garza abruptly flipped the notebook closed.

"Well, he is Eye-talian," Red offered.

"Oh yeah?" Garza asked with exaggerated suspicion, as if he and Red could unravel this conspiracy together. Marlin had to stifle a laugh.

"Hell, yeah, he is," Red said, happy to regain an audience. "And I don't need to tell you how those people are."

"No, Red, you really don't," Marlin said—before Red decided to share his thoughts on Hispanics and Asians, too.

A chirping sound filled the air, and Red flinched. "Take it easy," Garza said. "Just my cell phone."

Garza answered the phone, listened for a moment, then handed the phone to Marlin. "Your friend at the lab. He's got some more news."

CHAPTER THIRTY-SEVEN

Marlin walked over to the cruiser, the phone pressed to his ear. Richard Fanick had been a busy man. He had already lifted some prints from the money in the envelope, and was sharing the results.

"So it was a solid match?" Marlin asked. "No doubt at all?"

"Oh, yeah. I got more prints than I know what to do with. Complete latents, partials, you name it. Guy touched nearly every bill in the stack. Just him and Gammel, though. Not the other guy."

"All right, Richard. This helps me out a lot, and I owe you one for working the weekend."

"Hey, no problem."

"Seriously, next time you're passing through Blanco County, give me a call. I'll buy you the best barbecue lunch you ever had."

"It's a deal."

Marlin disconnected and turned to Garza. "We gotta go."

•   •   •

Garza and Marlin sped away in the sheriff's cruiser—and Red nearly collapsed. He sat on the front steps of the trailer and cradled his head. *Damn, that was too close for comfort.* Red thanked the Lord that he was blessed with a quick mind and a nimble tongue that helped him avoid trouble. Someone like Billy Don wouldn't have been able to handle the situation. But Red had played Garza and Marlin like fiddles.

Billy Don poked his head out of the trailer door. "They gone?"

"Yes, they're gone, no thanks to you. What the hell was you doing in there? Ropin' a goat?"

"So what's the plan?"

"We go directly to Judge Hilton and get a warrant," Garza replied. "I don't care if we have to chase him down on the golf course. Then the deputies will search Clements's house, while we go at him again, this time hard."

Marlin could think of no plausible reason why Clements would have handled Gammel's money—but if he had, he was obligated by law to tell them about it. Otherwise, he was obstructing an investigation. "You operating on the assumption that he killed Gammel?"

Garza sighed. "I have no idea. But he obviously knows more than he's telling. The question is, what does he know? And I keep trying to figure out how Sal Mameli is involved—or *if* he's involved. Kind of strange that Fanick found his prints on the envelope but not on the money."

"I suppose Mameli might have handled the envelope during a visit to Gammel's office. I'm sure they must have met a few times to discuss county projects. It could all be innocent. . . ."

Garza stopped at the one and only traffic light in Johnson City and gave Marlin a glance. "You really believe that?"

Marlin was weighing the question in his mind when he noticed a brown Jeep Cherokee coming the opposite way. Marlin pointed and said, "Isn't that Clements right there?"

Garza followed Marlin's gaze. "It sure as hell is. And it isn't even halftime yet."

The light changed and the Cherokee pulled through, Clements staring resolutely ahead. Garza waited a few seconds, then swung a U-turn and fell in behind him.

"Guess our plans have changed," Marlin observed.

"For the time being. Let's just see what he's up to."

Clements continued south on Highway 281, keeping it to the speed limit. When he left the city limits, he edged his speed up to seventy.

"We forgot to give him the standard warning about not leaving town," Marlin joked.

They caught Clements stealing discreet glances into his rearview mirror, but he did nothing out of the ordinary. Six miles down the road, Clements pulled into a roadside picnic area and came to a stop, Garza and Marlin right behind him.

"What now?" Marlin asked.

"Let's give him a few minutes."

Clements continued to sit in his Cherokee, both hands on the wheel, staring out the windshield.

"I'd say the man is trying to make a decision," Garza said.

"Sure looks that way."

Garza swung his door open. "Reckon we ought to see if he needs any help with it?"

Marlin popped his own door open. "I'd say that's the neighborly thing to do."

Both men exited the cruiser and began walking slowly up to Clements' vehicle. They could see him watching in the rearview mirror.

"Careful, John. He might be armed." Garza's hand was resting on his revolver.

Clements's chin fell to his chest, like a man defeated. Then he lifted his head, shoved the Cherokee into reverse, and came screaming back toward them. Both men jumped out of the way and the Cherokee slammed into the front end of the cruiser. Clements shifted into DRIVE and burned rubber back onto the highway.

* * *

Thomas Peabody sat in his hiding spot in the woods and surveyed the house. It was a long time until nightfall—several hours before he could take action—but he had patience. Oh, yes, he was a patient man indeed. He had waited a painfully long time to be in this position, and he wasn't going to ruin it by acting prematurely. His entire relationship with Inga was at stake. Soon he would be transformed in her eyes. Saving her from the attacker in the motel room had created a chink in her emotional armor—he had seen it in her eyes and felt it in her embrace. She was almost ready to become his soul mate; he was certain of it. Now he merely needed to define himself for her, once and for all. Then she would realize they were destined for each other.

As Marlin and Garza sprinted back to the cruiser, Marlin heard a hissing sound and noticed green fluid puddling under the front bumper. They hopped in and screeched onto the highway, lights flashing and siren blaring. Garza grabbed the mike and called for backup.

"He took out your radiator," Marlin said, one hand braced against the dashboard as they gained speed.

"I saw," Garza replied.

The speedometer was quickly up to ninety. A half-mile ahead, Clements's Cherokee came into view—stuck behind several vehicles in the left lane and a semi carrying a mobile home in the right lane. Seconds later, Garza was on Clements's bumper.

The drivers in the left lane began to drop their speed as they heard the siren . . . as did the driver of the big rig. Now the cruiser and the Cherokee were caught behind a cluster of traffic going fifty. Then Clements saw his chance: He nosed up mere inches from the semi and cut sharply left, almost clipping the front fender of a station wagon. The driver of the wagon tapped the brakes, slowing Garza, as Clements accelerated in the fast lane, gaining a few hundred yards on the cruiser. Finally, the wagon pulled to the right behind the semi, and Garza had a clear path.

"Road narrows," Marlin reminded him.

Garza nodded. The two southbound lanes merged to one, with a meager shoulder on the side. The cruiser crested a hill, and now they could see another semi carrying the other half of the double-wide mobile home. Clements was already on its tail, weaving left and right, trying to pass. Oncoming drivers blared their horns and swerved right as Clements tried to see around the semi.

Marlin smelled something burning and leaned to see the temperature indicator on the dashboard. Pegged on *H*. "Car can't take much more," he said.

Garza was riding Clements's bumper now, speed at sixty, and Marlin wondered if the sheriff was going to attempt the PIT maneuver—a move where the pursuing car nudges the rear quarter-panel of the lead car, causing it to spin out. The answer was clear when Garza found a lull in the traffic and pulled into the oncoming lane, edging up to the Cherokee.

Steam poured out from under the hood and Marlin knew the cruiser didn't have much longer. He craned his neck and looked back—but there were no other deputies in sight yet to continue the chase.

Just as Garza was about to use his right front fender to tap the Cherokee behind the left rear wheel, Clements jerked the Jeep onto the shoulder and began slipping past the semi on the right, picking up speed. The three vehicles were approaching a long leftward curve now, and Garza eased into the left lane to see if he could pass the semi. The road was clear for several hundred yards—except for a broken-down truck on the right shoulder, directly in Clements's path. With the way the road curved, and the semi's large load, Marlin knew Clements couldn't see what lay ahead.

Garza and the driver of the semi both spotted the imminent disaster and reacted: Garza pushed firmly on his brakes and put some distance between the cruiser and the semi. The semi began to drift over into the left lane to give Clements a chance to see the truck in his path.

But it was simply too late—and Clements was going too fast now.

He finally spotted the truck and tried to accelerate and cut back in front of the semi. He almost made it, but he clipped the rear of the broken-down truck in an explosion of glass and began to spin. The rotating Cherokee careened across the highway, bounced off a guardrail, and finally came to a stop in the middle of the highway.

But now Clements was sitting broadside in the path of the semi.

The driver was standing on his brakes, leaving trails of black rubber. Marlin winced: He could see Clements's terrified face as the semi closed in on the driver's-side door.

The semi finally began to lose its momentum and drop some speed. It was traveling no more than five miles an hour when it thumped into the Cherokee and pushed it for ten yards down the highway. But the sight of that massive metal grille closing in on him made Maynard Clements pass out cold.

CHAPTER THIRTY-EIGHT

By the time Marlin and Garza arrived at Blanco County Hospital, deputies were executing a search warrant on Clements's home and property.

The small hospital was quiet, as usual, but Marlin could sense a buzz of excitement among the staff. Rumors had already spread about Clements's involvement in the Gammel homicide.

Marlin and Garza proceeded to room 107, where they found Deputy Ernie Turpin posted at the door, as Garza had requested. Garza asked him for details.

"Couple of busted ribs, is all," Turpin said. "I been poking my head in there every few minutes. He's awake—I know that much—but not responsive to the doctors. They don't know if it's shock or what."

Inside, Marlin and Garza found Maynard Clements lying quietly, staring upward. His eyes moved in their direction as they entered, then continued to study the ceiling.

Garza pulled a chair up next to the bed, and Marlin hung back behind him.

After a few moments of silence, Garza said, "Maynard?"

Clements gave a small nod.

Garza pulled a small tape recorder from his breast pocket and hit the RECORD button. "Maynard, I'm going to record this conversation, okay?"

In a weak voice, Clements said, "I understand."

"Now, I'm going to read you your rights, just so we're clear on what the situation is here."

Clements didn't respond.

Garza recited the Miranda warning from memory, then asked Clements if he understood. Maynard gave another small nod.

"Please answer aloud, Maynard."

"I understand my rights," Clements whispered.

Garza let a few minutes pass, then quietly said, "Maynard, my deputies are searching your home right now. Your Cherokee, too. All your possessions. I've got a pretty good feeling they're going to find evidence tying you to the death of Bert Gammel."

Marlin noticed Garza had said "death" rather than "murder."

Garza continued: "See, no matter how clever you think you are, there's always something you leave behind. A tire track or a shoe print. Maybe a puddle of tobacco juice. That means DNA evidence, which is almost impossible to beat."

Clements gave Garza a quick glance, then went right back to looking at the ceiling.

Garza stopped for a moment and crossed his legs. "You grew up here, Maynard, so you know how the people are. You know the kinds of sentences juries come back with. And I'll be honest with you, Maynard: The district attorney is gonna go for broke on this one—because everything points toward Murder One. You understand what I'm saying to you here?"

Clements squeezed his eyes shut.

"But . . ." Garza took a small pause. "A confession could go a long way toward helping you out. The only thing the D.A. likes better than a guilty verdict is getting a guilty verdict without having to go to trial. If he can avoid—"

"I did it," Clements croaked—so quietly Marlin almost missed it.

Marlin felt a charge of adrenaline travel through him, a rush of excitement unlike any he had felt in years. But he struggled to remain perfectly still—like a hunter standing among a herd of deer who haven't sensed his presence—afraid that any movement would spook Clements back into silence.

"I know you did," Garza said softly. "Tell me about it."

Tears sprang from the corners of Clements's eyes and ran down his temples. Garza passed him a tissue, which Maynard accepted with his left hand, grimacing in pain.

"It's just like Marlin said: He was bribed, and so was I. But then it all went wrong."

Clements quit speaking then, for so long that Marlin wondered whether he had changed his mind about confessing. Marlin followed Garza's lead and simply waited.

Clements seemed almost unaware of the men in the room, as if he were talking to himself, when he finally continued, in a whisper: "We each got twenty thousand dollars in cash. We agreed to lie low for a while, not spend any of the money, until we were sure we weren't gonna get caught. But Bert couldn't do it. He got cocky, started showing off with the money . . . buying things, like that Explorer. He'd flash the money around, acting like a big shot."

A nurse peeked her head in the door, offered a quizzical look, and Marlin shook his head at her. The door slipped shut quietly behind her.

"Then what happened?" Garza asked gently.

"We had arguments about it. Several times. He said I was paranoid, that we were home free." Clements's face contorted in despair. "Then he tried to blackmail me. Said he wanted my share of the money or he'd go to the cops and tell them it was all my idea, that he had nothing to do with it. He double-crossed me."

Clements paused again.

"I can understand your frustration, Maynard," Garza said. "What'd you do about it?"

Clements wiped his eyes. "I shot him. I set up near his deer blind . . . and then I shot him."

Garza nodded and asked Maynard if he wanted anything to drink. Maynard shook his head.

Garza then asked Maynard to give him a recap of the morning he had shot Gammel, and Clements complied.

He had driven onto the Bar T Ranch—next door to the deer lease where Gammel hunted. He had picked a day when he knew the foreman at the Bar T would be out of town at a cattle auction. In the early afternoon, he found a good spot under a cedar tree. Then he waited for Bert Gammel to show up. He didn't bring any cigarettes because of the telltale smoke—and he was trying to quit anyway. But he was so nervous he needed something. So he had chewed some tobacco. "Guess that stuff *is* dangerous, huh?" Clements said, no trace of humor on his face.

Garza asked a few more questions until he had the full story. Then he went back to the bribery.

"What did you receive payment for, Maynard—you and Bert? What was the money for?"

An expression of pure shame crossed Clements's face. "To look the other way on some concrete that didn't meet code. The builder wanted to use a lower grade and pass it off as spec. To save a bunch of money."

"Who was the builder?" Garza prodded.

Marlin tensed. His back was aching from standing still for so long. *Just a few more minutes,* he told himself.

"It was Sal Mameli," Clements said bitterly, spitting the words out.

"What about Emmett Slaton?"

Clements looked confused.

"Was he involved in any of this?" Garza asked.

"No, not Slaton. Where did you get that idea?" Clements replied. "It was just Mameli. We met at Big Joe's for lunch one day and he gave me an envelope with forty thousand in cash. I counted it, and then gave twenty to Bert." Clements was beginning to blubber. "And the concrete . . . it's really not a big deal. It's plenty safe—I *know* it is—or I wouldn't have done it."

"I know you wouldn't, Maynard," Garza said. "You've always been a good worker for the people of this county."

Clements gave a small smile. "Thanks, Bobby."

Garza shifted in his chair. "Last question, Maynard, then you can get some rest: What was Mameli building? What was the concrete for?"

When Marlin heard the answer, his knees went weak.

"The dam," Clements said in a monotone. "The dam at Pedernales Reservoir."

"Yeah, that's right, Darrell," Garza said over his cell phone. "See if you can get Corey on Wylie's phone. If you can, tell him he's cleared. Uh-huh, we've got a full confession. Then pull everybody back and see if he'll come out."

Marlin couldn't hear the other end of the conversation, but he knew the dispatcher was having a tough time believing what his boss was saying. "No, I don't want you to go in—under *any* circumstances," Garza said firmly. "Just pull back and let him come out in his own sweet time. We clear? All right, then, I'm heading over to the Public Works Department for a few minutes and . . . no . . . no, I can't explain right now. Goddammit, Darrell, just do what I'm asking you, okay? I'll see you within the hour." Garza hung up. "I swear, just getting people to follow orders around here . . ."

"So, what's next with Mameli?" Marlin asked.

"I'll call the team at Maynard's house and see if they find the envelope where he said it would be. If we can pull Mameli's prints off that one, too, we'll be in good shape. We'll take a look at Mameli's bank accounts, see if he had any big withdrawals prior to his meeting with Maynard. Probably interview the waiters at Big Joe's, in case one of them can verify seeing the two of them together. I'd say it looks pretty solid, though." He glanced Marlin's way. "Listen, this is still your case if you want it. Just tell me how much you want to be involved."

•   •   •

Five minutes later, Marlin and Garza were standing in front of Toby Gardner, who was the Public Works Director, Gammel's and Clements's supervisor.

"Thanks for meeting us, Toby."

"Glad to help," Gardner said. "But I'm not sure what I'm helping with."

Garza turned to Marlin. "You want to fill him in?"

Marlin recapped their conversation with Maynard Clements, hitting the high points but omitting any details about the murder of Bert Gammel.

Gardner stared at Marlin incredulously. "Do you believe him?" he asked. "I mean, was he loopy on painkillers or anything?"

Marlin shook his head.

Garza said, "We have no reason to think he's lying . . . and plenty of reasons to think he's telling the truth. Unfortunately, I can't go into them all right now. It involves a case, and I'm not at liberty to—"

Gardner held up his hands. "Say no more. If you tell me it's true, then as far as I'm concerned, it's true."

"The question, then," Marlin said, "is, can we believe Clements? Is the dam a threat or not?"

Gardner frowned. "If that concrete's not up to code, I'd say we've got a big problem on our hands. See, these codes aren't arbitrary. Certain grades of concrete can withstand higher pressures, and—"

"No offense," Garza interrupted, "but you don't need to explain it to us, Toby. Just tell us what we need to do next."

Both men stared at Gardner, who stared back. "Oh, I don't think there's any question about that," Gardner stated flatly. "We've got to empty the reservoir."

Sal Mameli was drinking scotch, watching the evening news and waiting for Maria to serve dinner—but his thoughts were wandering. Once again, he was daydreaming of a tropical island—now more than ever—but he sure as shit didn't like the dark clouds looming on the horizon. There wasn't any goddamn sunshine in his life right now, that was for certain.

Everything should have been so easy.

Buy out Emmett Slaton, get every goddamn brush-cutting contract from here to Houston, then grab every last dime and get the fuck out. Screw the clients. Screw the creditors. But no, Slaton had to be a hard-ass, giving Sal no choice but to take him out. And this tree-hugging duo from who-the-fuck-knows-where. It was like they were sent here as a practical joke by some jamook, just to give him a major pain in the balls. At least the little leg-breaking bastard was out of the picture, on the run from the law. But the broad . . . she was still hanging around town, according to Vinnie. Sal had told Vinnie to give her a good scare—an *I'll kill all your loved ones* kind of scare, the type that makes people leave town in the middle of the night. Apparently, she didn't scare that easy. Sal had asked Vinnie about her this morning, and Vinnie had said, *She's a tough bitch, Pop. I'm still working on it.*

Sal hadn't liked the way that sounded. But, truth be told, that broad was on the back burner now, ever since this afternoon. He had more important things to do, like keeping a lid on this Slaton thing. He had to laugh, really. A shitstorm had hit Blanco County, but he had managed to keep his own dirty laundry buried. So far, anyway. He didn't like those two cops—well, that cop and that game warden—coming to his house. What was their problem, anyway? Sal's fingerprints on an envelope? *Get the fuck out of here with that*—that's what any decent attorney would say. *It proves nothing.* But it was Sal's piss-poor luck that Gammel had gone and gotten himself whacked, and that the cops had had to come nosing around about it. Yeah, so maybe he *had* bribed Bert Gammel, but Sal was in the clear on the murder beef. He'd had nothing to do with that. But the big question was, after the cops had asked him about Bert Gammel, why in the fuck did they bring up Emmett Slaton? That was the one thing that made Sal nervous. It didn't make sense.

Sal turned up the set as KHIL cut to a reporter—a good-looking broad with nice-sized jugs named Kitty Katz.

You gotta be kidding, Sal thought. Sounded like a stripper, not a reporter. Kitty was trying to look all serious and dramatic, standing in front of the courthouse.

> *"There has never been a chain of events quite like the past few days here in Blanco County—that much everyone can agree on. It all started nearly forty-eight hours ago when Jack Corey, a suspect in the murder of Blanco County employee Bert Gammel, shot a sheriff's deputy and began a standoff in the building you see behind me. For days, Corey has remained holed up with the wounded deputy, refusing to negotiate a surrender. But just moments ago, we received word that there is another suspect in the homicide, and the new suspect has indeed confessed . . ."*

Sal watched as the station cut to a clip of an earlier interview. Some goofy-looking deputy standing there, looking cocky in front of the camera. His name—DEPUTY ERNIE TURPIN—was superimposed on the bottom of the screen.

> *"We do have a full confession on record, but I'm not at liberty to identify the suspect at this time. But this does mean that Mr. Corey is no longer a suspect, and we are encouraging him to end the standoff immediately."*

The camera cut back to the reporter.

> *"So far, however, neither Corey nor the deputy have emerged. Meanwhile, there is still no development in the disappearance of local rancher and businessman Emmett Slaton, who has been missing since Wednesday. Anyone with information pertaining to the case is asked to call the Blanco County Sheriff's Department. Remarkably, another odd story has made headlines lately in this small, nor-*

*mally quiet county—the escape of a suspect in an
assault-on-an-officer case. The suspect, Thomas
Peabody . . ."*

Sal gave an involuntary yelp as a photo of Peabody appeared
on the screen.

*". . . remains at large. He was arrested after an al-
tercation at an assembly in the Johnson City High
School gymnasium. He resisted arrest, assaulting an
officer in the process, and later escaped in the confusion when the officer—you guessed it—brought his
prisoner to the sheriff's office here, just after the
current standoff began."*

The camera cut back to the reporter.

*"Strangely, Peabody is credited with breaking up
an attempted rape late last night, then disappearing
once more before deputies arrived."*

Sal winced. An attempted rape? What was that all about?
Goddamn—could they be referring to Vinnie? Did he try to
rape that bird-loving broad? That's all he needed, the cops
breathing down his neck on account of his hard-dick son. Time
to have a talk with the boy, tell him to ease off till further notice.

And what about this new suspect in the Gammel case? It
could take the heat off Sal, stop the cops from digging into
his connection with Gammel. Then all he'd have hanging
over his head would be Emmett Slaton—and Vinnie had sworn
on his grandmother's grave that there wasn't anything to worry
about there.

CHAPTER THIRTY-NINE

John Marlin couldn't remember the last time he had walked through his front door and smelled dinner cooking. Months, surely . . . since before Becky had made the move to Dallas. He called out to Inga, not wanting to startle her after what she'd been through.

"I'm in here"—her voice came from the kitchen.

He found her standing in front of the stove, dressed in a turquoise V-neck shirt and tan shorts. She had her long blonde hair pulled back, but a few tresses had escaped and gently framed her face.

"You're just in time," she said, turning and handing him a cold beer in a frosted mug. "I found a package of ground beef in your fridge and decided to make some spaghetti. I hope you don't mind."

Mind? Marlin thought. *Are you kidding?* "Smells great," he said. "But I should let you know: That's not beef, it's venison."

Inga said, "Huh," then leaned over the skillet and examined the saucy contents. "I was wondering about that. It smelled kind of different. I just figured—Texas cows." She shrugged. "What the hell, I'll give it a try."

Marlin was shocked. "I thought you were against hunting. A few days ago, in the cafe, you said something about Rodney murdering innocent animals."

"Well, this deer is already dead. Not a whole lot I can do for it now, is there?" She tapped a spatula against the side of the skillet and set it on the stovetop. "You think I'm a hypocrite?"

Marlin shook his head. "Hey, I'm not here to judge. I was just curious."

She checked the spaghetti bubbling in a large pot. "Five more minutes and we'll be ready to eat. You hungry?"

"Starving. And I really appreciate you—"

"Hey, it's the least I can do, you helping me out like this." She went to the refrigerator and grabbed a beer for herself. "So. Tell me about your day. Anything exciting happen?"

By dinnertime, Sal's nerves had started to calm down a little. The power of positive thinking—either that, or a shitload of scotch.

Angela was sitting to his left in her usual place, quiet, avoiding eye contact. Jeez, there was no pleasing this woman. It had been—what?—a solid week since Sal had made a little trip out to Maria's cabin, and Angela hadn't warmed up at all. Woman was as cold as a New Jersey winter.

Vinnie was to his right, not exactly a fountain of conversation, either. The kid had been acting kind of weird ever since the cops had come by. He still had a lot to learn. Most of the time, when the cops ask a bunch of questions, it's because they don't have any answers. So you just keep your trap shut and tell them to get the fuck out of your house.

Maria entered through the kitchen door, her hands in oven mitts, carrying a casserole dish. Sal tried not to watch her, but it was damn near impossible. She was dressed in a big, loose blouse, but there was no hiding that body. The woman was hot, there was no denying it. She went to place the dish in the center of the table, and Sal couldn't resist a peek down the front of her blouse. Just a quick glance before Angela could catch him. But then he saw something that put a lump in his throat and froze his eyes in place.

She was wearing one of those cheap homemade necklaces of hers. And hanging from it was the missing shell from his .35!

"Do you mind?" Angela asked.

Sal jerked his eyes toward her as Maria quickly left the room. "Wha . . . ?"

Angela scowled and stared down at her plate. "Honestly, Sal."

Sal attempted a gesture of innocence, then let it go. He ladled a large portion of casserole onto his plate and took a bite. "This food tastes like crap," he said.

"This tastes great," Marlin said, slurping down some spaghetti.

Inga nodded. "Thanks. I thought venison would be—I don't know—kind of gamy. But it's not."

"Oh, you'll get a batch now and then that's pretty strong, but not this one. Sometimes, it's all in how you prepare it."

"Anyway," she said, "you were going to tell me about this case you were working on."

As they finished dinner, Marlin told her everything he was at liberty to reveal, without using any names. He left out the remark Vinnie Mameli had made, and he also didn't mention anything about the dam. Garza wanted to keep that information under wraps until the dam had been inspected, in order to avoid unfounded panic about a dam burst.

By the time Marlin finished his tale, Inga had stopped eating and was staring at him. "So you basically solved a murder investigation by yourself?"

"No, not by myself. The sheriff—"

"Yeah, but you were the one who kept digging around and found all the evidence."

"Got lucky on a couple of things. But Bobby Garza was the one who got the confession. He has these questioning skills that they can't teach you at the Academy. Played the guy just right."

"Well, I'd say he was awfully lucky to have you around."

Marlin was embarrassed, and he tried to conceal it with a nod. "It was interesting," he said. "But now it's almost over and then I can get back to my regular patrol."

They cleared the dishes and made their way to the sofa in the living room. It was a beautiful evening, and a cool breeze drifted in through the open windows. They sat in silence for a few minutes, and Marlin felt at peace. He had been wondering if it would be awkward to have Inga in his home—but it felt completely comfortable. He knew there was an unspoken attraction between them, but there was also the beginnings of a friendship. He thought it would be best to keep it that way.

That's when Inga suddenly leaned over and kissed him.

It was gentle at first, but then their lips parted and their tongues found each other. Wordlessly, their mouths still pressed together, Inga straddled him and began to unbutton his uniform. She ran her fingers through his chest hair and moaned softly deep in her throat. Marlin pulled her shirt free from her shorts and she slipped it off over her head. She gazed into his eyes as she removed her bra, then placed his hands on her breasts, the nipples round and hard. They kissed again, and a few seconds later, he could feel her hands tugging at his belt buckle.

Angela finally went to bed after the weather report, as usual. Smashed on vodka, also as usual. Sal had tuned to an Austin station instead of KHIL because he was getting tired of hearing about all the shit happening in Blanco County. The last thing he needed right now was an update on the Emmett Slaton case. His nerves couldn't take it.

He had to get that shell, there was no getting around it. It was the only piece of evidence linking him to Slaton. Once it was destroyed, he could relax, let the cops sniff around all they want. But the thought of going into Maria's cottage sent chills down his spine. If she had half the powers of Aunt Sofia, she could put some kind of wicked-ass curse on him and make him fall dead in his tracks. And there was that damned cat, too. A thing of pure evil. If it attacked, he'd be done for.

On the other hand, he'd rather be dead than go to prison. If he could just talk some sense into Maria, keep her calm, maybe the cat would stay calm, too. It was the only option Sal had.

He gave it a good thirty minutes, then stuck his head into the bedroom. Angela was out cold.

He clomped down the hallway on his crutches and went out the back door. Good. There was still a light in Maria's window. He followed the path to her cottage.

Thomas Peabody double-checked his supplies, found everything in order, and set off through the darkness. He moved slowly, painstakingly. Stealth was imperative now. One small error could mean disaster.

Maria was sitting cross-legged on the floor, meditating, feeling more at peace with the world than she had in years. At the center of it all was this wonderful man named Smedley. He had been a sensitive, caring lover . . . though his sudden departure had left her a little puzzled. But he *would* come back—she was certain of it. Why else would he have left behind his badge and his gun? She had not known Smedley was a police officer, but now that she knew, it made her feel protected. She would have felt uneasy being involved with a police officer back in Guatemala, for they were often corrupt and immoral. But here in the United States, it was known as an honorable and noble profession. Holding the badge in her hand, caressing its gentle curves, gave her a feeling of security. The gun, however, made Maria very nervous. She had even draped a towel over it to help her put it out of mind.

Maria meditated for ten more minutes and was just about to go to bed when there was a knock on the door. She was startled at first, and she instinctively flinched.

Just as she was wondering if perhaps Smedley had returned, she heard Mr. Mameli calling out to her. It had been seven days since Maria had been subjected to Mr. Mameli's advances, and she had hoped he would no longer try to inflict his abuse. Obviously, though, Mr. Mameli had no intention of leaving her alone.

He knocked again, more firmly this time, and called her name once more.

Much to Maria's surprise, the feeling of dread that normally accompanied the sound of her employer's voice had vanished. In its place were anger and outrage and defiance. Her relationship with Smedley had somehow liberated her, transforming her meek submissiveness into a steely resolve. *Tonight,* she said to herself, *it will all end!*

Maria Consuelo García Rodríguez had had enough!

She made a move to lock the door but was not fast enough. The doorknob turned, and Mr. Mameli limped into the room on his crutches. He gave her a large, false smile, the type Americans were always giving.

"Go away!" she hissed at him. She suddenly remembered she was dressed in nothing but a long nightshirt that draped to her thighs—but instead of feeling a sense of vulnerability, she now felt empowered and strong. "You go now!" she hissed again.

He made a meaningless gesture with his hands. "Aw, come on, Maria. Don't get all crazy on me," he said, his eyes darting left and right. "I just need to get something from you."

Maria knew exactly what that *something* was—and she vowed that he would never "get it" again.

Sal was relieved that the cat was nowhere to be seen—but Maria was the problem right now. She had it all wrong. All he wanted was the damn bullet shell from around her neck. He could see it now, plain as day, glistening on her necklace.

·　·　·

Peabody made his way to the first BrushBuster, one of six hunched together on the west side of Sal Mameli's house. There was a structure on the east side of the residence—a cottage of some sort—but it was too far away to be of concern. He went to the closest tree-cutter and unscrewed the gas cap.

Mr. Mameli was blatantly staring at her chest now, and Maria responded by planting her feet squarely and giving him an icy stare. She was giddy with power, and she was delighted to see the fear in Mr. Mameli's eyes.

He took another step forward on his crutches, asking her to calm down. Nonsense! She would never be calm again in the face of oppression!

He reached out toward her breasts and she swatted his hands away. He flinched, like a small child caught misbehaving.

He reached again. And Maria was surprised by the harsh words she heard leaving her throat: "Go to hell!"

Peabody struck the match, touched it to the trail of gasoline on the ground, and sprinted like a jackrabbit back to the woods.

It was so close, just inches from his fingertips. If only Sal could make Maria understand. All he wanted was the shell—the god-damn shell. He reached for it again . . . and she cursed him! In a voice full of rage, the witch told him to go to hell! But it was more than her anger, it was the evil gleam in her eye that sent a shudder through his body and caused a tremble in his hands.

And at that moment, she fully unleashed her powers.

A series of deafening explosions ripped the night, and the earth rocked beneath Sal's feet. He fell to the floor and curled into a fetal position, waiting for some hideous winged demon to pull him into a fiery eternity.

He peeked through his fingers. Maria was silhouetted against the window, the sky behind her glowing an eerie orange.

· · ·

Marlin was lying in bed, Inga dozing beside him, when the phone rang. Ten-thirty. Could be a poaching call, but Marlin decided to let the machine get it. If it was important, he'd pick it up. He heard Bobby Garza's voice . . .

> *"John, it's Bobby. Just wanted to see if you were watching KHIL right now. Good news, buddy. Jack Corey has finally surrendered. He just came out about ten minutes ago and I wanted you to know. I'll fill you in tomorrow. It's gonna be a big day. I've got some guys coming from the Army Corps of Engineers to inspect the dam. Toby Gardner already has the floodgates open, and he says the reservoir should be down twenty feet in forty-eight hours. Just wanted to keep you posted. Good work, my man. Hell of a job."*

CHAPTER FORTY

Marlin's phone rang again at seven-thirty the next morning, rousing him from a deep slumber. It had been months since he'd slept so late. Beside him, Inga muttered something sleepily and pulled a pillow over her head.

He picked up the phone. "This is Marlin."

It was Garza, breathless on the other end. "John, can you hear me? It's Bobby." The connection was weak and full of static, but there was no mistaking what Garza said next. "It looks like we found him, John. We found Emmett Slaton."

Sal was on the couch, the television murmuring in the background, while he tried to recover from the hellish night he had had. He had almost pushed Maria too far, he knew that. Worse than that, he had gone about it all wrong, didn't use his goddamn brain. The truth was, there was no need to confront Maria at all. All he had to do was wait until she wasn't wearing the necklace, send her and Angela to the grocery store, then raid

Maria's room. It would be much easier that way, and he could avoid Maria's wrath.

He thought about last night, and it made him shudder. After the explosions, when the cops had finally left and the firefighters cleared out, he had freaked out a little in front of Vinnie and Angela. He had had a moment of stupidity and tried to make them see that it was all Maria's work, that she had used her powers to rain fire down upon him. But they had looked at him as if he was going fucking crazy and asked if he wanted to see a doctor. In the end, he had decided it was best to keep his knowledge about Maria's powers to himself. He accepted the sleeping pill that Angela had offered in the middle of the night, and eventually fell into a fitful, horrifying slumber.

He had had a nightmare, one in which Maria had caused him to slice open his own bowels with a rusty knife. He was forced to watch in terror as a pack of goats with razor-sharp teeth began to feed on his entrails. He was starting to sweat now, just thinking about it.

He heard a noise behind as Vinnie came into the room. "You get any sleep, Pop?"

Sal grunted.

Vinnie came around and sat next to him. Sal picked up the newspaper and pretended to read. He didn't feel like talking to anybody. Vinnie grabbed the remote and turned the sound up a little, surfing through the channels.

Sal could hear a news reporter babbling, but he wasn't paying much attention.

Until Vinnie said, "Oh, shit!"

Sal lowered the paper to see what the fuss was about.

As Marlin drove to Pedernales Reservoir, he replayed in his mind the amazing tale Garza had recounted for him. The team from the Army Corps of Engineers had arrived just after sunrise. They had closed the floodgates temporarily, to allow a team of divers to inspect the underwater portion of the dam. The divers entered the water at the boat ramp, and as they swam toward the dam, one of the team members spotted something large and yellow at the bottom of the lake. Something he wouldn't have seen if the water level hadn't already dropped so rapidly. He swam lower, and realized it was a submerged car.

It turned out to be a Porsche owned by a local kid named T.J. Gibbs. Marlin remembered citing Gibbs and Vinnie Mameli for four-wheeling on park property. Marlin had had some other troubles with Gibbs in the past: hunting without a license, shooting a turkey out of season. Mostly minor stuff. Garza had said there were no clues as to how the car had gotten there. They had tried calling Gibbs and got no answer.

The diver went down a second time to get a closer look. According to Garza, "The guy came up white as a sheet, John—saying there was a body in the car."

"Slaton?" Marlin asked, wondering what the rancher's body would be doing in a car owned by a punk like T.J. Gibbs.

"We're just now pulling the car out of the water," Garza said. "The body's in pretty bad shape, but from the description the diver's giving, yeah, it sounds like Slaton."

On the screen, Sal could see a tow truck pulling a car out of a lake. The lake looked like Pedernales Reservoir. And the car looked like T.J. Gibbs's Porsche. "What the hell?" Sal said. "Ain't that your friend's car?"

Vinnie nodded, his eyes glued to the television.

The camera switched to a clip of the sheriff.

> *"We were conducting a routine inspection of the dam when one of the team members spotted the submerged automobile. It has apparently been underwater for several days. I'm sorry to confirm at this time that we did discover a body inside the car."*

Sal turned to Vinnie, thinking, *Poor kid, having to find out about his dead pal this way.* His son looked close to tears.

"What the hell happened, Vinnie?" he asked gently. Vinnie didn't answer.

> *"I am able to confirm at this time that the deceased was not the owner of the car, and we are presently making efforts to locate him."*

"Well, that's a relief," Sal said, smiling, looking at Vinnie. But Vinnie looked far from relieved.

A reporter off-camera asked if the sheriff could reveal the identity of the deceased.

> *"I'm afraid I can't make any comments at this time."*

The same reporter asked if the deceased was in fact, the missing rancher, Emmett Slaton.

"Emmett Slaton?" Sal said. "What the hell's he got to do with dis?"

The sheriff paused. Way too long of a pause to suit Sal. A pause big enough to drive a fucking Cadillac through. Then he said:

> *"No comment."*

As Sal turned to Vinnie again, he felt himself hyperventilating. His head was spinning and his mouth was bone dry. He tried to laugh it off. "Tell me, Vinnie . . . tell me I got nothin' to worry about."

But Vinnie wouldn't meet his eyes. He just kept looking at the screen, his face a mask of shock.

Sal twisted toward him, ignoring the pain in his broken leg. He spoke softly now, trying to control his rage. "Tell me you didn't sink him in the goddamn water in dat goddamn Porsche."

And Vinnie—his only son, a future *capo* with balls the size of cantaloupes, the boy who reminded Sal so much of himself when he was a kid—said the worst three words Sal had ever heard: "I'm sorry, Pop."

Sal lunged at Vinnie, who squirmed away from his grasp. "You stupid son of a bitch!"

Vinnie leaped off the couch. "I screwed up, Pop! I'm sorry!"

Sal vaulted off after him, his lame leg buckling under him. "You lousy no-good bastard!"

Vinnie ran from the room, and Sal bucked and jerked on the floor, trying to climb to his feet. "You fuckin' lamebrain cock-sucker!"

Marlin found Garza near the boat ramps, in a swarm of deputies and staff members from the Corps of Engineers. T.J. Gibbs's ruined, muddy Porsche sat on the shores of the lake, surrounded by yellow crime scene tape that had been strung between county vehicles. A tow truck sat with its engine idling, the driver reeling in a dripping steel cable. The news-station vans were already back in full force, and Deputy Ernie Turpin was doing his best to keep the media back from the scene.

Marlin ducked under the tape and made his way toward Garza, who nodded him toward one of the patrol cars. They climbed inside and closed the doors. "Yeah, it's Slaton. Looks like he was shot several times. Lem's doing an autopsy later today," Garza said, referring to the county medical examiner.

"Any word from T.J. Gibbs?"

Garza gritted his teeth. "Someone called an hour ago, about an unmanned boat floating around. Before we could check into it, a guy across the lake called. Found a young white male floating, stuck underneath his boat dock. Gotta be Gibbs. And get this: He was wearing a scuba suit."

Marlin shook his head. He didn't even know what to say.

Garza rubbed his hands over his face. "What in the world's going on out here, John? It's like all hell's broke loose this week. I've never seen anything like it. You hear about the trouble at Sal Mameli's place?"

Marlin shook his head. "What now?"

"Somebody vandalized some of his machines last night—more like they blew 'em up, right there by his house. A miracle that nobody got killed. No leads on who did it, but my money's on Thomas Peabody."

Hearing that, Marlin was relieved nobody had gotten hurt. Marlin knew that if he'd been more careful with Peabody, the little jerk wouldn't be running loose.

Garza read Marlin's mind. "Don't worry, we'll catch him. Just a matter of time. He would have walked on bail anyway, even if he hadn't slipped away from you. So don't blame yourself for the mess at Mameli's place."

"Thanks." Marlin wanted to hear more about the present situation. "So what's the story on the Porsche?"

"Slaton was in there, along with his dog. In two pieces: It had been decapitated."

"You've got to be kidding."

"Some sick shit, I'm telling you. That probably explains the blood on Slaton's porch. Plus, we found two guns in the car, a forty-five and a thirty-five."

"A thirty-five? I didn't even know there was such a thing."

Garza nodded, getting excited. "That's our ace in the hole. There was only one model ever made—by Smith and Wesson, from 1913 to 1921. There was only something like eight thousand of them produced, so it's something you might see at a gun show. But at a crime scene? We're running the serial number, but don't hold your breath on that. We'll check for prints, too, but being underwater that long . . ."

"Any kind of connection between T.J. and Slaton?"

"We're looking into it." Garza must have seen a look of concern on Marlin's face. "I know what you're thinking: Just yesterday, we were speculating on whether Sal Mameli mighta had something to do with both Gammel and Slaton. Now we find Slaton in a car owned by one of Vinnie Mameli's runnin' buddies."

Marlin nodded. He didn't want his anger toward Vinnie Mameli to cause him to jump to any conclusions, but he felt it was an angle worth exploring.

Garza said, "I'm gonna take this real slow, John. One step at a time, with no screwups. If either Vinnie or Sal was involved, we're not gonna let them slip through the net, I promise you that."

Marlin asked about Jack Corey and Wylie Smith. "They're fine," Garza replied. "Both in the hospital getting checked out. One other thing: This isn't out yet, so you gotta keep it under your hat. . . ."

Marlin nodded.

"I saw Wylie late last night." Garza paused—and Marlin knew the sheriff didn't want to say what he was about to say. "He admitted to holding a gun to Corey's head. Just flat-out confessed to it. So, between you and me, he's a goner. Unofficially, he's already off the force—only he doesn't know it yet. Probably be some criminal charges."

Oddly, Marlin's spirits sank when he heard the news. He had never liked Wylie, but it was heartbreaking when a fellow law-enforcement officer strayed the way Wylie had. It was obvious Garza was bitterly disappointed that one of his deputies had nearly wrecked the life of an innocent man.

Garza continued, with a grim face: "Now I gotta figure out what to do about Corey. He's clear on the Gammel charge, and we can't really hold him accountable for the standoff."

"Hell, the county'll be lucky if he doesn't sue."

"Yeah, I can't say I'd blame him." Garza glanced out the window. "Listen," Garza said, "I've still got a lot of work to do around here. You can hang around and see how it plays out, or take off and I'll keep you posted."

Marlin reached for the door handle. "Think I'll go for a drive," he said. "Take a break for a while."

"I don't blame you."

The twin stories of Jack Corey's surrender and the discovery of Emmett Slaton's body were big news, justifying sporadic live updates on KHIL for the remainder of the day.

Unfortunately for Smedley Poindexter, the only thing playing on the television set in the headquarters of Slaton Brush Removal, Incorporated, was *Hee Haw*. The same clip. Over and over.

Smedley tried valiantly to hang on to his dignity. But within hours, he was a blubbering, pathetic wreck.

CHAPTER FORTY-ONE

John Marlin had never wanted to be anything but a game warden. After all, it was in his blood. His father, Royce Marlin, had been Blanco County's game warden for twenty-two years, up until the mid-1970s. Growing up, John used to watch in awe as his father pulled on his uniform, strapped on his handgun, and set off into the field. Then Royce would come home for supper and tell tall tales about his exploits that day, John's mother rolling her eyes at the exaggerations. It was a happy, exciting childhood—until Royce was killed by a poacher in 1976.

Even that didn't deter Marlin's drive to carry the warden's badge; if anything, it strengthened it. He had completed the game warden cadet academy in Austin in 1982, and then awaited his assignment. The state would relocate him to the first available position, whether it was in the piney woods of East Texas or the flatlands of the Panhandle. As luck would have it, Marlin was assigned to Blanco County when the previous warden retired. For twenty years now, Marlin had thoroughly enjoyed chasing poachers and enforcing game laws around his hometown.

But as he drove the back roads that sunny afternoon, he had to admit that the last week had been unusually rewarding. Nailing a killer like Maynard Clements was gratifying—and Marlin was rarely called upon to take part in a case of that magnitude. Marlin found himself thinking about Bobby Garza's open-ended offer to become a sheriff's deputy. There was no doubt it would be more exciting, with higher-profile cases.

What is this, Marlin wondered, *a midlife crisis*? He put the thought out of his head and puttered down rural roads for the next three hours, stopping at generations-old hunting camps, as well as some new ones. He checked licenses, made small talk with men he had known since birth, and decided that being a game warden wasn't so bad after all.

Just after noon, he drove back home for lunch. Pulling into the driveway, his stomach turned a flip as he saw a familiar car sitting next to Inga's Volvo: Becky's Honda Civic. He swore quietly. He had forgotten that Becky had planned to pick up the last of her things.

Before he made it to the front door, Inga exited, an odd smile on her face. She didn't say anything until they were a few feet apart. "You have a visitor."

"Yeah, that's what I gathered."

They stood in silence for a moment.

"Listen, John," Inga said, "if I screwed anything up for you . . ."

"No, there wasn't anything left to screw up."

"Becky and I talked for a while. I hope you don't mind."

Marlin wanted to groan. That was the last thing he wanted to hear. "Anything I should know?"

Inga shrugged. "She's a nice lady."

"Yeah, yeah, she is."

"I'm going to go into to town for a while, let you two talk."

"I appreciate it. You can come back for—"

Inga held up a hand. "Why don't I call first? Okay?"

Marlin nodded, and Inga walked to her Volvo, climbed in, and drove away.

Marlin turned toward the house, and Becky was already

standing on the front porch holding a box, wearing sweatpants and a T-shirt, her hair pulled back in a ponytail.

"Hey, there," he said softly.

Becky didn't reply. She set the box down on the porch and took a seat in one of the two rocking chairs, looking straight ahead.

Marlin eased into the chair beside her.

"You don't have to say anything," she said.

"I'm sorry. . . ."

She shook her head, cutting him off, and Marlin saw a single tear run down her cheek. She stared down at her hands. "I *am* surprised at how quickly this happened, I will say that much."

"That's not fair," Marlin replied, feeling a need to defend himself. "You haven't really *been* here in four months . . . and I'm not talking physically, I'm talking about up here." Marlin tapped his temple.

She leaned back in the rocking chair and finally looked him in the eye. "I know that. And I'm not sure how I could have changed it. With my mother . . . and the new job. . . ."

Marlin wished there was something he could say to make the awful ache in his chest go away, but he knew words alone couldn't do it. It would take time—for both of them. Finally, Becky laughed and said, "If I had known you had company, I would have put on some makeup."

Marlin tried to grin, but it didn't quite work out. "How's your mom?"

"Actually, she's doing okay—for the moment. The doctor says it could still be several weeks. I had to get out of there for a while."

They sat for a time, letting the sun warm their faces, listening to the doves in nearby trees.

"Becky," Marlin said, "I've told you before: You mean more to me than any woman I've ever met. I love you, and I only want you to be happy."

Her face was a mottled red now, the tears flowing freely. "I know that." She let one hand drift over and cover his—but it felt like anything but a lover's gesture. "I love you, too."

They rose, and Marlin helped Becky pack the rest of her things.

Thomas Peabody could see the BrushBusters from his vantage point—and it appeared that Emmett Slaton had owned a much larger fleet than Sal Mameli. Peabody counted eleven of the infernal machines. Surely the old man must have realized the irreparable damage he was inflicting on the ecosystem. Perhaps Slaton had disappeared because Mother Nature had smote him down, exacting punishment against those who would abuse her. Alas, someone else would come along and fill Slaton's shoes. Those machines wouldn't sit idle for long. Unless Peabody put them out of commission for good. It would be the pièce de résistance of his entire campaign. A replay of last night, with an extra little encore at the end.

The two rednecks in the trailer posed a small problem, but Peabody couldn't see how they could possibly disrupt his plan. It would all happen too quickly, and be too stunning, for them to react in time. He might need a few moments to hot-wire one of the BrushBusters, but he was certain he could accomplish it if he had to. He had learned all types of interesting skills from fellow activists. He had also learned that the men who ran these machines were often foolhardy enough to leave the keys in the ignition.

Afterward, Peabody's work would be done here. The rednecked sapsucker would be saved. He would gather Inga, load up into the trusty Volvo, and ride off into the activist hall of fame.

It was seven o'clock before Bobby Garza finally got back to his office and logged on to one of the terminals connected to the Department of Public Safety's computer network. After wrapping up the crime scene at Pedernales Reservoir—sending the body of Emmett Slaton to the M.E.'s office, and the Porsche, the guns, and the dead dog to the lab in Austin—he had left Bill

Tatum in charge of the investigation. Then he went home and slept for four hours. The Jack Corey standoff had thoroughly wiped him out, and he was emotionally and physically exhausted. After his short break, though, he felt renewed enough to dive back into the Slaton case.

He had checked in with Bill Tatum, who told him that the body found under the dock was indeed T.J. Gibbs. Tatum was on his way back from Austin after informing the Gibbs family of T.J.'s death. He had spent an hour interviewing the family, but could not discover any link between T.J. and Slaton. He also reported that none of the deputies had run a check yet on either of the handguns found in the Porsche.

Garza was disappointed, but he didn't quibble. His deputies had been stretched to the max in the last week, and they didn't need to hear his complaints. Especially when he had just awakened from a midday slumber himself.

So now, sitting at his desk in his office, he accessed the DPS network. He entered the first serial number, the one from the .45 automatic. After a few seconds, the owner was identified as Emmett Howard Slaton. Interesting, but a little disheartening. Garza was afraid the second gun would come back as Slaton's, too.

He typed in the second serial number and waited. This request took a little longer to process, but the results finally appeared on his screen. Garza frowned.

It was a familiar name, but he couldn't quite place it.

Who the hell is Roberto Ragusa?

Before he could figure it out, the phone on his desk rang. Someone was calling his direct line. Garza answered it.

"Good evening, Sheriff, my name is Eugene Kramer. I'm an attorney in Austin."

"How can I help you?"

"I believe you may know a client of mine. Sal Mameli."

"Yeah, I know Sal," Garza said, trying to put as much disapproval into his voice as possible. He expected the lawyer to protest his questioning of Sal about the bribery case. But Garza was in for a surprise.

The attorney said, "Mr. Mameli and I would like to arrange a meeting with you—as soon as possible. Vincent believes he might have some information regarding the murder of Emmett Slaton."

Marlin was enjoying another wonderful meal prepared by Inga, but he was afraid he wasn't very good company. He was preoccupied, replaying his conversation with Becky that afternoon.

"Great food," Marlin said.

Inga smiled. Marlin knew she could sense his mood. He was about to apologize when the phone rang. It was Bobby Garza.

"Can you meet me at my office at eight-thirty?"

"I guess so," Marlin said. "What's going on?"

"Something interesting has come up, and I want you to sit in."

Billy Don was happy to take a break and ride into town for supplies like Red asked. Shit, as far as Billy Don was concerned, this thing with Smedley was going nowhere. That's because Red had it all wrong. Ain't no way that guy worked for Sal Mameli. He was too damn nice for that. A couple of times, Billy Don had gone in and talked to him for a few minutes when Red was sleeping. Just another regular guy, friendly as can be. Billy Don hated the way Red was abusing him. In fact, Billy Don had snuck in and turned down the volume before he left, so poor old Smedley wouldn't go completely cuckoo from listening to that *Hee Haw* song. As long as Red didn't check the headphones, he'd never know.

Billy Don pulled into a convenience store and went inside. *Just don't go to that one owned by Ay-rabs,* Red had said. Hell, Billy Don didn't need Red to tell him *that.*

Inside, Billy Don began loading up a basket with potato chips, pretzels, Slim Jims, and little chocolate donuts. He even threw a package of Twinkies in for Smedley. Billy Don thought Smedley looked like the kind of guy who could appreciate a Twinkie now and again.

Billy Don was making his way toward the counter when the

front door opened and Kitty Katz, the TV reporter, walked in. Behind her was Darrell Bridges, the sheriff's dispatcher. They were giggling about something. Billy Don instinctively turned and strolled casually to the far side of the store.

Kitty and Darrell walked in Billy Don's direction but stopped at the soda fountain, where they began to fill some cups. Billy Don could tell from the way they were standing, brushing hips on occasion, that they had the hots for each other. It was quiet in the store, so Billy Don couldn't help but over-hear what they were saying.

"Aw, come on, Darrell. Just between you and me," Kitty cooed.

Darrell glanced around the store and Billy Don pretended to be studying a quart of motor oil.

"All right," Darrell whispered. "But off the record, okay?"

Billy Don couldn't see, but Kitty must have batted her long lashes at the dispatcher.

"It *was* Emmett Slaton's body in that car," Darrell said.

Billy Don wondered if his ears were playing tricks on him.

"And there were a couple of guns in there with him," Darrell went on to say. "A forty-five and a thirty-five. They're running ballistics down at the lab."

Billy Don quietly set his basket on the floor, took the long way around the store, and walked out the front door as quickly as he could.

CHAPTER FORTY-TWO

At precisely eight-thirty, Marlin watched Bobby Garza escort Sal Mameli, who was on crutches, his son Vinnie, and a third man—presumably Sal's lawyer—into the interview room at the Sheriff's Department. Marlin was sitting in an adjoining room, watching through a one-way mirror. Beside him were two deputies: Bill Tatum and Rachel Cowan. The lawyer, Kramer, had insisted that Garza conduct the interview alone. (*But, Garza had said, he didn't say anything about spectators.*)

"I hear you had quite a commotion out here," Kramer said, making small talk to break the uncomfortable silence.

"Word travels fast," Garza replied.

All four men took a seat around the lone table, Sal and Vinnie surveying the room as if they expected cops to be hiding in the corners.

"Before we begin, I would like to lay down a few ground rules," Kramer said.

Garza nodded.

"Mr. Mameli tells me that you paid him a visit yesterday on an unrelated matter. Considering that my clients are coming forth out of their own concern for the community, I will ask that you restrict your questions to the Slaton case alone. If any questions should stray from that topic, I will advise my clients not to answer. Are we clear on that?"

Marlin knew the lawyer was discouraging Garza from fishing for details about the bribery case. And possibly the attempted rape case, if Vinnie was involved.

Garza kept a poker face. "Agreed."

"Well, then. . . ." The lawyer gestured toward Vinnie, who looked as if he was about to vomit.

"I saw the news this morning," Vinnie said. "I saw T.J.'s car gettin' pulled outta the lake and everything. And, uh, the thing is . . . I kinda think T.J. killed that old man."

Red was sitting on the couch, keeping an eye on Smedley, flipping through a copy of *Juggs* magazine, when he heard Billy Don come roaring up to the trailer. A few seconds later, he felt the entire structure shake as Billy Don thundered up the steps and came bustling through the front door.

"Red!" he said. "Turn on the news! They found Emmett Slaton!"

Garza sat quietly for a couple of beats, his eyes boring into Vinnie's. "And why do you think that?"

Vinnie leaned forward, putting his elbows on the table. Then he changed his mind and removed them. "See, me and T.J. was out four-wheeling once, and we kinda wandered onto Slaton's place. We wasn't doing nothin', just riding through a coupla his pastures. But he came ridin' up in his truck and started screamin' at us, tellin' us we was trespassin'. Guy was pissed off, too. I thought he was gonna drop dead right then from a heart attack, he was so worked up."

Vinnie went on to say that Slaton and T.J. had been enemies ever since. Anytime they saw each other, they would exchange harsh words.

Garza asked when and where the incidents had taken place, and he took notes as Vinnie answered. Most of them, Vinnie said, had happened outside of various businesses in Johnson City. Apparently, T.J. and Vinnie had nothing better to do than park along Main Street and "just hang out."

"Did anyone else ever see these arguments?" Garza asked.

Vinnie glanced at the lawyer, who nodded. Vinnie continued: "Well, they wasn't really arguments, more like the two of them just cussing each other. T.J. would make engine sounds, you know, like four-wheeling noises, when Slaton would walk by. Slaton would glare at us and tell us to stay the hell off his land."

"You didn't answer my question," Garza said quietly. "Were there any other witnesses to these exchanges?"

Vinnie scratched his head. "None that I can remember."

The room was silent as Garza wrote something on the pad. "So," the sheriff said, "if you think T.J. killed Slaton because of this bad blood, do you have any idea how T.J. ended up dead himself?"

Vinnie lowered his eyes to the table. "Yeah, I heard about that this afternoon. I got no idea how that happened. Musta drowned somehow. He was always out on the lake, just fuckin' around."

Garza nodded abruptly, and it was obvious to Marlin that the sheriff thought everything Vinnie had just told him was worthless. "Anything else?"

The lawyer glanced at Sal, who finally spoke up. "Yeah, dere is one other thing. I think the kid was stealing from us."

"T.J.?"

"Yeah, T.J. We had a coupla things go missing after the kid had been at our house. My wristwatch, some cash on the kitchen counter, some of my wife's diamond earrings." Marlin could tell from Sal's facial expression that he hoped Garza would find that information very interesting.

Garza didn't. "Did you report it?" he asked.

"Naw. Didn't figger it was wort' the hassle." Sal laughed. "Figgered youse guys was busy enough already."

Garza slid his chair back. "All right, then. Thanks for coming in."

The deputies filed into the interview room, Marlin bringing up the rear. Garza had sat back down again, drumming his pencil on the table.

"What do you think?" Tatum asked.

"Total bullshit," Garza said.

Out in the parking lot, Sal rested on his crutches and shook hands with Eugene Kramer. He gave Vinnie a big smile. These small-town cops were so much easier than the Feds. And he had played them just right. Now they had a good reason to look at T.J. for the death of Slaton. And if they ever managed to trace Sal's .35-caliber back to him, he could simply say that T.J. must have stolen it. *Why didn't you mention the handgun in the interview?* they would ask. *I hadn't noticed it was missing yet,* Sal would say. It was perfect. He felt much better now, not so angry at Vinnie. "Well, dat went pretty well," Sal said.

Smedley liked the big guy, Billy Don, much more than Red. Billy Don was nicer, doing things like turning down the headphones and cutting Smedley loose to go to the bathroom when he needed to. But now, if Smedley could have freed himself from the chair, he would have jumped up and kissed Billy Don. Because he had just said the magical words: *They found Emmett Slaton!*

It was all over now. Red would have no reason to hold him anymore.

He listened as Billy Don told Red a story about being at a convenience store. Billy Don had overheard a cop talking to a reporter about Slaton's body. Oh, thank God there were still a few loose-lipped officers around!

Red turned off the DVD and switched the TV over to KHIL.

Sure enough, there was Kitty Katz, giving a live report. She was saying that a reliable source had confirmed that the body found in the car pulled from Pedernales Reservoir was Emmett Slaton, as rumored. She went on to say that the police had also found two handguns in the car—a .45-caliber and a .35-caliber.

Smedley wondered: *Did she just say .35-caliber?* Smedley was putting it all together, thinking that Sal Mameli was the only person he knew who owned a .35, when—

WOOOOM!

The trailer was rocked by the most enormous explosion Smedley had ever felt. It was followed by another. And another. And another—until Smedley thought the assault would never end. Finally, the explosions did stop, and now all three men were lying on the floor of the trailer, in a stupor, like G.I.s after a mortar attack. The interior of the trailer was bathed in an eerie orange glow.

"What in the fuck was that?" Red said, as he struggled to his feet.

Smedley began to grunt urgently, the tape still over his mouth, trying to capture the men's attention. Surely they would have the good sense to turn him loose before something worse happened.

Red swung the front door open and Smedley could feel the heat from the fires burning outside.

"Oh, Jesus," Red said, staring out the door as if aliens had just landed. "Billy Don, come take a look at this."

But Billy Don wasn't listening. Smedley was elated and grateful and relieved to see Billy Don coming toward him with a pair of scissors.

Red simply could not believe what he was seeing. The Brush-Busters were on fire. All of them. With flames shooting thirty feet high, big goddamn clouds of black smoke rolling into the sky.

Then he saw that he was mistaken. There was one solitary BrushBuster that wasn't on fire. And there was a man sitting in the driver's seat. Red couldn't be sure, because the fires were roaring pretty loud—but he thought he heard the BrushBuster's engine running.

Just then, their prisoner, Smedley, went pushing past Red into the night. Red didn't even try to stop him. He had much larger problems on his hands now.

Billy Don came up behind him and they stepped out onto the front porch. They watched as the man tried to operate the BrushBuster, first going forward, then putting it into reverse, backing away from the flames.

"Grab my forty-five," Red said. "On the kitchen counter."

"But Red—"

"Do it!"

Billy Don turned and went into the trailer. The BrushBuster made a left turn and seemed to be heading away from the trailer. *He's stealing my last goddamn machine,* Red thought. *That lousy sumbitch.* Then the man slowly swung around and came to a halt, eighty yards away.

Billy Don returned and handed the gun to Red.

"What the hell's he doing?" Billy Don asked.

Red shook his head, thoroughly confused.

The man seemed to be staring right at them, just watching them.

"You know, there's that mental hospital right up the road," Billy Don said. "Maybe he—"

Red held up his hand for silence.

Then there was a gnashing of gears as the man put the tree-cutter into DRIVE. He started slowly, then picked up speed. He was heading straight for the trailer.

"What's wrong with that crazy fucker?" Red said.

The BrushBuster was forty yards away now, and closing fast.

Red and Billy Don began to yell, waving their arms as if they could somehow ward him off.

The machine kept coming.

Red lowered his gun and fired a round at the machine.

Twenty yards.

Red fired again.

Ten yards.

And then they both dove for the inside of the trailer as the BrushBuster came smashing through the front door.

The chaos was incredible. Tremendous wrenching sounds as metal was twisted and torn. The sound of the tree-cutter's engine whining as it tried to plow forward. Red felt himself being tossed and jostled, like he was riding an inner tube down the rapids of a flooded river. He was aware of a tremendous pain in his leg.

Finally, the noise came to an end as the BrushBuster's engine sputtered and died. The tree-cutter was now sitting *inside* of the trailer, the floor sagging beneath it, the ceiling above crumpled.

Red looked down and saw that his left leg had been gashed by a ragged sheet of metal. He heard Billy Don moaning on the other side of the machine.

Billy Don knew his arm was seriously damaged, pinned under the BrushBuster's front wheel. But for some reason—maybe he was going into shock—he found himself mesmerized by the metal plate that was right in front of him, riveted to the machine's frame. He had never noticed it before. The plate was well lit by the fires burning outside.

"Billy Don, you okay?" Red called.

"I think I'll be all right." Billy Don said, still staring at the plate. On it, he could see all kinds of information about this particular model of BrushBuster. There was a serial number. Net vehicle weight. The size of tires you were supposed to use. Even the amount of gas the tank held. And at the bottom, there it was: the pounds-per-square-inch that the pincers applied.

"Hey, Red," Billy Don called.

"Yeah?" Red answered, grunting as he extracted himself from the wreckage.

"I know what the '3000' stands for now."

CHAPTER FORTY-THREE

Bobby Garza, the two deputies, and Marlin were sitting around the table now, drinking coffee, brainstorming about the Mameli case. They had stopped calling it "the Slaton case"; they were that certain one of the Mamelis was involved.

Ten minutes earlier, a lab tech from Austin had called with disappointing news. Both of the handguns in the Porsche had been dusted for prints. Both were clean. Likewise, Bobby Garza had thrown out the name Roberto Ragusa, but none of the deputies recognized it. They had run the name through the computers, and it was like the man had fallen off the face of the Earth. His last known address was in New Jersey, but that had been more than three years ago. Since then, there was nothing in the public records for Ragusa. He hadn't voted, renewed his driver's license, or even filed a tax return. The man was a ghost. Garza planned to make some calls to New Jersey in the morning, to see what he could find out. In the meantime, the deputies were rapidly running out of ideas.

"What about a warrant to search Mameli's house?" Marlin asked. Marlin was surprised nobody had suggested it yet.

"We don't have enough," Garza said. "You have to specify exactly what you're searching for and why you think you'll find it there. We don't even know what we'd be looking for."

The search-and-seizure laws were obviously more complex than the ones that allowed Marlin to search a poacher's vehicle.

"The question is," Bill Tatum said, "why would Vinnie make up all that crap? And why would Sal throw in that stuff about T.J. stealing from their home?"

"Misdirection?" Rachel Cowan suggested.

Garza stretched and yawned in his chair. "I think if we figure that out, we'll blow the case wide open," he said.

After another ten minutes and no forward progress, Garza pushed back his chair and said, "It's nearly eleven now. I say we call it a night. We're gonna have to keep digging on this, and I want you all fresh in the morning. Let's regroup at six A.M."

The deputies murmured agreement and began to stand.

"Of course, Marlin, I don't expect—"

"I'll be here," Marlin said, surprising himself.

Garza smiled. "Okay, then."

The deputies left the interview room, walked through the main room of the department, and stepped out the front door.

Bill Tatum started to say something, but Garza signaled for him to be quiet. A large engine could be heard in the distance. Tires squealed as the vehicle turned the corner onto Main Street, one block down from the sheriff's office. A few seconds later, headlights appeared and swung into the parking lot. Marlin recognized Red O'Brien's old Ford truck racing their way, more banged up that before.

The vehicle screeched to a stop directly in front of them. The driver's door swung open and an overweight, unkempt man emerged. His clothes were soiled, he needed a shave, and he had duct tape dangling from his wrists and face.

Breathing heavily, his eyes wild, the man said, "Sal Mameli killed Emmett Slaton. And I can prove it."

.   .   .

Red jostled and pulled and tugged—and finally managed to get Billy Don's arm loose. He felt plenty bad for his friend, because his arm was obviously broken. Red needed medical attention, too, probably some stitches on his leg. But they were both doing better than the lunatic who had driven the tree-cutter into the trailer. The man was slumped over the steering wheel, unmoving.

Red reached up and shook the man's shoulder. The man responded by sliding sideways out of the seat and falling to the floor.

"Oh, shit," Red said. He bent down and jostled the man's arm, but there was no response. "Aw, damn. Billy Don, I think I kilt him! Call nine-one-one!"

"I'd say it's too late for that, Red."

"How did you hear about the thirty-five caliber we found?" Garza asked. They were back in the interview room once again—the deputies, the sheriff, Marlin, and the man Garza had introduced as U.S. Deputy Marshal Smedley Poindexter. If Garza hadn't vouched for Poindexter, Marlin never would have believed he was a federal agent. Marlin always imagined a Fed would look like the cool characters in the movies: mirror shades, expensive suit, and an attitude the size of a Buick.

"It was on the news just thirty minutes ago," Poindexter replied, gently removing the last of the duct tape.

Garza let out a sigh, and Marlin knew that meant there had been a leak.

"And what is the evidence you have, if you don't mind me asking?"

Poindexter told them that Sal Mameli owned a .35-caliber handgun, a family antique, and that he had recently seen a shell from the gun hanging from the Mameli housekeeper's necklace.

Garza gave him a puzzled expression.

"See, she makes jewelry out of little odds and ends. She must have found the shell in Sal's house and decided to put it in her necklace."

Garza shook his head in confusion. "Look, you're losing me here. Start from the beginning. How do you know Sal Mameli?"

The marshal took a deep breath. "I'm afraid I can't comment on that. At least, not yet."

Everyone was fidgety and frustrated now, including Marlin.

"But you're saying the gun we found is Sal Mameli's?" Garza asked.

Poindexter said, "It *has* to be. How many of you have ever seen a Smith and Wesson thirty-five caliber?"

Rachel Cowan spoke up: "I think I did once, at a pawn shop."

"My point is, they're pretty damn rare," the marshal replied. "And what are the odds of one showing up in a murder case where the Mamelis are material witnesses, and then it turning out that the gun isn't Sal's?"

"But when I ran a check on that serial number," Garza said, "it came back as—"

He stopped in midsentence and everybody looked his way. Marlin had never seen Garza look as astonished as he did now. "Oh, crap," the sheriff said softly. "Roberto Ragusa. The mafia informant."

Someone gasped.

Everyone turned to Poindexter now. He shrugged and held his palms up, a *What can I say?* gesture. "I'm afraid I can't comment on that."

"Does this become a federal case now?" Garza asked.

"I'd say that's kind of a gray area," Poindexter replied. "He's a dangerous man, Sheriff, and I would feel obligated to participate in whatever action you might take. But if you feel the need to proceed . . ."

Garza glanced at Bill Tatum. "Get Judge Hilton on the phone."

"Uh, Bobby," Tatum said, "it's kind of late to—"

"Wake him up if you have to! Tell him we need a warrant. Immediately."

Tatum grabbed the nearest phone and began to dial. Poindexter spoke up in a sheepish voice: "Uh, I don't suppose one of you has a gun I can borrow?"

• • •

They went in two cruisers: Garza, Cowan, and Marlin in one, Poindexter and Tatum in another. When they were a quarter-mile from Mameli's driveway, they drove slowly with the headlights off.

It was now almost one in the morning. Judge Hilton had been grumpy as hell about being awakened, but when he heard the wild tale Garza and Poindexter laid before him, he issued the warrant and wished them luck.

Marlin had been on countless middle-of-the-night maneuvers, but nothing compared to this. His heart was thundering in his chest and his breathing was rapid.

The plan was for Garza, Marlin, and the deputies to serve the warrant at the front door while Poindexter covered the back. Poindexter had told them about Maria's cottage behind the house, and they wanted to make sure they contained Sal and Vinnie within the house. If they were forced to invade the home, Marlin and Poindexter were to guard the perimeter of the home until Garza, Cowan, and Tatum had the situation in hand. Poindexter had warned the team that Sal Mameli was capable of just about anything. *He might welcome us into his home with open arms, or he might start shooting as soon as he sees us.* Those comments hadn't raised the team's spirits any, but Marlin could tell that everyone was glad the marshal was being frank.

Garza pulled the lead car into the driveway, and the crunching of the gravel under the tires seemed as loud as firecrackers. As soon as the home came into view, Garza stopped the car. The team gathered between the cars to exchange a few last words, and Smedley gave them a general layout of the house.

Garza said, "We're just serving a warrant here; it's not a bust. I want you to be careful, but no guns drawn, understood?"

Nods all around, and then the group made their way up the driveway. When they were twenty yards in front of the porch, which ran the length of the house, Poindexter quietly split off and went around the side.

Garza waited a full minute, then motioned toward the front door. A weak porch bulb—yellow, to discourage insects—illuminated the way.

They stepped right up to the front door, and Garza didn't waste any time. He pounded on the door with the cushion of his fist. "Sheriff's Department! We have a warrant! Open up!"

A light popped on somewhere deep inside the house.

Garza pounded on the door again and repeated his command.

Half a minute passed, and then they heard shuffling behind the door. It opened about four inches. There was a chain dangling from the door to the frame, and Marlin could make out Sal Mameli, wearing pajamas, crutches underneath his arms, peeking through the crack. "What the hell is this?" Mameli said.

Garza held up a sheet of paper. We've got a warrant, Sal. Open up."

Sal's mind was buzzing, rocking and reeling in overdrive, and he could barely put together a coherent thought. It was Garza and Marlin and a couple of deputies banging on the door and screaming and yelling and now Garza was holding up a goddamn warrant.

They didn't give me enough time to get ready for this shit! Without even thinking, Sal slammed his body against the door and it closed with a bang. He let the crutches fall, then he turned and clomped down the hallway on his cast, thinking, *The shell, the shell—I've got to get to Maria and get that goddamn shell!*

Marlin would try to describe the next few minutes in his report the next morning, but as his adrenaline kicked in, he found that the sequence of events unfolded in a fuzzy, almost dreamlike fashion.

Sal was looking at them one second—and the next, the door slammed shut. Garza immediately began kicking at the door,

Tatum joining in, and Marlin found himself standing . . . watching . . . playing the role of a spectator.

It seemed that it was taking entirely too long, but then the door finally gave, and Garza, Cowan, and Tatum ducked inside, yelling loudly, guns drawn.

Sal opened the top drawer of the hutch to grab the handgun he had placed there just this evening for exactly this kind of thing and . . . Jesus Christ Almighty, it was gone! Vinnie must have grabbed it. Sal could still hear the cops hammering on the door behind him, and it was sure to give any second. He started to head through the living room to the back door, but then stopped and ducked into the kitchen, suddenly *knowing* that they would have somebody waiting at the back door. They came out in force, they came out in the middle of the night, so of course they'd have somebody at the back door. But Sal was too smart for that shit and he wasn't going to fall into their trap. He was going to go through the garage instead.

Marlin was standing on the front porch, jittery, feeling useless, when he saw a flash of movement from the corner of his eye. He took one step back and saw Vinnie Mameli squirming through a window that opened onto the far end of the porch, almost at the corner of the house. Marlin started to move toward him when he noticed the black steel in Vinnie's hand.

Before Marlin could even yell *Freeze!*—Vinnie swung the gun at him and fired.

CHAPTER FORTY-FOUR

Behind the house, waiting by the back door, Smedley was hoping and praying the operation would go down flawlessly. After all, he was sure to receive a reprimand for failing to report to Austin before the warrant was served. But Maria meant too much to him, and he didn't want to wait that long. He knew his superiors would want to study the situation, analyze it for a few days. Hell, they might even try to whitewash the entire situation. They certainly didn't want another black eye for the witness protection program. That's why this had to go smoothly, without incident.

Then Smedley heard a shot from somewhere near the front of the house. He drew his weapon.

Garza and Tatum were deep within the residence, trying to find Sal, when they heard the gunshot. The acoustics in the big stone house played tricks with the sound, and they couldn't tell whether the shot came from inside or outside the house. They began a room-to-room search, Garza wondering whether they might find Sal's corpse, dead from his own hand.

Marlin threw himself to the ground and heard the round ricochet off the stone entryway behind him. He instinctively rolled, anticipating another shot, but it never came. He sprang to his feet and saw that Vinnie had leaped the railing of the porch and was sprinting into the darkness.

Marlin had dropped his gun when he tumbled, and by the time he picked it up and drew his flashlight, Vinnie was out of sight. Marlin glanced through the open front door, unsure whether to remain where he was or go after Vinnie. Garza and the deputies were nowhere to be seen.

He went after Vinnie.

The waiting was almost too much for Smedley. Who the hell had fired that shot? What was going on in there? Was there an officer down? Should he abort the original plan and enter the home?

Then he heard a sound he instantly recognized. The groaning of the garage door as it worked its way up the tracks. They had forgotten about the garage door—and now somebody was coming out through it! The question was, should he go investigate or stay put? He decided he would work his way along the back wall of the house, peek around the corner to the garage, and still keep an eye on the back door.

He stepped gingerly because the area behind the house was rocky and uneven. He tripped a few times, making more noise than he would have liked, then finally arrived at the corner. He stuck his head around to take a look . . . and had a mere instant to see a shovel coming toward his forehead.

He felt the impact all the way down to his toes.

His knees buckled, but he managed to remain standing. But now he realized his gun hand was empty. Even through the double vision, he could see that the .38 he had borrowed was now in the hands of Sal Mameli, pointed straight at his face.

Then he heard another shot.

Garza and the deputies found the house empty, except for Angela Mameli passed out in the bedroom. Even the two gunshots hadn't roused her. They headed for the front door to see what the hell was going on outside.

Marlin weaved his way through a thick grove of cedar and oak trees, his flashlight extinguished, following the sounds of Vinnie's frantic rampage through the brush. Vinnie was in Marlin's territory now—in the dark, tramping through the woods—maybe twenty or thirty yards away. *Take it easy,* Marlin thought. *It's just like rounding up a poacher.*

Just up ahead, he heard the scratch of a branch against Vinnie's clothing. It was unmistakable, a sound he had grown up with. Vinnie seemed to have slowed down, too, waiting for a chance to ambush his pursuer.

Groping in the dark, Marlin found the trunk of a large oak tree and stood perfectly still behind it. Then he called out, "Vinnie, give it up!"

The response was another shot, which thumped into the front of the oak tree.

Marlin was breathing heavily now, struggling to remain calm, the pulse pounding in his temples. He took a deep breath—and heard it again. Just a scratch—but that was all he needed.

Marlin wheeled around the tree and fired three quick shots into the dark.

He heard Vinnie Mameli scream.

Smedley wondered if he was dead. He didn't feel dead. He heard screaming, but he was fairly certain that it wasn't coming from him. He was almost too afraid to open his eyes. But he did. He still had double vision, so he saw two Sal Mamelis rolling on the ground, cupping their groins.

Smedley craned his neck and looked behind him. He couldn't believe it. It was like something out of a million bad movies he had seen . . . where someone arrives in the nick of time to save the day.

It was Maria.

She was holding Smedley's gun.

She had just shot Sal Mameli.

Right in the balls.

Marlin waited a few minutes, until Vinnie Mameli's groans subsided. Then he knelt low and turned on his flashlight, prepared to dive for cover if necessary. But Vinnie was down, sprawled under the lower boughs of a cedar tree. Marlin carefully stepped toward Vinnie until he was just a few yards away.

He might have seen the final spark of life in Vinnie's eyes, but he couldn't be sure. In any case, when he knelt down to check his pulse, there was none. Marlin dropped his head and sighed, and he could feel his hand shaking as he slid his gun back into its holster.

After a moment, he returned to the house and called through the front door. Tatum responded, but his voice came from outside the house, near the garage. Marlin found Tatum and Cowan standing guard over Sal Mameli, who seemed to be in shock, lying on the ground. Blood saturated the crotch of his pajamas.

"Garza and Smedley?" Marlin asked.

Tatum said, "Garza's inside, calling for an ambulance. Do we need two?"

"Yeah . . . but no rush on the second one."

Tatum nodded. He gestured toward the small cottage behind the house, where every window now glowed with light. "Smedley's in there, with the housekeeper. Got clocked with a shovel. Bleeding pretty bad."

Marlin walked to the cottage and stepped inside. It was a

small structure, but clean and well-decorated. In the small bedroom, he found Smedley sitting in a chair, the pretty housekeeper holding a towel to his head. She was murmuring to him
in Spanish, but Marlin couldn't pick out any of the words.

"Smedley, you all right?"

Neither of them even looked his way.

A cat emerged from somewhere and began to rub against
Marlin's leg. A black bird in a cage bobbed up and down on its
perch, chirping, probably thinking it was morning already.
Marlin looked away, and then looked back at the bird. It
looked . . . familiar.

Marlin stood there awkwardly for a moment, watching
Smedley and the housekeeper gaze into each other's eyes, then
he turned and left them alone.

Sheriff Bobby Garza finally decided to accept assistance from
an outside agency. An investigative team from the Department
of Public Safety converged on the Mameli house within hours.
When Marlin spoke to Garza on Monday afternoon, the sheriff
was exhausted but confident.

A .35-caliber shell had been found on the housekeeper's
necklace, just as Poindexter had said. Three bullet holes pocked
the walls of Sal's den. One .35-caliber bullet, still in good condition, had been extracted from a stud. Luminol revealed the
presence of blood in many locations around the room, with a
large concentration in one particular area on the carpet. This,
Garza figured, was where Emmett Slaton had died.

Monday evening, Marlin drove Inga to the Mamelis' house. She
would be leaving in the morning, going back to Minnesota,
where Thomas Peabody would be buried. Inga had been
crushed by the news of her friend's death, and Marlin hoped he
could lift her spirits a little. He had warned her that he hadn't
gotten a good look at the bird, and he was pretty sure it didn't
have a red band on the back of its neck.

That seemed to excite her. "The males don't have that band when they're young. It appears when they mature sexually." Inga started talking about the possibilities—the opportunity to initiate a captive-breeding program—if only the bird turned out to be a male. Marlin was worried that she was in for a letdown.

He pulled around the house and parked by the garage, next to one lone van from the DPS. The investigation was obviously wrapping up.

He put his truck in PARK and sat for a moment. "I'm sorry it had to end up this way," he said. "With your friend . . ."

She smiled, then leaned over and gave him a hug. Marlin held her tight for several moments.

"Well," she said, wiping her eyes, "let's go see what we have."

They walked to the small cottage, and Marlin ducked under the yellow tape while Inga waited behind it. A moment later, Marlin emerged carrying the birdcage.

As he got closer, Inga's eyes widened. "Oh my God, John," she whispered. "Oh my God."

Billy Don and Red were watching the Cowboys on *Monday Night Football*, sucking back a few cold ones, but Billy Don felt like he was sitting in a funeral home. It was just that depressing. Billy Don hated to see Red feeling so low.

The day had actually started out pretty well. This morning, they had met with Smedley—who turned out to be a federal marshal after all! It had looked like they were in hot water up to their necks, but Smedley and Billy Don had shared a box of Twinkies and Smedley decided not to file charges.

Then the cops called, and Red found out he wasn't responsible for killing that little guy on the tree-cutter. The man's neck had been broken when he'd crashed into the trailer. Didn't have a single bullet wound.

But right after that, Red received some awful news from Emmett Slaton's lawyer, Harold Cannon. Turns out Mr. Slaton didn't have insurance on any of the tree-cutters. Cannon said the old man was so rich, he hadn't needed insurance.

That's why Red was moping over there, pissed off that his brand-new business had gone up in smoke last night. He wasn't even a vice president of anything anymore.

"Red, you want another beer?" Billy Don asked.

"Yeah, I guess," Red said.

Damn, the man was downright glum. Billy Don pulled two beers from the cooler sitting next to his recliner and tossed one to Red.

"What say I go in there and whip up some of my world-famous nachos? With extry jalapeños like you like 'em?"

"Whatever."

Billy Don came back fifteen minutes later with a cookie sheet loaded with tortilla chips that had been covered with re-fried beans, melted cheese, jalapeños, and sour cream. Billy Don started wolfing them down, and Red finally ate a few himself. That was a little bit of progress.

The game was a scoreless tie, and Billy Don was starting to get a little bored. He raised his arm and examined the cast around his left wrist. "Red, let me ask you somethin'," he said. "Why do they call this stuff 'plaster of Paris'? You think it's all made in Paris?"

Red grunted and shook his head.

"Because, to me," Billy Don continued, "that seems kinda dumb. I mean, why ship this shit all the way over from Paris when we could manufacture it right here in the U.S.A.? Damn unpatriotic, if you ask me."

"It ain't made in Paris," Red muttered.

"What was that?"

Red grabbed the remote and turned the volume down a tad. "I said it ain't made in Paris, you doofus. That's just a name they give it."

Billy Don tried to look skeptical. "Aw, come on, Red. Then why would they call it that?"

Red sighed and looked up at the ceiling. "Hell if I know, Billy Don," he said forcefully. "Maybe they named it after the inventor or somethin'."

"What, like 'Bob Paris'?"

"Yeah, maybe," Red said defensively, getting all stirred up now.

"Shee-yit, I don't think you know what the hell you're talking about," Billy Don said.

And *that* got Red riled. He swung his bandaged leg off the sofa and sat up straight, his jaw flapping ninety miles a minute now, giving it to Billy Don with both barrels. Billy Don wanted to grin, but he did his best to keep a straight face.

EPILOGUE

Susannah Branson, the newspaper reporter, was happy to have another crack at John Marlin. Not just for personal reasons this time, but for professional ones, too. The man was a local hero now—he and the sheriff. The cases they had been involved in were incredible. Front-page stuff. Susannah could envision her stories being picked up by the dailies in Austin, Dallas, Houston . . . maybe even New York and L.A. This was the kind of exposure that could finally skyrocket her career.

They met at Big Joe's Restaurant again, took the same booth, and sat down for a quiet interview. It was three o'clock on Thursday, and the restaurant was nearly empty.

"Thanks for meeting me again, John," Susannah said, giving him her best smile as she removed her tape recorder from her purse. "Sounds like you had a wild week."

Marlin smiled faintly. "You could say that."

They talked for nearly an hour about both the Bert Gammel bribery case and the Emmett Slaton homicide. Susannah was getting some magnificent material on tape, but there were still some things Marlin couldn't discuss. Like the autopsy results on T.J. Gibbs. The police were remaining quiet on that topic—but the buzz was that it wasn't a drowning after all.

"Tell me about working with the federal marshal, Smedley Poindexter."

Marlin proceeded to describe Poindexter as a committed, hardworking agent. "I've spent some time with him over the last few days, going over details on the cases, and he's really a fine man and a dedicated officer. The U.S. Marshals Service is lucky to have him."

"What about the gossip that he plans to move to Guatemala and open a beachside hotel? With the Mamelis' housekeeper?"

"I'm afraid you'll have to ask Smedley about that," Garza said, and Susannah suspected he knew more than he was telling.

"And the other rumor: that you're thinking about hanging up your game warden's hat and joining the Blanco County Sheriff's Department?"

Marlin laughed. "You've been talking to Bobby Garza, right?"

"Well," Susannah played along with his good humor, "you know I can't reveal my sources. Just passing along what I heard."

Marlin grabbed his coffee cup but didn't drink. "Well, to be honest, that's all it is: gossip."

"No plans to join the Sheriff's Department, then?"

"None whatsoever."

Susannah eyed him, trying to gauge his sincerity. After a few seconds, she was convinced.

"Okay, last question." She had gotten all the good stuff already. Now she just needed some filler. "Do you have any comment on yesterday's reading of Emmett Slaton's will?"

"Sorry, but I haven't heard anything about it."

"Oh, well, I guess you *have* been kind of distracted. It turns out that Slaton was wealthier than a lot of people realized. His lawyer held a press conference yesterday and announced that Mr. Slaton left more than fifty million dollars to the county. And it says here . . ." She rifled through some papers. "I know I have a transcript of the announcement somewhere. Here we go: The attorney said, 'The bulk of the money is to be used to renovate and expand the Blanco County Hospital.' Pretty exciting, huh?"

Marlin set down his coffee cup. "May I see that?"

Susannah handed the papers to the game warden, who began to scan them quickly. He looked up, grinning broadly. "That's fantastic news," he said. "When is all this going to happen?"

"From what I understand, they're going to start building as soon as possible. The city council says . . ."

John Marlin was sliding out of the booth. "I don't mean to be rude, Susannah, but I've really got to make a call."

"Sure," Susannah said, anxious to get in front of her computer and begin writing. She held out a hand and Marlin shook it. "A pleasure, as always, Mr. Marlin."

"Thank you, Susannah."

Susannah gathered her belongings, keeping an eye on Marlin as he went to the pay phone and slipped some coins into the slot.

Keep reading for an excerpt from
Ben Rehder's next mystery

FLAT CRAZY

NOW AVAILABLE FROM
ST. MARTIN'S/MINOTAUR PAPERBACKS!

Duke Waldrip was a damn resourceful hunting guide. In fact, he was so clever, his clients occasionally ended up with trophy deer mounts that weren't exactly authentic. Of course, the clients were unaware of this fact, but it was always at the back of Duke's mind that one of them might figure it out.

That's why he was a little uneasy about the man who was currently sitting in front of him—and there weren't too many things that made Duke Waldrip uneasy. As Duke liked to say, once you've done time in Huntsville, being outside is a walk in the fucking park. Most of the time anyway. Till shit like this came up.

The visitor—Oliver Searcy—had been a customer a few weeks ago, and he had called Duke early this morning, kind of rude, saying, "We have a problem." Duke had been in the middle of some important business—mounting a new scope on one of his deer rifles—but he put the screwdriver down on his desk and said, "What kind of problem?"

"I'll tell ya when I get there." Then, nothing but a dial tone. Well, shit. Duke didn't like problems, especially the kind

that would make a man drive nearly five hours from Houston.
Matter of fact, Duke wasn't particularly fond of Searcy, either.
The dickwad had first called Duke from Houston about a month
ago, in the middle of deer season. He said he'd heard Duke was
a hell of a guide, and he was in the market for a big buck.

"How big we talkin'?" Duke asked.

"At least one-seventy," Searcy replied. "If you think you can
handle it." He was referring to the standard scoring system for
trophy whitetails. One-seventy was the minimum to make the
Boone and Crockett record books.

"Oh, I can handle it all right," Duke replied, thinking, *Okay,
how am I gonna handle this?* Truth was, there weren't many
deer that big in Blanco County. Sure, there were a handful of
free-ranging bucks that scored 140, maybe 150 if you were
lucky. But if you wanted one of their big brothers, well, you had
to plunk down a lot of cash. Trophy deer like that were usually
kept on large game ranches, behind high fences, unmolested by
hunters. Those deer were protected like valuable livestock,
which was exactly what they were. Many of the ranches were
willing to make a commission deal with the guide—but Duke
didn't like to go that route. Why part with most of the money
when, with a little creativity, he could keep it all to himself? And
that's exactly what he had done with Searcy. Duke *did* make
good on his boast—sort of. The important thing was, Oliver
Searcy had gotten his deer and gone away happy. Something
had changed, though. Now Searcy was sitting in front of Duke,
looking none too happy at all. They were in Duke's two-room
office, right next to the feed store, which was closed today, it being Sunday. Duke was behind the desk, sitting in his big leather
chair, and Searcy was in one of the twin chairs in front of him.

So far, Searcy hadn't said a word, other than giving a gruff
"No" to an offer of coffee. Duke smiled and placed his hands
flat on the desk in front of him. "Okay, so what's up?"

Searcy didn't waste any time. "Last month, you said you
could set me up with a trophy deer."

Duke nodded.

Searcy said, "You acted like it wasn't a big deal, like you did it all the time."

"That's 'cause I do."

Searcy shook his head. "The thing is, I've been hunting all my life, and I know big deer are hard to come by. I asked for the deer of a lifetime, and you acted like you could find it for me"—Searcy snapped his fingers—"just like that. Then you take me to a ranch-and—*bam!*—first time out, I get a buck. It all seemed too easy. Now I know why."

Duke was sizing the man up, just in case there was trouble. Searcy wasn't a large man, only about five eight, maybe 160. Nothing compared to Duke's well-muscled six two. Plus, Duke's shaved head gave him a particularly menacing appearance. And his voice, full of gravel from twenty years of smoking, was a pretty good tool for intimidation, too. If things got rough, Searcy wouldn't be a problem.

Duke tried to act confused. "What exactly are you getting at, Mr. Searcy?"

"I'm a radiologist."

Duke didn't know what to make of that. "Yeah, so?"

"The deer mount you brought me last week—the 'outstanding trophy,' as you put it—it's a fake. I x-rayed it. Those antlers don't even go with that skull. They're bolted on."

Well now, aren't you a clever boy? Duke did his best to appear surprised. He contorted his face into an expression of Academy Award–winning amazement. He stood, walked around the desk, and sat with one butt cheek on the corner, now just a few feet from Searcy. "You gotta be shittin' me. For real?"

Searcy seemed nervous now, with Duke in such close proximity. He nodded. "Looks pretty realistic. You do good work."

Duke pointed one hand at his own chest, going for incredulous. "Me? You think I did it? Well, goddamn, I'm shocked, to be honest with you. I—it was probably the taxidermist I took it to." Not likely. Duke did all the taxidermy himself.

"The taxidermist," Duke continued, "that's who we oughta be lookin' at. They're experts at that sort of thing. Not me, that's for sure." Duke added a little extra head shaking, sort of an I-can't-believe-you-said-that gesture.

Searcy didn't buy it. That much was obvious. Especially when he reached under his coat and came out with a revolver. "I don't care who's responsible," he said, "as long as I get my five thousand dollars back."

Suddenly, Duke's raspy voice didn't seem like much of a weapon at all.

If Red O'Brien had known that the wetback he'd hired for the day was going to get hit by a truck, he probably would have insisted on a fatter one, one with a little more burrito on his bones. It might have cushioned the blow a little and the day wouldn't have turned into such a giant cluster fuck. Hell, a beefier guy might have walked away from it all.

But no, Red's friend Billy Don Craddock, who spoke the language some, had settled on this skinny little guy named Jorge, who was supposed to be damn good at rock work, and that was the important thing.

To be honest, Red wasn't all that crazy about using wetback labor, taking work away from genuine Americans. But in this case, as usual, Red couldn't afford to pay a regular white boy to do the job. It was one of those situations—what do you call it?—a catch-33. He'd wanted to hire some local worker, but they were all too pricey. He *didn't* want to hire the wetback, but the wetback was affordable. If Red didn't hire *anybody,* that meant he and Billy Don would have to take care of it all. And that settled that. What the hell. Mexicans were more cut out for that kind of work anyway.

Red and Billy Don had found Jorge early that morning, hanging around with the other illegals in their usual place—behind the Git It & Go convenience store. They'd buy orange juice and sweet rolls, then patiently sit with their backs against the brick wall, waiting for trucks to swing around the store. All those brown faces, none of them speaking hardly a lick of English. For the most part, Red had to admit, they were damn hard workers. They'd pick up manual labor at the rate of sixty bucks per day. Clearing cedar, hauling rocks, digging ditches—hell, they didn't seem to care what the work was as long as they could earn a few dollars and send it home to Mexico.

The problem was, Red was pretty sure Jorge was hungover as hell, and it worried him. The schedule was tight, and the last thing Red needed was a Mexican who couldn't pull his weight.

In the truck, heading toward the job site, Red was driving, Billy Don's three-hundred-pound bulk was on the passenger's side, and the scrawny wetback was squeezed in the middle. As soon as the doors had closed, Billy Don had begun jabbering away at Jorge in Spanish. To Red, each sentence sounded like one long word. If there were any subjects or verbs hiding out in that mishmash of sounds, Red sure couldn't find them. Plus, it made him feel left out, like when he'd get picked last for dodgeball back in grade school. So Red was trying to tune Billy Don and Jorge out, concentrating on the day's schedule, finding it hard to focus with the two of them rattling on.

Worse yet, every time Jorge opened his mouth, Red could smell last night's stale beer, stronger than bean dip. Then he smelled something even worse.

"Goddamn, which one a y'all cut the cheese?" Red groaned, rolling down the window.

"Jesus," Billy Don said, "it wasn't me," and opened his window, too. "Jorge told me he had *cabrito* last night. Plus a case of Budweiser."

Jorge just grinned, and Red gave him a frown.

"*No comprendo,*" the Mexican said.

"Well, tell him he better be ready for a long day. We got a schedule to keep," Red said.

Billy Don translated, and Jorge fired a string of words right back, looking Red's way and smiling.

Billy Don laughed.

"What'd he say?" Red asked.

"I think he said you are a serious man."

Red snorted. "Damn right I am. Serious as a heart attack." And then he ignored them both. He had more important things to think about as he eased his old Ford truck and a trailer onto the shoulder of Flat Creek Road. Mr. Owen Pierce, yes, *that* Owen Pierce, owner of the most popular chain of barbecue joints in Texas—wanted the stone entrance to his ranch rebuilt, and he wanted it done *now*. He had some sort of party coming up this weekend, lots of bigwigs coming out, and it seems Mrs. Pierce had decided just last night that the entrance wasn't quite up to par, thank you. "Kind of a last-minute thing," Mr. Pierce had said on the phone. "Think you can help me out?" Hell yes, Red could help out, for what the guy was willing to pay.

Red cut the engine, stepped out of the truck, and surveyed the elaborate limestone rock work on either side of the road leading into the ranch. Red didn't think it looked too bad. Sure, the concrete between the stones was crumbling in a few places, and there was a buildup of green mildew here and there. Nothing a little mortar mix and a few squirts of Clorox wouldn't fix. But Mr. Pierce wanted the whole thing torn down and reconstructed. In three days. "And let's make it granite this time," Pierce had said. "Mrs. Pierce likes the look of granite."

"Well, we're burning daylight," Red said. He gestured at Jorge. "Amigo, grab the jackhammer out of the truck and let's get busy."

Jorge stared back with bloodshot eyes.

"You know . . . ratatatat," Red said, making a jackhammering gesture with his hands.

The Mexican didn't budge.

Billy Don said a few words in Spanish, and that did the trick. Jorge grabbed the hundred-pound jackhammer, which weighed nearly as much as he did, and hefted it out of the truck like it was a toy.

Maybe he'll work out okay after all, Red thought.

But then the Mexican laid the jackhammer on the ground and leaned against the truck, moaning. Now he was bent over, grimacing, rambling on in Spanish.

Red removed his Dallas Cowboys cap with one hand and scratched his scalp with other. "All right, what the hell's wrong with him?"

"Our boy says his stomach don't feel so good," Billy Don said. "Must be the *cabrito*."

"Yeah, that or the goddamn case of beer," Red said. "You picked a real winner for us this time, Billy Don. You ever try to run a jackhammer after drinking all night?"

Billy Don shrugged.

Red and Billy Don watched as Jorge suddenly turned and scurried onto the ranch, tugging at his belt buckle, disappearing into some cedar trees.

"Well, hell's bells," Red said. "You found us a wetback with the runs."

Billy Don chuckled, then quit when Red glared at him. "Aw, give him a minute. He'll be fine. Just don't shake hands with him."

Red wasn't in the mood for jokes. "Well, let's quit wasting time. Gimme a hand with the generator."

The men pulled the generator out of the truck and carried it over to the stone ranch entrance. As soon as they had the generator running, they'd have juice for the jackhammer and they could tear this whole thing down in a matter of hours. The best thing was, Red could save the limestone and use it again on another job. Not only that, Mr. Pierce was *paying* Red to haul the rock away. Red was making money coming and going. Sweet deal. Now, if only the wetback would finish his business and get to work.

Red figured he'd have Jorge operate the jackhammer, the really hard work, while he and Billy Don used wheelbarrows to move the rock to the trailer. When they were ready to rebuild with the granite, he and Billy Don would have to provide the muscle, because Jorge had the masonry skills. Supposedly anyway. That remained to be seen.

Red opened the choke on the generator and was just about to pull the starter cord, when Billy Don said, "Here comes our granite."

Several hundred yards down the road, a loaded flatbed was slowly rumbling in their direction. *At least they're here on time*, Red thought. He yanked the starter cord and—in the instant right before the generator roared to life—there was a scream from the woods.

Red raised his head puzzled, and locked eyes with Billy Don, who was mouthing something to him. The noise from the generator was too loud, but Red didn't need to read lips to know that Billy Don had said, "Did you hear that?"

They looked toward the woods, and here came Jorge, naked from the waist down, running—as Billy Don would later describe it—like the entire Border Patrol was on his tail.

Red had no idea what had Jorge so worked up—maybe a rattlesnake or a wild hog. But he figured whatever it was, Jorge would stop running once he came back through the ranch entrance. Then, as Jorge zipped through the open gate and loped across the shoulder of the road, Red was pretty sure he was running for the safety of the truck. It was only in the tragic half second after Jorge passed the front of the truck that Red realized the Mexican had no intention of stopping until he reached Laredo. By then, it was way too late. There was no way to warn Jorge about the oncoming flatbed, the sounds of which were covered by the generator.

The truck driver would later tell Red he had been planning on *bypassing* the ranch entrance, so he could back up and dump the load. That's why he hadn't slowed down much yet.

But right now, all Red heard was the awful sound of the truck's worn-out brakes grinding, metal on metal, followed by a sickening thump.

Red and Billy Don rushed over to Jorge, who was now writhing on the pavement, his leg obviously shattered, bone exposed.

"Oh man," Billy Don said, instantly going pale.

"Didn't see him in time," said the driver, who had climbed out of the cab of the truck. "Just never saw him."

"It wasn't your fault," Red said. "Meskin ran right in front of you."

Billy Don knelt down beside Jorge, grabbed his hand, and said something in Spanish.

"¡Oo, mi Dios! ¡Chupacabra!" Jorge replied between

clenched teeth, followed by a bunch of other words Red didn't understand.

"¿Que?" Billy Don asked.

"What's he babbling about?" Red asked.

Jorge eyes got wide, and he said it again, much louder, "¡Chupacabra!" Then he made the mistake of looking down at his ruined leg and promptly passed out.

Billy Don looked up at Red. "What do we do now?"

"Well hell, Billy Don, we gotta get the boy an ambulance," he hissed.

But what he was thinking was, *There goes my goddamn schedule.*

Searcy wasn't exactly pointing the pistol at Duke, just kind of holding it in front of him.

This was the kind of situation Duke had always worried about. For years, Duke had made a comfortable living by finding ways to gain access to beautiful animals so that wealthy hunters like Searcy could shoot them. Duke thought of himself as a broker, a man who paired hunters with the animals of their wettest dreams. He had set people up with all kinds of trophies, but white-tailed deer were the biggest market by far. And yeah, sometimes Duke had to skirt a few laws to get what the hunter wanted. Other times, if he really wanted to make good money in this business, he had to think outside the box. Which is what he'd done two years ago, when he'd first pulled off one of the most brilliant and profitable swindles ever concocted.

It was so slick, nobody had ever figured it out. Until now. Frankly, Duke couldn't blame Searcy for being a tad peeved.

"Take it easy," Duke said, his palms toward Searcy. "No reason to get all crazy on me."

"I just want my money."

Duke spoke softly. "I can understand that. You got ripped off, and now you wanna set things straight. Who can blame you? Just don't take it out on the wrong guy."

Duke was thinking there still might be a peaceful way out of this. Just return the guy's money, smooth-talk him a little, maybe even offer to take him on a free hunt—just to show there were no hard feelings. Duke could afford to give up the cash. What he couldn't afford was a guy like Searcy bad-mouthing him around the county.

But Searcy pushed him even further into a corner.

"I'm walking out of here with my money," Searcy said. "I paid cash, I want cash back. Then I'm gonna talk to the game warden and let him know what kind of operation you're running."

Duke could feel his heart pounding. If Searcy made good on his threat, Duke would be facing a lynch mob. Once word got out, every hunter Duke had ever guided would double-check their mounts for authenticity, and several of them would find reason to be seriously pissed off. Once the authorities got involved, Duke'd be looking at a return to the joint.

Duke held one hand up in the Boy Scout's gesture. "Mr. Searcy, one last time, I swear to you, I had nothing to do with this mess." With his other hand, Duke was reaching back behind him, feeling for the screwdriver on the desk.

Searcy waved his gun in Duke's direction. "Go on, now. Get my money. I'm sure you've got it stashed around here somewhere."

Duke found something with his hand—but it turned out to be the stapler. "See, now, I don't have any problem paying you back. No sir. You deserve it." He was buying time, still fumbling with his hand. Where was that damn screwdriver! "But see, I don't exactly have it on me," Duke said.

"Bullshit," Searcy said, coming around with the revolver now. "You're lying to—"

That's when Duke's hand found what it was looking for.

It was the final day of deer season, and Blanco County game warden John Marlin was thrilled. Yes, the season was the most exciting part of the year, but it was also the most tiring. It was an around-the-clock job, checking hunting camps during the day, chasing spotlighters at night. The weekends were especially hectic, and he was lucky to get a couple hours' sleep each night.

Then there were idiots who shouldn't be let loose in the woods with firearms, like the two Marlin had just pulled over on the side of Highway 281, north of Johnson City. He had spotted blood on the rear door, saw that the driver was wearing camo, and decided to do a license check.

"Looks like y'all had some luck this morning," Marlin said as the driver lowered the window.

"Yes, sir," the middle-aged driver said, nodding, clearly excited. "Shot my first buck. I got him tagged and everything, no problem."

Marlin peered through the side window, seeing a medium-size six-point lying on a tarp in the rear of the SUV. "If you'll cut your engine for me, sir, I'd like to take a quick look."

The man complied, and Marlin opened the rear of the vehicle. It was eleven o'clock on a Sunday morning in early January. But this was Texas, where winter didn't have much bite, and today the temperature was hovering around seventy. The interior of the vehicle, with the sun shining in, was probably at least eighty.

"You planning on icing him down?" Marlin asked.

This time, the passenger replied. He could have been the driver's twin: middle-aged, wearing freshly creased camos and some sort of safari hat he had probably ordered off the Internet. "Think we need to?"

"That depends. Where you headed?"

"Back up to Dallas."

Marlin shook his head. Most hunters were knowledgeable, law-abiding, salt-of-the-earth types. In fact, Marlin would stack hunters, as a group, up against the general population any day. But occasionally he ran into a pair like this. Utterly clueless. It was a four-hour drive to Dallas, which meant the venison would have plenty of time to spoil.

"When you shoot a deer," Marlin said, "you wanna get the

carcass cooled down as soon as possible. This thing would be better quartered and in an ice chest. You realize it's a violation if you fail to keep the meat in edible condition?"

"Yes, sir, I understand that," the passenger replied. "I've hunted before."

Marlin examined the tag that was attached with twine to the animal's ear. There were small abbreviations for each month, plus the number 1 through 31, running along the border of the tag. "Then you should know you're supposed to *cut* the month and date out, rather than marking it with a pen," Marlin said.

"Well, uh, we were a little unclear on that," the man said.

Marlin glanced down at the Winchester he had noticed lying parallel to the deer. It wasn't in a rifle case, but was left to slide around in the rear compartment as the vehicle moved. That was dangerous in itself, but the hunters had made an even bigger mistake. "Whose rifle?"

"Mine," said the passenger.

"You mind?" Marlin asked, gesturing toward the rifle.

"No, go ahead."

Marlin lifted the rifle and worked the bolt. It was unloaded, but that wasn't what concerned him. Around the butt of the stock was an elastic band that was designed to hold bullets. This one was filled to the max.

"Guess you didn't do any shooting this weekend," Marlin said.

"I was waiting for a nice buck. Could have taken a couple of does."

"Good thing you didn't. This rifle is a thirty-aught-six and you're hunting with ammo for a three-oh-eight."

There was a brief pause as the hunters considered that fact.

"I, uh—is that a problem? I kinda figured since they were nearly the same caliber . . ."

"Thing probably would have blown up in your face," Marlin said. He heard the driver mutter, "Glen, you dumbass" under his breath. Glen, grimacing with embarrassment, opted to remain quiet for the moment.

Marlin was about to chastise the men further, when he heard